THE
SILENCED

Anders de la Motte is the author of the internation-
ally acclaimed Game trilogy, which has been published
in twenty-seven languages. The first book in the trilogy,
Game, won the First Book Award from the Swedish
Crime Writers' Academy and has sold more than
100,000 copies in Sweden alone. He is a former police
officer and director of security at two Fortune 500
companies, and currently works as a consultant on
international security.

🐦 @AndersdelaMotte
f Anders de la Motte

Also by Anders de la Motte

Game
Buzz
Bubble
MemoRandom

THE
SILENCED
ANDERS DE LA MOTTE

Translated from the Swedish by Neil Smith

HarperCollins*PublishersLtd*

The Silenced
Copyright © 2015 Anders de la Motte.
Translation copyright © Neil Smith 2017.
Published by agreement with Solomonsson Agency.

Published by HarperCollins Publishers Ltd

Originally published as *UltiMatum* in 2015 in Sweden
First published in Canada in 2017 by HarperCollins Publishers Ltd
in this original trade paperback edition.

HarperCollins books may be purchased for educational, business, or sales
promotional use through our Special Markets Department.

HarperCollins Publishers Ltd
2 Bloor Street East, 20th Floor
Toronto, Ontario, Canada
M4W 1A8

www.harpercollins.ca

Library and Archives Canada Cataloguing in Publication
information is available upon request.

ISBN 978-1-44343-636-6

Printed and bound in the United States of America
LSC/H 9 8 7 6 5 4 3 2 1

For Anette

Prologue

Even though she was only just past thirty, Detective Inspector Julia Gabrielsson had seen plenty of dead bodies. Probably more than most police officers, with the exception of the bull elephants in the far corridor of the Violent Crime Unit. The old guys with minty breath who appraised her figure unashamedly, used *password* as the password on their computers, and could never be reached after two o'clock. But she doubted that the closet alcoholics in the Tic Tac club had ever seen anything as disgusting as the body lying on the autopsy table in front of her. If you could actually call it a body.

Nine years had passed since her earliest visit to the Forensic Medicine Unit in Solna. Her first body hadn't wanted to make a lot of fuss. He lay there quietly in his apartment for a whole summer while the maggots slowly dissolved him onto the parquet floor, and she felt her knees wobble when the body bag was opened. The body on the slab in front of them was worse. Much worse.

She glanced at her colleague, Amante, who was standing beside her. His Adam's apple was bobbing up and down frenetically in his freshly shaven neck. Not exactly a gentle introduction. As long as he didn't actually throw up. She stepped back discreetly to remove her shoes and trousers from the danger zone.

Amante seemed to notice her looking. He turned his head and gave her an apologetic smile. The eyes behind his dark-framed glasses were brown and looked simultaneously friendly and mournful, which surprised Julia. Revulsion would have been much more expected. Or why not a hint of good old Get-me-out-of-here panic? That would have been perfectly understandable. After all, her new partner wasn't a proper police

1

officer but a civilian investigator. Infinitely more at home sitting in a cozy office surrounded by statistics than getting stuck in practical police work. The only question was why her fat boss had without warning foisted an oversensitive office clerk on her? She made up her mind to solve that particular mystery before the day was out.

The thin-haired pathologist in front of them leafed through his sheaf of papers but evidently failed to find the form he was looking for. Unless he was just searching for the right words with which to start his explanation. Somewhere in the depths of the Forensic Medicine Center an air-conditioning unit rumbled to life, making a subdued but ominous sound.

Amante swallowed again. Julia nodded at him and forced herself to summon up something that resembled an encouraging smile.

Just look away for a minute, she thought. *That's a perfectly understandable human response. The living don't like to see the dead. Don't like to be reminded of what lies ahead. Rich, poor, good or evil. Sooner or later we all end up lying there with cold, stiff limbs. All the same in death. That's why most people look away from the dead, say something unrelated, or make some stupid joke simply to break the silence.*

But not her. She belonged to a considerably smaller group of people. People who exploit the silence surrounding the dead. Observing. Listening. Understanding.

Everyone has a rhythm, a way they move through life. She learned that in her first year in Violent Crime. With some people you can see their rhythm fairly easily, but others require more concentration. Especially if you're trying to work out that rhythm in hindsight. Reading it from homes, belongings, bodies, and—not least—crime scenes. It's easy to let yourself be distracted. Do what most of her colleagues did and concentrate on the things that are yelling for attention. Weapons, accessories, blood, fingerprints. Obvious signs of violence and death.

That's often enough to get them quite a long way, but sometimes it takes more than that. Sometimes it takes someone like her, who stands completely silent, just listening carefully. Seeking out the tiny details that disturb the rhythm. A glass missing from a cupboard, a belt that's been fastened wrongly, a small bruise in an odd place, maybe just a lingering smell. Little things that appear to be utterly inconsequential to everyone except her, but that turn out to be the exact opposite when seen in context.

That was how Julia had built her reputation in Violent Crime. Not by talking, shouting orders, or cross-examining suspects. But by listening.

The dead body on the examination table hadn't yet said anything to her, hadn't revealed its identity or what sort of life it had lived. Which wasn't terribly strange, seeing as someone had gone to great lengths to make sure the corpse would stay silent.

To start with, the body was naked. And it had been chopped into fourteen pieces. Twelve of them were on the metal table in front of them. The pathologist had put everything in the correct place. Head, torso, upper and lower arms, thighs, shins, and feet. But because the pieces weren't joined together, the body looked like a macabre puppet, too absurd to be human.

The skin, which only partially covered the body parts, was gray and half-dissolved. In several places the bones jutted out. The fat, sinews, and muscles that ought to have been around them were either gone or transformed into a pale, soapy sludge out of which seawater was still oozing. It formed small pools on the stainless steel worktop before the law of gravity persuaded the water to start to make its way slowly toward the gullies at the corners of the table.

Where the corpse's face should have been there was almost nothing left. Just a jagged mosaic made up of splinters of bone, skin, and gristle. The eye sockets gaped empty, the nose was missing altogether, and from the shattered jaw the minuscule stumps of a few teeth poked out. As if the dead body were smiling at them. Grinning at its own wretched condition.

Julia cast another glance at Amante. Stupidly, he had gone back to staring at the body. He seemed almost to be forcing himself to keep his eyes on the leering skull. She wondered if it was a macho thing, that he didn't want to seem weak in front of her and the pathologist. In which case he was more stupid than he had seemed during their short conversation on the way there.

"The body was found in Lake Mälaren, just outside Källstavik, at a depth of twenty meters. But you already know that." The pathologist with the Donald Trump hair finally seemed to have found what he was looking for. "Judging by the state it's in, I'd say the body has been in the water for about four months. I'll be able to say more after tissue analysis. The bottom-feeders have had plenty of time to do their thing. Most of it has been . . ."

He gestured toward the corpse as he appeared to consider his choice of words.

"Eaten," Julia stated before he had time to make his mind up. Amante made a faint whimpering sound, then hid it quickly by clearing his throat.

"Male or female?" Julia said, even though she was already fairly sure of the answer.

"Hard to tell right now," the pathologist said. "My first impression is that we're dealing with a man. And the statistics back me up on that. But we won't know for sure until we've taken a closer look at the pelvis."

"And the t-tool . . . ?" Amante's voice sounded hollow. He licked his lips a couple of times but couldn't bring himself to finish the rest of the sentence. In spite of the cool air in the room, a tiny droplet of sweat had formed on his right temple, just below the arm of his glasses.

"Can you say anything about the tool that was used to dismember him?" Julia said.

"A very powerful motorized tool with extremely sharp teeth."

"A chain saw?" Amante said, making a fresh attempt, this time looking directly at the pathologist instead of down at the table, which seemed to help.

"A chain saw or possibly a reciprocating saw. I'll know more once we've examined the surface of the cuts."

The pathologist gestured toward the table again, but this time Amante was smart enough not to look down. Instead he quickly wiped the bead of sweat from his temple. *He's a fast learner: extra points for that,* Julia thought.

"And presumably it isn't possible to identify a cause of death as things stand?" she said, mostly as a statement of fact. As expected, the pathologist began shaking his head halfway through her question, which made his comb-over bob like a thin sail of hair.

"Considering the state of the body, it's extremely doubtful that we'll ever be able to identify the cause of death," he said. "Whoever did this . . ."

The pathologist adjusted his hair as he appeared to ponder how best to continue.

Julia cast a quick glance at Amante to reassure herself that he wasn't going to give in to the temptation to fill the gap in the conversation. But fortunately he kept his mouth shut and waited for the conclusion. A second bonus point: not bad for a civilian.

"Well . . ." The pathologist made a face, as if the words in his mouth tasted unpleasant. "I've worked here twenty-three years, Gabrielsson. Just like you, I imagine I've seen most of the things people are capable of, both toward themselves and others. Over the years I've had the dubious privilege of examining at least a dozen dismembered bodies. But this one . . . This perpetrator's different. Different from pretty much everything else I've ever come across. Just look here, for instance."

The pathologist pointed at the gap between the torso and one thigh, then at the corresponding gap between the upper arm and shoulder.

5

"No sign of hesitation on any of the cuts, not even when the perpetrator took the head off." He moved his forefinger to the even stump above the shoulders. "Depriving someone of their humanity so brutally doesn't normally happen without a degree of anxiety, and that's usually clearly visible on the body. Superficial trial cuts, abandoned or failed attempts that demonstrate the technical difficulty of handling the saw, but also the reluctance of the perpetrator. Disquiet at the terrible thing he or she is doing. Do you understand what I mean, Gabrielsson?"

Julia nodded. "But not this perpetrator. He didn't hesitate."

The pathologist adopted his bitter expression again.

"No, see for yourself. Thirteen very decisive cuts, one for each joint. All the way through, right through muscle and bone. Whoever did this was in full command of himself and the situation."

"What about the face, then?" Julia said with a frown, nodding toward the badly ravaged body. "The perpetrator seems to have been rather less in control there. How does that fit your theory?"

The pathologist shook his head hesitantly.

"This is purely speculation, but I'm fairly sure that the condition of the face doesn't reflect any emotional outburst. The perpetrator simply wanted to make sure that there was no way the body could be identified."

He pointed at one lower arm, then the grinning jaw.

"Both hands are still missing, and the facial features and teeth have been almost totally destroyed. Which, obviously, makes it impossible to check fingerprints or dental records, or circulate pictures of the victim's face. Admittedly that does leave us with DNA identification, but—even if we do manage to get a reasonably clean tissue sample—that presupposes that the victim's profile is already in the police database or that you'll find another sample to match it against at a later point in the investigation."

A few moments of silence followed. The air-conditioning

rumbled in the background. The low sound was like thunder, gradually creeping closer.

"Add to that the black garbage bags the body parts were wrapped in," the pathologist went on. "To start with, they were sealed with cable ties rather than tape. No sticky surfaces where forensics experts could find hairs or fibers. And as weights the perpetrator used ordinary gray stones found in any garden or stone wall. Nothing to go on there. And I found small holes here and there in the plastic, probably from a narrow knife blade. If I had to hazard a guess, I'd say there are probably similar holes on the torso of the body. We'll see once I've been able to stretch what remains of the skin across the stomach, but I'm fairly confident."

"How can you be?" Amante's voice sounded muffled. "How can you know that the perpetrator stabbed—"

"Because all the body parts were found in a limited area," Julia said. "In one of the deepest parts of the inlet. Probably in exactly the same spot where the perpetrator dumped them last winter."

The pathologist nodded.

"The gases given off by decomposition usually make bodies float to the surface after a week or two. A bit longer if the water's cold; it can take a few months then. In contrast to what most people think, bodies dumped in water usually get washed up on a beach somewhere, and then they get found by a member of the public. Your perpetrator stuck holes in the bags and probably also the torso, where the decomposition is most noticeable. That way the gases were able to escape and the body parts stayed where they were down on the bottom. And the holes would also make it easier for scavengers to get in and do their thing. We've got half a bucket full of various bottom-feeders that made their way inside the bags. A few more months underwater and there wouldn't have been much left."

"You're saying that our perpetrator is someone who knows exactly what they're doing," Julia said.

The pathologist held his hands up in front of him in a gesture that managed simultaneously to convey agreement and dissociation.

"Like I said, this is all speculation. All I can say is that this scenario is unlike anything I've come across before. If those two yachtsmen hadn't lost their anchor in that inlet and decided to dive down to get it, this poor soul would never have been found." He nodded toward the table. "Imagine the shock when they realized what they'd stumbled across down there in the darkness."

Amante cleared his throat again and looked like he wasn't having any trouble at all imaging the men's horror.

Julia ignored him and looked back at the table again, where the dead body grinned at her with its wrecked smile. She had to admit that the pathologist's theory was good. Logical, in light of the evidence. The perpetrator appeared to be extremely methodical, ice-cold in his thoroughness and attention to detail. But she still couldn't shake the feeling the grimacing face gave her. A feeling of rage, of hatred.

Someone wanted you to disappear, she thought. *Wanted to make sure you'd never be found. Someone you'd upset so badly that he destroyed your face. That's what happened, isn't it?*

The dead body didn't answer. Just went on smiling at her, as if her words amused him.

· · ·

Twenty-two pills. Twenty-two white, oblong pills that he'd paid for with just as many nightmare-filled nights.

David Sarac had surreptitiously googled *sleeping pills*. Taking into account his emaciated body and generally poor state of health, he had worked out that twenty pills would be enough for what he wanted to achieve. But with twenty-five there would be no doubt, so he had another three nights to struggle through. Three nights of lying curled up in bed, drifting in the indistinct borderland between sleep and wakefulness, while everything that had happened out on the island replayed in his head. Always in the same order. First the snow. Heavy flakes falling on a frozen forest. A silent, dark old house. Then a low bass note, a threatening rumble on the horizon, growing louder and louder as the winter thunder approaches. Then suddenly beams of light from headlights cutting through the trees. The sound of powerful engines, of gunfire and shouted orders. Flashes from gun barrels creating a ghostly shadow play as the howls of anger, pain, and terror grow ever louder.

The thunder keeps building in intensity in the background, swallowing up all other sound until it transforms into the roar of the flames consuming the old house. A rain of sparks flies through the night sky, and the stench of gunpowder, soot, and burning flesh makes his throat sting. Just when he thinks it's all over, when he thinks he's finally on his way out of the nightmare, he finds himself in the middle of it again. Feels the heat of the pressure wave as it knocks him flying. The bullet hitting him in the neck, filling his airways with liquid iron. The blood on the white ground. His own blood. That of others. All of it sucked up by the snow crystals around him, until he's lying on his back in a sea of carmine red. He hears himself laugh. A shrill laugh that sounds more like a sob. His head falls back on the snow. The world slowly starts to dissolve at the edges. Curling up like a burning photograph until it fades to black.

All this is your fault, David, the voices whisper.

It was your plan. Your fault.

Then the film starts over again. Unless he's lucky enough to wake up, that is. Wake up locked away in a nursing home in the middle of nowhere. "For your own good, David," as the senior consultant had said during their first conversation.

But he didn't complain, couldn't see any reason to do so. In a few days he was planning to leave it all behind: the island of Skarpö, the nightmares, and this place.

He scratched at the red scar running across his neck. Caught at it with his nails until it started to sting. The whispers were

9

right. He should have died out there in the snow along with the others. Should have drowned in his own blood. It would have been a fitting punishment for his sins. Some things were simply too broken to mend.

But instead, against all the odds, he had survived. Had made a mockery of the justice he had tried to implement. David Sarac, heroic police officer. The hero who had to be kept locked away in a secure unit *for his own good*. But what was the alternative? For him to tell the truth about what had happened out on Skarpö? The reason why all those men had died out there in the snow? That was hardly an option, either for him or his superiors. A public relations disaster that must be avoided at all costs. That was why he was where he was. Planning his own escape.

It had taken time to build up the stock of pills. The staff had been very vigilant during the first week. They followed their routines to the letter, forcing him to open his mouth and stick his tongue out every time he took a sleeping pill. He had been careful. Played along and gained their confidence. He couldn't afford to fail. If just one of the caregivers started to suspect, he'd find himself in the suicide wing and his plan would be thwarted.

He glanced out through the window. Between the trees he could just make out the little lake in the distance. He had explored the park during a couple of short walks when he was still considering other options beside the pills. But the light and all the sensory impressions out there had been too sharp. They exhausted his broken brain and forced him to stagger back into the safety of the building. But at least he knew that there was a fence and a heavy metal gate by the jetty. Floodlights, alarms, and cameras too, just as there were along the high brick wall by the road, and the double fence facing the dark forest on the other side. Barriers he wouldn't have to confront. Because now he had the pills. He closed his hand around the plastic bag. Moved the pills one by one through his fingers. Counted them again. Even numbers, odd numbers.

Odds and evens.

Sarac shivered and pulled the blanket up over his legs. In spite of the heat in the gloomy little room, his fingertips and the end of his nose were always cold. He looked down at the notepad on his lap and tried to put his thoughts into words. But as usual they wouldn't play ball. The senior consultant had suggested that he try to write down what he felt, and that was his task in advance of his next therapy session. Of course he could ignore the whole thing, tell the psychologist to go to hell and shut himself away in his room the way a couple of the other patients did. But he was keen to go on acting compliant for a few more days.

Janus, he had written. Not much to offer, really, and certainly not the sort of thing he was thinking of telling anyone.

I owe everything.

Debts I can't escape till the day I die.

The loop of music was back in his head again. The lyrics that had helped him unpick his stroke-damaged brain last Christmas. Helped him reveal his own secrets. And his sins.

Anxiety tightened its grip around his heart and lungs.

Debts I can't escape till the day I die.

He put the pad down and took the bag of pills out of the pocket of his cardigan. Moved the tablets around again like pearls on a strand.

Twenty, twenty-one, twenty-two. Only three more performances to go. Then the film of his life would be over at last.

• • •

Julia Gabrielsson turned the wheel and changed lanes abruptly as she put her foot down and with satisfaction felt the car respond instantly. It hadn't driven more than a couple of thousand kilometers and still had that new-car smell, which was obviously preferable to the odors that would become ingrained in the seats over time. Fast food, various bodily fluids, and, not least, tedium. She had worked out a long time ago that you had to push yourself forward on Mondays, when jobs that had come in over the weekend were allocated. That way you could get hold of a decent car so you didn't have to drive about in one of the worn-out old patrol cars that were parked in the far corner. So she always got in at six o'clock on Monday mornings and raided the key cabinet before going down to the gym. She made sure she was back in time for the morning meeting at a quarter past eight, alert, fresh from the shower, eager to get to work, and with the key to the best car in her pocket, while her bleary-eyed colleagues were sipping their first cups of coffee and wishing it was still the weekend.

She liked cars, liked driving fast. Dad used to practice his J-turns and controlled slides with her in the works parking lot every winter once she turned thirteen, and she had beaten the crap out of all the guys on the emergency response driving course. One of the many advantages of being the daughter of a police officer. It was just a shame Dad couldn't see her now.

She finished overtaking and pulled back into the right lane.

"How long have you been back in Sweden?" Julia took her eyes off the traffic for a few seconds. High time for a bit of mundane chat with the civilian. Get him to reveal who he was and, more importantly, what he was doing on her team, in her murder investigation.

"Three weeks, give or take," Amante muttered distantly.

"UN or Foreign Office?"

Amante shook his head. "Europol. Lampedusa. An Italian island in the Mediterranean."

"Yes, I know. Where all the refugee boats from North Africa end up."

Underestimating her general knowledge was a black mark, a big one that more than swallowed up the feeble plusses he had managed to scrape together so far. But she thought she'd give him a chance to correct his mistake. Or commit another one so that she could comfortably and guiltlessly file him away in the box marked *Dry Academics, Type 1A*.

"So you worked on refugee issues?"

"Yep. For two years," he said with an awkward little smile. He seemed to have realized that he'd come across as patronizing.

"And now you're here with us."

She paused, waiting for him to explain why. But Amante merely sat there without speaking. Clearly she was going to have to try a different tactic.

"We could certainly do with some fresh blood in the Violent Crime Unit."

That was perfectly true. The head of the unit, Pärson, held his protective hand over the old Tic Tac guys. He let them drink their way surreptitiously toward retirement at the end of the corridor. Or toward a fatal heart attack. The old men blocked the paths of other people's careers as successfully as they did their own arteries, so the division was roughly fifty-fifty.

"We've been on our knees since Skarpö," she added.

Amante looked up. "I was out of the country. Missed most of that. There were a lot of fatalities, weren't there? Two police officers?"

"Nine dead in total. And even more injured. Several different criminal gangs clashed out there, and three of our colleagues got in the way. We still don't really know why."

"Oh." Amante looked out of the side window. He wasn't taking any of the juicy bait she was dangling right in front of his nose. He seemed more interested in the buildings swishing past along Sankt Eriksgatan.

Strange. Pretty much every police officer Julia knew wanted to talk about Skarpö. Tried to get the details out of her, anything that, against all odds, hadn't yet been dissected and analyzed in the media or on the internal gossip network. About the gangsters and officers who had died out there, and above all about David Sarac, the heroic police officer who had survived.

"So what do you think of Eva Swensk, then?" she said in an attempt to find a fresh topic of conversation. "Our new national

13

police chief," she added, in a poorly disguised imitation of his dry tone of voice.

Amante turned his head toward her. "Do you know her?"

The traffic ahead of them slowed down. Julia changed lanes again and accelerated past a few more cars before skillfully pulling back into a gap. She gained five car lengths by the maneuver.

"No, I can't really claim I do. We've only met a few times. I listened to a couple of her talks when she was regional police chief. She's got a reputation for being tough and efficient. But I was still a bit surprised when Stenberg gave her the job. I thought it was going to be yet another man."

Or, to be more accurate, one particular man, she thought. For some reason Deputy Police Commissioner Oscar Wallin had lost the race to Eva Swensk. Wallin had done all the dirty work of the reorganization only to find himself unexpectedly— and to the delight of many—pushed aside when it was time for the minister of justice to appoint a new national police chief. She still wondered what had actually happened. But Wallin wasn't the sort of man you called up for a chat, so she'd had to contain her curiosity. It had been several months since she last heard from him, which left her feeling slightly disappointed.

Wallin was one of the few police officers she regarded as a role model. Someone who, even though he was only four or five years older than she was, had managed to make a rapid ascent through the otherwise sluggish police hierarchy. She had hoped to be able to follow him up to the top. But instead she was sitting here, babysitting an inexperienced civilian.

"The minister of justice doesn't seem afraid to try new tactics," Amante said, breaking her train of thought. "Did you read the article in *Dagens Nyheter* last week? Stenberg's on the offensive."

Amante's tone was a bit more engaged now, less robotic. This subject clearly interested him more than a straightforward massacre and a couple of dead officers.

"It'll certainly be interesting to see how many of Stenberg's ideas can actually be put into practice," he went on. "Anonymous witnesses, expanded possibilities to use infiltration, amnesties, or reduced sentences for perpetrators who stand witness against their fellow criminals."

"You don't believe in all that, then?" Julia said. "It already works that way in a ton of other countries. The police need more effective tools against organized crime; you have to admit that, surely?"

Amante shrugged his shoulders. "It doesn't really matter what I think. But people are saying that the Bar Association is likely to try to stop a number of the proposals. And if the opposition wins the election this autumn—"

Amante broke off abruptly. He blushed slightly, as if he'd suddenly realized he was talking too much. Julia put her foot down and changed lanes again, gaining a few more places in the queue. The maneuver made Amante grab hold of the handle above the passenger door. Julia smiled to herself. *Just wait until we get the lights and sirens on.* But that presupposed he'd be sticking around, which she doubted. Amante clearly wasn't an expert in either violent crime or murder investigations, and didn't seem remotely interested in the subject. He must have been recruited to the unit for some other reason. Because someone wanted or needed him there. Superintendent Pärson was a keen adherent to the path of least resistance. Everyone knew that the fat little bastard supplemented his horse-racing pot by tipping off the evening tabloids about ongoing investigations at advantageous moments. Yet no one was ever able to catch him. He knew exactly how often he needed to change his pay-as-you-go cell phone and Western Union account. And, perhaps most importantly of all, which people to stay on the good side of: whom he ought to do favors for, and when.

She glanced surreptitiously at Amante as they approached the heavy gates leading down into the garage of Police Headquarters at Kronoberg. She couldn't quite make sense of the rhythm she had picked up from him so far. His age was difficult to determine; she guessed at thirty-five or so. But he spoke in a rather stilted way, like someone considerably older, more like a politician than a cop. And the way he dressed was something else. A blue blazer with the gilded emblem of the Royal Swedish Yacht Club on top of a coral-colored sweater with a designer logo, just frayed enough at the collar to suggest that its owner had worn it when he sailed around Gotland. Pale slacks with a neat crease and hand-sewn boating shoes. But in place of the slicked-back, sun-bleached hair that would have matched his well-to-do summer wardrobe perfectly, Amante's dark hair was cut short. And he didn't have a salt-splashed suntan from Båstad or Sandhamn with lighter patches left by his sunglasses either. Amante's skin was swarthy, like someone from southern Europe. Or even farther south. His whole rhythm was full of contradictions, a syncopated beat that was hard to follow.

"Your surname," she said. "Is it Italian?"

"Spanish," he replied, slightly too quickly.

An image flashed through her mind. Something on the news, a row of smartly dressed EU politicians, something about the legal system. An articulate man making critical remarks about the government and minister of justice.

"Victor Amante. The EU politician?" She guessed the answer as she saw her new colleague squirm uncomfortably in his seat.

"He's my stepfather."

. . .

The quiet knock made Sarac slip the bag of pills under his pillow in a flash. It was designated rest time, so no one should be disturbing him now. Had the staff begun to suspect something after all? But a search team would hardly knock and wait politely to be let in before they turned his room upside down.

"Come in," he said as calmly as he could. He leaned back

against the pillow so that the bag of pills ended up behind his back. Damn, he should have slipped the bag back into the gap he had carved out behind one of the baseboards instead of hiding it in the first place he thought of like a startled five-year-old.

One of the caregivers, a man in his late twenties whose name Sarac thought might be Eskil, came into the room. Sarac noted that he closed the door behind him in a different way from usual. Carefully, as if he were trying to be as quiet as possible. Whatever Eskil was doing there, it definitely wasn't a search.

"Hello, David." The nurse glanced at the closed door, then put his hand in the pocket of his uniform tunic and held out a small white envelope. "For you."

Sarac frowned.

"Who from?" he said, without taking the envelope.

"The guy said his name was Frank."

"Surname?"

"He didn't say. Just that you were colleagues of some sort. That he'd been looking for you last Christmas but didn't manage to find you."

Sarac closed his eyes for a few seconds, searching his broken mind for an image that matched the name. He didn't succeed.

"What did he look like?"

"Dark hair, short, bit like a cop."

"Height, build? Other distinguishing features? You must be able to remember something?"

Eskil shrugged his shoulders. "I don't know. Normal height, normal build. Looked a bit like you, but not as skinny."

"And where did you meet this Frank?"

Eskil looked like he was getting fed up with all the questions. Instead of answering, he held the envelope out a bit farther. Waved it gently in front of Sarac's nose.

Sarac didn't move. He was trying to work out if the nurse's nervousness was because he had been threatened into doing

17

this, or because he was used to taking bribes and didn't want to get caught.

"Just take it, for God's sake." Eskil glanced over his shoulder again as if expecting someone to throw the door open at any moment. So he'd been bribed, then.

Sarac still didn't move. Could this be some sort of trap? Were they trying to trick him? Find out what he was planning to do? The distant rumble of his nightmares was suddenly back in his head. He put his hands over his ears and shut his eyes tight.

Eskil gave up his attempts to hand the letter over and tossed it onto the bed next to Sarac before heading for the door.

"I'll look in again in an hour in case you want to send a reply. Don't tell anyone, okay?"

"Sure," Sarac mumbled. "Actually, hang on . . ."

But before he had time to say more, the nurse had left the room. Sarac quickly put his hand under the pillow. The feeling of the plastic against his fingertips was strangely reassuring. It made the roar in his head subside.

The letter was lying on his bed, beside his left foot. He could read his own name in Times New Roman on the front. *Detective Inspector David Sarac*; nothing else. Unless there was something on the back. He picked the envelope up, turned it over, and held it up to the light. The back was blank, the envelope smooth and flat. It couldn't really contain anything but a sheet or two of paper.

He hadn't had any visitors for a long time, no contact with the outside world except for TV and the Internet. Perhaps Frank was yet another reporter trying to arrange an interview with him, an unusually creative one who was willing to bribe a staff member.

He slowly opened the envelope with his forefinger and pulled out a folded sheet of paper. At the top was a message in the same impersonal font as the envelope. Four lines, seven sentences, forty-six words. More than enough to make his heart beat faster.

He betrayed you, David. Swapped his future for you and Janus. Then he moved on while we bled and died out there on the island. No punishment, no consequences, straight to the top. How about a swap? Your secret for mine? A chance to get justice.

Sarac unfolded the bottom part of the sheet of paper. Two photos fell out onto the bed, landing upside down.

He turned the first one over. Husband, wife, two teenage girls dressed up for some sort of premiere. A good-looking, happy family smiling assuredly toward the photographer with perfect, dazzling media smiles.

His heart beat even faster. Spread out from his chest and up into his throat. He turned the second photograph over. Felt his hand tremble. He swallowed hard a couple of times.

The dead blonde woman was lying on her stomach across the black hood of a car. The pool of blood formed a sort of aura around her naked body. The force of her descent had been so strong that it almost welded her body to the expensive car. Transforming it into a single horrifying sculpture of skin, glass, and metal.

· · ·

"The dismembered body at Källstavik: What do we know?"

The waitress had barely put their plates down on the checkered cloth and walked off before Deputy Police Commissioner Oscar Wallin revealed the purpose of their meeting. Julia couldn't help smiling. Wallin hadn't changed. Straight to the point, no unnecessary beating around the bush. Just like her. That morning he had suddenly called after months of silence. Now she understood why. Or at least what he wanted to talk about.

"Aren't you going to ask me how I am or what I've been doing for the past six months?" Julia smiled, but Wallin's expression didn't change. "Anyway, you didn't have to ask me to lunch. Most of it's already been in the papers."

That was more accurate than she would have liked. No more than a couple of days had passed since her visit to the Forensic Medicine Unit, but the public already knew almost as much as she did. The evening tabloids loved summer murders, and their reporting followed the usual pattern. Yesterday there had been a few grainy pictures of police boats and divers, and a map covering the whole centerfold. *Where the body parts were found.* Quotes from *a source with inside knowledge of the investigation*, obviously her own boss, and today she had just read the assortment of speculation and confident assertions from the usual academic detectives who had never seen a dead body in real life.

This could be connected to the criminal underworld. Statistically, the killer is likely to have been known to the victim, and her personal favorite: *Dismemberment is a way for the killer to get rid of the body.*

Wallin put what looked like a perfectly judged mix of beef patty, potato, sauce, and lingonberry preserve in his mouth. He chewed slowly as he raised his eyebrows quizzically.

"The victim, according to the latest we've got from the pathologist, is a white male between thirty-five and forty-five," Julia said. "Just over one meter eighty centimeters tall, with short, dark brown hair. We may need to take that last bit with a pinch of salt. The crayfish didn't leave much of his scalp."

She fell silent. Wallin went on chewing, as implacable as ever. If the malicious rumors about his career contained any truth at all, there certainly wasn't any sign of it in his behavior or appearance. His boyish features, emphasized by his perfectly combed side parting, formed such an abrupt contrast to his tailor-made three-piece suit that it almost jarred. He looked like a boy dressed up as a grown man, he always had. Previously only the most deranged of his colleagues had made fun of that. Only in recent months had she heard his nickname spoken out loud in the corridors of Police Headquarters. Even by some of her superiors.

Manboy.

She didn't approve. Wallin was a talented policeman and an equally skilled administrator. But now others were enjoying the fruits of his labors, and the whole of his handpicked team had been transferred to the staff of the national police chief. All but Wallin himself, which most of his colleagues took to mean that he was going to be sidelined somewhere and never heard from again. She hoped that interpretation didn't turn out to be correct.

"Have you been able to identify the body?" Wallin wiped his mouth on his napkin with exaggerated thoroughness.

"Not yet. We've checked for a match on the missing persons register: nothing there. His hands haven't been found, so we haven't got fingerprints. Same with teeth and dental records. We're expecting DNA results from the National Forensics Lab by tomorrow at the earliest but probably on Friday, maybe even Monday. It's not at all certain that they'll be able to get any DNA. The body was in a very poor state."

"And the face? Could you release a photograph to the press? Ask the general public to get in touch with tip-offs?"

Julia shook her head.

"The perpetrator had a go at the face with a chain saw. It's completely unrecognizable."

At least for the time being, she added to herself. She considered telling Wallin about her backup plan. Let him know how good she was at her job. Six months ago she would have done so without hesitation. But for some reason she decided to wait. Besides, she wasn't even sure if what she was considering could actually be done.

"The experts in the tabloids are right, then," Wallin said. "You've got a real challenge on your hands with this case. You know the statistics as well as I do. Only six out of ten dismemberments get cleared up. A sixty percent chance that quickly shrinks to single digits if you don't manage to identify the body. And what would that do to your solving rate?"

The question seemed to be rhetorical, because Wallin turned

his attention back to his food without waiting for an answer. Julia stuck her fork into her Caesar salad, took a mouthful, and discovered at once that something was missing from the dressing. It took her a few seconds to work out what. Anchovies. What chef would make a Caesar salad without using anchovies? Presumably one who thought he could get away with it.

The murmur of conversation in the restaurant rose in volume as more and more diners sat down at the tables. One or two suits, but mostly neon-clad laborers. People who, like Wallin, had a preference for traditional Swedish fare. Personally she preferred Asian. Lighter food: less flour, cream, and potato.

Wallin went on eating calmly. He was evidently planning to make her ask.

"So, tell me! Why is the minister of justice's special investigator so interested in an old dismembered body?"

Wallin took a sip of his lingonberry drink and then carefully wiped his mouth again before leaning over the table.

"As you may be aware, the party has its training center in Källstavik. Several of the higher-ups rent houses on the grounds with access to the water, including the minister of justice's father-in-law, Karl-Erik Cedergren. A dismembered body in the water they go swimming in, just in time for the holidays, is a little uncomfortable, particularly when the tabloids are wallowing in the details. The minister's phone is going to start ringing, and when it does, I want to be prepared."

"You want me to keep you informed?"

He smiled at her, a crooked, slightly mocking smile. Yet Julia still found herself smiling back at him. She'd missed this. Missed their rather peculiar sense of camaraderie.

The first time she'd met Oscar Wallin was around five years ago. She'd been part of the team investigating an unusually grisly murder in the southern suburbs of Stockholm. The victim was a small-time informer, and the method resembled another case that National Crime was investigating. Wallin was involved in his capacity as National Crime's informant handler, and he was the only one who didn't shake his head when she, unlike all the alpha males on the investigative team, declared firmly that they were dealing with two different perpetrators and that the second was simply a copycat. When the forensics experts proved her right a week later, Wallin bought her lunch. Over a meal of stuffed cabbage leaves he asked how she could have been so certain. She explained that the two crime scenes were just too different. The perpetrators had moved through the rooms in different ways and did things in a different order. And, unlike all the other police officers she knew, Wallin seemed to be in no doubt about her abilities.

Two months later he had called her and asked her to take a look at the security camera footage of a robbery and compare it with videos of various suspects and images from where they lived. She had found it relatively easy to point out those whose movements and rhythms matched the robbers'. Not long after that, she was suddenly promoted to detective inspector and given her own room in the front corridor of the crime unit, and she slowly began to make a name for herself within the force. And even if Superintendent Pärson claimed the credit for having discovered and coached her, Julia was well aware of who her real mentor was.

Wallin had continued to contact her every now and then: sometimes to find out how she was getting on, but more usually to give her a new challenge or ask for discreet favors. Most recently last Christmas.

"By the way, what happened about that trace of blood I found in Sophie Thorning's apartment?" she said. "Did it help prove that someone else had been there the night she jumped?"

Wallin shook his head. "It turned out to be her own blood. I thought I'd told you that."

"No, we haven't spoken since I sent you my report. Not so much as a Christmas card by way of thanks." She pretended to be upset. That would have made most guys blush and start to stammer their apologies. She knew she looked pretty good and that this could occasionally be used to her advantage. But that sort of trick never worked on Wallin, which was another reason why she respected him. The only way to get Wallin's attention and respect was by delivering results.

"I've been busy," he said, without sounding the slightest bit apologetic, but more like he was chastising her for not realizing something so obvious.

"And the post of national police chief . . . ?"

Julia regretted saying it before it was even out of her mouth. Wallin's mouth narrowed to a thin line.

"If I'm allowed to say what I think, the minister of justice picked the wrong person," she added quickly.

Wallin sat silent for a few seconds, as if he was trying to work out how truthful her statement was. The thin line curved into a controlled smile.

"Thanks. Obviously, I'm aware that I'm being talked about. That people are saying I've been passed over, even that I'm heading toward the exit." Wallin shook his head gently. "Success breeds enemies, Julia. You'll find that out. Colleagues who are envious or bitter, who take pleasure in the few occasions when you fail, and who don't hesitate to spread all manner of rumors."

He leaned forward slightly and smiled more broadly, revealing his canine teeth.

"But I'm still here, as you can see. I've still got an office just a few meters from the minister's, and sooner or later everyone who's underestimated me will have to pay for that."

He held her gaze for a few seconds. Then straightened up.

"Enough about that. There's another reason why I wanted to talk to you. It's about your new colleague . . ."

Wallin wasn't the sort to do air quotes, but Julia thought she could almost see his fingers twitching on the checkered tablecloth.

"Omar Amante, lawyer, excellent grades at university, foreign service. If the predictions are correct and the opposition win this autumn's election, his stepfather will replace Jesper Stenberg as minister of justice. Which makes Amante junior the golden boy. The question is: Why has he suddenly appeared from nowhere to join you in the Violent Crime Unit?"

"What do you mean?" Julia frowned. A police car drove past outside in the street. Flashing lights and sirens. The sound bounced between the buildings, drowning out everything else for a few seconds.

"Amante left his job with Europol last Christmas," Wallin said as soon as the car had passed. "Six months before his contract was due to finish. One unconfirmed rumor is that he fell out with his boss. That there was some sort of scene that got hushed up. No one seems to want to talk about it. Either way, Amante disappeared off the radar for a few months. He wasn't in Sweden, and he wasn't at Europol's offices in The Hague. Then he suddenly shows up in Stockholm and lands in the middle of a murder investigation that has vague connections to the party. The same party that his stepfather is doing his utmost to eject from power."

Wallin leaned across the table again and lowered his voice.

"You've been saddled with Amante for a reason. And I'd dearly love to know what that reason is."

• • •

Sarac zipped his jacket up and pulled his hat as far down on his forehead as he could before looking at his watch again. Thirty seconds. This was madness. He was mad. Which made it all the more ironic that he was trying to escape from a mental institution.

He put his fingers on the door handle. Five, four, three, two, one . . .

He stepped out into the corridor. Walked without hesitation straight toward the door to the stairwell, not falling for the temptation of looking up at the spherical camera above it. The change of shift was under way and the likelihood of any member of the staff looking at the picture from the camera for the few seconds it took him to pass it wasn't very high. At least that was what he tried to tell himself to calm his pounding heart. Panic and fear were being temporarily held at bay by the tranquilizer he had swallowed just over half an hour ago.

This isn't a good idea, the voices in his head whispered. But the happy pills had rendered them impotent. Easier to ignore. At least for the time being.

The doors to the ward were always kept locked, and he fiddled with the key, got it into the lock, but couldn't turn it. He jerked and twisted it. For a fraction of a second he considered giving up. Going back to his safe little room, forgetting everything, and carrying out his original plan. Gulp down all those sleeping pills at once, tonight. Put an end to everything. But he knew that was impossible. He had to know the truth, had to know how everything fit together.

He suddenly felt the lock give with a clicking sound. The key Eskil had given him was evidently a cheap copy that took a bit of fiddling to make it work. He guessed that his new pen pal Frank had paid for it, just as he had paid for Eskil's services.

Sarac headed down the marble staircase, all the way to the basement. He managed to unlock the heavy steel door almost at once and found himself in a bare, low-ceilinged corridor. Another glance at his watch. Two minutes and ten seconds had elapsed since he began his escape. He quickened his pace, trying to make use of the surplus adrenaline while it lasted.

He stopped at the door marked *District Heating*. Once again he used the copied key to unlock the door and stepped inside a large, warm room full of pipes and meters. He stood still for a couple of seconds to get his bearings. Then he identified the incoming pipes and followed them to the far end of the room, just as he had been instructed to do. Another heavy door, and behind it a tunnel where the pipes disappeared into the darkness. He took a few steps forward. Felt for the circuit breaker but couldn't find it.

Suddenly the door behind him closed and everything went pitch-black. He was seized by panic as it broke through the chemical barrier protecting him from his anxieties and gripped his rib cage.

Why are you doing this, David? the voices whispered. *Why?*

He put his hand against the concrete wall, leaned forward, and took a couple of deep breaths. He caught the vomit when it was halfway up and forced it back down into his stomach. He stood there for a minute or so until the panic attack subsided. Then he straightened up and felt across the wall with his hand. His fingers nudged the circuit breaker and he turned it. A mechanical click echoed off the concrete walls of the tunnel and a sequence of fluorescent lights flickered slowly to life.

What if this is a trap? What if someone's waiting for you out there? Someone who wants revenge.

Sarac stopped. He'd had time to think through that scenario over the past few days. That and a handful of others. The possibility that his secret pen pal, the man calling himself Frank, didn't actually exist. That everything, the letter and photographs alike, was a fabrication intended to lure him from his hiding place. But for some reason during their brief correspondence he had become convinced that this wasn't the case. Besides, he had managed to persuade Eskil to take a surreptitious photograph of Frank, and had studied it carefully on the cracked screen of the nurse's phone.

Frank definitely existed. What he said was true. Someone had managed not to face up to his responsibilities so far. Had bought himself free from guilt. Had saved his own life and career by betraying Sarac.

Justice.

That was why he was now heading, for the first time in several months, out into the wide world. Exposing himself one last time to the frightening world that he no longer felt able to deal with.

Even if he was wrong, if all this turned out to be a trap

27

after all and Frank or someone else was waiting out there in the darkness to kill him, then they'd only be doing him a favor.

He put his hand in his pocket and closed his fingers around the bag of pills. Twenty-five of them now. Enough for him to pull the emergency cord whenever he wanted to.

It took him seven minutes to make his way through the tunnel and climb up the steps to the boiler room at the other end. The combination of the exertion and the heat in there left him drenched in sweat. He hesitated a few seconds before cautiously nudging the door open. To his left lay the main building and the illuminated yard that he had just passed beneath. To the right was the staff parking lot, and beyond that the security lodge and main gate. Twelve minutes had passed, in another three the change of shift would be over.

He inhaled the cold evening air and tried to focus. Felt the slight tremble in his muscles that told him that the rush of adrenaline that had brought him this far was ebbing away. But he was almost there now. All it would take was one last burst of effort.

The car was exactly where Eskil had said it would be, all he had to do was open the unlocked trunk and crawl inside. Close it and make himself as comfortable as he could in the dark. Exhaustion took over his body, his head.

The picture of the attractive family popped into his mind again, then the dead woman on the hood of the car. They were replaced in turn by pictures of a dark forest where the flare of guns firing flashed among the trees.

Are you really sure about this, David? the voices whispered.

• • •

Julia was about to fetch her last cup of coffee for the afternoon from the unit's staff room when her cell phone started to buzz. She answered with the phone clamped between her ear and her shoulder as she poured coffee into a chipped mug. For a moment she thought about being nice and getting a cup for

28

Amante, then realized that the phone call gave her an excuse not to. She could carry only one mug back with her.

"Hello, this is Katarina Lindgren from the National Forensics Lab."

Julia took hold of the phone with her left hand, then, with the mug in her right hand, started to walk back toward her office. She passed the closed door to the little cubbyhole that had been found for Amante. A claustrophobic, windowless room that was probably meant to be a janitor's closet. But he hadn't complained so far. Another tentative point.

Before her lunch with Wallin the day before, she had put Amante to work calling everyone who lived near where the body was found; there weren't too many. The number of permanent residents with an open view of the water was limited to four or five, and she strongly doubted that any of them would have anything to contribute. But a murder investigation was in part just a long list of things that needed to be checked, whether or not you actually thought they might turn out to be useful. And, usefully, the task was a way of keeping Amante occupied. Pärson had decided not to let her have more detectives until they had something to go on. He had blamed the summer holidays and the fact that they had other cases that were higher priority. In fact he was actually counting on her managing on her own, so that he would later be able to report good results to his boss.

"I'm calling about the unidentified body that was found in the water at Källstavik," the woman on the phone said. "I saw a note that you wanted to be informed the moment we found anything."

"Absolutely." Julie closed the door behind her, shutting out the voices of those of her colleagues who were already on their way home.

"We've found a match in the DNA register . . ." the woman began.

Julia put her cup down a little too hard, spilling some of the contents on the pale wood of the desktop.

". . . but I'm afraid I can't say much more than that."

"No?" Julia slipped onto her chair.

"There's a match in the register, referring to another case. It's not a complete match, just sixty-five percent compared to the usual ninety-nine. The sample we received was badly degraded. What that means is—"

"You've matched it to DNA that was found in another case, but never identified," Julia interrupted.

"Exactly. All I get on the screen is the fact that there's a match in the register, the percentage of the similarity between the samples, and the number of the case in which the other sample was found."

Julia got hold of a pen and paper. "Would you mind giving me the number?"

She wrote the digits and letters down, one by one, then stared at the familiar combination.

"Skarpö," she said. As much to herself as to the woman on the other end of the line.

Her brain was working at high speed, already starting to process the consequences of what she'd just been told. But she still forced herself to ask one more time:

"Just so I know I've got this right. Our dismembered body was present at the shoot-out on Skarpö?"

"That's certainly what the DNA sample suggests. The match came through a few minutes ago. I'm new here, so I don't really know what the procedures are, but I thought you'd probably want to know as soon as possible. I mean, there's been a lot in the papers and everything."

"You did exactly the right thing. Thanks very much for letting me know."

"No problem."

Julia ended the call. And realized that she was smiling. A line of inquiry, she thought. For a moment she imagined herself as a sniffer dog with its nose pressed to the ground.

And what a line of inquiry . . .

• • •

Sarac cautiously opened the door to his apartment. He breathed in the stale air with its smell of newly constructed Ikea furniture. Then he took a long stride across the heap of advertisements and newspapers, snuck in, and lowered all the blinds before switching on the weak lamp above the stove. He rubbed his hands together, trying to get some warmth back into his frozen fingers.

Even though it was his home, the apartment filled him with unease and he had to sit down and take a few deep breaths to control his anxiety—the new and deep-rooted varieties alike. He was safe there, he told himself, at least for a few hours.

Everything looked just as he remembered, yet he was still convinced that the apartment had been painstakingly cleaned. That anything suggesting that he was anything other than the heroic police officer David Sarac had long since been removed.

The clock on the microwave said 14:50, which meant that at best he had about three hours before the staff in the nursing home realized that he'd escaped, and maybe as long as three and a half hours before the news reached the right people. Not long, but long enough.

The envelope containing his passport, banknotes of various currencies, and the credit card he only used when traveling was still in the bottom drawer of his desk. He breathed a sigh of relief. The people who had cleaned his apartment obviously didn't think he was likely to want to run. He could hardly blame them. Only a few days ago he hadn't even wanted to go outside. That he had managed to handle the train journey to Stockholm was largely because Eskil had given him a healthy dose of tranquilizers that had protected him against the sounds, the lights, and, not least, the voices in his head.

In the pantry he found a packet of ramen noodles. As the water boiled he emptied the pockets of his borrowed clothes and put the train ticket, key ring, and bus pass on the kitchen table. Then, finally, the bag of sleeping pills.

He undressed and stuffed the clothes into a plastic bag he found under the sink. There were surveillance cameras at the Central Station that he hadn't been able to avoid. It wouldn't take long for them to find him. And police photos showing what he looked like. He dug out a pair of black jeans and a cotton shirt from his wardrobe. They were both too big, reminding him of how much weight he had lost. He ate the noodles straight from the pan, then washed down another tranquilizer with tap water. Oddly enough, the food tasted considerably better than anything he had eaten in the nursing home.

When he had finished he washed everything up carefully and put the trash in the bag containing the clothes. He was planning to dump it in a bin by the entrance to the subway, so that at least there wouldn't be any visible evidence that he had been in the apartment.

In the back of the hall cupboard he found a padded jacket and a black knit hat. Just as he had hoped, his own clothes made him look different. Just an ordinary Swede on his way to work.

He put the things on the kitchen table in his jacket pockets, turned out the light, and then slowly peered behind the blind. Everything looked quiet outside. He couldn't help glancing at the windows opposite. That was where they had watched him from last year. Waiting for his next move.

All your doing, your fault, the voices whispered.

· · ·

It was almost nine o'clock at night by the time Julia got all the boxes into her office. The corridor was deserted, its doors closed, half the fluorescent lights in the ceiling above the linoleum floor switched off. She liked working late. It meant she avoided unnecessary distractions, telephones ringing, colleagues knocking on her door when they didn't actually want anything.

The pictures were all laid out on her desk. First their unidentified body with its silent grin. She looked at him. No matter who he was and what he had done, no one deserved to die like that. Someone had stripped him of everything. His name, his dignity, even his humanity.

Below the pictures of the body she had lined up the photographs from Skarpö.

First the burned-out wreck of a house surrounded by snow. Black beams, a solitary chimney stack sticking up toward the sky from the foundations. Then a number of pictures that were far worse: charred bodies among the ruins, others outside in the snow. Lifeless, some of them with visible holes in their torsos or heads. Spent cartridges everywhere. Short ones from pistols, longer ones from assault rifles, red or blue ones from shotguns. The photographs were an all-too-visible reminder of just how violent the shoot-out had been.

Superintendent Peter Molnar lay on his back with his mouth wide-open, several of his dazzlingly white teeth shot out. The blood around his head formed a red halo. His eyes were staring blankly up at the sky. She'd seen the picture before, enough times for the shudder in her stomach not to feel quite so strong. Poor Peter. He'd been a good officer, someone most people spoke well of. Admittedly, he and the men on his team were the same tiresome alpha males whom the force seemed to be awash with. The guys who tried it on with her, one after the other, on the few occasions she had been stupid enough to visit any of the police bars. But Peter was at least both smart and funny. He knew when it was time to give up and go and hunt easier prey. And now his wife was a widow and his children left fatherless. She turned the photograph over.

Detective Inspector Josef Almlund's death looked more peaceful. She had known him too, of course. Peter socialized more with his second-in-command than with his own family. Josef had been a large man of few words, always ready to do exactly what Peter asked of him. Even lie to Peter's wife, if that was called for. Which it probably had been on a fairly regular basis.

Josef Almlund was sitting at one end of the house, leaning back against the foundations with his head lolling on his chest. The fire had burned his jacket and the hair at the back of his neck, but apart from that it almost looked like he was asleep. Having a bit of a rest before the fighting started again. She turned the picture over, just as she had with the one of Molnar. She paused for a moment, trying to shake off the images of the two dead men. She only half succeeded. She thought about David Sarac. The horrors he must have experienced out there. Watching his friends die around him. The last she had heard about Sarac was that he was in a nursing home in an undisclosed location. Hardly surprising, really.

Her cell phone buzzed, but she ignored it, just as she had a few minutes earlier. She knew it was Amante. He'd have to wait until morning, when she had a better idea of things. Besides, her conversation with Wallin was still in the back of her mind.

She gathered all the photographs she needed and put the others back in the evidence boxes. Now at least she had a time and a location to work with. On January 2, 2014, the dead man had been on the island of Skarpö, just outside Vaxholm in the Stockholm archipelago. According to the pathologist, the body parts had been in the water for approximately four months, so since late February or thereabouts. That left a gap of six, eight weeks between the Skarpö shoot-out and the time when the body parts were deposited beneath the ice.

She looked at the photographs from the Forensic Medicine Unit again. Stared at the mutilated smile.

"I'm getting closer," she whispered. "I'll soon know who you are."

Her cell phone started to buzz again, but she let it ring.

• • •

"Come in, David. I'm Frank." The man who had opened the door held out his hand toward Sarac, but he didn't take it. It was the same man from the grainy photograph Eskil had shown

34

him. The nurse was right: they did actually look quite similar. They both looked like cops. Or criminals. Or both.

He walked past the man into a shabby little office. The room couldn't be more than fifteen to twenty square meters in total. By one wall was a camping mattress and a sleeping bag, and there was a door that presumably led to a toilet. In the opposite wall was a dirty window facing the parking lot outside. Two overflowing Dumpsters were visible below, but, judging by the general state of the building, all construction work had been abandoned a long time ago. The whole of the run-down industrial estate felt badly neglected. Next to the bus stop Sarac had seen a couple of large signs proudly showing the future. Glass and concrete reaching for the skies. No 1970s barracks like this.

"It's all ready, just as we agreed." The man calling himself Frank gestured toward the two wooden chairs beside the camping table in the middle of the room. There was an open laptop on the table and, next to it, a camera mounted on a tripod.

Sarac took off his jacket and hung it on the back of the chair, then sat down. Frank put a photograph in front of him. The blonde woman on the hood, the same terrible image as the picture he had already seen, but from a different angle. Then a sheet of paper, a printout from the vehicle register with the name of the car's owner clearly circled. Then another picture. The good-looking family again.

Sarac swallowed. His heart was pounding so hard that he was having trouble breathing.

"He called me straight afterward. Crying like a little child," Frank said. "I went round and cleaned up. Got rid of all the evidence that he'd ever been there. And in return he told me about you. Who you met, how much you could remember after the accident. He was my source in the hunt for Janus. And he told me that you and Janus were out there on the island."

Sarac took a deep breath. So it was true. He'd been betrayed. Betrayed by his ultimate superior.

"You understand what this means, don't you?" Frank went on in a low voice. "What the consequences could be if you choose to go on with this? This sort of knowledge can be lethal."

"If I d-didn't . . ." Sarac cleared his throat. The bullet that had passed through his neck out on the island had damaged his larynx, making his voice unreliable. "If I didn't, I'd hardly be here."

Frank nodded, then went over to the small sink at the far end of the room and poured a glass of water, which he put down on the table. Then he sat down in front of the computer. Sarac took a couple of sips before looking up.

"Okay," Frank said. "Your turn. Your secret in return for mine, like we agreed."

The man pressed a key and a little red light lit up on the camera. "You can start talking whenever you like."

Sarac cleared his throat again and instinctively scratched the scar on his neck.

"M-My name is David Sarac. I handle informants for the Stockholm Police, and I was responsible for a secret source, an undercover agent called Janus. I was also responsible for the shoot-out on Skarpö in the New Year. Everyone who died and was injured out there was trying to get hold of Janus, to uncover his true identity. None of them succeeded."

He paused, then breathed in through his nose.

"I'm the only person who knows the truth. The only survivor who knows who Janus really is . . ."

• • •

Julia stood up from her chair. She hit her knee hard against the desktop and very nearly emptied the contents of her morning coffee across the collage of terrible images that had lain on her desk since the previous evening.

"Gone? How can a body just be gone?"

"Well . . ." The pathologist's voice on the phone was dry as dust. "I didn't say it was gone. I said it isn't here. There's a big difference. We aren't in the habit of losing bodies here in the Forensic Medical Unit."

The pain in her knee made Julia grimace. She was at the point of saying that she hadn't had enough coffee to deal with semantic pedantry but managed to stop herself just in time.

"Do you feel like telling me what *has* happened to the body, then?" she said as calmly as she could.

"Your colleagues came and collected it last night. They brought their own van and everything."

For a couple of seconds Julia's brain stopped working.

"My colleagues," she managed to say. "My colleagues moved our dismembered body?" She could hear how stupid she sounded.

"Exactly," the pathologist said. "Your colleagues in the Security Police. According to the night staff, they seemed to be in quite a hurry."

· · ·

The door to Pärson's room was open, but it wouldn't have made any difference if it had been barricaded from the inside. No one stuck their oar into her cases—not the Security Police, nor anyone else.

"What the hell is going on? Why have the Security Police taken my dead body?"

"And good morning to you too, Gabrielsson. I was just about to call you, so you've saved me the trouble. Please have a seat."

Pärson waved his fleshy hand toward one of the two chairs opposite his desk. Only then did Julia realize that Amante was already sitting in the other one.

"Well," he went on, "the news I was going to share with the two of you, which Julia has evidently already heard, is that the Security Police, in their great wisdom, have decided to ease our burden."

He smiled ever so slightly, just enough to crease his jowls.

"Apparently our dismembered body is connected to a suspected terrorism case. Some sort of defector. Syria or Iran or something."

"That's not true," Julia said, rather less calmly than she had hoped.

"No?" Pärson's happy smile faltered slightly.

Julia took a deep breath. "Our victim was involved in Skarpö. There's a match with his DNA in the register. We already knew that at least one person got away, so that's probably who we've found."

Pärson straightened up. The movement made his chair whimper under his weight. "And how the hell do you know that?"

"I spoke to the National Forensics Lab late yesterday afternoon," she said. She bit her lip and waited for the inevitable explosion.

Pärson's face turned from pink to red. "Why the hell didn't you tell me straightaway?"

Well, she thought. *Partly because you'd already left several hours earlier; partly because you get annoyed if anyone calls you after work about things that aren't a matter of life and death; but mainly because you would have seen a chance to make a bit on the side by calling the media, thereby making my job ten times harder.* For a few seconds she actually considered saying all this out loud.

"We were going to tell you first thing this morning," Amante said out of the blue. "We just wanted a chance to discuss it first. To be honest, neither of us believed that there was much urgency in a case where the victim had been dead for several months."

Pärson glared at him, and even Julia got the evil eye before he threw himself back in his chair, which once again protested loudly.

"Bloody hell. This sort of thing needs to be reported at once; that should be obvious, surely? A connection to Skarpö changes everything. The media are going to lose it completely. The phones will be ringing off the hook. Those soft-shoed bastards must have got one of their hackers to flag up the case in the computer system. And got advance warning as soon as the lab found a match. The Security Police have been waiting for an opportunity to muscle in on the Skarpö case ever since last winter. It's no wonder that they were so damn fast. I need to inform the head of Regional Crime right away."

"Why do the Security Police want to get a foot in the door of the Skarpö investigation?"

Pärson glared at Julia.

"Are you hard of hearing? They want to stake out their position in the new police authority. Show that they're worth their huge budget. If the Security Police manage to tie all the remaining loose ends in the Skarpö case and find the person who got away—the one we and National Crime have failed to find so far—it'll make us look like incompetent idiots. Thanks a fucking bunch for that, Gabrielsson. I promise you now, I'll be sure to tell the head of Regional Crime all about your exemplary work."

Julia tried to control herself. She didn't succeed as well as she usually did. And blamed it on the lack of caffeine.

"What about you, then," she said, "just letting the Security Police stroll in and take over everything? Without so much as calling me, even though it was my case. Who did you talk to at the Security Police? What unit? What case number did he give?" She stopped herself, aware that she had crossed the line, actually way beyond it.

"Now listen," Pärson said, leaning forward over his desk. "You've been in the force long enough to know that you have to take things as they come. Don't try to blame this on me. If you'd kept me properly informed, I could have told them to go to hell—just like I want you and your little pal here to do now, before I resort to physical measures."

As they were walking away from Pärson's room, Amante drew her aside in the corridor. They stopped in front of a faded picture of an archipelago landscape.

"Explain what just happened to me," he said quietly.

"I thought you'd worked it out," she muttered. "Our work-shy boss allowed someone at the Security Police—whose name he can't recall—to take over our case for reasons he can't remember. And right now he's calling his own superior and blaming the whole thing on us."

"So we're being taken off the case?"

"He didn't actually say that in so many words. Not that it really matters. Without the body we haven't got a case. No chance of making any progress. The National Forensics Lab has probably already received new orders to talk exclusively to the Security Police from now on, presumably for reasons relating to national security."

She fell silent and nodded at a colleague walking past them.

"Okay, that's pretty much what I thought," Amante said when the man was out of earshot. "Just wanted to make sure."

He leaned a bit closer to Julia as he glanced over his shoulder.

"I've got something I need to show you. It's about our body."

She raised her eyebrows and waited for him to go on. But Amante gave no indication of continuing.

"Okay," she said. "Let me get a cup of coffee. Your room or mine?"

Amante shook his head. "Not here. In my apartment. I'll make you coffee."

. . .

Sarac got up from the camping mattress, switched the computer on, and sat down at the table. He stretched to shake off the half doze that had more or less replaced real sleep for him. Time was running out, his tranquilizers would last another four days, but he hoped everything would be over by then.

Three days had passed since their exchange. Frank had left shortly after the video was finished. Packed his things, gave him the key to the office, and showed him how the computer and encrypted e-mail worked before taking his leave. This time Sarac did shake his hand. He knew who Frank was now, and why he had gone to such lengths to find out the truth about Janus. But instead of trying to steal it the way he had last winter, he had offered something in exchange. A fair deal between two equal parties. Quid pro quo.

So there he was, in a shabby little office in a ramshackle building that was waiting to be demolished. A perfect hiding place.

By now they must be hunting all over for him. They'd have tracked him via the security cameras at the Central Station, and one way or another they'd have figured out that he'd been back to his apartment. But there the trail would go cold. He had taken three different buses to get out here, using a different travel card each time. All bought at different places and paid for in cash, according to Hunter's instructions. He was safe here. Safe enough, anyway.

He had spent a whole day thinking about his next course of action. Then he made up his mind not to beat around the bush. He sent an encrypted e-mail revealing what he knew. What he wanted. But so far he hadn't received a reply.

He logged into his online e-mail account and, as he waited for the program to load, wrapped his fingers around the bag of sleeping pills in his pocket. He counted them one more time. Odds and evens.

Debts I can't escape till the day I die, the song in his head echoed, just as it had last Christmas.

The program opened up. There was a new message at the top of his in-box. He held his breath. Heard the music in his head get louder as he clicked to open the e-mail.

Curl your lip and make me want to live for one more day. Make me want to sleep through one more night.

An answer. One final task. His final task.

• • •

The apartment didn't look anything like what Julia had been expecting. The lobby of the building in Östermalm was imposing, with high arches and a heavy limestone staircase with a polished teak handrail. But inside the heavy door of the apartment the furnishings were considerably more spartan.

She should really have said no. Should have made her so-called partner tell her whatever he had to say up in Police Headquarters instead of wasting time going home with him. That she went along with him without a word of protest or even asking any questions was entirely Oscar Wallin's fault. Wallin's and that of her own wretched curiosity.

Sadly, Amante's apartment didn't provide any immediate clues regarding either him or his intentions. There were three bedrooms, two of which were completely empty apart from a few dead flies on the windowsills. In the third was a folding bed, two open removal boxes, and a small, old-fashioned television on the floor. No photographs, pictures, or anything else that said anything about the person who lived there. The only rhythm echoing between the bare walls was loneliness.

"Divorce," Amante said, confirming her impressions. "All my things are in storage. My ex-wife sent the wrong boxes here. Old vacation clothes." He gestured toward his yacht club blazer and sweater. "She knows I hate this jacket, so she probably did it on purpose."

He shrugged his shoulders as if to indicate that he'd said enough on the subject.

"There's coffee in the kitchen. Hot water in the right-hand tap. I'm just going to . . ." He nodded toward the toilet door.

"Sure, I'll sort it," she said.

The kitchen was, if possible, even barer than the rest of the apartment. And expensive. Marble counters, a big wine refrigerator, a gas range with six rings. Stepfather's money, she guessed. Maybe the apartment even belonged to him.

She couldn't see a coffee machine but did find a jar of instant and a few mismatched mugs covered with advertising logos. One of the German taps was marked *Heisswasser*. She tried it and, sure enough, got scalding-hot water straight from the tap. What an idea. She filled two mugs with water, added some powder, and stirred them with a coffee-flecked chopstick she found in the sink. She shuddered. The smell from the mugs wasn't enticing, but a splash of milk would make it bearable. She opened a large stainless steel door that she hoped belonged to the fridge. She found an open can of pea soup, a couple of greasy trays of Chinese food, and a can of low-alcohol beer. The huge kitchen was evidently completely wasted on Amante.

At the bottom of the fridge was a big yellow plastic cooler that looked brand-new. Amante had gone to the trouble of removing a couple of shelves from the fridge to make room for it, so at a guess it contained something that needed to be kept fresh. With a bit of luck there might even be some milk. She undid the straps on the side and opened the lid. She felt her heart stop for a few seconds.

She took a step back. Then another one. The fridge door slowly closed of its own accord and she was left standing with the lid in her hand.

Amante came into the kitchen.

"Did you find the coffee?" He caught her eye and stopped.

"Amante," Julia said, trying her utmost to sound calm. "Would you mind explaining why you have the head of our dead body in your fridge?"

• • •

Sarac had pulled on his jacket and hat. Turned out the lights in the little room. He looked at the time. Ten past five, and darkness was already settling on the parking lot outside the window. Time to get going. For some reason he felt different. Almost excited. He put his hands in his pockets and felt the bag of sleeping pills. On a sudden impulse he took it out and held it up against the weak light from the window. Twenty-five oval pills. He went over to the tiny kitchen area, opened the cupboard,

43

and tucked the bag away inside it. Then he walked out of the room and closed the door silently behind him. He was on his way now. On his way to put things right.

. . .

The coffee tasted just as disgusting as Julia had expected. But it was also the only thing in this whole situation that was remotely predictable.

"Sorry if I scared you," Amante said. "Let me explain. I called the National Forensics Lab yesterday. Spoke to a very nice young woman who was about to finish for the day. She said she'd spoken to you about the link to Skarpö a few minutes before I called. She asked if we actually spoke to each other in Violent Crime."

He took a sip of coffee and gave her a long look over the top of the cup. Julia said nothing, preferring to wait for him to go on instead.

"When the pathologist said we might not be able to identify our victim from DNA, I called a guy in Europol who I got to know on Lampedusa. He works as a forensics expert in Sarajevo. They've got a computer program that can create a three-dimensional image of a face from a layered X-ray of a skull. They use it to identify remains from the war. Obviously it's not a hundred percent, but enough to get a photofit." He took another swig of coffee. "The same thing must have occurred to you—that we could try to reconstruct his face some other way. That's why you called the Forensic Medicine Unit this morning, isn't it?"

She glared at him for a few seconds.

"The Museum of Medieval Stockholm," she said. "They've got a forensic anthropologist who came up with a wax model of Birger Jarl's face using just his skull a couple of years ago."

"Ah, smart." Amante nodded. "A proper model of the whole head probably works a lot better than just a photofit. But that would take longer. At least a month or so."

"And you couldn't wait that long. You needed to prove how smart you were."

A hint of a blush spread across Amante's neck. "I did actually try to call you yesterday evening. It wasn't that hard to work out why you weren't answering. You knew there was a link to Skarpö and you didn't want to involve the civilian once the case started to heat up."

Her turn to blush now, if she'd been the type. Which she wasn't.

"I figured out that everything would change as soon as the connection to Skarpö became common knowledge," he went on. "All manner of different police units and bosses would get involved. And the civilian would be the first person taken off the case. And I didn't want that, not after seeing the body. After seeing what our perpetrator had done to him." He stared at her; his anxious expression seemed to be looking for understanding.

Julia stifled a nod. Amante was saying the right things and he sounded entirely honest. But she wanted to hear the rest of the story before she made up her mind if he really was telling the truth.

Amante took a deep breath. "So, after I tried to call you last night, I drove out to the Forensic Medicine Unit. I paid the member of staff on duty two thousand kronor to let me borrow the head for twenty-four hours. I'd have gone as high as five, but he jumped at my first offer."

He pulled a face that was probably meant to look amused.

"The plan was to get the skull X-rayed and have it back in place by now. No one would have noticed anything and it would all have been a lot quicker than filling out forms and waiting for them to be processed. But then the Security Police appeared out of nowhere to fetch the body. Without even opening the bag, apparently, which was lucky for me."

"You must have realized that people were bound to ask questions about your photofit. Wonder where it had come from?"

He shrugged. "One thing at a time. A photofit would have been a big step forward. Paperwork can always be sorted out afterward, and it's not as if I've done anything illegal."

"Apart from bribing a public official, you mean?"

Amante smiled, a cryptic little smile that she couldn't really make sense of. Like so much else about him. If Wallin hadn't warned her, by this point she would have been convinced that Amante was telling the truth. But for now she still had her doubts.

"Two, actually, if we're being strictly accurate. An X-ray operator too—a guy I know from the yacht club. But I doubt either of them would be prepared to testify. All I did was pay what the Italians call a *tangente*. A sort of service charge, you could say."

"Did you learn that on Lampedusa? You know, that Italian island in the southern Mediterranean," she added, unable to stop herself.

He looked at her for a few seconds. His smile faded. He walked over to the sink and put his cup down.

"I learned lots of things on Lampedusa. More than I would have wanted." He turned his back on her as he rinsed the cup under the tap. Julia waited for him to go on, but Amante seemed to have clammed up.

"What do we do now?" The question was aimed at herself as much as him.

He turned the tap off and turned around.

"That was what I was thinking of asking you. As soon as the Security Police open the bag and discover that the head's missing, all hell's going to break loose. The smart option would be to go out to the Forensic Medicine Unit right away, pay the guy to sneak the head into one of the cold storage units, and forget the whole thing."

She looked at him, aware that he could easily have done that without her involvement.

Amante smiled faintly again and glanced at the time. "Or

we wait until ten o'clock before we decide what our next step's going to be."

"Why ten o'clock?"

"Because that's when we get to see what our dead man looked like."

. . .

Sarac was standing perfectly still in the darkened doorway. He resisted the temptation to reach out for the light switch he could see on the wooden wall. The forest behind him was dark and silent. The narrow unpaved track he had followed from the main road was only just visible at the edge of the trees on the far side of the turnaround. In the distance he could hear a raven call. The ghostly sound echoed between the trees, fading into a distant rumble. Unless it was just in his head.

The wind blowing off the ice-covered inlet cut straight through his clothes. He shivered and stepped in through the door. The soles of his boots scraped against the concrete floor. The smell inside made him think about the house on the island, and he waited for the usual accusing whispers. But for the time being the voices seemed to have fallen silent. Maybe the dead were huddled together in the darkness. Waiting for whatever was going to happen.

What *was* going to happen?

He didn't really know. All he knew was that he had reached the end of the road. That the whole Janus affair was going to end here, this evening, one way or another. That everyone involved would finally have to face up to the consequences of their actions.

The rumbling in his head grew louder. The winter thunder was getting closer. Then his thoughts were interrupted by another sound. A real one this time. It sounded as if someone was approaching. Taking cautious, creaking steps through the snow outside on the path. Sarac felt his heart beat faster.

Soon, he thought. *Soon it will all be over.*

A dark shape appeared in the doorway. Clearly visible against the white snow.

"David Sarac?" he heard a low voice say. And at that moment he knew how it was all going to end. The voice was firm, clear, not unfriendly. This was someone who had made up their mind. Then he saw a weapon aimed toward him. Saw it being raised. He closed his eyes.

Debts I can't escape till the day I die.

Time to pay his debts. Pay for his betrayal. Some things were simply too broken to be fixed.

"H-Here," he whispered. "I'm here."

A lightning flash, a frozen gust of wind right through his chest. The roar of winter thunder drowning his thoughts. Then nothing more.

• • •

The face on the screen looked real. Everything was where it should be, the proportions looked right. The nose, neither large nor small. The mouth with its hard, pursed lips, and the skin stretched across the cheekbones. The short, dark hair, the thin eyes. Even the eyelashes and brows were perfect, down to the last hair. Yet there was still something about the picture that wasn't quite right, something Julia couldn't put her finger on. But that didn't really matter. A clump of ice had formed in her stomach, its chill spreading throughout her body.

"A computer simulation will never be entirely accurate," Amante said over her shoulder. "The program uses measurements from the CAT scan—the size and angles of the bones in the face, eye sockets, and nose. Then it adds supplementary information such as hair and skin color. It all comes together to form an image that ought to be fairly close to reality. The only thing the program can't provide is—"

"Humanity," Julia said, turning toward him. "You're right: it's not a hundred percent. But I still recognize him."

She took a deep breath. *All hell is going to break loose now. A shit-storm of biblical proportions.*

"That"—she tapped the screen where the photofit of their dead man stared back at them with empty eyes—"that's Detective Inspector David Sarac."

THE
SILENCED

One

The smell coming from the kitchen woke Minister of Justice Jesper Stenberg. Bacon and eggs, freshly brewed coffee. Those thick American pancakes that the girls loved to drown in maple syrup.

He got out of bed and pulled on his robe. It was just past ten o'clock. He had slept for almost eight hours. Eight hours of deep sleep, just the way it should be. It had been several months since he last had any nightmares, which was as good a sign as any that his brain had moved on. That he'd put everything that happened last winter behind him.

In the bathroom he splashed his face with water. Tried out some of his most reliable facial expressions. Interest, concern, pensiveness. Everything seemed to be working and he winked at his own reflection.

As he walked down the stairs he heard voices from the kitchen. Karolina and the girls, of course, but among them a male voice that he'd hoped to avoid. But after the previous evening that was obviously a vain wish.

"Good morning, Jesper," his father-in-law said.

"Good morning, Karl-Erik. Morning, darling." He glued on a polite smile, kissed his wife on the cheek, and took the cup of coffee she held out to him.

"We thought you deserved to sleep in," Karolina said. "You did well yesterday—didn't he, Daddy?"

"Absolutely. The papers are unanimous in saying you did an excellent job. Even the opposition papers' lead articles express reluctant admiration."

Stenberg took a sip of coffee. Walked around the kitchen and kissed his two children on the head.

"We saw you on television yesterday," his youngest daughter said, looking up from her iPad.

"And what did you think?"

"You were really good. Mom let us play on our pads so we wouldn't wake you up."

Stenberg pulled out a chair and sat down opposite his father-in-law. Decided to preempt any criticism.

"I could have been more aggressive with the opposition. I could have made it even clearer that they're soft on crime and terrorism."

His father-in-law made a soothing gesture.

"You'll have plenty of opportunities to do that over the next few weeks. The main thing is that people saw you can handle a tough line of questioning. That you can keep a cool head and come across as solid and dignified under pressure and without a script."

"Statesmanlike. He was, wasn't he, Daddy?"

Karolina put a plate of bacon and eggs in front of Stenberg, half as much as he would have liked. He noticed her exchanging a quick glance with her father.

Karl-Erik got to his feet and patted him on the shoulder. "High time for me to get going."

"Don't you want breakfast?" Karolina sounded slightly disappointed.

"Thanks, but I haven't got time to stop. I just wanted to call in and congratulate Jesper on his performance. Boman's waiting out in the car."

"But why didn't you ask him in? Nisse's always welcome; he's one of the family. Isn't he?" Karolina gave Stenberg an encouraging glance as she followed her father out of the room.

"Of course, absolutely. Nisse's always welcome," he muttered after them.

Nisse Boman had been his father-in-law's driver and right-hand man for the past thirty years, if not more. Before that,

54

sometime in the Stone Age, he had been Karl-Erik's orderly in the military. Karolina had grown up with him around, thought of him as an extra dad. The sinewy little man was always polite, never behaving with less than military correctness toward those around him. He only spoke when he had something important to say, which wasn't very often. He was also considerate, almost protective toward Karolina and the girls. Yet there was still something about Boman that irritated Stenberg. Something about his eyes that was, in the absence of a better description, actively unpleasant. They were pale blue, cold. Almost like a fish's. They always seemed to be watching and judging him. And not in a way that did him any favors.

His wife came back into the kitchen.

"Daddy doesn't want to say anything to you yet," she said, and he could hear the excitement in her voice. "But he's having an informal meeting with the prime minister this afternoon. He's worried about the opinion polls. And the likelihood that people regard him as old and tired, especially now that he has to walk with a stick since the operation. Yesterday's interview was the final test, and you passed. The prime minister is going to ask if you're ready to stand by his side for the last part of the campaign. His unofficial crown prince."

Stenberg nodded. He could feel his face automatically delivering the right expression as his wife went on talking.

"All our dreams are coming true. After all our hard work. And sooner than we could ever have hoped. Prime Minister Jesper Stenberg—how does that sound? I've booked us a table at the Diplomat this afternoon to celebrate. Lina will stay on for a couple of hours to look after the girls."

Stenberg went on smiling at his wife. *Nothing can spoil this moment*, he told himself. *Nothing and no one.*

• • •

"Good afternoon, Minister," Oscar Wallin said in an exaggeratedly cheery voice as he walked into Stenberg's spacious office.

He stopped obediently behind one of the leather armchairs that were positioned at just the right angle for visitors to be able to see both the City Hall and the water of Riddarfjärden through the large windows facing Rosenbadsparken.

"Congratulations on your excellent performance on television last night. You looked like you owned the whole studio. That vicious little journalist really didn't have much luck. The lead article in my paper declared that you're the future of the party, possibly even our next prime minister."

"Hello, Oscar. Have a seat." Stenberg nodded toward the chair on the other side of the desk. "You wanted to see me?" he added before Wallin had a chance to go on with his predictable flattery.

Wallin opened the blue folder he had been carrying under his arm and put it down on the table between them with a flourish. Stenberg did his best to maintain a neutral expression.

"Well, I just wanted to update you on the body that was found in Källstavik last weekend. I thought it would be good for you to know. The body was found just a stone's throw from your father-in-law's country retreat. My guess is that sooner or later someone will start asking questions."

Stenberg waved one hand. "Of course. But keep it brief, if you don't mind."

Wallin started to talk, but Stenberg was only half listening. He knew that Wallin would let his secretary have a detailed memo. To show how clever he was, how industrious. The problem with Oscar Wallin was that he tried too hard, not least when he'd done something wrong, which made him look slippery and ingratiating rather than reliable and trustworthy.

He had begun to get seriously fed up with Wallin. His boyish appearance, the little water-combed curl in his hair, the breezy tone of voice. Not to mention that tired old thing he did with his folders. Wallin was intelligent—very intelligent, even, at least in some respects. But in others he was a complete idiot. Wallin had made a serious mistake last winter, biting the hand that fed him. But he didn't actually seem to realize that he ought to have handed in his resignation instead of prancing about in the corridors, trying to find things to do and look important.

For a couple of days last Christmas, Stenberg had been worried. Wallin indicated that he had found a trace of blood in Sophie Thorning's apartment. He had kept the documentation inside one of his blue folders and intimated that he could link Stenberg to Sophie, possibly even to her suicide. At first he had considered giving in to Wallin's demand and appointing him as the new national police chief. But then he calmed down. Realized that Wallin was actually playing poker and was bluffing. Wallin had seen to it that dozens of prominent police chiefs had lost their jobs and privileges. Without political protection his career in the police authority was doomed. Probably within the entire justice system, actually. And the only person protecting Wallin was Stenberg himself.

So he had seen through the bluff and consequently deprived Wallin of his dream job. And there was nothing Wallin could do to stop him. It was three days until he appeared in Stenberg's office with a servile smile and a blue folder under his arm. But by then Stenberg had begun to doubt that there had ever been a trace of blood at all.

He had contemplated going whole hog and firing Wallin. Or, even better, giving him a tedious job in some inquiry and letting his career gradually wither away. He had already slashed Wallin's budget and seen to it that he had lost his colleagues. All it would take was a single stroke of the pen, and he'd be gone.

But that blue folder Wallin was carrying was still a signal. If Wallin was utterly humiliated, there was a risk that he'd start talking to John Thorning, reveal that Stenberg had been having a secret affair with John's daughter for years and that Wallin strongly suspected that Stenberg had been there when she killed herself.

Stenberg daren't take the risk of his former mentor becoming his enemy. He still needed John's support, not least because he was general secretary of the Bar Association. So Wallin was allowed to keep his office, at least for the time being.

Wallin was still talking. He was halfway through a lengthy description of how bodies decompose in water. Something about bottom-feeders eating the dead bodies.

Stenberg couldn't help thinking of Sophie, of how her beautiful, slender body was lying in a coffin deep below the ground. Skin and tissue slowly turning to wax. If the worms hadn't gotten there first.

He felt suddenly nauseous. He stood up abruptly and went over to one of the windows. The smoke from the steamers by the City Hall was drifting on the breeze above Riddarfjärden.

Just a few meters outside his window a seagull hung in the air, almost motionless. It stared at him with empty, dead eyes.

* * *

When Oscar Wallin closed the door of his office his watch struck the handle with an alarmingly loud noise. It had been a Christmas present to himself, a Patek Philippe, exactly the same as the one Jesper Stenberg wore. Before he sat down behind his desk he anxiously checked to make sure the diamond-polished glass wasn't damaged. His mother had commented on the watch when they had dinner recently. A gift, he had told her, for professional accomplishments. "From the minister?" she had asked, but her tone revealed that she already knew the answer. He had managed to avoid the trap.

Six years ago he helped organize an apartment on Gärdet for her, just a stone's throw from his own. He moved her out of the dull suburb where his father had exiled them to a three-room apartment, ninety square meters with a view of the city center. He'd had to pull a lot of strings to get it, but obviously the apartment wasn't the same thing as a grand villa, which it hadn't taken her many minutes to point out.

All through the years when he was growing up she had waited. Every evening she had forced him to dress for dinner. "Your father will call soon, you'll see, and you must promise to be a good boy this time."

The fact that the professor had replaced her with a woman fifteen years her junior, and that the villa was now inhabited by his new family, appeared to make little difference. She had gone on waiting, hoping, and nothing he did could possibly replace what had been taken from her.

As a teenager, he had sometimes gone back to their old home, creeping through the garden gate and standing there in the darkness, looking in through the big windows. The home where he was no longer welcome. The perfect family he wasn't part of. Dad, mom, daughter, son. Even a golden retriever that didn't have the sense to bark on the occasions it found him out there in the garden. It just licked his hand and waved its tail stupidly, as if it expected him to play with it.

He still looked up his father's family from time to time. His half brother and half sister had gone to fancy schools, had traveled the world and studied abroad. Unlike him, they had no student debt and hadn't had to do part-time work and evening courses with sweaty cheese sandwiches and thermos-flask coffee. Even so, they were no more than drones. Idiots with no ambition to achieve anything, to make a lasting impression.

He had always known that he was different. That he was destined to achieve things. Great things. In that way he and Jesper Stenberg were pretty similar. They weren't content merely to exist, but knew they were meant for something more than just an ordinary life. They set ambitious goals and did whatever it took to achieve them. Not long ago Jesper had been his role model. A man he regarded as his mentor. Now everything had changed. He hadn't understood that Stenberg had appointed Eva Swensk as national police chief in order to gain support within the party. Instead he felt let down, overlooked, just as he had as a teenager. And he had been stupid and clumsy enough to try to force Jesper to change his mind. And since then their friendship had soured badly.

All Wallin had wanted to do was prove the extent of his loyalty. That he was the right man to keep Stenberg's secrets, and that he could do so even better as national police chief. But Stenberg had misunderstood his intentions and stripped almost everything he had built up away from him. His privileged access, his staff, all the power that made his colleagues fear him. The same colleagues who used to beg and plead for a five-minute meeting now kept their distance from him or openly mocked him.

His relationship with the minister of justice had been seriously damaged; he couldn't deny that, even if he was doing his best to improve things. In a number of discreet ways he was trying to get Stenberg to realize that his secrets were still in safe hands and that he could be trusted. Evidently that tactic had failed, judging by the conversation they had just had.

But he still had his job in the Ministry of Justice. That meant he still had a chance. He looked up at the framed quote from Robert Kennedy on his wall:

> *Only those who dare to fail greatly, can ever achieve greatly.*

He had failed. That was all there was to it. But he wasn't beaten yet. One way or another he would make his way back to the top. He would climb higher than anyone could imagine. His colleagues and everyone else who had underestimated him over the years would have cause to think again. He had licked his wounds long enough, playing the role of obedient lapdog. It was high time for a new strategy.

He pulled a business card out of the top drawer of his desk, picked up the phone, and dialed the direct number written on the back.

A male voice answered on the second ring. A short, confident bark.

"John Thorning."

"Hello, this is Detective Superintendent Oscar Wallin. I was wondering if you had time for that meeting we talked about."

Two

Superintendent Pärson's office was twice the size of Julia's. But it felt smaller. Possibly because of the physical bulk of the room's occupant, or the stacks of documents covering practically every available surface. Or simply because of the distinct smell of sweat that seemed to force out all the oxygen.

"That isn't David Sarac." Pärson tapped the photofit picture with the yellow nail of his index finger.

"How can you be so—"

Pärson interrupted Julia by holding up one fleshy hand.

"To begin with, unlike certain other people in this room, I've been a police officer long enough to know that photofit pictures can never be trusted. I must have seen hundreds over the years, and when we eventually get our hands on the culprits, they never match."

"But this one's different," Amante said. "This isn't based upon witness statements but X-rays and measurements of the skull—"

"Which you bribed your way to get ahold of out at the Forensic Medicine Unit," Pärson interrupted again. "I must say, that part of your little presentation is of particular interest to me. That's a fair number of notations in your record already, Amante. Misconduct and two cases of bribery. Not bad for your first week."

Pärson grinned and leaned back.

"Don't worry. You meant well, and besides, I've got an arrangement with your stepfather. But keep your nose clean from now on, is that understood? There are limits to the amount of protection I can give you."

Amante moved his head in a way that could be interpreted as a half nod.

"But Amante is actually right: this is nothing like an ordinary photofit." Julia didn't manage to say more before Pärson held his paw up once again.

"The second and possibly more significant reason why our photofit phantom can't be David Sarac is that I happen to know exactly where Sarac is."

Julia sat with her mouth half-open. "Okay," she managed to say. She exchanged a quick glance with Amante.

"Sarac has been in a home for patients suffering from PTSD since he left the hospital last winter," Pärson said. "He's barely capable of walking and talking on his own, and then only for short periods. That's why you haven't seen any interviews with our heroic detective. He's incapable of going anywhere without suffering panic attacks, pissing and shitting himself."

"And we're completely sure about that?" Julia said.

"Yep. Secure psychiatric care. Sarac won't be out of the nuthouse for years, if ever. So he couldn't have been at Källstavik in February, which means he wasn't murdered, chopped up, and dumped under the ice. Besides, I've had time to check the DNA match that made the Security Police get such a hard-on about taking over the case. A sixty-five percent match is crap. That means there's only a slightly greater probability that the victim was at Skarpö than that he wasn't. Both I and the head of Regional Crime are more than happy to hand that sort of speculation and guesswork to our spook friends."

Julia bit her top lip. She had been expecting Pärson to fall off his chair with shock when he heard their revelation. Instead he was sitting there on the other side of the desk, grinning at them in an unpleasantly supercilious way. As if they were two crazies in tinfoil hats.

She looked at the photofit again, then at Amante. He avoided her gaze. Could they really be that wrong? But the grinning skull in her head didn't agree. The dead man was

David Sarac, no matter what Pärson claimed. She just couldn't prove it at the moment.

"Listen, Gabrielsson." Pärson sounded more friendly now, almost paternal. "You're a good police officer—one of the very best, I'd say. I'll be retiring in a couple of years, selling my apartment and moving to Thailand to drink myself to death with garish cocktails. If you play your cards right, this lovely desk can be yours. But if the head of Regional Crime gets the slightest whiff of this business with the skull, well, you're smart enough to work out the rest for yourself. Kollander's paranoid about his reputation, especially now that he's expecting the national police chief to reward him for his efforts. He'd get rid of you quicker than you can say *ass-kisser*."

Pärson tilted his head slightly.

"I know you, Gabrielsson, I know what this is about. If it would make you happier, I can give the case a new code. Make it look like it was being investigated by one of the alcoholics in the end corridor until the Security Police took over. That way your solving rate won't get messed up."

She didn't respond.

"Good, that's all sorted, then. Now, make sure you get that fucking head back to the Forensic Medicine Unit as quickly and discreetly as you can. Send our intrepid bribemaster general in while you wait in the car." Pärson grinned at his joke. "As soon as the skull's back, start the weekend early and go home. On Monday I promise you'll have a nice new murder to get your teeth into. And with that, I think we can put this whole episode behind us. What do you say, Gabrielsson?"

• • •

The bodyguard—Stenberg thought his name might be Becker—opened the car door. The man was looking away the whole time, focused on their surroundings. Stenberg got out of the car and stretched gently. He shaded his eyes with his hand and gazed out across the water, toward the Vasa Museum and Gröna Lund amusement park. A couple of young women in short summer dresses and high heels walked past on the pavement. One of them smiled at him and he couldn't help smiling back. And why not? It was Friday afternoon, the working day was over, the sun was shining, and Stockholm was looking at its most beautiful.

Inside the restaurant Karolina was waiting at their table.

"Hello, darling," he said, and leaned forward to kiss her. She tilted her head to one side and let him kiss her on the cheek instead of the lips.

"I've already ordered. Veal for both of us. Salad rather than potato gratin." She looked up and noted his expression. "You've let your belt out a notch, and the camera added a few more kilos yesterday."

She nodded gently toward his stomach and revealed a row of perfectly white pearly teeth between lips red with the lipstick she had just stopped him from spoiling. Karolina was his rock, the only person he could trust unconditionally. She was strong in every sense of the word.

He sat down, spread the large linen napkin over his lap, and took a sip of water.

"How has your day been?" he asked.

"Fine. The phone keeps ringing. Two different charities are trying to recruit me, and I'm inundated with lunch invitations. If it carries on like this, I'm soon going to need an assistant." Karolina winked at him.

"I could put someone onto that if you like."

"It's too soon. An assistant would make it look like we're taking developments for granted."

The waiter appeared with their starters. The thick carpet and subdued conversation of the other guests almost drowned the sound of him approaching.

"You're right," Stenberg said once the waiter had left them. "I'm just worried about you."

Karolina patted his hand. "I'll manage. Now eat; the veal is supposed to be wonderful."

Stenberg returned her smile, then glanced up briefly as two familiar men walked in through the doors facing Strandvägen and stopped at the maître d's little podium. One was Oscar Wallin, the other John Thorning. The men were laughing, as if one of them had just said something amusing. They were behaving like old friends and Stenberg felt his good mood sink.

"How lovely to see you," John Thorning said with a surprised smile.

"Yes, what a surprise." Karolina repeated the trick with her cheek so that Thorning could kiss her on both sides. "It's been ages. How are you and Margareta?"

John Thorning replied something that Stenberg didn't hear. He was fully occupied trying not to glare angrily at Wallin.

"I didn't know that you and John knew each other," he said.

"Oh, we've had a few dealings. John suggested we get a bite to eat together, and as luck would have it he had a gap in his schedule today." Wallin nodded toward Thorning.

"Yes, I wanted to thank Wallin personally for his efforts last winter. That supplementary investigation into"—Thorning made a slight gesture with his hand—"Sophie's tragic passing. You told me that Wallin helped to iron out the question marks that had been troubling me. So I thought that the least I could do was to offer a bite to eat in return." John Thorning patted Wallin's shoulder. "And it's a good idea anyway, having an early dinner on a Friday. It makes the weekend feel longer, don't you think? And the boat to Sandhamn leaves from just outside here, so I'll be sure of getting home okay."

Stenberg forced a smile. This meeting was obviously no coincidence. Wallin must have checked his diary with Jeanette. He would have to talk to her about that.

"We won't disturb you any longer, Jesper," John Thorning said. "You and Karolina need a little time to yourselves, and Oscar and I have a lot to talk about. I'm very interested in how things are going with your plans. We should meet again. Soon. I'll ask my secretary to call Jeanette."

They shook hands, and with an effort of will Stenberg managed to squeeze out another smile.

"John's looking brighter," Karolina said as they sat back down. "He seems to have put that sorry business with Sophie behind him."

Something in her voice made Stenberg start. An undertone, a trace so insignificant that he wasn't even sure that he'd really heard it. He stared at his wife, but she looked exactly the same as usual. She smiled at him. Bright red lipstick, white teeth. For a millisecond he got it into his head that Sophie was sitting on the chair opposite him. Looking at him with her shattered eyes. He shuddered and blinked hard a couple of times to make the image disappear.

"Aren't you feeling well, Jesper?" his wife asked.

. . .

Julia sat with her lower arms resting on the wheel as she fiddled with her cell phone. Both side windows were wound down to keep the summer heat from turning the car into an oven. Even so, she could feel her blouse sticking to her lower back, and she started the engine and air-conditioning the moment she saw Amante emerge from the Forensic Medicine Unit.

She'd had time to make four calls while he was in there, all with similarly disappointing results. No one could tell her where David Sarac was being treated. Or, to be more accurate, where he had been treated before someone murdered, dismembered, and dumped him in Lake Mälaren. Because she was still convinced that they were right and Pärson was wrong.

"All sorted out?" she said.

"Yes." Amante sat heavily in the passenger seat and closed the door. "My good friend in there promised to put the head in an empty compartment in cold storage. One of his colleagues will find it within the next few days and call the Security Police. A regrettable mistake, blah, blah, blah . . ."

"And how much did that cost you, then?"

"Do you really want to know?"

Julia didn't answer. She just took the hand brake off and let the car roll slowly out of the parking lot. Suppressed an urge to put her foot down and force Amante to grab for the handle above the door.

"Are you planning on telling me what Pärson meant earlier?" Amante said after several minutes' silence.

"Which bit?" she muttered.

"What he said about your solving rate."

She glanced at Amante, but nothing in his tone of voice or expression suggested that he was teasing her. The best idea would obviously be to keep quiet. Follow Pärson's advice, get shot of this mess, and put the whole case behind her.

"I've got the best clearance rate when it comes to murder investigations," she found herself saying instead. She heard the note of pride in her own voice.

"In Violent Crime?"

She shook her head. "In the whole country, actually. Almost all the cases I've investigated have ended up solved."

He turned toward her and she could sense his skepticism.

"We're talking solved from a police perspective," she added. "Not necessarily guilty verdicts. In two of the cases the perpetrators are dead. And in two more they've fled abroad and can't be brought to justice because of that. And in one . . . in one the perpetrator was released on appeal, unfortunately."

She bit her top lip gently. Thought about saying that the appeal was successful because of an unusually sloppy prosecutor, but decided against it.

"Either way, I've concluded all my investigations. Answered all the questions and worked out what happened, who did what and why."

"I get it. So Pärson's going to shuffle a few papers to keep this from affecting your statistics."

"Something like that," she mumbled.

"Great," Amante said in a tone that suggested he meant the exact opposite. Silence fell inside the car as he studied her.

Julia pulled up at a red light. She went on staring straight ahead to avoid meeting his gaze. Even so, he seemed to have read her mind.

"You still think Sarac is our victim, don't you?"

She realized she was biting her lip again and made a mental note to stop doing that.

"I haven't seen any evidence to prove that he isn't. The fact that Pärson says Sarac is locked up is one thing, but I know him well enough to assume he hasn't called to check. If he even knows where to start. I've made a few calls myself, but no one seems to know where Sarac is."

She turned to look at Amante.

"What about you? What do you think?"

"I was actually thinking of asking if you had any plans for the weekend." He smiled that cryptic little smile again, and for a moment she thought he was going to ask her out.

"Why?" she said, more abruptly than she intended.

"Well, if you're free, I wondered if you fancy a little trip up north."

"Where to?"

"Pick me up at one o'clock tomorrow and you'll find out."

The car behind them blew its horn and Julia realized the lights had turned green.

Three

A monotonous four-hour drive—that was what Julia's Saturday afternoon had consisted of so far. Back roads, fir forests, and wildlife fences.

This wasn't how she had imagined the weekend. She had been planning to work out, finish the book she never seemed to get to the end of, go to the movies, or do one of the other things that got her through weekends when she wasn't working. Instead she was sitting behind the wheel, glancing at Amante as he watched the GPS bubble on the screen of his smartphone.

"Turn right here." Amante pointed toward an anonymous-looking side road. "One kilometer of country road, then we're there."

"Okay."

She wondered how he'd found out the address of the nursing home; she'd even asked him about it when she picked him up outside his apartment. But, as usual, all she got in response was that tentative little smile.

About half an hour earlier they had stopped at a gas station to look at the map and see what Amante's smartphone could tell them about their destination. The satellite picture showed what looked like a manor house with two wings. Surrounding the main building was a large park that stretched all the way down to a small lake. If you zoomed in really close, you could just make out the walls and fences surrounding the entire property. But as they approached the facility, none of that was visible apart from a section of wall, a security lodge, and a large metal gate. All you could see from the gate was tall, well-established trees in the park beyond.

Julia drove slowly into the visitors' parking lot and turned the engine off.

According to Google, the home had originally been built as a sanatorium. Over the years it had been an adult education college and an old people's home. According to one five-year-old article, it had been sold and turned into a nursing home, but that was about it. It wasn't even possible to find a phone number for the main switchboard, so, whatever they were doing there, they were keen to avoid publicity—which seemed fairly logical if they were treating patients with PTSD. The female security guard behind the glass hatch was similarly welcoming.

"Sorry." The speaker fixed in the reinforced glass gave the guard's voice a metallic clang. "All visits need to be authorized in advance. Those are the rules."

Amante raised his ID higher, pressing it against the glass.

"Like I said, we're police officers, and we're conducting an investigation. It's extremely important that we see David Sarac."

"If it's that important, then you should have spoken to the senior consultant and got him to arrange a visit. Anyway, you're not a police officer; it says you're a civilian investigator on your ID."

Amante took a sharp breath, but Julia put her hand on his shoulder before he could say anything else. Arguing with a guard was never a good idea. She recognized the type all too well. Low-level employees who were given a tiny bit of power and made the absolute most of it. She stepped forward and held her own ID up against the glass just as Amante had done.

"I'm a police officer," she said. "And, like my partner just said, it's very important that we see one of the patients here. His name is David Sarac."

The guard leaned closer to the glass. Read her name on her

ID. "Look here, Detective Inspector . . . Gabrielsson. You see those signs?"

She pointed to a yellow rectangle with black lettering hanging above her head. Then at another one a short distance away on the heavy metal gate.

"This is a secure site. That means no unauthorized access. Under any circumstances. And seeing as neither you nor your colleague appear on the list of names, that means you aren't authorized, whether you're police officers or not. Those are the rules. People have lost their job for less."

"What sort of nursing home gets classified as a fucking secure site?"

Amante's sudden outburst took Julia by surprise. She squeezed his arm and got him to shut up. The guard glared at him.

"We look after soldiers here: people who have been in wars. According to the Security Police, that makes it a potential target."

Amante opened his mouth to reply, but Julia squeezed his arm again, harder this time. What was wrong with him?

"Rules are rules," she said to the guard. "Obviously we appreciate that you're just doing your job. You'll have to excuse my colleague: the case we're investigating is pretty serious. A lot of pressure."

She looked over toward the metal gate. The sign on it was bright yellow, but it was already bleached by the sun. And the barbed wire on top of the wall didn't look new.

"We'll call the senior consultant and come back tomorrow." She bustled Amante a couple of steps toward the car before she turned round again. "By the way, how long has the home been classified as a secure site?"

"Since sometime last winter," the metallic voice replied.

"Do you remember which month?"

The guard glared at Julia, then at Amante.

"Early March. Why?"

"Oh, no reason. Just curious. Thanks for your help." She nodded to Amante to get in the car. She didn't say anything until the doors were closed. But he beat her to it.

"Coming here was a long shot—I said that before we set off—but maybe if we wait until it gets dark—"

"And do what?" Julia interrupted. "Climb over the wall? Break in through a door? Smash a few windows at random?" She shook her head. "We have no idea what the inside of the building is like. And if our suspicions are right and Sarac is our dead body, then we're looking for someone who isn't even in there."

Amante looked suddenly sullen. "Sorry I dragged you up here for nothing. We could have waited till Monday, I could have asked my contact to get hold of the senior consultant's number. I got carried away . . ."

Julia held up a finger to get him to stop talking. The metal gate was slowly swinging open. A car drove out, followed by another one. Then a motorcycle. The vehicles stopped and a man in uniform emerged from the security lodge to check the backseats and trunks. He even insisted on looking behind the motorcyclist's visor and seeing some ID before he allowed them to leave.

The vehicles passed their parked car. Two men in the first car, a lone woman in the second one. It wasn't possible to determine the gender of the motorcyclist. All three vehicles turned left at the junction a short distance away.

"They're very conscientious with their exit checks," Julia muttered. She looked at the time. Quarter past five. Probably a change of shift. Suddenly she had an idea. She turned the key in the ignition and roared off, following the three other vehicles.

They caught up with the motorcycle just before the small village that consisted of little more than a cluster of bungalows and a gas station. The motorcycle turned off at the gas station and pulled up at its little hot dog stand. Without saying anything to Amante, Julia got out of the car. She walked toward the stand, but when she was almost there she pulled out her phone and pretended to take a call. The biker, a man in his fifties, had taken his helmet off and was chatting to the attractive woman in the stand—she was maybe half his age—before she put together his order. The smell of fast food reminded Julia that it had been a while since she had eaten anything.

She waited until the man had gotten his food, put his helmet back on, and driven off before walking up to the window.

"Hello," she said.

The woman behind the counter returned the greeting.

"Regulars, eh?" Julia said, nodding toward the disappearing motorbike. "I've just come from the nursing home. It was the staff who told me to come here."

She smiled, trying to come across as friendly and unthreatening as she read the menu.

"Well . . ." The young woman hesitated over her reply, but Julia's smile seemed to convince her. "You could say that. Some of them stop off here practically every night."

"Best place for an evening burger, the girl in the gatehouse said. You probably know her: fair hair, keeps herself in shape. Maybe a little grumpy?"

"Mia. Yes, she can be a bit sullen." The young woman gave a wry smile and Julia reflected it back to her.

"Mia—that was it. Smart too. You seem to know what's going on as well. Who works where and so on."

"This is a pretty small place: everyone knows everyone else. The doctors live in town, but most of the other staff up there come from around here."

"You don't happen to know if anyone's left recently?" Julia said. "Someone who maybe lost their job last winter, something like that?"

Another long shot, based on something Security Mia had said. *People have lost their job for less.* But Julia could tell from the evasive look in the young woman's eyes that she'd guessed right.

She leaned over the counter and held out her police ID. She saw the woman's eyes open wide.

"It's vital that we talk to that person, right away."

• • •

The man looking out from the gap in the door was wearing underpants, a T-shirt, and a grubby dressing gown, even though it was late afternoon. His eyes were red and a cloying, burned smell that Julia recognized all too well drifted out across the crooked front steps. She cautiously took hold of the door handle from the outside.

"Eskil Svensson?"

"Why do you want to know?"

"Food delivery from Isa in the kiosk." She held up the plastic bag and let it dangle from her forefinger. The smell from it made her stomach rumble.

The man in the robe seemed just as hungry as she was. He reached out one hand for the bag without letting go of the door with the other.

At that moment Julia tugged the door toward her, which made the man lose his balance and tumble out onto the porch, where he landed at their feet. Before he had time to react, she put one knee against the back of his neck and twisted his arm behind his back. Then she winked at Amante.

"Police," he said, sounding rather breathless. "We'd like to ask you some questions."

Four

"The girls are watching television. I was thinking of going for a run round the Altorp track. I'll be gone an hour at the most. Then I thought we could have a nice, cozy evening together."

Stenberg's wife came into his study with a cup of coffee in her hand. She put it down at a safe distance from the keyboard, leaned over, and kissed him on the head.

"You look tired." She ran her hand through his hair, forcing him to look up from the screen. "Is it anything in particular? Anything you want to talk about?"

"No," Stenberg muttered. "Just a lot going on."

"Is the prosecutor general causing trouble again?"

He nodded absentmindedly and looked at the screen again.

"The prime minister trusts you, Jesper, now more than ever. The fact is that the whole party trusts you, so you can't let little things like that get in your way. We need a modernized justice system; we've needed one for ages. Otherwise people will gradually lose faith in the system. The contract between citizens and the state, all the things we discussed ad infinitum at law school. You already had a vision back then, a conviction that made people take notice of you. It made *me* notice you."

"I know, darling. But trying to reform state institutions is a constant uphill struggle: various government and other entities everywhere having their say on things, with everyone terrified of losing influence."

"What about Wallin? Can't you let him do some of the heavy lifting?"

Stenberg felt his jaw tighten. Even here at home in his study, his inner sanctum, Wallin cast his baleful shadow.

Karolina raised her eyebrows. "Is it Wallin who's the problem?"

Damn. She knew him far too well. Noticed the slightest change in his expression. She could even hear things he didn't say. Keeping his affair with Sophie Thorning secret all those years had taken all his willpower and concentration. Yet he knew he probably wouldn't have been able to lie if Karolina had confronted him, if she'd asked straight out if he was being unfaithful and looked at him the way she was right now. Fortunately she never had.

He filled his lungs, then slowly breathed out through his mouth.

"What's this all about?" Her tone of voice was perfect, a fitting combination of concern and empathy. Karolina would have been a brilliant lawyer, but instead she had put his career ahead of her own. Taken on the role of supportive wife and mother to his children. Her grandfather had been foreign minister; her father, Karl-Erik, was a member of the party's inner circle. She had opened doors for him that he could never even have dreamed of. And how had he thanked her? With betrayal, lies, and infidelity.

For a couple of moments the feeling he had had last winter was back, the conviction that he ought to tell her everything. Beg for her forgiveness. But he couldn't ask that of her. It wasn't Karolina's responsibility to lighten his burden.

"Oscar Wallin . . ." He took a sip of his coffee to make what he was thinking of saying sound less loaded. "He's very ambitious. You saw him with John Thorning. Wallin is forming new alliances, and, to be honest, I've started to have doubts about his loyalty."

Karolina leaned against the edge of the desk.

"Wallin couldn't be national police chief. We agreed on that. You, me, and Daddy. Appointing Eva Swensk gained you support within the party, support you're going to need in the future. We're going to need . . ."

She paused and stroked his hair again. He liked her hands, even though she herself didn't. Those long, strong fingers. The hands of a person who could be practically anything she wanted to be.

"Right now it's more important than ever to think strategically. You have to see things in a longer perspective, not just focus on the present. If you're convinced that the goal is the right one, you mustn't hesitate to make unpalatable decisions. Keep your eye on the prize."

He shut his eyes. He'd seen this trick before and was starting to get a bit tired of it. Karolina's lips were moving, but the voice coming out of her mouth belonged to someone else.

"If we win the election, the prime minister will probably step down at the next party conference. Go out at the top. And if we lose . . ."

She pulled out a chair and sat down next to him.

"If we lose, he'll have to accept the consequences and resign at once. Either way, the party will be looking for a younger, more energetic successor. Someone whom can reform politics the way he's reforming the justice system."

"You're absolutely right," Stenberg said, but more and more often these days he wasn't sure whom he was replying to: Karolina, or her father.

• • •

Julia Gabrielsson held up the little plastic bag of marijuana she'd found on Eskil Svensson's coffee table. Waved it slowly in front of his pallid face.

"So, to sum up: a mysterious man calling himself Frank contacted you early in February and paid you to take messages to and from Sarac inside the home, and then a bit more for helping Sarac escape. But that's as much as you know."

Eskil was sitting on the sofa between her and Amante, shaking his head.

"And you don't know where this Frank came from or what he wanted with Sarac?"

"Like I said, he showed up in the pub one evening and started buying me drinks. Then he asked for a favor. It didn't sound too difficult and the money was good. Then it sort of grew . . ." He pulled a pained expression and seemed to be avoiding looking at the bag of marijuana between Julia's fingers.

"And you started to acquire a taste for the money. I get that." She put the bag down on the table in front of Eskil. "This is quite a stash. I'd guess about a year in prison, wouldn't you say, Amante?"

"Maybe two," he said somberly as he stared at Eskil. "Possession with intent to supply—that's serious stuff."

Julia was having trouble keeping a straight face. Amante was a fast learner.

Eskil turned even paler. His Adam's apple bobbed up and down.

"Come off it. That's my weed. I'm not some fucking dealer. Look, I've told you all I know. The only thing I did was get the master key copied. Then we decided what time was best if you wanted to escape without being spotted. Sarac got out and hid in the trunk of my car during the shift change. Then I let him out at the railway station and gave him a train ticket, a travel card for Stockholm, and a bit of cash. That's all."

"And then you got caught," Amante said.

"No, for fuck's sake! Haven't you been listening?" Eskil threw his arms out. "They accused me of stealing drugs."

"The sleeping pills and tranquilizers that you gave Sarac."

"That's right. I understand the tranquilizers. I mean, the guy wasn't well. But he already had a bag full of sleeping pills, so I can't see why he wanted two more. But he said it was important—that he needed to have exactly twenty-five before he left. Otherwise he wasn't going anywhere."

"So it was the pills that got you the sack?" Julia said.

79

"Shit, you two are unbelievable," Eskil groaned. "Aren't there any entrance requirements for joining the police? I've already told you what happened. No one fired me. They couldn't prove anything, so I was given six months' wages in return for handing in my resignation. I didn't want to work there anyway. You've seen what it's like there. It's a fascist setup. The staff have to give urine samples, all kinds of crap like that . . ."

"This mysterious Frank," Julia said. "Tell us about him again."

Eskil let out a theatrical sigh.

"Like I've already said a thousand times: he and Sarac had been on that island together last winter. Where a load of people got killed. That's why he wanted to talk to Sarac."

"And you don't remember anything else about Frank apart from the fact that he might have had a slight accent, paid well, and acted like a cop?"

"No. I mean, it's several months ago now. Actually, he did have a bit of a limp, even though he looked like he was in good shape."

Julia started waving the bag of weed again. "What do you think about getting a sniffer dog out here?" she said to Amante. "Turn this apartment upside down. Maybe ask the neighbors if they've noticed drug dealing going on here."

"Do you want me to call right away?"

"Probably just as well. Eskil here isn't exactly a rocket scientist. I doubt we're going to get anything else useful out of him."

She turned toward Eskil and could almost see the cogs turning inside his head. Amante slowly got to his feet and pulled out his cell phone.

"Wait," Eskil said. "Wait, for fuck's sake! I've got something you might want to see."

He started to dig about in the pockets of his dressing gown. He fished out a smartphone with a cracked screen and started to look through it.

"Here," he said eagerly, holding the phone out to Julia. "Sarac made me take a picture."

The screen showed a grainy photograph of a man with sharp features. He was half facing away and seemed unaware that he was being photographed.

"That's Frank. See what I mean about him looking like a cop?"

Five

The rain started falling just as they passed the sports ground on the edge of the village. Tiny drops to start with, barely enough for Julia to switch the windshield wipers on. But gradually the rain got harder, wiping out the distinction between the summer's evening and the forest spreading out on either side of the road.

"What do we do now?" Amante said. "Call Pärson and tell him that Sarac isn't in the home after all? That we've got a picture of the man who lured him out and probably killed him?"

Julia shook her head.

"It's too soon to talk to Pärson. This is the Security Police's case now, and you heard me promise to let go of it completely. And seeing as it was Pärson who tried to convince us that Sarac was in that home, I'm not entirely sure where he stands. But regardless of who we go to with all this, it would be better to wait until we've got something more definite than a grainy digital photograph and a first name."

"So what are you thinking, then?"

"I don't know yet. I need some time to think."

Besides, I'm still not entirely sure where you stand either, she thought. *You seem a bit too eager to press on with this case.*

"Sure," Amante said. "We've got at least a four-hour drive home, so take as much time as you need." He started fiddling with the car radio and managed to find three different commercials before he ended up with a soppy Whitney Houston ballad.

They were approaching a junction beside an old house. From a distance it looked almost abandoned, but as they drove past, Julia could see the ghostly glow of a television in one of the windows.

"Just think, people choose to live out here," she said, mostly to give her brain something else to think about for a few minutes. "So far away from absolutely everything."

"A surprising number of people are prepared to die for the chance to do that," Amante muttered.

"What did you say?"

He looked up. Didn't seem to have noticed that he'd spoken out loud.

"Just that a surprising number of people are prepared to risk their lives to get here. Hundreds of thousands of them."

Julia saw an opening and decided to make the most of it.

"Lampedusa must be a nightmare. Isn't it? I can understand if you'd rather not talk about it."

"At its worst, there were two boats arriving each week." Amante's voice was lower all of a sudden, more monotonous. "Well, maybe not boats, exactly. Some of them were little more than a small hull and an engine. The bigger ships were even worse. No food, no toilets, hardly any drinking water. Cargo holds so packed that the air sometimes ran out down there. Did you know . . ."

The words seemed to catch in his throat.

"Did you know that dead people can stay on their feet if they're packed together tightly enough? Rigor mortis turns them into statues. Men, women, children, whole families. If you listen carefully you can almost hear them still calling for help."

He turned away. The radio went on playing the slushy song.

"Three thousand dead each year, but the EU is reducing the funding. They'd rather spend billions of euros rescuing banks than spend a few million saving people who happen to have the wrong color skin."

"And you said that out loud to someone who didn't like it?"

He smiled that little smile again. "More times than I should have. A lot more."

"So what happened?"

He shrugged his shoulders. "Not a damn thing. The boats kept coming, people kept dying."

"And you were transferred?"

"You could put it like that."

Something in his voice told her the conversation was over, and she resisted the temptation to ask any more questions. At least for the time being.

They passed a road sign. Just under three hundred kilometers until they were home. Sooner or later she would have to make her mind up. It would be difficult to carry on with this case on her own. Besides, she was starting to appreciate Amante's company, albeit slightly reluctantly. The smile that was so hard to read. The unconventional way he went about tackling problems. The way he quickly adapted to different situations. But, perhaps most of all, the way he talked about the victims, the dead.

"My dad was in the police," she said. "My grandfather too. They didn't really talk that much about police work at home. Mom didn't like it. She probably didn't want me to hear their stories. But I still realized—worked out that what they did was something different, something you couldn't really understand if you hadn't experienced it yourself. That was probably what made me want to become a police officer. To start with, I thought it was all about adrenaline. About putting yourself in danger. It took me several years to realize that it was actually about something else entirely. About seeing people when they're at their very worst. Drunk, distraught, furious, humiliated, beaten up, raped, or dead. About seeing that and trying to do something about it. About failing more often than succeeding, but still not giving up."

She fell silent, thinking about Sarac's mutilated body. And his distorted grimace.

Amante said nothing. But she was sure he was listening carefully—that he understood exactly what she meant. The light of the car's headlights reflected off a pair of eyes at the side of the road. She noticed a fleeting movement and switched her foot from the accelerator to the brake, but the animal was gone. A cat, or maybe a fox?

"You said you didn't know all the details about Skarpö," she said. "There were two other people who were found out there with Sarac. Right beside him, to be more accurate."

Amante turned to look at her. "Who were they?"

"The first one was a woman, Natalie Aden. She worked as Sarac's personal assistant after his car accident. Her intervention saved Sarac's life. We should at least talk to her. Show her Frank's picture and see if she recognizes him. But I think we ought to start with the second person. If anyone can identify Frank, it's probably him."

"Who are we talking about?"

"Atif Kassab. Seven years ago he was a notorious member of the Stockholm underworld. A nasty bastard. He retired and left the country with his mother. Didn't show up again until last winter, at his brother's funeral. Looks like someone managed to persuade him to go back to work." She dimmed the lights as a car came toward them. "Kassab blew Superintendent Peter Molnar's brains out on Skarpö, along with another three people, and took a couple of bullets himself. It looked like he wasn't going to make it for a while, but thanks to Natalie Aden's actions he survived as well."

Unfortunately, she added to herself.

"Kassab said nothing when he was questioned, and kept quiet all the way through his trial: never said a word about why he was on the island or who had hired his services. He was given a life sentence—didn't even bother to appeal against it."

"Strange."

Julia nodded. "Very. But there are plenty of things about Skarpö that are strange. Atif Kassab is being held in one of the 'phoenix' high-security units south of the city. It's a long shot, but I suggest we go and see him as soon as possible."

"So we're going to ask a cop killer for his help?"

"Yes, to track down another one," Julia said. "What do you think?"

Amante didn't answer, but from the corner of her eye Julia caught another glimpse of that cryptic smile.

Six

Phoenix. The bird that catches fire, dies in the flames, and is then reborn out of its own ashes with shimmering new plumage.

The name couldn't be more inappropriate. No one in the prison was transformed into a better version of himself and emerging as a new, well-adapted individual with sparkling new feathers, ready to be embraced by society. The majority would end up back behind bars within a couple of years, for crimes just as bad as the first time around.

Maybe that was the cycle of repetition that the name hinted at? A sort of ironic wink: *We all know how this is going to turn out, don't we?*

Atif Kassab pushed his breakfast tray aside and laid three cards facedown on the table in front of him. He noticed himself looking up at the camera in the ceiling above him. One of several hundred. The phoenix units were built to house the most dangerous prisoners in the country, those deemed most likely to try to escape. No doors or gates led to the outside world; the only way out was through an underground tunnel that led to another unit. A prison inside a prison.

He looked at the men at the other tables in the dayroom. Fifteen of them in total, an interesting mix of murderers, drug dealers, and bank robbers. They weren't all particularly dangerous or likely to abscond. The state had overestimated the capacity needed in the phoenix units and had had to dilute their occupants with ordinary criminals to keep the smart new facilities from sitting half-empty.

But a number of the men had no boundaries at all. In the wrong situation they could be lethal, both to themselves and those around them. The big, square guy at the table in the middle, the wall-eyed one called Rosco, was the current unofficial boss of the unit. Rosco had come over and introduced himself in the first few days. Shook hands gangster-style, spouted a load of names of people Atif didn't know and gangs he'd never heard of. In here he was a cop killer, someone viewed with respect. But the conversation was about more than mere pleasantries. Rosco was evaluating him, trying to work out if he was a threat, if he was going to upset the balance of power.

Atif had no interest at all in prison politics. He kept himself to himself, read books, and worked out in the small gym. Rubber straps and Pilates balls. No weights, nothing that could, according to Prison Service regulations, turn already dangerous criminals into mountains of muscle. But the exercise on offer was enough for his body to recuperate gradually from its injuries. The doctors had removed four meters of gut, drained almost a liter of blood from his torso, and patched up a number of less serious injuries. He had survived, and he knew whom he had to thank for that. He hoped he would be able to convey his thanks in person one day.

Atif stared blankly at the cards in front of him, then closed his eyes. He tried to conjure up an image of his house back home in Iraq. The scent of the almond tree in the back garden. The starry sky up above. But in spite of the fact that he regularly tried to keep the memory alive, it was getting hazier, losing its color, like the old pictures in his mother's well-thumbed photo albums. Pale imitations of what had once been. Something that was now lost. He wondered how she was. If she was still in the nursing home in Najaf, or if his aunt had moved her farther south, away from the fighting in the north. He'd written a couple of times, hoping to hear if the money was arriving each month. But he hadn't yet received a reply.

Atif turned the first card over. The seven of hearts. Tindra had turned seven three weeks ago. He'd sent her a card. He came close to writing that he missed her, that he'd do anything to hear her voice, no matter how briefly. But he didn't want her to come here. To have to go through all the security checks just so they could sit on opposite sides of a table. He still wouldn't be able to hold her.

Besides, her mother would never let her visit him. Cassandra needed to keep him as far away from her as possible, a decision he couldn't blame her for. He had wounded and killed people last winter, people who had families, friends, and business acquaintances outside the prison walls. People who were waiting for a chance to get their revenge. But as long as Abu Hamsa was protecting Cassandra and Tindra, no one would dare do anything. Which was rather ironic, to put it mildly, given that the old man was his worst enemy. Abu Hamsa had manipulated him, commissioned him to track down a ghost when it was actually the old man himself who had had Adnan killed, leaving Tindra without a father.

Abu Hamsa had sent him a message via Cassandra. *Don't tell the police anything, serve your sentence, follow my instructions.* She hadn't needed to say more than that. Didn't have to utter the words that were hanging in the air.

Or else . . .

So Atif had played along. He followed Abu Hamsa's instructions obediently, played patience and waited to be dealt the right cards. Something that changed the field of play.

Atif moved his hand to the card next to the seven of hearts. But before he could turn it over, the door of the dayroom opened and the head screw, Blom, walked in. He looked like a cover boy from *Men's Health*. High cheekbones, spray tan, and short, tinted hair in a gentle wave across his forehead. Right behind him, between another two gym-pumped screws, Atif could just make out a birdlike little man in prison clothes that were too big for him.

"Good morning, gentlemen," the head screw said, as always slightly louder than necessary. "This is our latest resident. Perhaps you'd like to introduce yourself, Gilsén?"

Blom stepped aside. The little man remained where he was between the two guards, clutching the paper bag he was holding in his hands. The smell of his fear managed to overpower Blom's body lotion.

The senior guard waited another few seconds. Exchanged a malicious glance with his colleagues.

"Well, I daresay you'll all have time to chew the fat later on. Follow me, Gilsén, and we'll get you installed in your suite. It's probably not quite up to the standard you're used to."

The guards lumbered out of the dayroom with Gilsén between them. Atif watched the men over at Rosco's table lean closer to each other, covering their mouths so that the cameras and microphones wouldn't pick up what they were saying.

A few minutes later the guards returned without Gilsén. Atif watched them from the corner of his eye. Waited.

The head screw glanced quickly at Rosco. The square man looked up and for a moment seemed to meet Blom's gaze. Then the guards left the dayroom.

Atif turned the next card over. Ace of spades.

He held it in his hand for a few seconds. Imagined he could almost hear Abu Hamsa's hoarse voice.

Follow my instructions.

Or else . . .

A heavily built, tattooed blond thug—Atif had never bothered to remember his name—and a bearded Turk of much the same caliber stood up from Rosco's table. They slipped off toward the cells without any hurry. As they passed Atif, one of the men nodded toward him. Atif didn't return the greeting. Instead he turned the third card over.

A joker. He must have forgotten to remove them before he started to play solitaire. He picked it up and carefully folded it until it formed a solid little rectangle that he put in his top pocket. Then he got slowly to his feet and followed the two men.

· · ·

If you take an ordinary pencil, sharpen it properly, and strengthen the shaft by wrapping tape around it fifty times, you'll have made a primitive but functional weapon. A single stab won't be fatal—at least, not if you're inexperienced, are in too much of a rush, and aim for the heart and snap the pencil against a rib. Someone with more experience would aim at the softer parts of the body, the sides of the torso or the throat. Then make several shallow jabs and hope to hit an artery or an organ full of blood, like the liver or kidneys.

But if you're really serious, you work in pairs. Attack the torso and throat at the same time. And stab so many times that the victim is eventually left swimming in his own blood.

The two men who opened the unlocked door to Joachim Gilsén's cell were both experienced and serious.

"Hello, Gilsén, we'd like a word with you," the tattooed man said, stepping aside to let his associate in.

The little man leaped up from his bed. Saw the improvised weapons in the man's fists.

"Guys, w-we . . ." He held his hands up in front of him, but the two men shepherded him toward the far corner of the cell.

"Hang on a m-minute. We can talk about this. I've got money, I can get . . ."

The tattooed man put his hand on Gilsén's chest. Pushed him slowly, almost gently, back against the wall.

"H-Help! Help me, someone!"

The bearded man grabbed hold of Gilsén's jaw and forced his chin up until the man's cries became a gurgle. He raised the weapon toward his exposed throat.

"Tell us about the money . . ."

Atif kept his arm almost completely outstretched, using the

91

force in his hip and the speed from the two rapid steps that carried him into the cell. He hit the bearded man in the back of the neck, right where the nerves, muscles, and spine meet. A silent, brutal blow that reverberated all the way from his clenched fist to his teeth. The bearded man collapsed like he'd been hit by a sledgehammer.

The tattooed man turned around with a look of astonishment as Atif kicked him in the crotch. He fell to his knees and dropped his weapon as his hands went automatically to his crown jewels. Atif grabbed hold of his bull neck and kneed him in the face. He let the inert body fall to the floor and took a couple of steps back.

"Are you . . . okay?"

Gilsén didn't answer; he just stood there, glued to the wall with his eyes wide open. Atif felt the adrenaline burning in his throat and struggled to subdue the nausea it brought with it.

"Are you okay?" he repeated, gently touching the little man's arm.

Gilsén took a gasping breath that sounded almost like a sob.

"They, they tried . . ." He stared at the two men on the floor and the weapons lying by his feet. One of the men groaned feebly and Gilsén hurried toward the bed in horror. He slumped down onto it, wrapped his arms round his knees, and began to rock back and forth.

In the distance an alarm sounded.

"W-Why?" Gilsén stammered a few seconds later. "Why did you help me?"

Atif straightened up. "Let's just say that someone outside is concerned about your welfare."

"Abu Hamsa. The deal . . ."

Atif waited for the rest, but before Gilsén could go on, the cell door was yanked open. Blom rushed in, followed by three more guards with drawn batons.

"Hands in the air, Kassab!" the head guard shouted. In one hand he was holding a can of pepper spray the size of a small fire extinguisher. Atif obeyed and had already laced his fingers together behind his head when Blom pressed the button.

Atif's eyes caught fire and his airways shrank to the size of straws. The pain made him double over. Bloody hell, an eight, verging on a nine. One of the guards struck him on the thigh with his baton as hard as he could. Gym muscles, more air than real strength, and the blow was nowhere near as painful as the spray in his eyes. But Atif played along, groaning out loud and staggering. Better that than have the idiot continue to hit him and maybe take aim at something more sensitive than his thigh muscles.

The guards threw themselves at him, tugging at his arms. They tried to kick his legs out from under him, in line with the self-defense manual. Atif put up no resistance, letting them force him down against the concrete floor. He twisted his head to one side and through a cloud of tears saw Gilsén still rocking back and forth on the bed.

A joker, Atif thought as the guards put cuffs on him. A card that can mean absolutely anything.

Seven

The underground tunnel leading from the ordinary prison into the phoenix unit was several hundred meters long. At intervals along the roof sat dark spherical cameras, which, along with the airlocks, suggested that people there took security extremely seriously. Yet Julia and Amante had found it considerably easier getting in there than in the nursing home the day before. Her police ID, a quick check on the computer to make sure she was who she claimed to be, and then they got the green light. She had been worried that someone would ask why they had turned up unannounced on a Sunday. Maybe even get it into their head to call Pärson. But none of that happened.

She had sat in when Atif Kassab was questioned last winter. Just as an observer rather than as lead interviewer. As usual, she sat quietly and let others do the talking while she concentrated on observing Kassab. But neither she nor the lead interviewers got much out of it. Kassab's body language was almost as taciturn as his verbal responses. The only time Julia detected any sort of reaction was when his sister-in-law, Cassandra, and niece, Tindra, were mentioned. That caused an almost imperceptible change in him. His threatening air of pent-up energy softened slightly, only to switch back the moment the interviewer changed the subject.

Their escort showed them into a small room with a dark-glass observation window set into one wall. Shortly afterward a very fit, suntanned man appeared in the doorway. He was holding a folder under one arm.

"Blom," he said by way of introduction. "Prison Service, assistant director."

"Julia Gabrielsson. This is my colleague Amante." As the two men shook hands, she saw the light go on in the room on the other side of the observation window, illuminating a table and two chairs. Three men entered the room, two prison officers on either side of Atif Kassab.

"What's happened to him?" Julia watched as the guards roughly pushed Kassab down onto one of the chairs. His face was red and swollen and his eyes were streaming.

"You mean the cuffs?" Inspector Blom grinned. His exaggeratedly white teeth, combined with his muscular body, jerky movements, and chemical suntan, made him look a bit like an action figure. "Just a security measure. Kassab was involved in a little altercation this morning."

"What about?"

"Nothing much. There usually aren't any reasons, at least none that seem logical to us normal people. It could be anything: a gambling debt, someone looking at him the wrong way or sitting in his place in the dayroom. Maybe someone pinched his dessert."

Blom was still smiling, evidently waiting for her to respond. He turned toward Amante when she failed to oblige.

"Everyone here in our phoenix unit is extremely dangerous. They can appear nice and calm—pleasant, even. But it's not a good idea to turn your back on them. Especially not that one." He nodded toward the room on the other side of the glass.

"How long has he been here?" Amante said.

"Three months, give or take."

"Has he been involved in altercations before?"

Blom shook his head.

"Visitors?" Julia said.

"I thought you might want to know that." Blom opened the folder he had been carrying under his arm and leafed through to the right page. "Three visits in total. Two from his lawyer and one from a Cassandra Nygren. It says here that she's—"

"His sister-in-law," Julia said. "Or rather she used to be the partner of Kassab's younger brother Adnan before he died last year. They have a daughter, Tindra. Kassab's niece."

Blom nodded. "He has a picture of her in his cell. One of the few personal items he's got, apart from a few books. If it had been me, I'd have asked for a couple of pictures of the mother as well. She's definitely worth a look." He grinned at Amante, but the smile vanished when he saw the look in the other man's eyes.

"Take those cuffs off. And our conversation isn't to be recorded or observed, is that understood?"

Blom squirmed slightly.

"Our internal rules are very clear: everything that happens in the unit, with the exception of conversations with lawyers, is to be documented and stored."

"Kassab is going to be questioned as a witness in an ongoing murder investigation." Amante's expression and tone of voice left little room for doubt about what he thought of the other man. "As long as that investigation is going on, discussions relating to it remain confidential, according to the Code of Judicial Procedure. Your internal rules—"

"Don't cover police interviews," Julia finished for him, flashing Amante a sharp glare. "So if you wouldn't mind removing Kassab's handcuffs and asking your colleagues to leave the room . . . And, as we've already said, all cameras and microphones need to be switched off."

Blom glowered at Julia, then at Amante. Then he left the room without a word.

• • •

"You look a bit the worse for wear, Kassab," said the short-haired blonde who'd introduced herself as Gabrielsson.

Atif shrugged. He stared down at the table between them

in the claustrophobic little room. Tried simultaneously to blink away the tears that wouldn't stop running.

"Tear gas or pepper spray?"

He looked up. Screwed his eyes up to focus better, but that just made it worse. "Pepper."

Gabrielsson nodded. "We got to try it in self-defense. Hurts like hell. And I'm sure we only got a tiny dose compared to what He-Man out there gave you." She gestured toward the dark glass in the wall. "I heard that the other two are in the infirmary. I'm guessing you don't want to say what it was about."

Atif didn't answer.

"Still not very talkative, I see," Gabrielsson said.

He went back to staring down at the table. His eyes were stinging, tears still running down his cheeks. He been put in an isolation cell immediately after the fight. Hadn't been given a chance to wash off the damn pepper spray. Now it seemed to have caught in his skin and beard, making his whole face burn, which was obviously what the screws intended.

The cop put a photograph on the table in front of him.

"Do you recognize this man?"

Atif looked at the picture. Blinked a couple of times. There was something wrong with the picture, something about the eyes, but he still recognized the man.

"That's David Sarac."

Gabrielsson exchanged a glance with her colleague, who for some reason hadn't introduced himself.

"What about this one?" She put another picture down. A grainy photograph taken with a cell phone, showing a man who was half turned away.

Atif stared at it for a few seconds. "No."

"Are you quite sure?"

"Never seen him before." Atif pushed the photograph away. "If that's all, I'd like to go back to my cell now."

"Maybe we could help you somehow."

Atif screwed his eyes up. "You've shown me your pictures,

97

asked your questions, and got your answers. Can I go back to my cell now, please?"

"Take another look, please." Gabrielsson tried to push the photograph toward him again, but Atif ignored her.

"We're done here," he said, looking up at the camera in one corner of the ceiling.

A sudden sound made him start. There was a small yellow jar on the table in front of him.

"Here," Gabrielsson's colleague said. "It'll help with the pepper spray."

Atif met the other man's gaze, then slowly picked the jar up. "Vaseline?"

"The pepper sticks to it. Smear a decent amount on and leave it for five minutes. Then wipe it all off with a paper towel. Do it a couple more times if it doesn't seem to work. But don't try using water."

Atif looked at the cop. Tried to work out if he was making fun of him. He couldn't see any sign of that. "Thanks," he said, putting the jar in his pocket. "What did you say your name was?"

"Amante."

"North African?"

"Spanish."

Atif squinted at the man. The reply was quick—a bit too quick. "You look more Arabic than Spanish. Tunisian, Moroccan, maybe. Do you speak Arabic?"

"Maybe."

There was something about the guy that didn't make sense. His blonde colleague was a cop, down to her fingertips. But this man was different. Atif went on watching him for a few more seconds.

"You're not a cop, are you? It's obvious from your eyes. Your whole style, actually."

Amante shrugged his shoulders. "Does it matter?"

Atif thought for a moment. Then decided to play along.

"Okay, what's this about, then, Vaseline?"

"We've found a body. A dismembered body, in a very bad state." Amante leaned over the table and tapped at the grainy photograph of the man looking away from the camera. "We think he's involved, but all we know about him is that he calls himself Frank and speaks with a slight accent."

Atif looked at Amante, then at Gabrielsson. He pulled the photograph toward him and looked at it, more carefully this time. When the blonde cop had put the picture down he hadn't recognized the man. But now, as his tears softened the man's sharp features, he suddenly saw who it was.

"A dismembered body, you said?" Atif glanced at the other photograph, David Sarac, but with the wrong eyes.

Amante nodded. "Do you recognize him?"

Atif thought for a moment. Then he leaned back in his chair. "I'm sorry to disappoint you, Vaseline, but I've never seen him before in my life."

•   •   •

Julia waited until the prison had disappeared from the rearview mirror before she said anything.

"Do you usually go around with Vaseline in your pocket?" She took her eyes off the road and pulled a face to let Amante know she was joking.

"I get a rash on my wrists," he said without looking up from his cell phone. "Vaseline's the only thing that helps. My therapist says it's psychosomatic. That's why I don't like handcuffs."

Julia tried unsuccessfully to work out if he was teasing her. First she'd had to rescue Amante when he flared up out of nowhere and came close to telling the head screw where to stick his internal regulations. And then, out of the blue, he suddenly managed to get Kassab to open up. He handled the interview almost like a professional. She couldn't make any sense of him.

"So what do you think?" she asked.

"I think it's going to be a cold night. Might even get some rain. The wind's swung around to the north."

"And if we forget the weather forecast for a moment and focus on Kassab?"

"He knows perfectly well who Frank is."

Julia nodded. She'd picked up the same signals. Eyes widening slightly, the faint but unmistakable change in Kassab's body language.

"I agree. Kassab lied, and didn't really try to hide it. Almost as if he wanted us to realize that he knew but wasn't going to say anything."

Neither of them spoke for a few seconds.

"Was he right, by the way?" she said.

"Who?"

"Kassab. When he said you look like you come from North Africa."

"My biological father is from Morocco. My mom left him when I was ten." Amante turned away, his tone of voice suddenly unforthcoming.

"Okay," Julia said, in the absence of anything better. She stifled an impulse to ask more questions that wouldn't be answered. Another little piece to add to the puzzle of Amante. The question was whether it left her any wiser or just more confused. He was looking more and more like a thousand-piece jigsaw puzzle where half the picture was made up of dark clouds.

They reached the main road and she turned right toward the city.

"So you don't think we'll get any further with Kassab?" she said, to shift the conversation back to safer territory. Amante took the bait after just a few seconds.

"No . . . not unless something happens that suddenly makes him want to talk to us. But I can't really imagine what that might be."

Nor can I, Julia thought.

Eight

It had been raining for about five minutes, when there was a crackle in the Sniper's earpiece. A surprisingly cold summer rain, pattering rhythmically on the paneled roof around him and forcing him to pull up the hood of his dark Windbreaker. Rain and cold didn't usually bother him. He had been freezing cold before. In trenches where the mud stiffened to form ice-cold armor around your body. Among the trees on the damp slopes by the Sarsang Reservoir and in the mountains above the Lachin corridor, where he had stuffed his mouth with snow to stop his clouded breath from giving away his position. And then on the rooftops above the ruins of Agdam, where the wind cut right through his clothes and sometimes carried with it the cries of the dead.

Much later, when his first war was over, he went on freezing, in countries and places that had already faded from memory. Yet there was still something about this rain that he had never experienced before. A new sort of chill. It didn't really surprise him. The whole of this country was cold, even in the summer. The light, the colors, the people. The peculiar jagged language that came out of their mouths. Efficient, functional, so free of emotion if you compared it to his own beautiful mother tongue.

When had he actually started to get nostalgic, to think more about the past than the future? He didn't know. But he was fairly sure that his conversations with Father Ivor had some-thing to do with it.

Two hours had passed since he lay down on the groundsheet and unfolded the support for his rifle. Even though it was almost midnight, a thin strip of light was still lingering on the horizon. As if the day refused to be beaten, thus denying him the darkness he had been counting on, and which would have made him invisible up there. It troubled him and had made him consider abandoning the job. But then he heard the voice in his earpiece.

"Under way," it whispered.

Time to make his mind up. He was more visible than he had anticipated, more exposed than felt comfortable. But rain made people look down. Turn up their collars and open umbrellas, concentrate on avoiding puddles ahead of them. Besides, this was no ordinary job. A favor—that was how he preferred to look at it. One life in return for saving another. Or several, to be more accurate.

With a practiced hand, the Sniper removed the rubber covers from both ends of the large telescopic sight and laid his cheek against the butt of the rifle. The plastic was cold and smooth against his skin, exacerbating the chill from the rain. In spite of the hazy nocturnal light, the image was crystal clear. A street, a row of parked cars, a few illuminated windows, a restaurant.

According to the gauge, the distance was forty-eight meters, and the difference in elevation eleven meters between the street and the roof where he was lying. He had already adjusted the sight in light of all the data the expensive instrument had given him. It was a luxury that he could only have dreamed of as a young conscript equipped with an old Mosin-Nagant rifle with a battered telescopic sight. Even so, he found himself looking back on those days more and more fondly. He toyed with the forbidden thought that what he was doing now wasn't the same thing as back then. That the people in his sights weren't enemies but targets he was firing at for a price, and that his soul, in spite of all his donations to the monastery, was therefore irrevocably lost. Father Ivor would have said that was because he no longer took the trouble to remember his targets' names but instead actively tried to forget them.

A large, dark-colored Audi glided along the street and pulled up outside the restaurant. The driver remained in the car as the front passenger door opened. The Sniper trained the crosshairs of the sight on the man and followed him as he stepped onto the pavement. He was thickset, muscular in that way that made his clothes look like they didn't fit properly. The bulletproof vest that the man was presumably wearing under his leather jacket only emphasized the impression of stiffness.

The Sniper moved the crosshairs to the bodyguard's head and adjusted one of the settings so that his angular head almost filled the lens. He felt his pulse quicken and took a couple of deep breaths to slow it down. The rain went on drumming on the roof.

The bodyguard down below looked about him, then walked slowly around the car and took a large black umbrella from the boot. He put it up, then opened the rear passenger door wide and took a couple of steps toward the front door of the restaurant. Then he stopped and slowly scanned the facades of the buildings on the other side of the street.

For a moment the Sniper thought their eyes met through the telescopic sight. A shiver ran down his neck, all the way to his stomach. If everything had gone the way he had planned, the bodyguard would have had no chance of seeing him. His night vision would have been disrupted by the streetlamps, and the night sky would have made him blend into the dark rooftop. But as it was, things were very different.

The bodyguard continued to stare up toward him. His mouth opened slightly, as if he was about to say something into the microphone in his collar.

The Sniper held his breath. Waited.

He let his finger slide over the trigger. Carefully squeezed the cold metal until he felt it reach the sweet point. He had been spotted a couple of times before and had naturally planned for that eventuality. He just had to get up in a crouch, work through the five practiced hand movements that would get the rifle and groundsheet into his rucksack, then walk calmly toward the exit. The car they had given him was parked a block away, and he could be on his way to the airport within five minutes, maximum. The only trace of his presence would be a rapidly disappearing dry patch on the paneled roof.

The thought calmed him down. He let go of the trigger and stretched his forefinger as he continued to study the man below. Waiting for his next move.

The bodyguard turned around, opened the restaurant door, and held it open. There was movement within. The Sniper moved the rifle and put his finger back on the trigger. A man stopped in the doorway. There was a blonde woman on his arm. Behind her he could make out another well-built bodyguard.

"The target is leaving," the voice in his earpiece said. "Proceed. I repeat: Proceed."

The Sniper moved the rifle another few centimeters and squeezed the trigger halfway. He noticed his heartbeat again and took half a breath to settle it. Time switched gears. Suddenly everything seemed to happen in slow motion.

The rain went on drumming an irregular, chill rhythm on the black roof. The woman below laughed. The sound echoed between the buildings. Bloodred lipstick, white teeth.

An infinitely drawn-out second passed.

Two.

Just as the pair stepped out onto the pavement—the instant before they would be hidden by the bodyguard's large umbrella—he fired.

Nine

Julia wasn't properly awake when she got hold of her phone as it buzzed about on her bedside table. The central number of the Violent Crime Unit flashed on the screen.

"H-Hello?"

"What the hell are you playing at, Gabrielsson?" Pärson was shouting so loudly that Julia had to hold the phone away from her ear. She felt across the bedside table and found the light switch, then her alarm clock.

Ten past two on Monday morning. Pärson was still bellowing.

"—that you and a fucking civilian went and questioned Atif Kassab in prison on your day off. Would you care to explain to me what the fuck is going on?"

"We were following up the last leads regarding the dismembered body in Källstavik, boss." She did her best to keep her voice calm. Placed extra emphasis on the last word, because she knew Pärson liked it when she played subordinate.

"The dismembered body? You mean the case the Security Police are investigating? The case that I ordered you to drop on Friday?"

Julia got out of bed, rubbing her eyes with the back of her hand.

"Well . . ." she began as her brain tried to come up with a suitable response.

"Shut up. I don't want to hear it. You and I will have to have a talk about this at a later date. Right now you need to get some clothes on and come into the office. We've got a shooting in the city center. An execution, to be blunt. The victim was shot in the head by a sniper when he and his mistress were leaving a Michelin-starred restaurant. The media are all over it, the head of Regional Crime is on his way over in person, and the national police chief's people won't stop phoning. I need every detective we've got, even the ones who can't follow orders."

"Understood," Julia muttered. "I'll be there in fifteen minutes."

But Pärson had already slammed the phone down.

• • •

Atif had only been locked up with Joachim Gilsén for a few hours before he realized one thing very clearly: he loathed the man. He loathed his squeaky voice, his salesman's grin, his habit of sucking his crowned teeth like they were sweets. He loathed the nervous way Gilsén moved his head the whole time. Twitch, twitch, twitch, like a bird. Not to mention the crap he talked. A drawn-out monologue of rationalizations, excuses, and evasions.

"The way I see it, those greedy bastards only have themselves to blame. Do you get it?"

A twitch of the head.

"It's hardly my fault that their money burns holes in their pockets."

Another twitch, followed by a grin.

"It's really us taxpayers who helped them make a profit, thanks to all the deductions they can claim for property expenses. We've helped stuff millions into their bulging bank accounts."

Double twitch.

"All I do is take some of that back. I mean, who's stupid enough to believe they can get a guaranteed fifteen percent return? The idiots are practically begging to be turned over."

A scornful grin, followed by tooth sucking, which was making a whistling sound from the corners of Gilsén's mouth.

Atif sipped his morning coffee. The clock on the wall said

it was five minutes past eight. Less than twenty-four hours in isolation with Gilsén felt like a week. And of course there were no distractions. No newspapers, no Internet, no television. He hadn't even been allowed to take any books from his cell. Naturally, the whole thing was the idea of the sadistic Blom. A chance to give him a bit of extra punishment. And on top of that, he had to keep an eye on Gilsén. By now news of the fight would have reached beyond the walls. Whoever had paid Rosco and his guys to murder Gilsén would raise their bid. It was only a matter of time. And it wouldn't make the slightest difference that Gilsén was being kept in here with him for his own protection. Just like last time, the screws would turn a blind eye at just the right moment. Because while Gilsén was sharp as a razor blade when it came to business, he was seriously fucking stupid. During his time in custody he had managed to make numerous complaints against prosecutors, police officers, and prison guards. He had written long diatribes to the judicial public advocate, the European Court of Human Rights, and the media about how badly he was being treated by the judicial system and how his rights were being infringed in all manner of ways.

Atif had read the papers and therefore had a pretty good idea about the little man's business dealings. Gilsén mostly targeted retired businessmen, golden oldies who had just sold their companies and were sitting on pots of money. He had a flashy office on Strandvägen, complete with sexy secretary and all. He offered dinners and trips as he persuaded his victims to lend money at an extortionate rate of interest. Ten, sometimes fifteen percent, and as surety for this they were given shares worth three times the amount in some sham company.

Gilsén's opening gambit was smart—Atif reluctantly had to admit that—and the next phase was also pretty clever. He made payments for the first couple of months, enticing his greedy victims to invest more and more of their millions into his projects and to recommend him to their friends. The little bastard was so convincing with his porcelain smile and verbal diarrhea that he persuaded his victims to carry on transferring money long after they ought to have realized that things weren't right. Yet still no one reported him. Because as long as Gilsén kept answering the phone and feeding them excuses, there was still hope that their savings could be rescued. Besides, they still had the shares they had been given in exchange.

But Gilsén had grown careless. He boasted about the nature of the business to his secretary-slash-mistress, and when he later dumped her she sent a recording of the conversation to the police. Ironically, it was Gilsén's own drivel that finally made his victims realize that they had been duped. That sort of poetic justice appealed to Atif.

Oddly enough, neither Abu Hamsa nor any of his associates had been drawn into the trial, even though Gilsén's complex financial transactions had been made via Hamsa's currency exchange business. Gilsén maintained that he had been working alone, and the prosecutor never managed to work out who Gilsén's original backers had been, or where the money eventually ended up. All they had managed to salvage were a few paltry millions sitting in a current account. The rest was gone. And even though Gilsén was extremely talkative, he steered well clear of more contentious subjects.

So why would anyone want to kill him? If Gilsén hadn't blabbed by now, he probably wasn't going to. The golden goose would be out in a couple of years and could start laying new eggs.

Presumably Gilsén had picked on the wrong victims. The only question was who and in what way? And why did Abu Hamsa want to keep the little shit alive at all costs? Gilsén must know something that could improve his own position, and it wouldn't take much to squeeze the little man's secrets out of him. The problem was that Atif didn't dare touch him. Not while Abu Hamsa was holding Tindra and Cassandra hostage. So he would have to wait. He passed the time thinking about the previous day's visit and trying to work out if he could exploit the fact that he knew who the man in the grainy photograph was.

If only he could have a bit of peace, that is.

"Kassab, Kassab!" Gilsén snapped his fingers in front of his face. "Where did you go, my friend?"

Atif looked up and grinned back and him. And clenched one fist under the table.

"What were you thinking about? Penny for your thoughts."

You don't want to know, Atif thought, taking another sip of coffee. *You really don't want to know.*

• • •

Jesper Stenberg hung his jacket up on the stand next to the double doors of his office and put his briefcase down on the floor beside his mahogany desk. He completed his morning routine by going over to the tall windows and looking out. The leaves of the trees surrounding the little triangle of grass that someone had rather optimistically named Rosenbadsparken were slowly taking on a deep-green color. In a couple of weeks the torrent of tourists would be at its height: even now, a little after nine o'clock, they were flooding across the bridges toward Gamla stan, the palace, and the island of Riddarholmen.

He should really have gone with his family to their country retreat out in Källstavik. He could be lying in the hammock, relaxing with a book. Going for evening dips in the lake with the girls down by the jetty. The whole Astrid Lindgren thing. But he knew that was an illusion, something better in the imagination than in real life. Country life was Karolina's thing, not his. She even thought their villa in Danderyd was a bit too close to the city. Karolina had pretty much grown up in Källstavik. But he got restless there after just a couple of hours. The rustling of the trees and lapping of the water always gave him cabin fever.

Besides, he didn't feel like listening to yet another of his father-in-law's lectures. He liked the man and appreciated all his efforts and favors. But recently there had been rather too many suggestions: "Bear that in mind, Jesper." "It's important that you don't do this, Jesper." As if he were a child, or at best a complete novice who couldn't manage the most basic tasks without being coached. The old man seemed to have suppressed the fact that Jesper had been a successful lawyer for seven years, and before that had spent three years as a prosecutor at the International Criminal Court in The Hague.

But what bothered Stenberg most was probably Karolina's behavior. The way she toyed with him, constantly manipulating him in line with her father's instructions. Karolina worshipped her father. She'd set him on such a lofty pedestal that the old boy could practically touch the sky. One single bad word about Karl-Erik—a single sigh or raised eyebrow—was enough to get him in trouble. Karolina's relationship with her father had always annoyed him. It was like a secret club to which he was occasionally admitted but where he could never become a member. Perhaps it was that feeling of exclusion that had led him to carry on with his affair with Sophie . . . Maybe that had nurtured his need to have something of his own, something they weren't part of. But he knew that argument was something of a retrospective construct. The shamefaced married man trying to rationalize his mistakes.

His coffee was already waiting on the coffee table and he poured himself a cup before settling down at his desk. He wondered briefly if he could postpone the meeting. Come up with some sort of excuse. But he needed an update about the night's events in case he was asked about them. Just as well to get it out of the way. He pressed a button on his phone.

"Ask him to come in."

There was a short knock, then Wallin was standing in his room.

"Good morning." The same ingratiating tone as usual.

"Sit down, Oscar." Stenberg nodded toward one of the armchairs on the other side of the desk. He had neither the time nor inclination for small talk. "What else do we know about what happened last night?"

Wallin opened his obligatory blue folder.

"At 23:57 yesterday evening the command center received a report of a shooting outside a restaurant at Regeringsgatan 26. An all-cars alert was issued, and patrol 1940 was first on the scene, at 00:03, according to the report . . ."

Stenberg made a circular motion with his hand. "Fast-forward, please."

"Of course." Wallin smiled and leafed through the folder. "As I said on the phone, the victim is Fouad Nazari, sixty-seven years old, better known as Abu Hamsa. The person who shot him was on the roof of a building on the other side of the street. No forensic evidence so far, and my guess is that there won't be any either. This was a professional job. A single shot to the center of the head. Probably half-jacketed, maybe even hollow-tipped, considering the result."

Wallin paused, evidently waiting for Stenberg to say something.

"Go on," he said.

"The bullet expanded on impact. Created a pressure wave through the skull that blew the victim's occipital lobe off. Judging by the pictures, it wasn't a pretty sight."

Wallin put down a photograph of a woman in a white coat spattered with blood.

"Thank you, that's enough." Stenberg gestured to Wallin to remove the picture. He realized from the other man's smile that he'd walked straight into the trap. Another blonde, blood-stained woman he wanted nothing to do with. He swallowed and quickly collected himself.

"What do we know about the victim? You said earlier that Nazari wasn't just anyone."

"Abu Hamsa was a well-known figure. Officially he owned

a group of relatively small businesses. A handful of foreign exchange bureaus, a solarium, part ownership of a recruitment company, and a number of bars. All we've got in police files is a couple of traffic violations. But Abu Hamsa had long been regarded as one of the biggest players in organized crime. Something of a mediator, someone the other factions trusted and did business with. Hamsa's name has cropped up on the edges of a number of different investigations, most recently the Gilsén case."

"Gilsén? The fraudster, you mean?" Stenberg straightened up. He knew both the prosecutor and the defense lawyer in the case and had followed the trial carefully in the media.

"The mafia's banker, that's right. Joachim Gilsén and Abu Hamsa knew each other well. Hamsa was questioned when Gilsén was brought in. It seems probable that he helped launder money through his exchange bureaus, but the prosecutor didn't think there was sufficient evidence to bring charges. And Gilsén refused to testify."

"Okay," Stenberg said, in an attempt to move the conversation on. "A known gangster with links to an even better-known fraudster has been shot by a sniper on a street in the middle of the city. I assume that the resources of the Stockholm Police are out in force?"

"Of course, which makes sense for a number of reasons." The schadenfreude in Wallin's voice was unmistakable. "I happen to know that no fewer than five members of Parliament have links to addresses in the close vicinity. Mostly pied-à-terres, but also more personal connections. Children, mistresses, lovers . . . One of the MPs is also the deputy chair of the Justice Committee, so the national police chief has probably received a number of calls already today."

Stenberg sighed quietly to himself. That had become an almost obligatory ingredient in Wallin's recent presentations. After the blue folder and the veiled allusions to Sophie, it was time to snipe at the national police chief.

"All the news media are leading with the Abu Hamsa murder, and of course they're linking it to Skarpö. We managed to contain the negative PR on that occasion thanks to the geography and bad weather. But this case is very media-friendly. Cell phone pictures, pools of blood, witnesses, and buildings spattered with blood. Shaken and half-cut diners happy to be interviewed for online streaming. As I see it, the commissioner's erstwhile colleagues in Regional Crime have got a particularly hot potato on their hands. If Kollander and his gang don't solve this case in the next week or so, they're going to be in pretty hot water."

"Is there any connection, then? To Skarpö?" Stenberg asked.

"Well, there aren't really any clear similarities." Wallin shrugged his shoulders. "But there's already speculation about a power vacuum and turf wars. That could be true, of course, but I'm more inclined to think it's connected to the Gilsén case. There's actually a rather interesting connection between the two cases, even if it is rather tenuous."

"And that connection is?" Stenberg said. He was tired of this game now.

"There were four other people with Abu Hamsa when he died. Eldar Jafarov, who's a combination of driver and right-hand man. Two hired bodyguards—bulky guys who've been on a lot of weird courses in the States."

"Get to the point, Oscar."

"The fourth person was a woman. Cassandra Nygren. She's the one in the picture you saw. Around thirty, bartender, croupier, and glamour model. Bleached blonde, nipped and tucked, well upholstered. The mistress type, if you take my meaning."

Stenberg didn't answer. He realized he had clenched his teeth together. Another discreet little reference to Sophie Thorning. Another reason for stuffing Oscar Wallin's career into the freezer the first chance he got.

"Cassandra Nygren," Wallin went on. "She has a child by an Adnan Kassab, who was killed in a shoot-out after a failed robbery in the western district last fall. Little Tindra, seven years old, and her father's brother is Atif Kassab, the hit man who was convicted of four murders out on Skarpö, among them Superintendent Peter Molnar."

Stenberg quickly dropped the revenge fantasy he had just conjured up. He straightened his back. Wallin went on:

"I also happen to know that Atif Kassab is currently in isolation after a fight in a phoenix unit. Apparently he dispatched a couple of fellow inmates to the ER. Either way, Kassab's only company in isolation is another high-profile prisoner that he, according to the incident report, appears to have taken under his wing. Care to guess who?"

"Joachim Gilsén," Stenberg said. He had to admit, Wallin was occasionally more than just a pain in the backside.

"I said it was an interesting connection. And Abu Hamsa didn't usually have any bodyguards apart from Jafarov. So he must have been genuinely concerned for his safety. My guess is that Hamsa knew someone was out to get both him and Gilsén and took measures to protect them both. Unfortunately, he was only fifty percent successful. It'll be interesting to see what happens next."

Stenberg nodded as he observed the man in front of him. Wallin was an unpleasant, manipulative little shit, but there was no doubt that he took his job extremely seriously. Or that he could still be of some use.

. . .

The screws let Atif out into one of the ten small segments that the circular exercise yard had been divided into. Through the wire fence he could see Gilsén a few segments away. He was walking anxiously back and forth. When he caught sight of Atif he looked up and raised one hand in greeting. Atif ignored him. The distance between their segments was too large for them to be able to talk, which suited Atif fine. See but don't hear.

114

The door to the segment next to him opened and a rectangular man stepped out into the shadow of the building. Rosco.

He sauntered over to Atif, nodded to him, and then leaned against the fence separating them.

"Cigarette?" Rosco pulled a packet of Marlboros from the top pocket of his prison shirt. Atif shook his head.

Rosco lit a cigarette and took a deep drag before looking over at Gilsén's segment. The little man had started doing push-ups, but it didn't seem to be going well, and after just a few he moved on to what were probably meant to be sit-ups.

"Pathetic little shit," Rosco said. "He'd sell his own mother if the price was right."

Atif didn't answer. Rosco took another drag.

"You've heard about Abu Hamsa?"

Atif tilted his head slightly. Met the other man's gaze. Or half met it.

"Bad way to die. Skull blown off in the street, even though he had bodyguards and everything. No one's safe anywhere."

Atif remained silent.

"There's no reason for us to fall out, Kassab. Whatever deal you had with Abu Hamsa, it's just as dead as he is now. The old man was fucking your sister-in-law; he was doing that long before your brother died. You can't be protecting him out of loyalty . . ."

Rosco raised his eyebrows questioningly, and Atif looked over at Gilsén once more. He was bending his knees now, with his arms stretched out. He looked utterly ridiculous.

"They'll be looked after," Rosco said. "Cassandra and the little girl. No one will touch them, not as long as you and I are in agreement."

He picked a strand of tobacco from his tongue. Spat on the ground.

"What do you say, Kassab? Have we got a deal?"

Atif turned slowly toward the thickset man. Looked at him hard for several seconds.

"I'll take that cigarette now," he said.

Atif was lying on his bed with his fingers laced behind his head. His body felt better with each passing day. His muscles were slowly growing, more sinuous than bulky. Just the way he wanted. Stamina was always better than raw strength. You had to think long-term, have enough strength left for the last round.

The only thing he didn't like about his body was the gray hair that was starting to appear at his temples and on his chin. Coarse, almost like horsehair. A discreet reminder that nothing lasts forever and that his days, however you chose to look at it, were numbered. He wouldn't be getting out for at least another fifteen years. He'd be past sixty by then. An old man. And Tindra would be over twenty, a grown woman with a life of her own. A life that probably wouldn't have any room for an ex-con uncle she hadn't seen since she was a little girl.

He thought about how much he'd like to see her again. Hear her voice, feel her little arms around his neck. Her breath against his cheek. Now . . . soon. While she still remembered who he was.

An hour ago the screws had done their evening round. Locked him and Gilsén in their cells before closing the section for the night. Giving him a chance to be alone with his thoughts.

Abu Hamsa had been shot in the street. A single shot in the center of his head. That sort of operation was risky; it required a professional. Someone who was flown in and out of the country, and demanded serious money for their services. That sort of job also attracted unwanted attention, from both the public and the police. Why not make things easier for themselves? Get Abu Hamsa inside one of his restaurants after it closed, at the races, or, even better, when he shuffled out in his slippers to fetch the morning paper. Any small-town nobody could do a thing like that for a tenth of the price without attracting apocalyptic headlines. Someone wanted to show their power, their strength. But who, and what for?

Rosco was right: Abu Hamsa was dead, and their agreement had died with him. At midnight Gilsén would be getting a visit from Rosco and his guys, and whatever secrets the little man still harbored would be revealed. All Atif had to do was look the other way, pretend nothing was happening. Go on sitting out his time obediently. Time he didn't actually have.

He changed position, put his hand in his pocket, pulled out the folded playing card, and slowly opened it out. Three hard folds dividing the colorful joker into eight identically sized sections.

The clock behind the thick plexiglass screen above the cell door clicked. Two hours left until midnight, precisely . . . now. A short signal echoed through the facility, and then the lights went out. Atif lay still for a couple of seconds, listening to the dense silence. The windows lay deep within the thick walls, making it almost impossible to see the stars. They were up there, waiting for him, just like Tindra. As long as he kept a cool head and thought long-term. Played his cards in exactly the right order. He slowly folded the joker again and put it back in his pocket. Then he got to his feet and crept silently over to the door of his cell.

Ten

Senior prison officer Benny Blom knew the man in the cell was dead before he even opened the door. Yet he still found himself holding his breath. He'd been through all this before: the kneeling, forward-leaning posture, the swollen face and bulging, vacant eyes. The stench rising from the pool of piss on the floor around the man's bare knees mixed with a more cloying stench from his underpants. Even the improvised noose—a pair of Prison Service sweatpants tied to the bars on the window, and now the only thing holding the body up—was familiar. All in all a neat job, just as agreed, and nothing to trouble his conscience. Not for very long, anyway. The man in the noose had chosen to play the game of his own volition, and there were plenty of victims and relatives who would think he'd gotten just what he deserved. And after a couple of weeks in Thailand any lingering pangs of guilt would be blown away, Blom knew that from experience. Because he was one of the good guys, in spite of everything. Someone who helped to uphold justice.

Even so, he did his best to act suitably surprised in front of his colleagues. Took a couple of cautious steps into the cell and extended one hand toward the dead man. Just as he expected, the skin was waxy and ice-cold. Any attempt at CPR would be pointless. Not to mention disgusting, considering the black, half-bitten-off tongue sticking out of the man's lips.

He turned around to the guard who had fetched him from the staff gym and was now standing in the doorway with an equally wide-eyed colleague.

"Stone dead." Blom pulled his hand back. "And he's been

dead awhile, so there's no rush. Get Control to call the police and say another one's decided to check out."

Blom gestured to the two men to leave, then backed away slowly in the same direction. When he was sure no one was watching, he pulled out his phone and took a couple of quick pictures of the body. Just as well to have proof that he had kept his side of the deal.

Suddenly he heard someone calling for his colleagues out in the corridor. A low, muted voice that he couldn't quite place.

It took a couple of seconds for Blom to realize that the voice was coming from the cell next door.

"Tell the cops I know what happened. That I want to talk."

• • •

Julia Gabrielsson had folded her arms on her desk, leaned her head on them, and closed her eyes. She'd dozed off for a while until her phone woke her. For a few moments her brain fumbled for a time and place. After some hesitation, it came to the conclusion that it was Tuesday morning and that she was in her office at work.

She hadn't gotten much sleep in the past twenty-four hours. The big deployment following Abu Hamsa's murder lasted until well into Monday evening, and Pärson had kept her until midnight before letting her go home to get a couple of hours' sleep. She wasn't counting on getting any overtime for that marathon shift.

Her phone was still ringing and she picked up the receiver. Pärson, naturally.

"My office, three minutes."

She got to her feet, picked up her mug of coffee, and set off toward the women's restroom. Pärson was seriously pissed off with her—that much was obvious; he wouldn't have demoted her to desk duties otherwise. He'd got her searching databases, something any civilian employee could have done, and the result was a long list of people who were in some way connected to Abu Hamsa. Sixty-two of them so far. At the top of the list were the old man's daughter, Susanna, and her husband, Eldar Jafarov, who also happened to be Abu Hamsa's bodyguard. Presumably they'd be taking over the business from Abu Hamsa. Unless the people behind his murder had other plans. They were likely to find out which fairly soon.

She splashed some water on her face and tipped the cold coffee into the basin. Time for a more thorough chewing out for her and Amante's little adventure. She wondered who had talked. Probably that gym-pumped prison officer. But did Pärson also know about their trip to the nursing home?

Of course, she could give an account of what they'd discovered. Explain that Sarac had absconded and show the picture of the mysterious Frank who had helped him. But she was still hesitant about involving Pärson. She'd much rather wait and see how much he knew before revealing what they had found out.

Julia refilled her mug, took a deep breath, then knocked on Pärson's door. The "engaged" light was already glowing angrily.

"Come in."

The bags under Pärson's eyes seemed to have bred, and the smell from his nylon shirt was even more acrid than usual. On one of the chairs in front of his desk sat a tall, thin man in an impeccable uniform. Freshly ironed white shirt, heavy gold cuff links that matched the epaulettes on his shoulders. Staffan Kollander, head of Regional Crime, in person.

"Sit." Pärson waved toward the free chair.

Julia smiled tentatively at Kollander and received a reserved nod in response.

"There's been a development. Related to the Abu Hamsa case."

Pärson's tone of voice made it clear that she wasn't yet back in favor, but she still felt relieved. This wasn't about her and Amante's freelance jaunt. She wouldn't have to reveal any of their discoveries yet.

"Early this morning a man was found dead in his cell in a phoenix unit south of Stockholm," Kollander said. "For the time being, the evidence suggests suicide. But the victim is linked to Abu Hamsa. And . . ." He paused, and fixed his gaze on Julia for several seconds. ". . . there's a witness. The occupant of a neighboring cell says he has information. He claims it could lead to a breakthrough in the investigation into Abu Hamsa's murder."

"That . . ." Julia cleared her throat. "That sounds promising."

"But we have a slight problem," Pärson muttered. "This so-called witness is demanding to talk to Amante in person, just the two of them. Otherwise he won't say a word. And the interview also has to take place here in Police Headquarters and not out at the prison. Ridiculous idea." Pärson glared at Julia as if all this was her fault.

"Naturally, under normal circumstances we never agree to ultimatums. But Superintendent Pärson and I agree that the current situation is a little"—Kollander formed his thin fingers into an arch and slowly drummed his fingertips against each other—"out of the ordinary."

"Precisely," Pärson said. "The van is already on its way here from the prison. We're preparing an interview room. Amante hasn't turned up this morning and he's not answering his phone. You've got an hour and a half to find him and brief him on the case. Gilsén's body is on its way to the Forensic Medicine Unit; we should get a preliminary report from them before lunch." He scratched his ear with a stubby little finger, then inspected the result.

"I don't quite understand," Julia said. "Why does the witness want to talk to Amante?"

Pärson and Kollander exchanged a glance.

"Apparently he and the witness are already acquainted," Pärson said smoothly. "But that's something you and I can talk about in more depth on another occasion, Gabrielsson."

Julia carefully closed Pärson's door behind her and took her cell phone out, but waited to make the call until she was back in her own office. An inmate of a phoenix unit who wanted to talk to Amante directly. That could only be one person. But why did he want to talk to Amante and not her? What did he have to say? There was only one way to find out.

• • •

"You've reached the Care Center. This is Natalie Aden. How can I help?" Natalie opened the page containing the doctors' schedules on the computer as she listened to what was troubling the old dear on the other end of the line. "We've got a vacancy tomorrow, Wednesday at twelve o'clock, would that be convenient?"

The physiotherapist with the dimples sauntered slowly up to the counter. For the fifth time today, if Natalie's counting was accurate. That was at least three too many. Even so, she had nothing against his presence.

"Great, so we'll see you tomorrow at twelve o'clock."

She ended the call by gently pressing the side of her cordless headset.

"Just wondered if you'd like a coffee," the physiotherapist said.

"Definitely." She surprised herself with how happy she sounded. The physiotherapist was the same age as she was, a little under thirty. Maybe not massively handsome—his eyes were slightly too close together and he had a bit of a belly—but there was something about him that appealed to her. Something that made her feel happy every time he invented yet another obviously fake reason to visit reception.

"Okay. A splash of milk, no sugar?" he said.

"No, I'm sweet enough." She bit her lip but was too late to stop the cretinous comment slipping out.

The physiotherapist flashed his dimples. "I can't disagree with that."

He turned and walked off toward the staff room.

Shit. She had to play it cool. Stick to the role of extremely competent and practically indispensable receptionist she'd been playing for the past few months, instead of a women's magazine cliché.

She'd applied for the job on the off chance. She tweaked her CV and a few other documents to make herself look qualified enough; then, once she'd got the job, surprised herself by actually enjoying it. Answering the phone, making appointments. Giving little bits of advice to the regulars whose ailments she'd already learned. Okay, it wasn't the doctor's job she'd once dreamed of, but it was pretty close. Here she was, putting in the hours on a regular job. Who'd have thought it?

Considering what she'd been through just a few months before, it all felt rather surreal, but in a good way. She pulled her ChapStick from her pocket and ran it quickly over her lips while she waited for the physiotherapist to return.

The main door opened and a thin, swarthy man came in. His club blazer looked as if he'd slept in it, and the worn tennis shirt under it had obviously seen better days. Taken together with the slightly distant look in the eyes behind his glasses, his clothes told her what he wanted long before he opened his mouth: *Time to get a new prescription for lithium and tranquilizers.* Natalie clicked to bring up the doctors' schedule again and highlighted the psychiatrist's. Damn, she was good at her job.

"Hello, welcome to the Care Center. How can I help?" She smiled her best receptionist's smile. Waited for the man to confirm what she already knew.

"Natalie Aden?" the man said, and something in the way he said her name brought her up short.

"Why?" she said before she had time to think.

An ID badge appeared in front of her. Police. Natalie stiffened. Had her boss found her out? Called the cops without saying anything? Hang on, though. Would they really send a detective to deal with something as basic as a fake résumé?

"My name is Omar Amante. I work with the Stockholm

Police. We're trying to find someone in connection to a murder investigation. A David Sarac. You were out on Skarpö when he was wounded, weren't you?"

The relief that had begun to spread through Natalie's body stopped abruptly.

Now keep quiet about the real reason you were on that island, Natalie. Don't say anything you don't have to . . . Don't ask questions.

"I've already told you everything I know." She met the policeman's gaze. She was surprised at how depressed he looked.

She heard voices from the corridor: the physiotherapist and her boss, both heading in her direction.

"Look, no one here knows I was out there. I've tried to put it all behind me."

"But you were David Sarac's personal assistant, weren't you? His caregiver?"

"Only for a few weeks. We barely had time to get to know each other. I haven't spoken to him since then. Is he okay?" she added. And regretted the question the moment it slipped out.

The detective didn't answer. Even so, there was something in his face that told her Sarac was far from okay.

He put a grainy photograph down on the counter in front of her and smoothed out the edges to stop it rolling up.

"Do you recognize this man?" Those sad eyes lingered on her; they seemed to pick up the slightest change in her expression. The voices in the corridor were getting closer.

An unknown face, half turned away. Time for her relief to get a bit of a boost. But anxiety still had an icy grip on her insides, turning into the cold of last winter.

She could see it before her. Sarac leaning back against a tree. The gun in his hand, the blood spreading on the snow. The smell of smoke, powder, and something else. Mortal dread.

The physiotherapist and her boss came around the corner. They'd be at her desk any moment now. And would notice something was wrong, start asking questions.

"I've never seen this person before," she whispered to the detective. She was used to acting at being believable and making a lie sound genuine. Considerably less used to doing the same with the truth. She had to say something, do something—anything—to make him believe her. To make him leave. At once, before everything was ruined.

"Are you quite sure? He says his name is Frank. He and Sarac knew each other. It's very important that we find him."

Natalie shook her head hard. She quickly rolled up the photograph.

"So that's your appointment, booked for Monday. Thanks for calling in," she said, slightly too loudly. She quickly held out the photograph, tilted her head, and mimed the words *Please, go*.

The detective looked as if he was about to say something, then suddenly there was a muffled buzzing sound from the inside pocket of his crumpled jacket. He made no effort to answer it, just went on looking at her with that sad expression until the physiotherapist put a mug of coffee down on the counter right next to him. A splash of milk, no sugar. Because she was sweet enough.

"Thanks very much for your help, Natalie," the detective said, taking the photograph. He discreetly exchanged it for a business card with a handwritten phone number on the back.

It wasn't until later on that she realized that the detective had talked about David Sarac in the past tense. As though he no longer existed.

Eleven

The interview room was no more than ten square meters in size. A claustrophobic, windowless cube. Julia looked at the screens in front of her. There were a number of different cameras in the room, showing the man inside from a variety of angles.

She saw Amante step into the cube and put the folder she had given him forty-five minutes ago on the table. He pulled out his chair and moved it away from the table before sitting down, partly out of view.

"Adjust the angle slightly," Kollander said to the technician who was sitting at the keyboard. The man turned a knob and Amante reappeared in the center of the middle screen.

"You wanted to talk to me, Kassab," Amante said inside the room, making a little sound meter close to Julia start to move.

"I didn't think you were going to show up, Vaseline."

Amante shrugged his shoulders. "Well, I'm here now."

Kassab looked up toward one of the cameras. Then another one. "Are there many of them?"

"Who?"

"People watching. I can imagine there's a fair number of them."

"I honestly don't know."

The right answer would have been five, Julia thought. Herself, Kollander, the technician, Pärson, and another officer with a pockmarked face whose name she couldn't quite remember. Probably one of Kollander's errand boys.

Kassab looked hard at Amante. "You look more tired than when we met the other day. Looks like you've been sleeping in those clothes. Your partner, that blonde woman, was she the one who told you to come? You answer when she calls, don't you? I would too."

Pärson shot Julia a quick glance that made her squirm.

"What did you want to say?" Amante said. "And why did you want to talk to me in particular?"

Kassab shook his head.

"Not so fast, Vaseline. You have to answer a question first." Kassab leaned forward slightly. "What's your first name?"

"Why do you ask?"

"You know what my name is." Kassab gestured with his hand, making the cuffs rattle.

Amante looked at him for a few seconds.

"Omar," he said.

Kassab nodded with a look of satisfaction. "Okay, Omar. I'll tell you how Gilsén died, and why. But first . . ."

He held his hands up and tugged at the chain. Julia saw Amante hesitate.

"Come on, we're inside the prison on top of Police Head-quarters. Six floors up, and there must be at least ten cops in the nearest rooms." Kassab tugged at the chain again. "Please, take them off."

"I don't have a key."

"No? I thought all cops had one on their key ring."

"I don't like handcuffs," Amante muttered. His tone of voice made Julia glance at the others. She wondered if they had noticed anything, but none of them seemed to react.

"Okay, we'll have to ask someone else." Kassab held his hands up and stared into one of the cameras. Waited.

In the observation room Pärson looked at Kollander.

"Do as he asks," Kollander said to the pockmarked officer. The man left the room and appeared shortly afterward on the screens.

"Here." He handed a key to Amante before closing the door behind him.

"Big Brother is watching us," Kassab said as Amante fiddled clumsily with the lock of the cuffs. His fingers slipped on the metal and for a moment Julia considered going in to help him. But before she could make up her mind, Amante managed to get it open.

Kassab rubbed his wrists. The red marks from the cuffs were clearly visible on the screens. *Pulled far too tight,* Julia thought. *Must have hurt badly after a while.* For some reason she guessed that the gym-pumped prison officer she had met the other day was responsible.

Inside the interview room Amante put the cuffs on the table, sat back down, and opened the folder.

"Joachim Gilsén," he said. "Tell me. Why did he die?"

Kassab straightened his back. Julia found herself doing the same.

"Gilsén ran a Ponzi scheme where he swindled rich pensioners. Abu Hamsa helped by running the transactions through his currency exchange business. In the background were a number of serious criminals who stood for the initial costs and cashed in the excess."

"We know that already." Amante looked down at the folder. "But the prosecutor evidently didn't think he had enough evidence to bring charges against anyone apart from Gilsén."

Kassab nodded. "But what you and the prosecutor don't know is that Gilsén and Hamsa secretly skimmed off a share before passing on the profits. When Gilsén was arrested, Hamsa tried to conceal that—and seems to have succeeded, at least to start with. But someone must have talked."

"And that was why he was murdered?"

"The type of people Gilsén and Hamsa were working with don't like being taken for fools. It makes them look weak. And in that business weakness isn't allowed. So Hamsa and Gilsén had to pay for their betrayal, and preferably as publicly as possible."

"Weren't you supposed to be protecting Gilsén?"

128

It was Kassab's turn to shrug. "My job died with Abu Hamsa."

"But Gilsén appears to have killed himself. H-Hanged himself using a pair of trousers, it says here," Amante said, tapping at the folder Julia had given him. She noticed his Adam's apple bob in an involuntary gulp.

Kassab shook his head.

"Smoke screen. The autopsy will prove otherwise. Gilsén talked before he died. I'm sure of that."

"Talked about what?"

"The money. He was forced to reveal the details of the account where he and Abu Hamsa siphoned off their cut."

"How do you know that such an account exists?"

"Gilsén told me. About fifteen million, he estimated."

"Why didn't Abu Hamsa empty the account himself? And have Gilsén killed to remove the risk to himself?"

Very good question, Julia thought. Amante was doing better in there than she had expected.

"Because Gilsén had gotten himself some insurance. The only person who could get at the money was him, and if he died in mysterious circumstances, the police would receive a hard drive containing enough information to convict Abu Hamsa. Say what you like about Gilsén, but the little shit was smart."

"But not smart enough?"

Kassab grimaced. "When Hamsa disappeared, the rules of the game changed. Gilsén's insurance became worthless and he was left unprotected."

"So you're suggesting someone crept into Gilsén's cell unnoticed, forced him to reveal the details of the account, and then hanged him with his own trousers. All in one of the most heavily supervised facilities in the country."

"I'm not suggesting anything. I'm telling you exactly what happened."

A short silence followed, both in the interview room and the room where Julia was sitting. The only sound was Pärson's heavy breathing.

129

"You don't believe me," Kassab said. "Not entirely, anyway."

Amante didn't answer.

"Check the recordings from the cameras out at the prison. I bet the ones in our section stopped working just after ten p.m. and didn't start working until the following morning. The locks on the cell doors stopped working too. Check the computer records. I bet they'll blame a fault in the network, an overloaded system, something like that."

Julia noticed Kollander and Pärson exchanging a glance again.

"And if that's the case?" Amante said.

"Come on, Vaseline. A man is found dead the same night that the cameras are switched off and the cell doors are unlocked. And you're still not convinced it was murder?"

"Who?" Amante said.

Kassab threw his hands out and gave a wry smile.

"Who killed Gilsén?" Amante repeated.

"You're going to have to work that out for yourselves."

"Are you trying to tell me that you've set this whole thing up and now you're *not* going to say who the murderer is?"

But Kassab went on smiling.

"If you want something in exchange—a more comfortable cell, better food, a computer with free porn—well, congratulations, now's your chance." Amante gestured toward the cameras. "Just say what you want. I'm sure Big Brother can sort it out."

Julia saw Kollander pick up a pen. But inside the interview room Kassab slowly shook his head.

"I've told you that Gilsén was murdered and why. The rest is up to you. I'm not a snitch, I'm not after any special privileges, and this conversation is over now."

Kassab leaned back and seemed to concentrate on one patch of wall.

Amante sat silent for a while, apparently at a loss as to what to do. He looked beseechingly up at the cameras as if expecting someone else to take over. Kollander and Pärson leaned their heads together. They spoke so quietly that Julia could hear only fragments of what they said.

"Send someone else in . . . Put pressure on him."

"Waste of time . . . never said a word throughout the whole of the preliminary investigation . . . not a snitch."

The two men's whispered conversation continued. Inside the interview room Kassab stood up.

"Well, then." He turned around and put his hands behind his back. It took a moment for Amante to understand. He got to his feet, walked over to Kassab, and started to fumble as he put the cuffs on. The two men were standing close together and Julia raised her head anxiously. But Kassab stood nice and still.

Julia could see his lips moving slightly but couldn't hear what he was saying. Pärson and Kollander were too busy with their own conversation to notice anything.

Kassab made a slight gesture with his head, seeming to want Amante to move even closer. Amante hesitated for a moment. His fingers slipped on the cuffs again. He had had trouble taking them off a short while before, and it was clear that he was even less eager to be the person who put them back on.

Kassab turned his head a little. He pushed back toward Amante and said something else, but the needle on the sound meter barely moved. Amante appeared to be listening with fascination, and he leaned forward slightly. The men's bodies touched. Kassab was still whispering. Julia stared at the screen, trying to make out what was being said.

All of a sudden Kassab straightened up.

"You know, Vaseline, life's like a fucking card game," he said, loud enough for Pärson and Kollander to interrupt their conversation and look up. "And wogs like you and me are nearly always left with a handful of crap cards."

Kassab turned toward the camera, his eyes were almost entirely black. He seemed to be staring straight out of the screen.

Julia found herself holding her breath. And she probably wasn't the only person in the room to do so.

"But sometimes you get a joker," Kassab said slowly. "A card that can mean absolutely anything, as long as you play it at exactly the right moment."

Twelve

"Well, that was a nice little outing you organized for us all, Kassab." Blom grinned at Atif from the opposite seat. "Didn't the cops like what you had to say? Is that why you're coming back home with us? Rumors about you being a snitch are already spreading around the unit, so I'd watch my back if I was you. It would be a shame if there was another death."

Atif didn't answer, just looked out of the rear window instead. The police van was no more than seven or eight meters behind their minibus, in spite of the speed. Presumably the cop driving it didn't want to risk a worked-up rush-hour driver pulling in between them.

He turned to look forward, ignoring the moronic grins of Blom and his colleagues. Between the shoulders of the two men in the front seats he could see a road sign for Vårby, and the silhouette of the brewery a few hundred meters farther ahead beside the motorway. He stretched his neck and felt the sinews creak.

"We'll soon be back, but you'll be too late for food," said the guard sitting beside Blom. "You spent too long in the toilet. Having a loose stomach has cost you your supper."

The man was sitting so close that their knees were almost touching. The smell of the garlic pizza he had evidently eaten for lunch had long since taken over the air in the minibus.

Atif looked at the cuffs around his ankles and flexed his feet a little. He felt the driver ease up on the accelerator ahead of the long bend.

"By the way," the garlic guard said. "You've got some sort

of crap on your face. Didn't want to mention it before in case you were sensitive about it. But you're all shiny around your eyes. Some sort of skin cream, or what? Did you touch up your makeup before we came?"

Atif looked up and met the man's gaze. Felt the minibus enter the long S-bend of the Vårby bridge. A flash of water below them.

"It's Vaseline," he said, and stretched.

• • •

Julia had been in Staffan Kollander's office a few times before and it hadn't taken long to detect the rhythm of a vain, pedantic man. Although, to be honest, one look at the shiny desk was enough: it was at least two sizes too big for the room.

Amante and Pärson were both sitting opposite Kollander when she slipped in and took up position just inside the door. Neither Pärson nor Kollander objected, presumably because they were fully occupied with Amante.

"So Kassab didn't say anything else of interest?" Kollander said.

Amante pulled a face that Julia had learned meant no.

"Kassab complained a bit about me putting the cuffs on too tightly, so I loosened them a touch. Then I asked if that was okay, and he said yes. That was pretty much it."

"That's what I assumed," Julia said, without really knowing why.

Kollander looked up. Only now did he seem to notice that she was in the room. He arched his hands in a different power posture and drummed his fingertips slowly together.

"And Kassab gave no clue as to who murdered Gilsén?" he repeated unnecessarily.

"We've watched the recording four times," Pärson muttered. "Kassab says he doesn't want to inform on anyone. Gilsén was murdered because he and Abu Hamsa swindled some other guys out of their money. So there is a link between the two murders, just as we suspected."

"That doesn't help us if we don't know who ordered the killings," Kollander growled. "And to find that out, we need to know who the murderer inside the prison is. Assuming that there *is* a murderer, of course."

"Hasn't Forensics come up with anything?" Julia said as neutrally as she could.

"We're still waiting for a preliminary statement from the Forensic Medicine Unit," Pärson said. "Right now we have no evidence that Gilsén was actually murdered. Kassab could just as well be making it all up—saw a chance to escape the tedium for a few hours. All that crap about playing cards . . ."

"What about the other inmates in the unit? And the cameras being switched off? The unlocked doors?"

"We're in the process of looking into that."

There was a knock on the door. The pockmarked policeman who had helped Amante earlier walked in.

"This fax has just arrived from the Forensic Medicine Unit." He put some sheets of paper down on the desk and Kollander quickly pushed them over toward Pärson.

"The preliminary investigation of Gilsén's body suggests that he could have been unconscious before he ended up in the noose," Pärson said after glancing at the first page.

"*Could* have been unconscious?" Kollander said. "So they don't know for sure? In other words, we still don't know if it was murder. Is that how we interpret it?"

"Wait a minute." Pärson turned the page. "The pathologist evidently found a foreign object in Gilsén's throat. It looks like he was trying to swallow it, unless someone forced it into his mouth."

"What sort of foreign object?" Kollander said.

Pärson continued reading.

"The key," the pockmarked policeman whispered to Amante. "My key for the cuffs—can I have it back?"

"Sure." Amante felt his trouser pockets without taking his eyes off Pärson.

"What sort of object?" Kollander repeated, more impatiently this time. "What was in Gilsén's throat?"

"A folded-up playing card." Pärson frowned.

"I don't understand," Kollander said.

"Gilsén had a playing card in his throat," Pärson repeated. "Apparently it was a . . ."

"Joker," Amante said slowly. He stood up, turned his pockets inside out, and gave Julia a sorrowful glance.

"A card that can mean absolutely anything, as long as you play it at exactly the right moment," she muttered as her stomach clenched tight.

The four men in the room stared at her.

"Call the escort vehicle," Pärson snapped at the policeman. "Right away!"

• • •

Atif's fist hit Blom full force on the bridge of his nose. The cartilage shattered beneath his knuckles and a thin spray of blood shot up toward the roof of the minibus. Garlic Guard gaped in surprise and didn't seem to know what to do, but Atif ignored him and threw himself at the senior officer. He had carefully slipped the cuffs behind him onto the seat after unlocking them with the key he took from the Vaseline cop, but his feet were still cuffed, making it hard to keep his balance. He felt around the senior officer's waist and grabbed the pepper spray from his belt.

Blom gurgled and made an attempt to stop him, but his heavy limbs didn't seem to want to obey him.

Atif managed to free the can and aimed a hefty dose of pepper spray straight in the face of Garlic Guard. Then toward the driver's seat. The orange mist hit the front seats, the windshield, and the guard in the passenger seat, who had unfastened his seat belt and was on his way into the back of the minibus. Atif

136

went on spraying, hitting the back of the driver's neck and ears, and didn't stop before the passenger-seat guard threw himself at Atif's chest and they both fell to the floor of the van.

One of his feet gave way and his eyes and nose were stinging. The minibus was filled with a burned-tasting orange fog. Atif heard voices howling with pain, one of them right by his ear. He rammed one knee up as far as the shackles would allow, and struck something soft. He hit the man in the ear with the bottom of the can of spray. Once, twice. The canister cracked and flew across the floor, still dispersing its contents into the minibus.

The vehicle lurched and the passenger-seat guard rolled off Atif. Atif got to his knees, trying to breathe as shallowly as he could. He wiped his face with one arm, rubbing off some of the layer of Vaseline. His vision cleared slightly. He felt someone grab at his leg and heard the driver shout something unintelligible, then there was a jolt as the minibus hit the central barrier and abruptly changed direction. He just managed to throw himself on the floor again as the driver put his foot on the brake and he flew through the bus, tumbling over prone bodies and thudding into the back of the driver's seat.

All the air went out of him; his lungs were burning. Something warm and sticky was trickling down his neck and he tried to get up, but his foot wouldn't do as he wanted. The pain was a four, maybe even a five. A hand grabbed hold of his shirt and he glimpsed a shape through his tears and tried to aim a punch at it. He missed completely.

The vehicle lurched again, harder this time. The driver let out a panicked scream. Other voices joined in, merging into a single howl.

A moment later the minibus crashed through the barrier on the right-hand side of the bridge at full speed, skidded over the edge, and plunged into the water.

Thirteen

Natalie crossed the street. In one hand she held a bag containing milk, a microwave dinner, and the glossy magazine that was her guilty pleasure, and in the other her cell phone. She'd already scrolled down to find the number. Oscar Wallin, aka Rickard: her handler, the police officer who had placed her undercover with David Sarac last winter in order to find out the true identity of the person behind the code name Janus. And who later, once everything had gone to hell, did his utmost to hide his own involvement in the matter.

He had threatened to reveal her former deceptions, take everything she had away from her, if she breathed so much as a word about why she was really out on the island. At the time she had believed him. Accepted his demands, gritted her teeth, and lay low. Apart from one short interview with the police last winter, she hadn't talked to anyone about Skarpö.

Not until today, when that detective with the Buddy Holly glasses and air of melancholy showed up and started asking questions. She hadn't heard from Wallin in several months, hadn't seen any dark police car parked beneath her windows since early that spring. Presumably he had better things to do than keep an eye on her.

But maybe it still made sense to call him. Tell him about the visit, explain that she hadn't said anything, that there was no need for Wallin to worry. She had more to lose now than last winter, more things to worry about. Besides, a phone call would give her an excuse to ask about David Sarac. She had felt a nagging anxiety ever since the visit, an anxiety that wasn't entirely rooted in her fear of being uncovered and fired. She wanted to hear that Sarac was okay, that Buddy Holly had accidentally used the wrong tense when talking about him.

She opened the door to her building. Some of the kids must have had a water fight in the stairwell, because the steps were covered in splashes of water. As she got farther up she saw that some of what was on the steps wasn't water. Nosebleed, she guessed. Damn kids.

She stopped outside her door. The splashes, red and transparent alike, continued on up the stairs to the attic. A junkie, she thought. Not the first time, and almost certainly not the last. Another idiot hoping to find something valuable up there among the chicken-wire storage compartments. Objects of value that all the other petty criminals before him had somehow mysteriously failed to find. She could only hope that he liked Christmas decorations, battered paperbacks, and old skis.

She put the bag down and inserted the key in the lock. She thought about calling the police but doubted that something like this would be considered a priority. The cops were hardly likely to kill themselves racing to get a junkie out of an attic. On the other hand, what if someone was dying up there while she sat and drank coffee in front of *Paradise Hotel*? She started slowly climbing the stairs again. She still had her phone in her hand; she got rid of Wallin's number and tapped in 112 instead. She held her thumb over the green dial button.

Two more steps . . . three. The landing up above was as gloomy as the inside of a Hollister store. She thought she could detect movement next to the door to the attic. She took a few more steps and saw a pair of shoes. A sharp smell of pepper made her nose itch. Then she saw legs, a pair of green jogging trousers. A well-built man was slumped heavily against the attic door. His face was turned away, and between his head and the wall was a blood-soaked rag. It looked like he was asleep.

Natalie raised her phone but stopped herself. The man slowly turned his head.

"I was beginning to wonder when you were going to show up," he said.

. . .

Atif felt the needle being pushed through his scalp for a seventh time. Natalie tied off the stitch with a practiced gesture.

He grimaced as she stuck the needle in again.

"Sorry, but I haven't got any local anesthetic at home," she said. "How badly does it hurt, on a scale of one to ten?"

"Two," he replied quickly. Then wondered why he was lying. "Four," he corrected.

"You took a hell of a risk. What if you'd been knocked unconscious in the crash? You could have drowned."

"But I didn't."

"No, but you've lost a lot of blood. There's still some pepper spray stuck in your hair; when we're done here you're going to have to take a shower. And while you're at it, I'll try to find you some clothes. I presume you don't want those ones washed."

She nodded toward the sealed plastic bag containing his wet prison clothes over by the door.

Atif was about to shake his head when it occurred to him that that wasn't a good idea.

"So, why were you so sure I'd help you? How did you even know where I live?"

"Your address was in the report of the preliminary investigation from Skarpö. I was actually thinking of managing on my own, but I needed a backup plan in case I injured myself too badly. Anyway, the Vårby bridge was a good place to crash."

"So I'm the backup plan." Natalie sounded as if she was teasing him gently, but Atif couldn't be sure without seeing her face. "And what would you have done if I'd resisted the temptation to patch you up again?"

"I've got a relative who's a vet. If worst came to worst . . ."

140

"So you rate my nursing abilities higher than a vet's? That's good to know."

He was quite sure she was making fun of him now, but wasn't really sure how to deal with it.

"Like I said, I've got money. Or I will soon. I'll transfer twenty-five thousand to an account of your choosing. Ten for medical help, ten for your silence, and five for clothes. Okay?"

"And I'm supposed to trust you? Let you have everything on credit until further notice?" Natalie tied off the last stitch and cut the ends.

"Do I seem like the type who wouldn't keep his word?"

Natalie looked at him for a few moments.

"No, you don't. But, on the other hand, most men seem pretty fucking honest when they're sitting in nothing but their underpants."

She kept a straight face for a few seconds; then, when her face cracked into a smile, Atif found himself joining in, to his own surprise. The impression he had gathered out on the island last winter hadn't changed. There was something about this woman he liked. Respected, even.

"So, what happens now?" Natalie got up from the armrest she had been sitting on. "The divers will have been down to inspect the wreck of the minibus by now. The cops will have worked out that you didn't drown, so there'll be a nationwide alert for you."

Atif nodded. "I was expecting to be hunted. Counting on it, actually."

"I don't get it."

"My niece . . ."

Atif stopped. There was no reason to explain his whole plan to Natalie. Quite the opposite, in fact: he ought to say as little as possible. But he couldn't help it.

"Tindra," he said, and thinking about her made him feel better instantly. "There are people threatening her and her mother. Using them to put pressure on me. But if I'm on the

141

run, Tindra and Cassandra's apartment will be the first place the cops look. There'll be surveillance units in cars and in neighboring apartments, maybe even a rapid response team around the corner. As long as I'm on the run—"

"Your family is safe." Natalie nodded. "Not a bad plan so far. After that?" She went over to the little open-plan kitchen and started to dig around in the freezer. "Sooner or later the cops will get fed up of watching your family. Particularly if they work out that you've fled the country. Here, put this on the wound for a bit: it'll make the blood vessels contract."

She tossed him a bag of frozen peas, then returned to the sofa with two bottles of beer and handed one to him. When he looked up at her, she held his gaze for a few moments.

"You're not going to leave the country, are you?" she said. "Not without your family."

Atif took the bottle and took a couple of swigs. The beer washed the last of the pepper spray and seawater from his throat. The coldness from the bag of peas was spreading through his head, slowly diminishing the pain.

Natalie continued to look at him. She seemed to be studying his whole body. The pale skin left by the removal of the tattoo on his shoulder, his misshapen left ear. The scars and irregularities on his arms, legs, and upper body. All of a sudden he felt naked, exposed to her gaze. As if all his secrets were suddenly visible and the red-haired woman in front of him were reading them one after the other. He removed the bag from his head and took a couple of gulps of beer to shake off his awkwardness. He could feel the last of his energy draining away. He tried to straighten up and fight against exhaustion.

"You can crash on the sofa tonight," Natalie said. She interrupted him when he began to protest. "Don't be stupid. You wouldn't even make it down the street in the state you're in right now. And if the cops caught you here, near where I live, it wouldn't take them long to work out who patched you up. Stay till tomorrow, get some proper rest, have breakfast, then you can

142

blend into the rush-hour traffic on the subway. Breakfast and a bed for the night are included in the twenty-five thousand. And I'll clean the stairwell up too. Deal?"

"Deal," Atif mumbled. He lay down and closed his eyes for a few moments, trying to think about Tindra. About the night sky above the desert, and the constellations he'd be able to point out to her.

No more than a minute later he was fast asleep.

• • •

Natalie looked at the sleeping man on her sofa. She didn't really understand why she'd let him in. Any normal person who found a blood-smeared escaped murderer would have made a quick about-face, locked the door of their apartment, and called the cops. Whereas she had done the exact opposite, helping him down the stairs and sitting him on the sofa while she fetched her well-stocked medical kit and patched up his injuries.

Maybe she did it because she'd already patched him up once before, for far more serious injuries. By the very narrowest of margins she had saved his life and for that reason felt somehow responsible for him. Besides, he owed her, and even if she didn't know him—even if he hadn't said a word about it so far—she was absolutely certain of one thing: Atif Kassab wasn't the sort of man who took that kind of debt lightly.

Fourteen

Jesper Stenberg looked at his heavy wristwatch. Wednesday, lunchtime: in one minute and fifty seconds it would be twelve o'clock and John Thorning would walk through the door of the restaurant. John was anal about punctuality and had an almost uncanny ability to appear exactly on time. Never early, never late. Just on time.

The restaurant had been refurbished; nowadays it was furnished with light furniture and pale wood. But the grand old staircase was still there. Stenberg followed it up to the next floor with his eyes. He felt a brief shiver of excitement that vanished the moment he heard John Thorning exchange a few friendly words with the maître d' over by the door.

Stenberg quickly adjusted his facial expression. He had put off this meeting for far too long, but he could not avoid his former mentor any longer. Especially not when Wallin was clearly cozying up to John.

Listen, smile, and promise nothing, as Karolina had needlessly pointed out to him.

"Jesper, great to see you at last. How are your nearest and dearest? Karolina seemed to be in fine form. I heard she'd registered to take part in a bicycle race around Lake Vättern and the Vansbro Swimrun this summer. She's already done the Lidingö run a couple of times, hasn't she? She's almost done all four Swedish Classics."

Stenberg smiled and murmured politely in the right places as he shook John Thorning's outstretched hand. His handshake was just as firm and dry as ever. They sat down at the table.

"And I see you've got the Security Police with you." John nodded with amusement toward Becker, who was sitting over by the door.

"Comes with the territory, I'm afraid." Stenberg smiled apologetically. Just as he had noted the other day, John looked considerably brighter now than he had last winter. He'd regained the weight he had lost following Sophie's death and had acquired a healthy suntan, and both his voice and eyes were back to their former sharpness. John gestured toward their grand surroundings.

"I don't know that I've been here since the firm's Christmas party. How long ago was that, now, four years?"

"Three," Stenberg said. "It's been closed for refurbishment. New owners too."

"Ah, that'll be why I don't quite recognize anything. But I do remember that the party was a great success. We hired a big band, I seem to recall."

We did, Stenberg thought, smiling at his old mentor. *And your psychotic daughter gave me a blow job in one of the upstairs bathrooms while you were dancing the fox-trot with my wife. Sophie liked sick games like that. But that was then. I'm no longer the Thorning family's puppet.*

"In a lot of ways, everything was much simpler back then, wasn't it, Jesper?"

Stenberg didn't answer, just sipped his mineral water instead. He would have preferred something stronger, but it wouldn't have been fitting for the minister of justice to be seen drinking alcohol at lunchtime on an ordinary weekday. Thinking about Sophie and the Christmas party had given him a bit of an erection, and he drank slowly to calm himself down.

"But enough of that," John Thorning said. "What's past is past. That was really what I wanted to say to you. As you no doubt noticed, I went through a very tricky patch last winter. Losing a child . . ." He held his hands out. "But I'm back now. Business as usual, for both the firm and the Bar

145

Association. I have no intention of slowing down, certainly not now that we've got the chance to achieve so many good things together."

Stenberg made sure he kept smiling. Deep down he had been hoping that John would tell him that he was going to retire and spend the rest of his life playing golf on Mallorca, that Sophie's death had somehow made the old bastard realize it was time to stop. But when he looked into John's eyes when they met by chance the other day, he had begun to suspect that it was a forlorn hope. And now there was no doubt at all. *We've got the chance to achieve so many good things* together. That was a pretty good summary of what he least wanted to hear.

"I'm very pleased to hear that you're feeling better. It can't have been easy for you and Margareta. Karolina and I have thought of you both a lot." Stenberg paused, then lowered the warmth in his voice slightly and turned up the sharpness. "Naturally, I'd be delighted to hear your thoughts. I've always considered you my mentor . . ."

Stenberg trailed off involuntarily. Maybe it was his lingering thoughts of Sophie that made him lose concentration. John wasn't slow to exploit his hesitation.

"Splendid. I've already got a number of things I'd like to discuss with you. The appointment of Eva Swensk, for instance. Most unfortunate, in my opinion. You need a more loyal national police chief, someone who doesn't glance at other people when you give them orders. Oscar Wallin would have been an excellent candidate. What made you overlook him?"

Well, Stenberg thought. *To start with, the fact that Wallin is an unreliable little sociopath who isn't afraid to blackmail his boss.*

"Oscar was on my list. But there were a lot of factors that had to be taken into consideration."

"You wanted to ally yourself with Carina LeMoine and her section of the party. I'm guessing your father-in-law advised you to do that. Said it would be important in the future." John Thorning shook his head. "I'm afraid I think Karl-Erik

146

was mistaken. You should have held back, waited until things looked clearer. You should have focused on the tasks in front of you instead of dreaming about shortcuts to the top. There's still plenty to do. Just look at Skarpö and that restaurant shooting the other night. Dead police officers, gang warfare, snipers in the middle of the city. That's where your focus should be right now, Jesper. That's where you can do the most good."

John Thorning leaned forward across the white tablecloth.

"Besides, Carina LeMoine isn't a kingmaker happy to sit on the steps of the throne. She's got plans of her own. And no one really knows what the prime minister is thinking. The only thing you can be sure of is that he's following events very carefully. Biding his time."

The waiter brought their starters and the conversation paused briefly. Stenberg took the opportunity to pull himself together. He had hoped to escape this. Being given a lecture by someone over sixty. But John Thorning hadn't finished.

"You're becoming a pawn in a bigger game. A game you're not ready for. Not yet, anyway. Without good advisers you'll end up being outmaneuvered, all your good ideas will come to nothing or, possibly even worse, will be credited to someone else. Instead of being the great reformer of the legal system, you risk becoming a mere parenthesis."

Stenberg was on the point of saying something but stopped himself. It wasn't what John Thorning was saying that annoyed him most, but his tone. That patronizing You-don't-know-what-you're-doing tone that John sometimes deployed against inexperienced prosecutors and lawyers. He had experienced it himself when he first joined the firm, but that was a long time ago now, and he was now the country's minister of justice, for fuck's sake.

He really felt like telling John Thorning to go to hell. Explain that he had merely made use of him. That the days when he had played the subordinate protégé of the Great Lawyer were over now and that he, whatever the old windbag might claim, was already the prime minister's running mate and successor. It was time to demonstrate that he was in full command of the game these days.

"What do you suggest, John?" he said, so calmly that he surprised himself.

"Make me your confidant. Use me as a sounding board; try all your new ideas out on me before you get going."

Stenberg nodded slowly. He could see Sophie naked in front of him. The way she put his hands around her neck and told him to squeeze just as she was coming. And not let go until she was finished, no matter if she begged and pleaded.

"And if I choose to turn down your kind offer?"

Thorning started slightly. His smile changed from confident of victory to vaguely impressed.

"Well, Jesper, let us speak bluntly for a moment. I was the one who discovered you, who turned you from a promising young lawyer into the country's minister of justice. Your father-in-law prepared the way, I'll admit that, but it was my support and my network of contacts that made the difference. The prime minister wasn't sure; he was leaning toward Carina LeMoine. But I persuaded him, got him to realize that you were the best option."

John Thorning tapped his forefinger gently on the table.

"Turning your back on me would be very unwise. The opinion polls aren't good, and at a time like this the party can't afford to lose old allies. Regardless of what the prime minister might have promised you, he'll have to think again if he and the party begin to suspect that my support for you is wavering. And there wouldn't be much you or your father-in-law could do about that."

Thorning took a small pill bottle out of his inside pocket, shook out one tablet, and put it in his mouth. He quickly swallowed it with a sip of water, then raised his glass in a toast.

"To favors, and favors returned, Jesper. That's how politics works."

Stenberg smiled coolly. He was fighting an urge to smash the Perrier bottle in John Thorning's self-satisfied face.

"Here's what I'm thinking." Thorning's voice had softened slightly. "We meet regularly, once a week, to discuss things. You tell me your plans and I contribute my opinions and experiences to help you reach the best possible solution. We could meet in your office. After all, you are the minister of justice."

* * *

Julia pressed the phone harder against her ear to counteract the poor reception. All the antennae in the area seemed to cancel each other out and form a dead zone in that particular part of the grounds around Police Headquarters. But she didn't have time to find a better place for the call. She moved slightly and stepped between two parked police cars.

"So Kassab murdered Gilsén so he could run off with the money?" Wallin's satisfaction was suddenly much clearer.

"Yes, that's what it looks like," Julia said. She was still shaken by the previous day's events and had hardly slept during the few hours she'd been home before coming back to work. Kassab had fooled them—fooled the lot of them, but perhaps Amante most of all.

"This is absolutely priceless." Wallin sounded as if he was about to burst into laughter. "A convicted cop killer commits another murder inside one of the country's most strictly guarded facilities and then escapes using a key he stole from a colleague from Regional Crime. A civilian employee who, against all regulations, was permitted to question him alone. And now four prison officers are in the hospital. Do we know what happened to Kassab?"

"The divers have been down to the minibus this morning and confirmed that it's empty, so we definitely know he got out," Julia said. "A tracker dog found traces of blood on one bank late yesterday evening, but the trail went cold when they reached a built-up area. We've issued a national alert and Kollander has ordered surveillance on Kassab's sister-in-law, Cassandra Nygren. He's evidently very attached to his niece, so we're assuming that he'll try to contact them."

"Assuming? Right now Staffan Kollander is on his knees praying that Kassab is stupid enough to contact his family instead of fleeing the country. If the media find out that the head of Regional Crime was manipulated by a cop killer, Kollander's next job will be a one-man investigation into the thickness of police authority writing paper."

Julia didn't respond. Wallin's schadenfreude was making her feel uncomfortable. The fact that a convicted murderer was on the run, and had also killed again, was definitely nothing to be happy about.

"What about golden boy, then? Amante. What's happening to him?"

"Suspended until further notice on Kollander's direct orders." Julia grimaced at her own reflection in a car window. The rings under her eyes were clearly visible. She was exhausted; all she wanted was sleep. But she'd promised to keep Wallin informed. Best to get that out of the way before she went home to bed.

"I should think so too," Wallin said. "That idiot should never be allowed anywhere near a police investigation again, no matter who his stepfather is. Civilians should never be allowed to do real police work. Things always go to hell."

"But Amante acquitted himself pretty well in the case of the dismembered body." Julia realized that she was now in defense mode. Sure, Amante had been fooled. But he should never have been put in that situation. She should have been in the room, should have insisted on it. Not let Pärson and Kollander overrule her.

"Come on, Julia. You worked together for three or four days at most before the Security Police took over the case. How much did Amante manage to contribute in that time?"

"He managed to identify the victim," she said before she had time to think about it.

"Did he? You haven't mentioned that. When did this happen?"

"A few days ago. But seeing as it was only as a result of a photofit, we wanted to get confirmation first."

She bit her lip. She knew what question was coming next.

"So, who is he, then?"

Julia took a deep breath. The grinning skull in her mind's eye. The words ready in her mouth. Time to unleash the shit-storm.

"David Sarac," she said.

The phone went quiet for a few seconds.

"How long have you suspected that?" Any amusement in his voice was gone now.

"Like I said, only a few days."

"And you chose not to tell me until now?"

"To be honest, I haven't had time. And, anyway, we weren't entirely sure."

This last bit was a white lie, but she needed to reinforce her position with something more than the I-haven't-had-time defense. She could have called him as early as Saturday evening. But she wanted to have more to tell him, wanted to identify the mysterious Frank so she'd be delivering not only an identified victim to Wallin but also a potential perpetrator.

"We spoke to Pärson on Friday but he dismissed the whole thing," she went on. "He was adamant that Sarac was locked away in a nursing home, so there didn't seem much point calling you."

"But if I know you at all, you wouldn't have let yourself be persuaded by Superintendent Pärson's assurances."

"No. We checked out the nursing home over the weekend. Sarac escaped at the end of February, at roughly the same time that our dead body ended up in the water. One of the caregivers helped him escape. According to the caregiver, a man named Frank organized the whole thing and paid for Sarac's escape.

We didn't get any further than that, and, to be honest, I was going to call and tell you on Monday, but then we had the Abu Hamsa murder, followed by Kassab's escape . . ."

Silence on the line again. Then a crackling sound as Wallin moved the phone closer to his mouth. His voice sounded almost confidential all of a sudden.

"David Sarac left Sweden on February twenty-fifth. The national police chief and a couple of close confidants are the only people who know that. According to the senior consultant at the nursing home, Sarac was in a poor state and showed no interest in the world around him. But on the morning of February twenty-fifth he was suddenly gone. All we know is that he traveled home to Stockholm to pick up his passport. And the last trace we have is in Frankfurt, where he caught a flight to Belgrade the same evening. Once he was outside the EU's jurisdiction, there wasn't much we could do to find him. We couldn't issue an international warrant, seeing as Sarac isn't suspected of a crime. So it was decided to hush it up for the foreseeable future."

"Wow," Julia said, in the absence of anything better. She was trying to take in what Wallin had said, make this new information fit what she already knew. If they had hushed up the fact that Sarac was gone, that meant Pärson was telling the truth, that he genuinely believed Sarac was at the nursing home. The news that had escaped was much too juicy a tidbit for the fat bastard not to have leaked to the press.

"Yes, that's one way of putting it," Wallin said. "Have you got anything more than a photofit to prove that the victim really is Sarac? Fingerprints or a definite DNA match?"

"No, the DNA from the victim is a match for some found on Skarpö but not a specific individual. And the percentage of the match is lower than usual because of the condition of the body. But the photofit Amante managed to get is based on an X-ray of the skull, so it's pretty reliable. I'm sure it's Sarac. The dates match as well. The body is supposed to have been in the water since the end of February, beginning of March. Sarac must have come back from Belgrade pretty quickly."

Another silence on the line, and for a couple of seconds Julia wondered if they'd been disconnected. Then Wallin spoke again.

"If what you say is true, and the victim really is Sarac, then all hell's going to break loose. We need to tread very carefully, Julia. There's a lot at stake here. My suggestion is that you keep digging. We need to be one hundred percent certain before I can take this any further. Naturally, you can't say anything to Pärson. This has to stay between us. Have you talked to anyone else?"

"We've questioned two possible witnesses from Skarpö. Atif Kassab, who we visited on Sunday."

"Okay, that explains why Kassab specifically asked to speak to Amante. Who was the other witness?"

"Sarac's personal assistant, Natalie Aden."

• • •

Oscar Wallin put his phone down slowly. He sat at his desk for a long time as he tried to digest what Julia Gabrielsson had just told him.

David Sarac was dead. He had been a good police officer. But his stroke and the car crash had changed him, turning him into a babbling wreck rather than the hero he had been made out to be. Everyone had been astonished when he actually managed to escape. Now Sarac had been murdered. And for the time being only Wallin, Julia Gabrielsson, and that nightmare, Amante, knew about it. The question was: How could he exploit the information to improve his own situation? That would take a good deal of thought. But in the meantime he had another matter to deal with. Natalie Aden needed to learn to follow the rules.

He picked up his cell phone and scrolled through until he found the right contact. But just as he was about to press the button and make the call, he hesitated. He thought he could smell burning. He went over to the window, which was open slightly. Down on the pavement a council employee was killing weeds with a steam-powered weeder. He was heading toward a large green dandelion that was poking up between the paving stones. Wallin stood there with his phone in his hand and waited until the flame had made the plant boil to death in its own fluids before he made the call.

Fifteen

The drive leading up to the villa was blocked by Karolina's and Karl-Erik's cars, so the driver let Stenberg out on the street. It was almost seven o'clock in the evening and all he really wanted was to soak in the bath, pour himself a stiff whiskey, settle down in front of the television, and try to shake off his discussion with John Thorning. And suppress the images of Sophie that seeing her father had conjured up. But instead he was going to have to face his domestic inquisition.

His bodyguard, Becker, walked all the way to the front door with him. Nisse Boman stood smoking beside Karl-Erik's big, dark Volvo. The wiry little man was holding his cigarette inside his cupped hand so it was barely visible, and tucked it behind his back when Stenberg and Becker walked past, as if what he was doing wasn't really allowed or at the very least something he'd rather not be seen doing. Stenberg had seen the soldiers who guarded the trials at The Hague smoke the same way.

He gave Boman a curt nod and received the same in return. Boman didn't attempt any small talk, and he had chosen to stay outside even though Karolina was bound to have tried to persuade him to go in. In turn, Stenberg had long since given up any attempt to get the other man to accept him. Over the years they'd developed a sort of gentleman's agreement that made their encounters more or less bearable.

Stenberg said good-bye to Becker, closed the front door, and stopped in the hall. He took a couple of deep breaths before venturing into the kitchen.

In spite of the summer heat, Karolina had lit the fire. On

the other hand, it wasn't an ordinary wood fire but twenty tiny, decorative gas flames that—together with the heavy, New England–style cupboard doors and the limestone worktops from Gotland—had cost more than Stenberg cared to remember.

Karolina and Karl-Erik were sitting at the big kitchen table. Karl-Erik was at its head, Karolina to his right. They had their heads close together. Another secret meeting, clearly. When Stenberg entered the room, Karolina stood up and walked over to him.

"How was your meeting with John?"

He kissed his wife on the cheek, put his briefcase down, and shrugged his jacket off before replying.

"Fine."

"'Fine'? That's a nice, detailed description." His father-in-law had loosened his tie, his shirtsleeves were rolled up, and he had one of Stenberg's whiskey glasses in his hand. "Sit down, Jesper."

Karl-Erik gestured toward a free chair, and Stenberg stood still for a moment. He was being offered a seat at his own table, by a man who was drinking his whiskey. Marvelous.

Karolina appeared at his side with another glass, put it in his hand, and nodded gently at him to do as he was told. He hesitated for a few more seconds, long enough for one of her eyebrows to rise. *Don't be childish, now, Jesper.*

Reluctantly, he pulled out the chair and sat down.

"So, tell us, how did you get on with John?" Karl-Erik said.

"He seemed quite bright. Like he used to be, I'd say."

Stenberg drank a sip of the amber-colored liquid. Sophie had thrown a whiskey glass at him, he suddenly remembered. It almost hit him in the face. He closed his eyes tight, trying to suppress the flare-up of memories.

"Yes, I've heard the same thing. One of my colleagues happened to see him in court the other day. He mangled the opposition, apparently."

Happened to see. That suggested a degree of coincidence

that had almost certainly not been the case. Karl-Erik liked to stay informed. He didn't like surprises or secrets unless he was instrumental to them. He always wanted to know. For a few moments Sophie was back inside Stenberg's head.

"So, what did John have to say, then?"

Stenberg took another sip from his glass. Then he put it down on the table, rather harder than he intended. The noise made his wife raise her chin.

"He raised the subject of Eva Swensk's appointment. John doesn't think she was a good choice, even if he understands the thinking behind it. According to him, I ought to focus on the ministry of justice. Not aim . . . higher. At least, not at the moment."

Karl-Erik nodded slowly. Karolina fetched the crystal carafe and refilled their glasses.

"Anything else?"

You mean: Did he suggest he was likely to cause problems? Stenberg thought.

"He stressed that the Bar Association is an influential body. And that he would be following developments carefully."

"In other words, he wants a seat at the table. Or, to be more accurate, he's demanding one," Karolina said drily.

Stenberg was about to reply but closed his mouth when he noticed that Karolina was looking at her father rather than him. Karl-Erik leaned back in his chair.

"Loyalty is a good thing, Jesper. John did a lot to help you."

Yes, he did point that out, Stenberg thought. *Just like you did just now. And he was ill-mannered enough to say so openly.*

"But times have changed," his father-in-law went on, gently swirling his whiskey. "I'll take a few soundings. See if we can come up with something that will keep John occupied elsewhere."

Karolina got in before Stenberg.

"Don't you think he'd see through that, Daddy? John Thorning's hardly a novice, after all."

"Everything has a price, my dear. You just need to find out what it is. And John is a vain man. I'm sure he wouldn't turn down a fine title. An ambassador's post, something of that sort."

Stenberg emptied his glass. From the corner of his eye he saw Karolina and her father exchange a glance. It lasted only a moment or so, but he still realized instantaneously what it meant. This was something they'd already discussed without him and without actually reaching agreement. Even so, they weren't asking him what he thought. Didn't want him to cast the deciding vote.

"Do we know anything more?" Stenberg asked in an attempt to change the subject. "About the prime minister's plans? When he's thinking of making it all public?"

His father-in-law shook his head. "The prime minister isn't usually especially forthcoming. Not even with his closest confidants. But the pressure is building for him to do something about the poor poll ratings. You're the solution to the problem—we agree on that. But for some reason he seems to want to wait before taking the formal decision. And while he waits, the opposition is gaining more ground."

"Who's our principal opponent?" Karolina said. "Who's their candidate for the Ministry of Justice?"

The same question Stenberg had been about to ask, but she was a fraction of a second ahead of him.

"Victor Amante, no question. His career in the EU makes him the obvious candidate. Even if Victor did earlier declare that he'd prefer to stay in Brussels . . ."

"But not anymore," Stenberg said, finally getting a word in.

"No, it looks like he and his team have started to make preparations back at home. Building alliances within the judicial establishment. His stepson has recently been smuggled into Regional Crime here in Stockholm. Right under Staffan Kollander's nose."

"You think Victor Amante is using his stepson to get information about Kollander and Swensk?"

Karolina was one step ahead again. Stenberg tried not to let it bother him.

Karl-Erik shrugged his shoulder. "Amante junior was the last person to question Atif Kassab before he escaped. Which is pretty remarkable, seeing as he isn't a police officer, and has received no training in interview techniques. This isn't official, but Kassab stole a handcuff key from Amante's pocket and used it during his escape. Unless Kassab is recaptured soon, this business is likely to cost the head of Regional Crime any hope of landing the top job that the national police chief has planned for him. Not a fatal blow, perhaps, but certainly a black mark against Eva Swensk. Kollander is one of her most trusted allies, but she won't have any option but to park him on the sidelines somewhere."

"Could Victor Amante have planned this?"

Stenberg realized how revealing his question was the moment he said it. Damn, he should have known all this. This was his area of responsibility, his fiefdom. Wallin usually kept abreast of this sort of thing for him. But, just as he had suspected, Wallin's loyalty could no longer be trusted.

"Obviously I can't know for sure. But it's certainly a very unfortunate coincidence."

Karl-Erik didn't sound the slightest bit patronizing. But when Stenberg looked at Karolina, she gave him a smile that confirmed his suspicions. It was her Don't-worry-darling-you're-doing-fine smile, and it meant the exact opposite.

Sixteen

Atif was dreaming about a tiger. An animal he had once seen in the run-down zoo in Baghdad. A scrawny old male with a scabby coat that one of the zookeepers was trying to get to perform stupid tricks. Jumping up onto small stools, sitting on its hind legs, and waving its front paws at the audience. The tiger obeyed—it seemed almost tame—and the keeper became overconfident. He made the tiger open its jaws while he stuck his head in its mouth. Presumably he had done the trick hundreds of times before and it had always gone well.

A week later the tiger bit the zookeeper's head off. According to the newspaper, it took five pistol shots to get the tiger to let go of the body, and another three to kill it.

In Atif's dream the tiger is lying in front of him in a forest clearing. The animal is breathing heavily in the heat. Its chest is rising and falling, its mouth half-open, revealing the fleshy tongue behind the row of teeth. There are dark, rust-red stains around its gray nose.

The animal stares at him, holding his gaze. Sweat is running down Atif's back, soaking his T-shirt. On the ground in front of the tiger is a bloody rag. A pair of Prison Service sweatpants tied to form a noose.

The tiger goes on staring at him. Its eyes are dark and glossy. The smell of blood and something he can't quite identify is overwhelming him. Made worse by the heat. He realizes that it's fear. Atif's fear.

"Amu! Amu!"

Tindra is calling for him. He hears the girl come running

through the woods. Straight toward him. Straight toward the tiger.

He wants to shout at her to stop, turn around and run away as fast as she can. But all he can get out is a weak gurgling sound. It sounds like a purr.

The tiger pricks up its ears, then gets to its feet with surprising agility. The beast goes on looking at him for a few more seconds. Then it turns and leaps into the bushes. Straight toward Tindra. Atif's paralysis lifts and he races off, rushing after the tiger, into the darkness.

• • •

The shrill scream woke him. Made him sit up on the sofa. The sound continued even though he was awake, and transformed into the squealing brakes of a bus outside the window. The sheet beneath him was wet and for a moment he thought it was blood. Then he realized he was freezing and sweating at the same time. Nausea hit him like a punch in the gut and he staggered to the toilet as quickly as his injured foot would let him. Drooping over the edge of the bath, he emptied his stomach of beer and seawater.

Outside in the street another bus braked to a halt. Unless it was a little girl screaming inside his head. Running from a beast that was getting closer and closer.

He felt a hand on his shoulder. An electronic thermometer was inserted into his ear. He heard it peep as it registered his temperature. Not that it was really necessary. They both knew what had happened. Why he was still in her apartment.

"Thirty-nine point two," Natalie said. "Up even more from yesterday. The wound's infected and you need penicillin pretty urgently unless you want blood poisoning. I can get some, but it'll cost you. It's prescription only."

He wanted to say no. He'd already stayed a night longer than he had planned. Thirty-six hours had passed since his escape, and by now he ought to be well on his way to getting

161

Cassandra and Tindra out. But he had to face facts. In this state he couldn't even make it down the stairs, let alone plan any sort of rescue.

"Three thousand more," he muttered. "Five," he said when Natalie didn't reply at once. "And the same again if I can stay another night.

Natalie shrugged.

"Sure, Richie Rich. I'll be back at five. Take an acetaminophen and drink lots of water in the meantime. Don't pick at the wound, and don't throw up on the sofa. Okay?"

"Sure," Atif said. "No problem," he added after what felt like just a couple of seconds. But she had long since gone.

• • •

Six rows of chairs. Fifteen police officers, Julia and Pärson included. All with cups of coffee and their eyes focused on the movie screen. The head of Regional Crime was standing in front of them.

"Good afternoon, everyone. We'll start with a brief run-through of the situation." Kollander adjusted his stance, moving his highly polished shoes as if he was having trouble standing still. "What shall we take first? The perpetrator?"

He looked at Pärson, who was spread out across two chairs in the front row. The smell of his nylon shirt was for once less pervasive, but Julia was sitting several rows behind him.

"We have no forensic evidence at all apart from the bullet. And that seems to have been homemade. You've all seen the photographs from the crime scene. The bullet mushroomed like none I've ever seen before."

Most of the officers in the room nodded. The evening tabloids had already made the most of the pictures.

"The perpetrator is long gone, probably back in the Caucasian republic of his choice," Pärson went on. "We're checking the passenger lists of all the airlines, but our chances of finding a match are basically zero."

"I see." Kollander rocked on his feet again. "What about a motive, then?"

"Well, if we're to believe Kassab . . ." Pärson paused for a couple of seconds, giving Kollander time to squirm uncomfortably. ". . . the motive was revenge. Abu Hamsa and Joachim Gilsén were stealing money from other criminals, and now they're both dead."

"And who's taken over Abu Hamsa's businesses? That ought to give us a few suspects."

Pärson turned and looked back across the seats. "Gabrielsson, can you tell us more about that? Seeing as you're responsible for the in-house part of the investigation."

"Sure."

Julia leafed through the notepad in her lap. Pärson had upgraded her slightly since their last conversation. But there was still no sign that she was back in favor. On the other hand, at least he didn't seem to have told Kollander about her and Amante's freelancing. Not yet, anyway.

"I've spoken to the Intelligence Unit and called a number of my own sources. They all say the same thing. The exchange bureaus and restaurants are all carrying on as normal. No new faces anywhere. Abu Hamsa's eldest daughter, Susanna, is still running the bureaus, and her fiancé has been seen at their other premises."

"Eldar Jafarov," Pärson added. "He was at the crime scene. A combination of driver, bodyguard, and right-hand man to Abu Hamsa."

"Thank you, I know," Kollander said drily.

But Pärson seemed unconcerned. "So whoever it was who killed Abu Hamsa, they haven't yet made any moves to take over his businesses. Is that a fair summary of the situation, Gabrielsson?"

Julia nodded. "That's right. But both Susanna and Jafarov are surrounded by bodyguards, so they're obviously worried. Their villa out in Älvsjö looks more like a fortress these days."

"I see," Kollander said. "And Atif Kassab? What's happening there?"

"We've deployed all available resources," Pärson said. "Comprehensive surveillance of his sister-in-law and niece, and we're checking every address he's been linked to in the past. His passport has been blocked and we've issued a warrant via Interpol. We're conducting extensive internal searches to try to find other connections that might be worth investigating. But my guess is that he's already left. That he's stolen or bought a car and is on his way down toward Iraq through Europe. He got the details of the secret account out of Gilsén, then strangled the little bastard. So he's not short of money: he has enough to be able to live like a king down there."

Several of the officers in the room nodded, particularly Pärson's gang of supporters from the far corridor. Julia opened her mouth to protest. She stopped herself, but not quickly enough.

"You were going to say something, Gabrielsson," Kollander said. Pärson turned around again and glared at her.

"It's just . . ." she said. "Well, I don't think Kassab's gone yet."

"And why not?"

She could feel the other officers looking at her. "Kassab had practically no personal belongings in his cell. Just a few books and a photograph of his niece."

"And?" said one of the older detectives behind her, sending a waft of mint toward the back of her neck.

"Whoever killed Abu Hamsa and tried to kill Gilsén wasn't only out for revenge. They also wanted to get hold of the money that had been stolen from them. About fifteen million, according to Kassab."

She decided the best strategy was to try to get Pärson on her side.

"It's just like you said, boss. If what Kassab said when he was being questioned is true, then he's the one sitting on the money now. Several million, and there are plenty of people with a claim to it. Dangerous people. Kassab knows that. He knows that if he leaves the country, his sister-in-law and niece will be fair prey. That's why I think he's still here. He's trying to come up with a way to get his family out."

Kollander looked at her, then his face contorted into a grimace of agreement.

"I think you're right, Gabrielsson. Kassab is probably still in the Stockholm area somewhere. The only question is who finds him first. Us, or the people who want the money."

A low murmur spread through the room, and as far as Julia could tell, most of them agreed with her. Out of the corner of her eye she saw Pärson looking at her. She didn't like the expression on his face.

• • •

As a result of this information, Southern Homes Ltd is issuing you with a formal warning. Further complaints of this nature may constitute legitimate grounds for cancellation of your rental agreement in accordance with the Rental Housing Act, chapter . . .

Natalie lowered her smartphone and swore so loudly that the old lady in front of her on the bus jumped.

Oscar Wallin. Even if the e-mail came from her housing association, it was obvious that he was behind it. Information from the police authority regarding suspected criminal activity. Thank you very much!

She should have phoned him the other day, and probably would have done if Atif hadn't turned up and given her something else to think about. How the hell could Wallin have found out that she'd talked to the Buddy Holly cop? Was he still watching her?

She glanced around nervously, first checking out the other passengers on the bus, then the cars in the evening rush-hour traffic behind them, but failed to see anything to confirm that particular suspicion. Then common sense caught up with her.

If she was being watched, the Rapid Response Unit would have kicked her door in long before now. But according to the papers the hunt for Atif was still going on, so far without any result. So Wallin must have gotten the information about Buddy Holly's visit some other way, and not through direct surveillance. Maybe he had flagged her name in some computer system, unless someone had simply talked. Or else he was just bluffing.

She read the e-mail again. The sender's address looked as though it belonged to her housing association, and it said that a copy had been sent by regular mail. The warning was probably genuine. Wallin had stitched her up. She held her breath for a few moments, tried to control her anger and think.

She could live with a written warning from the landlord. This was Sweden, after all, and it took more than a nudge from the police to evict someone. Her former boyfriend was a full-time dealer these days, and he still had his apartment in Bagarmossen even though he operated from home. So this was just a warning shot, but—bearing in mind the identity of the man sleeping on her sofa—it was probably a good idea to call Wallin before things got out of hand and he really did get someone to watch her.

She got off the bus at her usual stop, a couple of hundred meters from home, and pulled up his number.

The number you have called has not been recognized. Okay. Maybe that wasn't so strange. She knew Wallin used to use a pay-as-you-go cell phone to call her, and guessed he had several of them, so he probably ditched them at regular intervals just to be on the safe side.

She tried the main police switchboard. "No, we haven't got an Oscar Wallin here," the prissy receptionist replied. "Try the Ministry of Justice."

He picked up on the first ring, which surprised her. Almost as if he was sitting there, waiting for the phone to ring.

"It's Natalie. I got your warning. Just wanted to let you know that there was no need for it. I'm sticking to the terms of our agreement."

A few seconds of silence.

"Really?"

"Yes." His patronizing tone annoyed her. She hadn't done anything wrong. He was the one who'd made himself difficult to reach. He was messing with her.

"I tried calling you right after that Amante guy came to see me at work, but your old number doesn't work," she lied. "So this whole thing with the damn housing association was uncalled-for. What if I'd lost my apartment?"

"What exactly did you tell Amante?"

He didn't seem remotely troubled by how angry she was, which just made things worse.

"Nothing but what I said when I was questioned last winter. He showed me a picture of a man called Frank and asked if I recognized him."

"And?"

"I didn't. And even if I did, I wouldn't have said anything. After all I've done for you, you could have made the effort to call me before you decided to start fucking up my life. You ought to trust me, for God's sake!"

The line crackled and his voice got closer. As if he was holding the phone right next to his mouth.

"Now listen very carefully, Natalie. My dad once had a dog. A golden retriever called Balto. He got it to guard the house. But the stupid dog didn't understand its job. Didn't bother to bark if anyone it didn't recognize appeared. One night an intruder set fire to the garden shed, but Balto didn't make a sound. Dad had him put down the following day."

A few seconds' silence.

"You can play at being a normal person all you like," Wallin went on. "But we both know who you are. You're a con artist, someone who tricks people out of their money. You're pretty good at it, but I'm better, and I'm the police officer who found

167

you out. I own your secrets, which in turn means that I own *you*. And the moment you stop being useful to me, guess what happens?"

Natalie didn't answer. Her pulse was thudding in her temples, and a bitter taste arose in the back of her throat.

"Tell me," he demanded. "Tell me where we stand."

"Er . . ." She cleared her throat, hoping he'd let the matter drop. Laugh and hang up.

"Tell me, Natalie."

She took a deep breath and closed her eyes.

"You . . . own me."

"Good. Never call me on this number again, is that understood? If I want you, I'll be in touch. I know where you are. Was there anything else you wanted to say?"

She wanted nothing more than to end the call. But she had to ask, otherwise this whole humiliation was pointless.

"David Sarac," she said.

"What about him?" Wallin's voice was perfectly neutral.

"Is he okay?"

"That depends on how you look at it. He's in a nursing home up in the north. It'll be a while before he gets out of there."

"Are you sure about that?"

"As sure as anyone can be."

The call ended before Natalie had time to say anything else. She stared at her phone for a few seconds. Wallin was hard enough to read when you were face-to-face with him, so over the phone it was almost impossible. But the nagging anxiety growing in her gut convinced her that he was lying.

Seventeen

Amante opened the door just a couple of seconds after Julia knocked. Almost as if he had been standing in the hall, waiting for her. The security chain was on, and it took a little while before he managed to undo it and open the door fully.

"Come in, come in!" He waved Julia into the bare hallway.

She took a good look at him. His blazer and tennis top had been replaced by a stained T-shirt worn over a pair of gray sweatpants. He had called her at work an hour before, saying he had something she needed to see. He was so insistent that she hadn't been able to say no, even though she had her hands full. She was starting to regret the decision.

Amante was sporting three days' worth of stubble and had bags under his eyes, and there was something unsettled in his gaze. After closing and locking the door, he stood still for a few moments and seemed to be listening for sounds in the stairwell.

"How are you?" she said, obviously not expecting anything but the reply she received.

"Fine, thanks. Go in."

He practically herded her into the kitchen ahead of him. There was a laptop on the marble counter, along with a printer that, judging by the box on the floor, was brand-new. An array of documents and enlarged photos was spread out around the computer. One of them was the photofit of David Sarac, another showed what must be the photograph from Sarac's police ID, and a third Eskil's grainy cell phone picture of Frank.

But it was the next photograph that made her gasp. The fourth picture showed a man in his thirties staring directly into the camera. She compared the photograph with the image from Eskil's cell phone. The man was older now, but there was no doubt about it.

"Allow me to introduce Frank Hunter," Amante said. His voice seemed more stable, almost the same as usual.

"H-How—" She broke off, realized she already knew the answer. "Kassab. Kassab told you who Frank was while you were putting his cuffs back on. That's why you didn't notice when he took the key from your pocket."

Amante nodded glumly.

"Why didn't you say anything about this to Kollander or Pärson?"

"I had no way of knowing if it was just a diversion, if Kassab was trying a double bluff. Besides, it's our case, not Kollander and Pärson's. It's our responsibility to . . ." He fell silent, and his eyes began to flit about again.

"What exactly did Kassab tell you?"

The question seemed to make Amante focus. "He said Frank Hunter was a security consultant from the former Yugoslavia. He also said that Hunter had been out at Skarpö. That he was there to get David Sarac. Or, rather, to *discover his secrets*. That was more or less how Kassab put it. My Arabic is a bit rusty, and he was talking quietly and very fast."

Julia studied the photograph again. Sharp features, watchful brown eyes, dark hair cut in a military style. If you compared him with the photograph on Sarac's police ID, it was clear that Eskil had been right: it was easy to mistake Frank Hunter for a cop.

"Where did you get this picture of Hunter? It's not a passport photograph, is it?"

Amante shook his head.

"It took quite a bit of work, but the way things are right now, I've had some time on my hands. I couldn't find Frank Hunter in our databases: no criminal record, never been suspected of anything. So I checked with my former employers, Europol.

Nothing there either. But then I remembered what Kassab said about the former Yugoslavia. So I got one of my contacts in The Hague to go up to the ICTY, the International Criminal Tribunal for the former Yugoslavia, and see if there was anything in their records."

"And he could do that, just like that?" Julia already knew the answer. But one bribe more or less hardly made any difference anymore.

Amante pretended not to have heard. "That photograph was taken six years ago when Frank Hunter was given a temporary pass as an independent contractor. Employing people like him isn't that unusual, not in countries where the local police are weak or less than willing to cooperate. My contact managed to get hold of the invoices from the company Hunter worked for."

"Called?"

"Bloodhound Incorporated. But precisely what the company or Hunter were doing for the ICTY is strictly confidential. In total they invoiced for about three hundred thousand euros, so presumably they were supplying some fairly advanced services."

"I'm guessing you've googled them." Julia nodded toward the laptop.

"Of course. Bloodhound is registered in Malta. According to its website, the company offers security solutions and consultancy. I tried calling and reached an answering service. Quarter of an hour after I left a message with the receptionist, a guy called me back to see what I wanted. When I asked for Frank Hunter, he started to interrogate me. Who I was, where I was calling from, what I wanted, and so on. His English was good, but I still got the impression that it wasn't his mother tongue. He could have been Swedish, even. He seemed to be trying to figure out how I'd tracked Frank Hunter back to them. So I hung up."

He scratched his stubble and appeared to be waiting for Julia to say something.

"Okay." She dragged the word out to give herself time to

think, to digest all the information Amante had thrown at her and test it against what they already knew. Even if his working methods were unorthodox, to put it mildly, it was impossible not to be impressed by what he had found out in such a short time. But there was still a long way to go.

"So this Frank Hunter could be our perpetrator?" She studied the photograph again, trying to sense whether that might be true. Had this man killed David Sarac, dismembered his body, and destroyed his face? She conjured up the image of Sarac and his shattered grin again. But he didn't give her any help this time either.

"It's not that much of a leap. Hunter was on a mission to get hold of Sarac and uncover some sort of secret as early as last Christmas. And now he's succeeded."

"Hmm." Julia bit her top lip. "What I can't quite make sense of is why Hunter would have waited two months before trying again. And how did he manage to get Sarac to agree to leave the nursing home to meet him? Sarac wasn't stupid, so whatever bait Hunter was using, it must have been something important. Something that persuaded him that it wasn't all a trap. And I've found out something else too. Sarac used his passport in Frankfurt the evening after he escaped. He must have come back for some reason. But if Hunter wanted to kill Sarac, why not do it as soon as he got out of the nursing home? There are tons of lakes up there in the forests. Places that are much better for dumping a body than a busy stretch of water in Lake Mälaren."

"Who told you about the passport and Frankfurt?" Amante looked at Julia curiously, and she took her time considering how best to reply.

"You're not the only person with contacts," she said, attempting one of his secretive smiles.

Amante continued looking at her for a few moments. Then he nodded.

"You're right. There are still a lot of the pieces missing from this puzzle. So if we sum up what we know so far, and leave Sarac and Hunter to one side for a moment . . ."

Amante held up his thumb, as if he was about to start counting.

"To start with, we've got a dismembered body that was dumped under the ice. The perpetrator went to great lengths to make both discovery and identification as hard as possible. But then those two guys went diving for their anchor and the body was found. Sheer luck on our part, and a serious bit of bad luck for the perpetrator."

He added his forefinger.

"Then the perpetrator has more bad luck. The DNA test turns out to match a trace from Skarpö, which should set off all the alarms. But before anyone has time to react, the Security Police appear out of nowhere and take over both the investigation and the body."

Middle finger.

"But the DNA match is pretty weak. Pärson and his boss lose interest and are happy to see the Security Police left holding the baby instead of Regional Crime. A transferred case doesn't spoil the clearance rates, does it?"

Amante lowered his hand and shrugged.

"The body's gone; the investigation's adrift somewhere in police bureaucracy. No one cares who the victim is, who killed him, or why. The perpetrator's bad luck has suddenly, and coincidentally, turned into extremely good luck after all."

He hunched over the papers spread out on the worktop. Stared at Hunter's picture the way Julia had done shortly before. Then at the picture of Sarac.

"But you and I don't believe in coincidence, do we?" she said.

Amante slowly shook his head. "I think the perpetrator may well be someone who can see what we're doing. Possibly even someone with enough knowledge and contacts to make both the body and the case vanish, and with very good reason to make that happen. And for some reason I can't quite explain, I don't think Frank Hunter is our killer. Kassab didn't say anything explicitly, but I still got the impression that he thinks so too."

"You know how this sounds, don't you? A conspiracy inside the police force, mysterious security companies, bodies disappearing. You just need a few men in dark raincoats watching your apartment and you can get the tinfoil out and start making yourself a hat."

Amante's cryptic smile was back.

"That was the old days. Why follow someone when all you have to do is keep an eye on their cell phones? We use official police phones and SIM cards; we use the wireless network at headquarters whenever the software needs updating. Sneaking in an invisible app that would regularly pinpoint our whereabouts can hardly be that difficult. At least, not for someone with the sort of contacts we're talking about."

Julia held her hands out as if to say that she wasn't about to argue.

"So, what happens now? Pärson's keeping me busy with the Abu Hamsa investigation, and you're suspended. Besides, as we keep saying, we haven't even got a case."

"Well, I can always carry on independently. I haven't got anything else to do. I'll do a bit of private detective work, now that I've gone to the trouble of making myself a tinfoil hat."

Julia couldn't help smiling.

"Right now I'm trying to find out if Bloodhound is linked to any companies in Sweden," Amante went on. "Frank Hunter, or whatever his real name is, must have been lying low after Skarpö. He must have had a hiding place to recharge his batteries while he figured out his next move. Who knows, that could even have been where he and Sarac met. If I can find that address, we'll be another step ahead."

Another step closer to our perpetrator, Julia thought.

When she stepped out of Amante's front door shortly afterward, she heard the sound of an engine starting. She took a couple of steps out into the street and just caught sight of a dark-colored car driving off at full speed. For a brief moment she wished she'd left her cell phone in the office. Then she thrust the thought aside. One tinfoil hat in this investigation was enough.

Eighteen

Atif is sitting in a small, hot interview room. He's being held down by hand and ankle cuffs. His breathing is labored. Sweat is running down his temples and the back of his neck. His chest and back are bare. He licks some salt from his beard. It feels softer than usual. Almost like fur.

The lead interviewer comes in. It's not Vaseline, or the blonde. In fact it isn't any of the many cops he's met over the years. No, the man who sits down on the chair opposite him is Joachim Gilsén. He sucks a little on his crowned teeth, makes a birdlike movement with his head, manages to make him feel uncomfortable instantly. Ashamed, angry. Something else he can't identify.

"Why?" Gilsén says. "Why did you kill me?"

Atif has no intention of answering. He's going to sit out his brain. Wait until it gets fed up and plays a different scenario. Or, even better, decides to settle into neutral and let him get the deep sleep he needs.

But suddenly he's standing outside the room. Looking at himself through the mirrored glass.

"You were dead anyway," his dream self says inside the interview room. "You only had another hour or so left."

"How did you know that?"

"Because Rosco told me out in the exercise yard. They came just before midnight. Three of them, maybe more. I heard them stick a wedge under my door. As a precaution in case I didn't keep my side of the bargain. Then they opened the door to your cell."

"By which time I was already dead," Gilsén whines. "Because you murdered me, stole my secret. Hanged me from the bars like some fucking suicide."

"I had to make it look like suicide: I was afraid they wouldn't fall for it. I thought they'd figure out what I'd done and come into my cell. When they removed the wedge, I was standing next to the door. Ready to fight for my life."

"But no one came."

His dream self shakes his head. His face slowly cracks into a smile, baring his teeth in a leer that looks more bestial than human.

Then he's back in the room. Back inside his body. The smell in there overwhelms him, making his nostrils flare. A smell of fear, of prey.

"Y-You promised . . ." Gilsén whimpers. He stands up and walks quickly toward the door. But the room has changed: suddenly it's a rectangular little box, with no doors, no one-way mirror.

Gilsén bangs on the wall where the door was before, screaming for help, and waves at the camera in the corner of the box. But no one comes.

Atif gets to his feet, and the shackles holding his arms and legs pull tight, contorting his body into an unnatural upright pose. He roars out loud: humiliation, impotence, rage, and a desire for vengeance.

Only one way out, Amu, Tindra's voice whispers inside his head while Gilsén beats his fists on the wall until they bleed.

Only.

One.

Way.

Out.

His body contorts, changes. The shackles around his arms and legs loosen and fall to the floor. He howls again, and his voice becomes a bellow that merges with Gilsén's shrill screaming, which sounds like the shrieking brakes of a bus. Or the scream of a little girl running for her life.

"Atif."

Someone is pulling at him. He turns and lashes out with one arm. Hits something with the back of his hand. A cry of pain, for real.

The living room sofa. Natalie was sitting a meter or so away, with one hand over her cheek. The cocky look in her eyes was gone, replaced by something he didn't like.

"Sorry," he managed to say. "I was dreaming . . ."

She lowered her hand. Her cheek was red, her eye half-closed. He got to his feet and pulled his clothes on. His body felt easier now, he was getting better.

"I'm really sorry," he muttered. "Just give me ten minutes, then I'll get out of here."

He struggled with one sock. His foot was less swollen now. His wounded head was no longer thudding so badly; it felt almost okay. Natalie was still glaring at him.

"And where were you thinking of going?"

"I've got a relative in Södertälje who'll put me up."

"Okay, so you swap my sofa for a different one. What then?"

"Sort out fake passports. Get my family out."

"And how are you planning to go about that? Do you think the police watching them are likely to overlook a bearded, two-meter-tall man missing half an ear?"

He didn't answer, just pulled his trousers on and began to fold the duvet and damp sheet. Getting Tindra and Cassandra out was the big challenge. If everything had gone according to plan, he'd have found a solution by now, instead of lying here in fevered delirium. Every hour that passed was an hour closer to the moment when the cops gave up and abandoned his family to the people hunting him.

"I'll think of something." He made himself look at her. Her cheek was less red now. Her eye looked almost normal. "Thanks for everything you've done, Natalie. I'll transfer the money as soon as I can. Within a couple of weeks at most. Look, I really am sorry about—"

"Sit down!" She pointed at the sofa.

He didn't move.

"Sit down, Atif," she repeated in a slightly gentler voice. "You're in no state to leave, not yet." She rubbed her cheek. "Besides, you still can't do a decent bitch slap. Let me know if you'd like a lesson."

She held his gaze until he returned her smile. Then looked at her watch.

"I need to get to work now. There's breakfast in the kitchen."

She took a couple of steps toward the door, then stopped.

"By the way, have you heard anything about David Sarac?"

"Not directly." He paused before replying. Not much, but enough for her to notice. "Why?"

"Someone showed up at work the other day. A cop, or rather a civilian investigator called—"

"Amante."

"How the hell did you know that?"

"Because he and his partner paid me a visit too. They're investigating a dismembered body. Showed me a photograph."

"Frank," she said. "Do you know who he is?"

Atif nodded. "He employed me to kill a guy last winter."

"Who?"

Atif grimaced. "You already know who."

"Sarac?"

Atif nodded.

"So you think . . ." She seemed to have trouble getting the words out.

"I think someone's been more successful this time."

• • •

Natalie had to wait until the day was almost over before one of the examination rooms was free. She needed somewhere quiet to make the call from, without any distractions or risk of being overheard. The medical center's soundproof examination rooms were perfect in that respect. Just as she was about to sneak off, the physiotherapist with the dimples appeared. He lolled on her reception desk wanting to chat. Normally she would have liked that—would even have thought it cute. But not today. She didn't have time for that sort of distraction, and after a couple of minutes she was obliged to come up with an excuse to get away.

She locked the door and switched on the red lamp to indicate that the room was occupied. She sat down on the examination table and took a deep breath.

He answered on the second ring.

"You lied to me, Oscar." She stood up, almost unconsciously.

"I told you not to call here. You're supposed to wait for me to contact you."

"Sarac." Natalie kept her voice as calm as she could. "He's dead, isn't he? He's the one in the papers, the dead body that was found in Lake Mälaren."

"What makes you think that?"

"That's why Amante came to see me. Sarac's dead, but you're keeping it quiet."

The brief pause before he replied told her all she needed to know.

"I thought I made myself clear regarding both your wild theories and this type of conversation. You don't call me—"

"Why not, then?" she interrupted. "Because you own me? Sorry, but you can forget that. All I have to do is call the newspaper hotline of my choice and all hell will break loose. The whole Skarpö story will be dragged up again, and this time there'll be more questions. I might even consider answering some of them this time."

"I'm warning you, Natalie."

"Warn me as much as you like. You can even tell me that pathetic story about the fucking dog again if it'll make you feel better. But the way I see it, we're one-all as far as secrets go. We could call it a balance of fear; what do you think?" She ended the call before he had time to reply.

. . .

When Natalie got home she found Atif in the hallway. He looked considerably better than that morning, which improved her already good mood even more. Two miracles in the same day. She'd put Wallin in his place *and* had practically brought someone back from the dead.

"On your way out?"

He nodded.

"I need to see someone. An old friend. He can help me get a few things."

"Okay." She looked at him. Sunglasses, the hood of his jacket pulled up over a baseball cap he must have found in her closet. "Is there anything I can say to persuade you to wait a day or two, until you've built your strength up a bit? That infection isn't gone yet: you could soon get worse again."

Atif shook his head.

"The clock's ticking. The police won't go on watching Cassandra and Tindra forever."

"I understand." She looked at his clothes again. Out of everything she'd bought him, he had to pick that. He might as well be carrying a sign saying *Dangerous* and *Wanted*.

"Come back in for a few minutes," she said.

"What for?"

"I'm going to try to make you look a bit less suspicious." *If that's actually possible,* she added silently to herself.

Nineteen

"I can't get over how peculiar you look." The old man in the bed fiddled with his hookah. He put the mouthpiece between his cracked lips and took a couple of deep drags that made the water in the container bubble. He held the mouthpiece out toward Atif, who shook his head.

"No, thanks." He caught a glimpse of his own reflection in one of the many framed family portraits covering the walls of the rancid bedroom. Zio Erdun was right. He really did look very different. Natalie had shaved his beard off. Replaced his cap with a skater's beanie that she pulled down over his deformed ear and bandage. She complemented this with a football shirt, a pair of baggy jeans, and a ton of leather bracelets that made him look like either a failed rapper or someone having a midlife crisis. But anything was better than looking like a wanted murderer.

"You want to know what happened to Fouad, I suppose." Zio Erdun was one of the few people who used Abu Hamsa's real name. Abu Hamsa literally meant "Hamsa's father."

Fouad's firstborn son, Hamsa, had died in an accident. A drunk driver ran down the boy and his mother, Leyla, and was given eight months for causing death by dangerous driving. It was four years before someone out picking mushrooms found what was left of the drunk driver's body. According to rumor, his fingers and toes had been cut off before he took a bullet to the head.

Abu Hamsa was questioned, and obviously denied any involvement. He presented a solid alibi. But everyone knew it was him, and everyone knew who had wielded the pliers.

Zio Erdun had been one of Abu Hamsa's heavies. Someone

Atif and plenty of others used to regard with equal amounts of fear and admiration. But there wasn't much left of that man now. The body, once built like a block of cement, was now a skeleton. His transparent skin was pulled tight across his cheekbones and nose, and his fingers resembled bony claws. An elaborate drip beside the bed occasionally made small bleeping sounds to indicate that it had released another dose of painkillers, which explained the glassy expression in the sunken eyes. The old man was dying. And had been for some time.

"Only if you feel you want to tell me," Atif said. That wasn't actually the only thing he wanted to know, but he had to be patient.

The old man took another puff and squinted at him through the cloud rising from the hookah. The sweet smoke made Atif's nostrils twitch. Marijuana mixed with tobacco.

"You mean you'd go quietly if I chose to stay silent?" Zio Erdun winked at him. "You're not usually the type to take no for an answer."

Atif shrugged his shoulders. "I suppose I've gotten older and wiser."

"Do you think that little bastard Gilsén would agree?" The old man cackled, but his laughter immediately turned into a violent coughing fit that left him gasping for breath. He gestured toward a table holding a plastic glass and some napkins. Atif handed them over and the old man coughed out a reddish-yellow lump of phlegm into the glass before wiping the saliva from his beard.

"Cancer," he gasped. "Started in my prostate, of all places. The fuck gland, can you imagine? The doctors gave me three months to live, but that was over a year ago. Doctors—what the fuck do they know? I'm going to survive. Show them how wrong they are. You can see I'm winning, can't you?"

He coughed again and brought up more phlegm. He reached for a bottle of water and took a couple of deep swigs. Atif waited while Erdun composed himself again. Beneath the smell of the hookah he could detect other things. Urine, unwashed body, rotting flesh.

"If anyone else had asked the same question as you, I'd have told them to go to hell. But you've always been a good boy, Atif. A man who keeps his word. Besides, I haven't really got anything to lose by talking to you. I mean, what could possibly be worse than this?"

The old man grinned, revealing a row of nicotine-yellow teeth. Atif wasn't sure what to say.

"Why was Abu Hamsa trying to steal money from people? He didn't usually take that sort of risk."

The old man nodded. "Fouad was always smart. Never aimed too high, always took care to protect himself. He visited me a lot; used to sit on that stool there, just like you. He talked about packing it in, retiring. But the time wasn't right. Business wasn't going well. The cleaning company owed back taxes, he'd put a fair bit of money into a gym, and the Leyla Restaurant was swallowing money as usual. Of course Fouad should really have gotten out a long time ago . . ."

The old man cleared his throat and took another puff on the hookah.

"But he'd named the restaurant after Hamsa's mother. In memory of happier times. So selling it wasn't an option. He used to be able to cover the losses with other income, but then came the whole Janus business. Suddenly no one was doing deals anymore. Fouad was here just before Christmas. He didn't say anything, but I could see he was worried. He needed cash, fast, to save him losing everything."

"And Gilsén offered a quick, easy solution?" Atif said.

Zio Erdun took a sip of water.

"Like I said, Fouad was a wise man. A cautious man. He should have been content with what Gilsén was already delivering. And told the greedy little rat to stick to the agreement. But Fouad and his family were in danger of being left penniless. So he took the risk."

The old boy fell silent as his eyes drifted off.

"And then Gilsén was caught," Atif said. "I think Abu Hamsa tried to negotiate with the people they'd stolen from. Come to some sort of arrangement that could save their lives. Is that what happened?"

The old man didn't answer, just took another puff from the hookah.

"He tried but he didn't succeed," Atif went on.

"No, evidently he didn't."

"Who shot Abu Hamsa, Zio?"

Zio Erdun shrugged his shoulders. "There's a guy called 'the Sniper.' Some relation of Eldar's, I seem to remember. Your age, or thereabouts. We used him a couple of times. Smart, ice-cold, doesn't make mistakes. Head shots are difficult; there aren't many who'd take on a job like that."

"Who commissioned him?"

There was a quiet knock on the door and the same young man who had reluctantly let Atif into the apartment stood in the doorway. He was holding a coffee tray in his hands. His eyes flitted between Atif and the old man.

"Put it down there, Kenny." Erdun gestured toward a small table, half covered by an array of drugs. The young man put the tray down and glowered at Atif. He had the sort of defiant look you only found in young men of twenty or so. As if the world belonged to them, and everyone else was making demands on their time and assets.

"I need more tobacco," Zio Erdun said. "Can you run down to the corner? Take some money from the bureau in the hall."

Kenny stood where he was for a few seconds. Then he turned around and sloped out of the room, slowly, to prove that he was going because he wanted to, not because he'd been told. Atif was seized by an almost irresistible urge to grab the young man's trousers by the waist and hoist them up so they sat where they should.

Zio Erdun nodded toward the door. "My grandson. His

mother named him Kenny, thought a more Swedish-sounding name would make things easier for him. Kenny . . ." He snorted. "That's an English name, for fuck's sake. And it didn't help. He still spends most nights out. Dreams of becoming a real gangster."

"Bit like me, then," Atif said. "And you too, perhaps?"

"Yes, sadly." Erdun sighed. "And look at what fine role models we are. I'm a skeleton in a diaper, and you look like a regular pussy."

The old man grinned again and Atif found himself smiling as well, albeit mostly out of politeness. There was something in the way Kenny had looked at him that he couldn't quite let go of. He was sure Erdun's grandson was the sort who eavesdropped behind doors if he got the chance. Atif's face had been on the television and in the papers, and Zio Erdun had addressed him by name.

He looked at the time on the screen of the cheap pay-as-you-go cell phone Natalie had given him. It would not make sense to stay much longer. He needed to get to the point, have his suspicions confirmed, and then ask the old man for help. Over the years he had done a number of favors for Zio Erdun. He had been wise enough never to turn him down and never to ask questions, never even ask for payment. Now he hoped that the old man would help him in return. Zio Erdun was old-school, still believed in all that business about honor.

Atif thought about Tindra, shut up in the apartment while the police hung around in their cars and watched them from neighboring apartments. Watching, waiting for him to show up.

"Who do you think commissioned the Sniper?" he repeated.

Zio Erdun looked at him for a few seconds. "Why do you really want to know?"

"Because the same people are threatening my family. Threatening *me*."

"And you want to strike first, just like in the old days?"

Atif shook his head.

"I want to get my family out and disappear. But to do that I need to know who's after me. And I need to find someone who can get us passports. I was hoping you might be able to help with both."

The old man took another puff, then shook his head.

"You've certainly changed."

Atif looked at his phone again. Seven minutes since Kenny walked out through the door. Plenty of time to make a call. He felt a sudden urge to grab the old man and shake some answers out of him. Then realized that probably wasn't a good idea.

Erdun moved his jaw sideways, as if he was ruminating over his words before uttering them.

"What Fouad did was wrong. He was a man everyone trusted. Which made his fall from grace all the harder. Everyone turned against him. Do you understand what I mean, Atif?" There was a bitter note in the old man's voice. "I can see that they had to act, but a man like Fouad shouldn't have to die like that. If I'd been well enough . . ."

He had another coughing fit. He cleared his throat deeply and spat a bloody lump of phlegm into the plastic glass. Ten minutes had passed. The smoke shop was in the same gray block as the apartment. Kenny should have been back by now.

"Who were they, Zio?" Atif tried to sound calm.

"Who do you think? Who would be forced to fight a war that couldn't be won? Who would lose everything—their livelihood, their future, even their lives—for a stubborn old man's mistake?"

Atif sat stock-still. "You mean Abu Hamsa was sacrificed?"

"What I mean is that Fouad's daughter Susanna and that gorilla she married sat down and negotiated. To avoid war, they promised to punish Fouad for his betrayal and hand over the millions he and Gilsén had stolen. Maybe a little more as compensation for the trouble caused. And in return . . ."

"In return, Susanna and Eldar were allowed to keep Abu Hamsa's businesses," Atif said.

"Susanna is her father's daughter. She knows that business comes first. She already runs the exchange bureaus where the money was laundered. Even if Fouad had managed to keep his and Gilsén's project secret from her, a lot of people would assume that she knew. So she was forced to act quickly." Erdun spat again. "Susanna has always been good at getting what she wanted, ever since she was little. The smartest member of the whole family."

"And now she's managed to stay alive and keep the businesses."

"Yes, but there's a problem." Erdun grinned, showing his yellow teeth, and held a long, thin finger in the air. "You, Atif. You're sitting on Gilsén's millions, aren't you? Without that money, Susanna and Eldar can't keep their side of the bargain, and the people they've been negotiating with aren't known for their patience. Another week, at most, then the deal will be as dead as Susanna and Eldar. Unless they find you first, of course. In which case I'll see you all in hell soon enough."

The old man's chest made an unpleasant rattling sound, and it took Atif a few moments to realize that it wasn't another coughing fit but laughter.

Twenty

The subway station was ten minutes from Zio Erdun's apartment. A quick walk between the huge gray concrete housing blocks. Or at least as quick as the infection in Atif's body would allow.

Dark walkways, rows of windows from which he could be watched as he followed the narrow path through the bushes. He had passed the smoke shop, where he peered in through the window. No sign of Kenny. The streetlamps were casting a pale light across the path. That hardly helped his situation. It made him perfectly visible and simultaneously ruined his night vision. And made the shadows between the bushes and trees impenetrable.

A scraping noise made him turn around. It sounded like a shoe dragging on asphalt. But he couldn't see anyone on the path either up ahead or behind him. He tried to lengthen his stride, but his wounded foot protested. In a couple of hundred meters he would have reached the station.

They were waiting for him just around the bend. Three guys, two of them sitting on the back of a bench. The third was standing in the middle of the path. Kenny, of course.

Atif turned his head slightly. Saw that another two had appeared behind him, cutting off his escape route. They all looked roughly the same. Young, no more than eighteen, twenty years old, with the same defiant look as Kenny. Hoodies, jeans or sweatpants, with the crotch pulled halfway down to their skinny knees. Clenched fists in pockets; knife or gun? Probably the latter. But which one was carrying it?

189

"Hey, man," Kenny said as Atif approached. "Stop. We want to talk to you!"

Atif stopped. The pair on the bench jumped down and sauntered over to him. Relaxed, confident. This was their home turf, and they were five against one.

"Isn't your grandfather waiting for you?" he said quietly.

Kenny snorted. "The old man hardly knows what day it is. His home nurse will be there soon to change his diaper."

"You shouldn't talk about Zio Erdun like that."

Kenny spat on the path, close enough to spatter Atif's shoe.

"And what the fuck do you know about that? The old man's a wreck. Should have been dead long ago. Would have been best for everyone."

"We were thinking of giving you a lift home," said one of the guys who'd been sitting on the bench. Somalis, Atif guessed. Or possibly Eritreans.

Atif shrugged and took a step toward him. "Okay. Where's the car?"

"Er . . . over there."

Atif's willingness seemed to surprise the Somali.

"So what are we waiting for?" Atif started to walk in the direction indicated by the Somali, forcing the guy to step aside to let him past. It took a couple of meters for them to catch up with him, the Somali on one side, Kenny on the other. The other three lumbered along obediently behind them. Atif could hear them whispering excitedly.

By the time they reached the parking lot, their confusion had switched to triumph. Kenny unlocked a red Mazda and jumped into the driver's seat. One gone, four left outside the car. Three hands still in jacket pockets. The Somali opened one of the back doors and let one of his friends in.

Three left, two hands in pockets.

"Get in." The Somali nodded to Atif, then at the backseat.

Atif shook his head slowly. "I'd rather sit in the front; I'm a bit too tall to sit in the middle of the backseat."

The Somali stared at him, and the other two suddenly looked bewildered. Another hand emerged from a pocket. Empty. One of the Somali's hands was the only one left now, which was logical. He seemed to be the leader of the group, so he was the one carrying the weapon.

"Get in!" the Somali said once more.

Atif opened and closed his hands and turned his body slightly so he was standing with his back against the hood of the car.

"No," he said. He held the Somali's gaze.

The young man stepped forward. Accepted the challenge. Did his best to outstare him, but he didn't stand a chance, even if it took him a couple of moments to realize that. He pulled his hand clumsily from his jacket pocket. A pistol, as expected. The final argument of an idiot.

The Somali pressed the gun to Atif's forehead, holding it at an angle as if he were in a movie. Atif didn't move a muscle, just went on staring at the young man.

"In the car, fuck-face!" the Somali yelled. His voice cracked a little with excitement. The idiot evidently thought he'd won.

Atif noted the position of the others out of the corner of his eye. Kenny and the other guy were still sitting in the car, just as he had hoped. The two outside the car were grinning confidently. Rows of perfect teeth.

"You watch too many movies," Atif said.

"W-What . . . ?" The Somali eyes flickered momentarily. "Okay, get in the car, motherfucker. Otherwise I'll blow your head off!"

"You don't hold a gun like that," Atif said with exaggerated calm. "At least, not if you want to hit anything. And you never press the barrel to someone's head. Do you want to know why?"

Before the Somali had time to answer, Atif's hand flashed up and clasped the guy's hand and twisted it. He squeezed the young man's fingers with all his strength and broke his index

191

finger against the edge of the trigger guard as if it were a dry twig. The moment the Somali opened his mouth, Atif punched him in the throat, turning his scream into a gurgle.

One of the two men behind the Somali took a step forward and whipped a butterfly knife from his pocket. But by the time he'd managed to pull the blade out, Atif was already aiming the barrel of the pistol at his chest. The guy stared at him, then at his friend. Then at the Somali who was rolling around on the blacktop.

"Drop the knife," Atif said. "On the ground, nice and gentle. Then kick it under the car."

The knife clattered over the asphalt. Atif backed away, then turned toward Kenny and the other guy inside the car.

"Out! Both of you!"

The young men obeyed instantly.

"Keep your hands where I can see them; that goes for all of you."

Kenny and his friend walked jerkily around the car and stood beside the other two. The Somali on the ground was whimpering and gasping, but none of his friends seemed the least bit interested in helping him. They stared at the gun, then at each other. The fear in their eyes was unmistakable. Atif aimed the pistol at Kenny.

"The rest of you can go," he said. "Now. Right away."

They were already twenty meters away before Kenny found his tongue.

"P-Please." He held his hands up in front of him. His arrogant attitude was utterly gone now. His lower lip trembled, and he had tears in his eyes.

"Down on your knees."

Kenny did as he was told. His hands were shaking, and the tears began to trickle down his cheeks.

"P-Please," he sniffed. "You know my grandfather. You're old friends."

Atif took a step forward. "Where were we going?"

Kenny opened his mouth, but seemed too frightened to understand the question.

"Where were you going to take me? Who?"

"E-Eldar. Eldar Jafarov. In Älvsjö. We were going to get fifty thousand. I mean, I . . . we don't work for him. A friend told us. Please, don't shoot . . ."

Lights started to go on in the nearest block of apartments. Atif could see figures moving in the windows. Someone would call the cops anytime now. He looked down at the sobbing Kenny and waved the barrel of the pistol.

"Run along home to your grandfather. You get to stay alive thanks to him."

The young man staggered to his feet.

"Actually, wait a moment!" Atif said.

Kenny looked like he was going to shit himself again.

"Pull your pants up."

"W-What?"

Atif raised the gun slightly and nodded encouragingly. He waited until Kenny's pants sat where a normal person would have them.

"There, that's better. You can go now."

The Somali had gotten to his feet, with his back against the car door. He was clutching his throat with both hands and breathing raggedly. Atif aimed the pistol at his face.

"Another rule of having a gun is that you never point it at someone if you're not prepared to shoot them."

He stared at the young man and waited until mortal dread appeared in his eyes.

"Bang," he said. The young man whimpered. A large wet patch spread across the front of his pants. Atif put the pistol in his pocket and set off toward the station.

Twenty-One

"Resign? But I don't understand . . ." Natalie stared at her boss on the other side of the desk. She had suspected something was wrong when Lena called at short notice to ask her to come in on a Saturday. She'd had a whole bus ride in which to persuade herself that there probably wasn't anything to worry about. An activity which turned out to be a complete waste of time.

"I received a phone call yesterday evening. A policeman who told me that you have a previous conviction for stealing drugs from a hospital where you were a trainee doctor. But there's no mention of that on your résumé, nor in the criminal record statement you gave us. How do you explain that?"

Natalie lowered her head. Tears were stinging behind her eyelids. Being found out was bad enough, but what made it even worse was Lena's tone of voice. More disappointed than angry.

"You've done an excellent job here, Natalie. My colleagues and I really have appreciated your cheery demeanor and the caring way you've handled our patients."

Lena sighed, then pushed a sheet of paper across the desk.

"The other partners wanted instant dismissal, but I persuaded them to let you resign instead. I want you to sign this, empty your locker, and hand your keys and pass card over to me before you leave."

Natalie looked at the document, but the letters blurred together and formed an indistinct mass. She grabbed a pen and scribbled her signature. Then she stood up. Her brain was babbling excuses, even considering begging and pleading, but she nipped those thoughts in the bud before they turned into words. She knew who was behind this. That fucking bastard Oscar Wallin. She shouldn't have called him again, and she definitely shouldn't have provoked him the way she had. But the realization that Sarac was dead had upset her, made her want to take it out on someone.

She looked down and pressed her hand against her eyes to hold the tears in. Wallin would have enjoyed seeing her humiliation, and she wasn't about to give him that satisfaction, even if he wasn't there.

"A real shame it had to end like this." Lena held out her hand. "Good luck."

On the way out, Natalie ran into the physiotherapist with the dimples. She turned away before he had time to react.

It wasn't until ten minutes into the bus ride home that the shock faded and she began to think clearly.

Revenge! And nothing feeble either, like scratching Wallin's car or ordering porn to be delivered to his office. This attack on her demanded locusts, frogs, and hailstorms. She wanted to hurt him so badly that he really felt it. Because of him, she was on her way back to square one. Or, to be more accurate, square zero. No job, no income, and no prospects. *Welcome to the rest of your life, Natalie!*

She considered following through with her earlier threat and calling the first paper she thought of to tell them everything she knew about "heroic policeman" David Sarac. Tell them what she had really been doing out on the island and who was responsible for her being there.

But there were two reasons why she stopped herself. The first was that she would be forced to drag David Sarac down into the shit. He had been her patient, her responsibility. And during their time together she had come to like him, to care about him. She had put herself in danger for his sake. In order to get at Wallin she would have to repeat the whole of Sarac's whispered account of the Janus affair. The words he had spat out into the snow while she did her best to stem the bleeding and save his life. The confession of a dying man.

The second reason was more practical. She was harboring a wanted murderer at home on her sofa, a man Wallin and all his little cop friends were searching for everywhere. As long as she was doing that, she couldn't go to the police or anyone in the press.

She'd assumed that Wallin would understand the concept of the balance of fear and leave her in peace. But she had evidently underestimated him. He was never going to let go of her, never going to let her get away.

Fact: as long as she was within reach of Wallin, she'd never stand any realistic chance of making a new life for herself and would always be looking over her shoulder. She would always be worrying that everything could be taken away from her at any moment.

Conclusion: her only option was to leave the country and start again somewhere new, beyond Wallin's reach. Thailand, maybe. She'd thought about that before but had no great desire to sleep on an inflatable mattress, hand out nightclub flyers for foam parties, or trick tourists into hiring clapped-out mopeds. That sort of thing was for twenty-year-olds who didn't know any better. A place of her own, that was more her style. A bar, maybe a strip of beach where she could rent out beach chairs and little cabins to backpackers. But that sort of thing took capital. A lot of capital.

What she needed was a three-stage rocket. Take her revenge on Wallin, get hold of capital, leave the country. Easy peasy . . .

Unless it wasn't quite as difficult as she imagined. After all, she did have one advantage that she'd been lacking only a few days before. All she needed was a good plan, her irresistible charm, and a bit of luck.

As agreed, she gave the distinctive knock before unlocking the door to her apartment.

"Honey, I'm home," she said, and received a grunt in response. She'd heard him get back late the previous night. She'd even had time to start worrying about him. Whatever he had been up to, it seemed to have worn him out.

She put the paper bag containing her things from work down on the kitchen worktop. The mug with the words *World's Best Receptionist*, her contract of employment, the job description and letter in which she had resigned "voluntarily." The remnants of what had been her ordinary life.

She looked at the things for a few seconds and swallowed hard, then opened the cupboard under the sink and threw them all into the garbage.

• • •

The run-down office block lay next to a junkyard and another abandoned building that, judging by the rusty sign, had once belonged to a wholesale greengrocer. At least half of the premises in the little industrial estate on the outskirts of Sollentuna were empty, and big, glossy signs by the entrance announced that the area would be covered with housing within a couple of years.

Julia followed Amante up the stairs. The paint was peeling from the walls and the whole stairwell smelled of damp.

"How come your friend knew about this place?"

"She helps lawyers track down concealed assets during bankruptcies and divorces. Safe-deposit boxes, cars, boats, machinery, property—anything. She gets a percentage of whatever she finds."

"And now she's found Frank Hunter's hiding place?" Julia wasn't convinced. But something about Amante's body language told her she probably wasn't going to get a better answer.

"That remains to be seen, doesn't it?"

They reached a landing with three doors. Two of them had names of businesses crossed out, but the third was completely anonymous. Amante dug out a key ring and tried one of the keys in the lock. It didn't fit, nor did the second. But the third one slid in and the lock clicked. Julia opened her mouth to ask where the key ring had come from, but Amante preempted her with a slight shake of the head. *Don't ask; then I won't have to lie.* She wondered how much it had all cost. A lot, probably. But money seemed to be the least of Amante's problems. He looked better today. At least he appeared to have had a shower and changed his clothes.

The office consisted of a single room with a small kitchen area and bathroom. The blinds were down and the room smelled stuffy. By one wall lay a camping mattress with a sleeping bag on top of it. In the middle of the room were two wooden chairs, a small camping table, and a camera tripod. On the table stood a laptop, with an unplugged charger on the floor alongside.

"He must be a minimalist." Julia heard how tense she sounded. She shouldn't be here, obviously. She ought to be up at National Crime taking part in the investigation into Abu Hamsa's murder and the hunt for Atif Kassab. But Pärson was still insisting on wasting her talents on deskbound duties, and she hadn't been able to resist the temptation to come out here. See with her own eyes if this was the right place.

"What do you think?" Amante said.

Julia didn't answer. Instead she opened the door to the bathroom. She found a large first-aid kit on top of the toilet's cistern. She opened it and noted that several rolls of gauze bandages, one roll of tape, and half a bottle of disinfectant had been used. She went over to the mattress, opened the sleeping bag, and found rust-red stains down toward the bottom of it.

"The person who slept here had a leg injury. Probably below the knee."

"Eskil said Frank had a limp, didn't he?" Amante said.

Julia straightened up and stood silent for a few seconds.

"We're on the right track, aren't we?" he added. "Should we set up a cordon? Get Forensics out here to look for clues?"

Julia didn't answer. She was still uncertain. Amante had a point. In a normal murder case that would have been their next move. But this one was as far from normal as it was possible to get.

"Clues about what?" she said. "Sarac certainly wasn't dismembered in here. In fact, there's nothing to tell us that Sarac ever set foot in the place."

"So should we get Forensics? Look for his fingerprints?"

"If we did that, I'd have to talk to Pärson. Tell him we've continued breaking every rule in the book. Reveal that we know Sarac's escape was hushed up even though my source asked me to keep quiet. I'm only going to do that if we find something definite. Something that can't be misinterpreted and won't lead to us being instantly transferred to the property store."

Julia made a sweeping gesture with her arm.

"This is just a shabby office building where someone's been sleeping. That's how Pärson will see it, and it's certainly not the sort of thing he's going to send Forensics to examine on a Saturday afternoon."

She was aware of how flimsy her argument sounded. But Wallin was right. They couldn't go to Pärson with this, not until they had watertight evidence. Maybe the computer could tell them something. Amante had started fiddling with the laptop and charger and was trying to connect them to a socket in the wall.

Julia went over to the tiny kitchen area and looked at the drainboard. One glass and one plate, both carefully washed. No remnants of food in the sink. The garbage can was empty and the fridge contained nothing but a few small packets of soy sauce. Nothing with a best-before date. Nothing to give them any clues about the person who had been living there.

She closed her eyes and tried to empty her mind, tried to detect the rhythm of the room. But it was hard, much harder than usual. Maybe that was because the room used to be an office, that the person sleeping there had never made it their own. Unless there was something else bothering her.

Amante swore loudly. "The laptop's password protected."

Julia opened the cupboard above the sink. She found a crumpled plastic bag with something inside it. She carefully emptied the contents onto the drainboard. It took her a few moments to register what she was looking at. Sleeping pills. White oval pills, twenty-five in total. Sarac's smile appeared in her mind again.

"You were here," she said half out loud. "You and Frank Hunter met in this room." And this time she was almost certain that Sarac's ravaged face nodded at her.

Twenty-Two

He could still see her falling. See her hanging between ground and sky with her eyes open wide, her mouth gaping, for a moment almost weightless. And then he heard the sound when she stopped being weightless. A muffled, awful sound—a sigh rather than a bang. The sound of something breaking. Something that could never be mended.

Then the dry voice inside his head.

A necessary sacrifice.

It was her or you.

You had no choice.

Only when the voice became a scream—a scream that burned in his chest, tearing his vocal cords and echoing off the bedroom walls—did Jesper Stenberg wake up.

• • •

He unlocked the front door from inside and opened it. The moment the small box on the wall began to beep, he realized that he'd forgotten to switch the alarm off. He had thirty seconds before a whole fleet of police cars began racing toward the villa. His sleepy fingers slipped on the buttons and it took him two attempts before he managed to get the beeping to stop.

He let the dog out, fastened his robe, and stepped out onto the driveway barefoot. The pavement was still cool, but that would soon change. Even though it was only six o'clock in the morning, the sky was bright blue and the sunlight so strong that he had to shade his eyes with his hand. He fetched the Sunday papers from the mailbox and slipped back inside the silent house, accompanied reluctantly by the little spaniel. Karolina and the girls wouldn't wake up before eight. They'd pad down to the kitchen and eat breakfast together in front of children's summer vacation television shows.

He wished the same could apply to him. Wished he could get a whole night of dreamless sleep so that his weary brain had a chance to recuperate. But that was a vain wish. The nightmares were back, stronger now than they had been last winter.

A fourth night in succession in which Sophie Thorning's naked body fell in slow motion before landing on his windshield with a heavy thud. Her white skin cut by hundreds of pieces of glass, the broken, accusing look in her eyes as she lay there just in front of his face. In the dream she was still alive. Her shattered lips moving, forming words.

"You're finished, Jesper. I'm going to crush you. Crush you and your whole fucking family." The next moment the windshield fell in and her body collapsed on top of him. Hands feeling his legs. Sharp fingernails digging into his thighs, feeling their way upward.

The dream scream was still echoing inside his head; it felt so real he could almost taste its bitterness in his throat. He caught a glimpse of his reflection in the glass door of the wine cooler. His hair was sticking up, his posture was slovenly, and he had bags under his eyes. Hardly the image of a virile young man who was going to breathe new life into the party.

Stenberg switched on the coffeemaker, sat down at the kitchen table, and spread the papers out in front of him.

It was all because of John Thorning. His old mentor was finding his way back into his life again. Treating him like an underling, dragging up thoughts, feelings, and memories that he had tried to put behind him.

Half the point of his relationship with Sophie had been about her father. Having to sit and take Thorning's orders and patronizing comments had been far more bearable when he knew he was fucking the boss's daughter. And Sophie knew that—even used to play on the fact when they were together.

There was no doubt that she had been a manipulative, deranged, crazy person, but she had also been his secret. The only thing in his life that his mentor, father-in-law, and wife didn't know about and couldn't control. His affair with Sophie had made him feel a bit smarter than them. More alive, more in the moment.

But now that she was dead, Sophie had become a weakness. His only weakness. And as long as John Thorning was trying to put pressure on him, he would keep being reminded of that. And would experience her death all over again, night after night.

He rubbed his eyes, poured himself a cup of coffee, and started to leaf through the top paper as he sipped the hot liquid. The article on page four made him start, and spill some coffee down his chin and into his lap.

A number of the evidently ill-considered proposals sent out for consultation by the minister of justice are at odds with the Swedish legal tradition, and risk creating a society in which the individual citizen's integrity and right to impartial treatment by the judicial system are seriously jeopardized.

He forced himself to read the article through twice. He felt suddenly nauseous. Fucking hell . . .

He read the names of the article's authors one more time. Ten lawyers, none of them real heavyweights or even particularly well-known. Nor among the best of their profession, which was some comfort. But one name on the list stuck out. Per Sörensen. He knew Per. He was young, smart, and ambitious, and one of John Thorning's acolytes. The timing of the article was perfect in a number of respects. On Sunday mornings almost everyone read the papers, and even though there were only months to go until the election, politics had shut down for the summer. All the professional commentators were bored and on the lookout for something juicy to pounce on in webcasts or social media. And the party's big summer gala was due to take place the following Thursday. Party dignitaries, senior civil servants, and businessmen—they would all have read the article and the ensuing discussion and analysis. Some of them with concern, others with a degree of schadenfreude, but all the same he would have to smile blithely and shake them all by the hand.

Taking the accumulated evidence into account, there was only one possible conclusion. The article was a warning shot, a taste of what would happen if he continued to keep John Thorning outside the decision-making process.

His cell phone began to vibrate. His press secretary's number. It was just as well to take the bull by the horns.

"Hi, Cecilia. Yes, I'm up, and, yes, I've read it."

Stenberg stood up, opened one of the kitchen cupboards, and pulled out a box of acetaminophen. He popped a couple of headache pills out onto the worktop.

"No, I don't want to make any comment . . ."

· · ·

Sunday morning had turned into afternoon, and Natalie had managed to drink two cups of tea, eat half a packet of cookies, and regret doing so at least five minutes before Atif emerged from the bathroom. He had showered and shaved, and the look in his dark eyes showed that he was clearly on the way to recovery.

"Good morning!" She poured him a cup of tea and waited patiently until he had drunk half of it before presenting him with the proposal she had spent the night working on. The exit strategy that would get her far away from there. Far away from Oscar fucking Wallin.

"Your plans are going a bit slowly, aren't they?" she said, and suddenly she had his attention, just as she had hoped.

"Look, I'll be gone from here by tomorrow at the latest."

Natalie held one hand up.

"It wasn't an accusation. Just a statement of fact. You're still not back to normal, and considering that you've been asleep for over twenty-four hours, your meeting can't have gone quite as well as you might have hoped."

Atif looked like he was about to protest, so she kept her hand in the air.

"I was thinking of making a suggestion. Something I think could help both of us. I'm sick of this shitty country. I was already thinking about moving abroad before you turned up. To Thailand: get myself a little bar or something, so I don't have to freeze my ass off for five months of the year. But to do that, I need capital. You, on the other hand, need a way to contact your family and explain what's going on, so they're ready when the time comes. And, even more importantly, you need a plan to get them out of their apartment and then out of the country. Right now there must be half a dozen cops watching Cassandra and Tindra, just waiting for you to show up. What you need is someone who can move freely without rousing any suspicion. Someone who can help you come up with and put into action a plan that will work." She paused to apply some ChapStick to give him a bit of time to think.

Atif sat in silence, drumming his fingers against his teacup.

"How much?"

"One million for my services, and the same again for the plan," she said, tapping her notepad, which was full of scribbled notes. She quickly went on before he had time to be overwhelmed by the size of the amount. "The offer also includes me getting the cash for you to pay for all the things you'll need. Plane tickets, fake passports, hotel, new clothes. I've done the math and you're going to need at least fifty thousand, probably more."

Natalie almost smiled when she thought about where the money would be coming from. But that was one detail she had to keep to herself. Even if she said so herself, her plan was a work of genius. The question was: Would Atif go for it?

He emptied his cup, then slowly put it down and moved his chair a bit closer to hers.

"Tell me what you had in mind," he said.

Twenty-Three

Julia Gabrielsson had shut the door of her office and switched on the red lamp to indicate that she was busy. Not that she expected anyone to disturb her on a Monday morning, even under normal circumstances. And at the moment almost all of her colleagues in Violent Crime were out hunting not one but two murderers. Everyone apart from her and a couple of civilian employees who were managing the deskbound part of the investigations.

More database searches, more additions to the Excel file detailing Abu Hamsa's network of contacts, and even more frustration. She had considerably more important things to be doing. David Sarac had been in that office. He had probably met Frank Hunter there not long before he was murdered. But there were still plenty of pieces missing from the puzzle. Sarac's passport had been used in Frankfurt the evening after he escaped. But, according to all the evidence, Sarac was in a very poor state. How could he have managed to escape and travel abroad on one and the same day? And why had he come back, and how? Until that piece of the puzzle was put into place, it was almost impossible to make any further progress.

Her phone rang and she grabbed the receiver.

"Hello, Julia, this is Johan Zachrisson at IT-Secure. It's about that laptop you asked me to look at."

"Wow, that was quick. How did it go?" She straightened up. If they were lucky, the computer found in Hunter's hiding place could answer a lot of their questions.

"Well, it's a bit mixed, to be honest. The reason for the quick response is that there isn't much on the hard drive. But I can at least tell you a few things."

"Okay." She reached for a pen and paper. "Go ahead."

"To start with, the laptop's brand-new, hardly used. Judging by the dates on the drive, the owner first used it at 3:46 p.m. on February thirteenth. After that, it was used regularly until February twenty-eighth. But since then it hasn't been connected to the Internet, no programs have been updated, and there haven't been any changes to any files. Nothing at all to indicate that the computer has even been switched on."

"Hmm." Julia jotted the information down on her pad. February 28, three days after Sarac left the country, which meant that Hunter must have remained in the hiding place for that long at least. Why? What had he been waiting for? And why the hell would Sarac have gone to Belgrade?

"The laptop was mainly used to look at the news online," Zachrisson continued. "I've made a copy of the browsing history for you, but there's nothing exciting in it. He seems mostly to have been interested in Swedish domestic politics. The only exception was a travel site, and he only visited that once."

"Lufthansa," she said. "A flight from Frankfurt to Belgrade. February twenty-fifth?"

"Yes. How did you know?"

A thought was slowly growing in her head. Something Eskil the nurse had said about how Hunter's appearance seemed to float somewhere between pictures of Hunter and Sarac. And blurred into what Amante had said about Hunter's work.

"Did the user communicate with anyone?" she asked without answering Zachrisson's question.

"He did, but I'm afraid I can't say who. He used an encrypted webmail program called Inkognite. I've come across it a few times before. Inkognite doesn't save anything locally in the computer. You have to log out each time, and when you do so, Inkognite erases almost all traces of activity from the computer. It takes a practiced eye even to detect that the service has been used. You basically need to know the exact IP addresses. The user connected to Inkognite about ten times, so it seems likely that he was both receiving and sending e-mails."

"And when was the last time?"

"February twenty-eighth. But before that something interesting happens. He created a Word document on February twenty-sixth that he probably sent as an attachment via Inkognite. I'm guessing, because he erased the document from the computer shortly after signing into Inkognite that same day. Or at least he thought he'd erased it."

"But?" Julia had an idea where he was heading.

"Emptying the wastebasket isn't enough to make something disappear. The computer doesn't erase the document itself, just the path leading to it. The document is still on the hard drive until the computer needs the space and overwrites it with something else."

"And seeing as the user stopped using the laptop two days later . . ."

"The document is still on the hard drive. I'll send you a link where you can download everything and read it for yourself. Then there was one other little thing."

"What?"

"Well, I'm not entirely certain, but I think the user attached an image along with the document he sent. I've found evidence suggesting that. There are no images stored on the computer, so it must have come from some external source."

"You mean a camera?"

"Camera, cell phone, memory card. Some type of external storage device that can be attached to a laptop. If you haven't found anything like that, keep an eye out. I've got a feeling that picture's important. I'm sure you'll agree once you've read the document."

Julia wrote down *EXTERNAL MEMORY*, then added a series of exclamation marks and underlined the words several times.

"Anything else?"

"No, I think that's about it. I'll call if I come across anything else."

"Thanks, Johan. When do you think I can have the link to the document?"

Her computer made a subdued two-note bleep.

"You just got it."

She ended the call and followed the instructions. The download took barely thirty seconds. As soon as it was done, she opened the Word document. She read its contents several times, then leaned back slowly in her chair.

Twenty-Four

Julia sat down heavily on one of the bar stools in Amante's kitchen. The keys to Hunter's hideout were lying on the middle of the island unit.

"No sign of an external memory?" Julia said, even though she already knew the answer. He would have called her at once if he'd found anything, not wait until she had time to call in and see him several hours later.

"I'm afraid not. I went through the place in minute detail, but I couldn't find anything that explains what that's about." He pointed at the Word document from the laptop. The message on it was only two sentences long.

You betrayed me. Pay your debt.

There were two words missing. The ones David Sarac's voice had been whispering inside Julia's head since the day before. Words that had no doubt cost him his life.

Or else . . .

"Is this all about money?" Amante said. "A blackmail attempt that got out of hand? It sounds like it."

"I don't think so."

Julia put the pictures of Sarac's mutilated body down beside the note. The feeling she had had since the very first time she saw that macabre smile was back. The murder was an act of rage. Ice-cold and controlled, but nonetheless: rage. This wasn't about money but something much more important.

"Sarac was thinking of committing suicide," she said. "That

was why he was carrying those pills around with him. But Hunter must have been offering something important enough for Sarac to postpone his plans, abscond from the nursing home, and make his way to that office to meet him."

"I'm with you that far," Amante said. "But what happened after that? Sarac and Hunter talk for a few hours before Sarac leaves the country. Two days later Hunter sends what looks like a blackmail letter from his laptop. At a guess, he's received some kind of information from Sarac that he's trying to make use of. A photograph, maybe?"

Julia didn't answer. The thought that had started to grow since she spoke to the IT security guy had now firmly taken root. She was beginning to get an idea of how everything hung together. But she still lacked evidence.

"Either way, not long after that, Sarac returns to Sweden by some unknown means, seeing as his passport isn't logged anywhere after February twenty-fifth," Amante went on. "Someone murders him and disposes of his body parts in the water at Källstavik. And that's what I can't make sense of: If Hunter sends the blackmail letter from his laptop while Sarac is in Belgrade, why is that the point when Sarac gets murdered? And where has Hunter gone? Has he been murdered as well? Are there more bodies out there in the water?"

"Okay," Julia said. "That number you had for Bloodhound—have you still got it?"

"Sure."

"Can I have it, please?"

Amante read out the number as she tapped it in. After a few moments of silence the call went through. A double ringtone.

"Bloodhound Incorporated. How may I assist you?" a cool receptionist's voice said.

"Frank Hunter, please."

"I'm sorry, but we don't have anyone here by that name. I can connect you to someone else if you like. Who may I say is calling?"

"David Sarac."

A Muzak medley began to play. "Best of Bossa Nova" by James Last, or something like that. Julia noticed that Amante was observing her with interest. He could do with a shave and a haircut, she thought. And some new clothes.

"Hello," a male voice said. "Who am I speaking to?"

Amante was right. The man's English was good. Yet there was still something in the way he stressed his sentences that suggested that it wasn't his mother tongue.

"This is Detective Inspector Julia Gabrielsson from the Crime Unit of the Stockholm Police," she said in Swedish. "Do you still have David Sarac's passport?"

There was silence on the line. Amante went on watching her.

"What makes you think I'd have someone else's passport?" the man at the other end said slowly.

"Because Sarac gave it to you on February twenty-fifth and you used it to leave the country. You look similar enough for that to work. David Sarac is dead; he was murdered a few days later. But perhaps you already knew that."

Another silence, and for a couple of seconds she thought the man had hung up. Then he spoke again.

"I'm sorry David Sarac is dead. But I had nothing to do with that. The fact is that I admired him in many ways."

"Was that why you bribed one of the nurses to smuggle him out from the nursing home? To express your admiration? The nurse took a surreptitious photograph of you, so we know it was you who organized the whole thing."

The man who had called himself Hunter sighed.

"Oh, well, that's what happens when you're forced to improvise. Good help is hard to find. Unfortunately I didn't have a lot of choice. Thank you for telling me this; I've been wondering how you tracked me down ever since I spoke to your colleague the other day. Amante—that was his name, wasn't it?"

"You met Sarac in your little hideout in Sollentuna," Julia said. "He gave you his passport and possibly something else.

213

In return you told him something, something that led to his death."

"If you're trying to make me feel guilty, you might as well give up," Hunter said drily. "Sarac knew what he was getting into. He was fully aware that things might end the way they did. I suspect that part of him was hoping that they would. He was in a bad way: his demons were getting the better of him. It took an immense effort of will just for him to come to our meeting."

"What was the meeting about? What sort of deal did you come to?"

There was a click on the line, a faint electrical sound that echoed against the background hiss.

"We exchanged secrets. He confirmed something I had long suspected regarding one of his informants. Something that reassured my employers and made it possible for me to resume my work."

"Which employers?"

Hunter snorted, a mixture of a laugh and an exhalation. "You hardly expect me to tell you *that*, do you? Let's just say that they're the sort of people who don't like having their affairs disrupted, especially not by undercover police informants, and who are prepared to go to great lengths to protect their interests. Thanks to Sarac, I was finally able to persuade them that their business interests were no longer threatened and that I had therefore fulfilled my mission."

"You filmed him, didn't you?"

"That was what we agreed."

"And in return you gave him one or more photographs. And perhaps something else?"

"Sarac was out for justice. That was what Skarpö was all about, even if it took me a while to realize that. Sarac wanted to punish everyone who had acted unjustly, himself included. He hadn't expected to survive, and the fact that he did was a great disappointment to him. But there was one other person who

214

evaded their responsibilities, someone Sarac wasn't aware of. I told him and gave him the opportunity to put that right. One last chance to take revenge on the person who had betrayed him."

There was another crackle on the line, and Julia had to wait a moment before asking the question she needed an answer to.

"What did you tell him? And who or what was the photograph of?"

"I've already revealed more than enough. Sarac made a deal to find out a secret, and it cost him his life. There's an awful lot at stake here, far more than you can imagine. You should be careful. Don't trust anyone. And as far as Frank Hunter and Bloodhound are concerned, the trail ends here."

Another click, louder than the others. The background hiss was suddenly gone, replaced by mute silence.

"Hunter?" Julia said. She could tell from the echo that the call had been disconnected.

She dialed back and waited for the cool receptionist to answer. But instead she heard a three-note signal and an automated error message.

This number is no longer in use.

• • •

Amante put two mismatched coffee cups down on the marble counter. He stirred his for a while as he absorbed the phone call with Hunter.

"Do you believe him?" he said. "I mean, in theory it could all be a smoke screen. A way for Hunter to confuse us while he covers his tracks. It could still very easily be him who killed Sarac."

"Well, in theory you're right," Julia said. She couldn't help mimicking his tone slightly. "If this were a normal murder investigation, we'd issue a warrant for Frank Hunter's arrest. Go through Interpol and try to get him extradited from Belgrade or wherever he's hiding at the moment. But I don't think

215

Hunter, or whatever his real name is, is the sort of man who'd let himself be found. That was pretty much what he implied right at the end of the call. And . . ."

"This isn't a normal murder investigation," Amante filled in. "So what do we do now, Julia? If we dismiss Hunter as the perpetrator, that really only leaves one possibility: the person Sarac sent the e-mail and photograph to. The person whose secret he threatened to reveal. Is it really completely impossible to trace the recipient?"

"Yes. I called back and double-checked after I'd received the letter, but the IT guy was completely certain on that point. The e-mail isn't going to lead us to the murderer. Sarac sent the letter and picture on the twenty-sixth and presumably received a reply by the twenty-eighth at the latest, when the computer was used for the last time. Shortly after that he was murdered. But we still don't have any idea who he sent the e-mail to or what the picture or pictures were of. Nor how Sarac and the murderer met. They could actually have arranged a formal meeting somewhere."

"Unless the killer found him some other way," Amante muttered.

Julia's phone started to vibrate. Pärson's number. She ignored it.

"Work," she said. "We've still got our hands full with Abu Hamsa and Kassab."

Amante scratched one of his wrists, then the other, and it suddenly occurred to Julia that he had used her first name.

"We've made a lot of progress," she said. "More than we could have imagined. But in some murder cases you have to pause for breath. Let things settle while you wait for an opening to appear."

Her phone fell silent. Amante went over to the window and looked out.

"If we believe what Hunter said about Sarac, then presumably we have to believe the rest too."

"What do you mean?" she said.

"That bit about us being in danger."

"He didn't say that. He said we should be careful."

"That call, then. Why did it end so abruptly?"

"Hunter hung up. Didn't want to say anything else."

Amante shook his head. He went on looking at the street outside.

"It could just as easily have been cut off by someone else. Someone who was listening to your conversation and didn't want Hunter to say more. You heard what he said. That there's a lot at stake. More than we can imagine. Put that together with the rest of it. Sarac's murder being hushed up, the way his body was moved. If Hunter's right, then we're not safe."

All of a sudden Julia wasn't sure what to say. "Well . . . I don't think we should read too much into—"

Her phone began to vibrate once more. Pärson again. Maybe she was being forgiven, unless he just wanted her to go in and continue mapping Abu Hamsa. Either way, she couldn't afford to antagonize him any further. And Amante's behavior was making her feel uneasy.

"I've got to take this," she said. But Amante didn't seem to be listening. Instead he just went on scanning the street below.

Twenty-Five

The whole thing was really almost ridiculously simple, Natalie thought as she reversed her Golf into one of the spaces next to the garage's service department.

The woman was in the phone book, and once you had a name and address you only had to contact the tax office to find out their ID number. Completely anonymously, and without any requirement to explain why you wanted it. The Swedish principle of freedom of information at its best.

From then on it had been pretty straightforward. Make a few online applications for credit cards, which she'd done on Monday, then allow time for them to be processed, then a bit more for the post. According to her calculations, four or five days in total ought to be enough, which meant that from the day after tomorrow she'd have to be in position out in Gärdet when the mail was delivered.

Best to wait until the mailman had disappeared inside the neighboring building. Then all she had to do was riffle through the bags of mail on his bicycle and grab the envelopes containing the credit cards. The day after, you did the same thing again to get hold of the letters containing the PIN codes, then all you had to do was select a suitable cash dispenser and voilà: you'd got yourself your very own printing press for banknotes.

But, in comparison to the payout, the risk of being caught was a bit too high for her taste. You'd be found out if the mailman happened to come out of the building early, or if the cash machine had been upgraded and fitted with a security camera. That was why she'd decided to give up this sort of fraud and had instead applied herself to other, considerably more profitable projects that entailed a smaller risk. That had gone better than expected, at least until Oscar Wallin had worked out what she was doing. And it was thanks to him that she was now forced to go back to her old ways again.

She hung around outside the building to get a glimpse of the woman when she was over at Gärdet the previous day to check the postman's times and routines. She didn't really know why. Maybe it was to salve her conscience, to persuade herself that she'd change her plans if her intended victim looked like a nice old lady. But she was spared all that. The old bag had cold eyes and a sharp set to her mouth that was easy to recognize.

Natalie got out of the car and went over to the cabinet containing the car care implements without hurrying. This could take a while.

• • •

She'd had time to wash and wax the Golf, pump the tires, check the oil, vacuum the whole inside, and read half of *Aftonbladet* before the first cops appeared at the garage. Two fit, slightly too-handsome guys in cargo trousers, boots, and hooded jackets who parked their anonymous dark-colored car around the back of the building. They walked purposefully through the door and headed straight for the restrooms. All detectives, no matter how talented they were, needed TLC: toilet, lunch, and coffee. All she'd had to do was work out where the nearest garage to Cassandra's apartment was, then hang around waiting for nature to take its course.

Barely ten minutes later the men came out again, visibly relieved and with a plastic bag containing emergency provisions—sweets, she guessed—and each clutching a mug of takeaway coffee. They stood and chatted for a while next to their car, made a couple of calls, probably to their respective other halves, while they drank the coffee. Neither of them gave her more than a cursory glance.

A couple of years ago that would have annoyed her. She looked a bit too ordinary, blended into the background, as one drunken guy had once told her. His words had hurt her deeply, and she put a lot of effort into trying to change. She spent hours in the gym, tried all manner of diets and beauty tips. But eventually she came to appreciate her ordinariness. Not standing out had its advantages. The way no one could describe what you looked like, even if she'd been standing right next to them, maybe actually exchanged a few words. Neither the woman behind the till in the garage nor the two slightly too-handsome cops would remember her, she was sure of that. Nor her poor little Golf, either, which would make it fairly easy to follow them back to the place they were watching the apartment from and mark it on a map. She needed to know exactly where all the cops were when it came to the third stage of the plan she and Atif had agreed on.

First identify the locations of all the cops, which was what she was currently doing, then find a way to communicate with Cassandra and prepare her, and then get them out of the apartment and take them straight to Arlanda Airport with their new passports.

Atif had basically accepted all her suggestions and only made minor adjustments that were all well reasoned. She actually liked his blunt way of expressing himself. And he wasn't exactly unattractive. His body was sinewy and in decent shape, and all the scars weren't as off-putting as he seemed to think. She got the impression that Atif Kassab didn't have a lot of experience when it came to women, or at least not with relationships. He was actually rather shy, which was kind of cute in a way. It was almost a shame that he was fifteen years older than she was. *As well as being a wanted murderer,* the voice of common sense said in her ear. *Because you're not about to turn into some prison bitch living under the ridiculous delusion that dangerous men can be redeemed by the power of unconditional love, are you?*

She shook the thought off and folded her newspaper. The break seemed to be over, because the handsome cops slowly got back in their car and went back the way they had come. Following them was easy. The two men saw themselves as hunters on the trail of their prey. It didn't cross their minds that their role had just been usurped by a red-haired young woman in a battered old Golf whom they had barely noticed, even though she had been sitting just ten meters away from them.

Twenty-Six

Dinner was over, coffee had been served, and the big band had started to play. Over by the stage, where the thick carpet had been replaced by shiny parquet flooring, a dozen couples were already dancing, and in the rest of the room party members were hobnobbing with a mixture of elite businessmen, senior civil servants, and general directors. Sweaty handshakes, alcohol breath, backslaps, and slightly too-loud laughter.

"Jesper, lovely to see you." The prime minister pressed Stenberg's hand, fixed his watery eyes on him, and would surely have grasped him by the elbow if his left hand hadn't been busy with his cane. "How are you? Is everything under control?"

"Absolutely. Couldn't be better."

"Good. Listen, I'd like a chat with you. Find out a bit more about how you and Karl-Erik see the future. But that will have to wait until next week. I think we can grant ourselves the luxury of relaxing a bit this evening, don't you? Set aside any thought of problems and setbacks."

"Definitely." Stenberg held his boss's gaze firmly without giving away how disconcerting he found the man's power games. Obviously the point of what he had just said was the opposite of its apparent meaning. Keeping him on tenterhooks, showing him who was in charge. That he couldn't take anything for granted.

The prime minister let go of his hand. "Have a good evening. If it weren't for my knee, I'd have been hoping for a dance with your beautiful wife. Karolina really is a gem." He gestured toward Karolina, whose back was visible a short distance away, then patted Stenberg on the shoulder and limped back to his table, where his own wife, freshly permed and dressed to the nines, was waiting with the rest of the old man's entourage.

Stenberg continued toward one of the bars in the corner of the large room, which had been his original goal. He was normally good at this sort of occasion, coached to perfection by Karolina. But this evening his professional but intimate smile wasn't sitting quite right. His timing was off, his thoughts and mimicry slightly late, like a dubbed film. He kept imagining sly glances and inaudible comments everywhere.

He had done what he had to, kept his mask in place all the way through dinner, and now all he really wanted was to go home, have a couple of whiskeys, and fall asleep in front of the television. But he knew Karolina would never allow that.

The hour after coffee is the most important, that's when you forge real contacts. Doubtless another of Karl-Erik's many pearls of wisdom that she was so generous about sharing. He had left her with Eva Swensk, engaged in conversation with the recently appointed national police chief while he escaped to fetch drinks. Naturally they already knew each other, presumably from some women's network. Karolina knew everyone who was worth knowing.

All this was child's play to her. Karolina had been born into the smart salons of politics, whereas he had had to fight his way into their warm embrace. He had struggled for years, licking his way toward the top and smiling admiringly at plenty of incompetent idiots to get where he was today. He had earned his place in this room, and—unlike most of the people in attendance—had worked his way there rather than plotting a path through the youth movement or quietly and obediently making coffee at thousands of pointless meetings. He had found his own way into the corridors of power and had no intention of leaving them. No intention of letting himself be exiled to a life of anonymity as a lawyer, where the only chance of being noticed would be if some particularly

223

vile suspect picked him as his public defender, or if daytime television wanted to interview him when he eventually published his obligatory autobiography. But a few minutes in the spotlight weren't enough, not for someone who'd been as close to the top as he had.

He had been minister of justice for less than a year but had already accomplished more than his predecessor had in the previous seven. Yet there were still plenty of people in the party who treated him like a newcomer. An outsider, a pretty boy with a decent pedigree—that was how they regarded him. An obedient tool who could be exploited for their own aims.

He caught a glimpse of John Thorning some distance away. To avoid catching his eye, he leaned across the bar and the bartender came over to him at once, as usual. One of the advantages of looking the way he did. Like a winner.

"Two dry martinis, please!" He turned around to see if he could locate Karolina, but instead he found another woman standing right in front of him. Blonde hair, porcelain skin, green eyes. For a fraction of a second his brain was convinced he was staring at Sophie. Then he realized it was Carina Le-Moine, unofficial leader of the party's younger phalanx.

She had cut her hair: now she had almost the same style that Sophie used to have.

"Are you okay, Jesper? Your face is completely white."

"It's nothing," he muttered. He leaned forward to air-kiss her on both cheeks, Östermalm-style, the way far too many people had started to do. As if they were in Paris rather than a tarted-up conference venue on the Stockholm waterfront. And Carina LeMoine had her very own way of conducting the ritual. She stretched it out, did it slightly too slowly, which had the effect of setting the second kiss somewhere between a Continental greeting and something else. Something far more intimate. Even if he was prepared for her perfume, the smell still made his heart start to beat a little harder.

Narciso Rodriguez—the same as Sophie wore.

He turned sideways and leaned against the bar again. Carina LeMoine took a step closer and did the same. Standing a little too close to him for Stenberg to feel entirely relaxed.

"You look tired. Are you sure everything's okay?" Carina had to raise her voice to make herself heard over the growing hubbub. "Are you sleeping all right?"

"Absolutely." Stenberg tried to force out a smile to make his lie seem more believable. To judge by the look on Carina's face, he didn't succeed very well.

The bartender put his drinks down on the counter beside them. Before Stenberg had time to object, Carina LeMoine picked up one of the glasses and raised it toward him in a toast.

"To the future. And new alliances." She put the glass to her lips a little too slowly. Stenberg realized he was staring at her mouth. He downed his drink.

"Another?" the bartender asked as he put his empty glass down. Stenberg didn't answer, and the bartender appeared to interpret his silence as a yes.

Carina LeMoine leaned forward. "Not long to go now, Jesper," she said close to his ear. "Two months to go until the election. Time to get moving. Our collaboration will be significantly more extensive from now on. After Eva Swensk's appointment, I owe you a favor."

Her cheek brushed his ear fleetingly. Or was it actually her lips? The back of her hand touched his thigh and stayed there for a fraction of a second.

His erection came out of nowhere and made his crotch almost ache. How long had it been since he had had sex? Three weeks? Longer? He couldn't quite remember. He'd had other things on his mind, and Karolina didn't usually take the initiative when it came to that.

Carina LeMoine was manipulating him—he understood that, of course. Yet he still found it hard to come up with an effective antidote.

The bartender put a fresh drink down and Stenberg took a

225

couple of quick sips. He forced himself to put the glass down without finishing it. Out of the corner of his eye he saw his father-in-law approaching.

"So this is where the youngsters are having fun."

"Hello, Karl-Erik." Carina LeMoine kissed Stenberg's father-in-law on the cheeks just as exaggeratedly slowly as she had kissed Stenberg, who experienced a sudden pang of something that felt oddly like jealousy.

"Jesper and I were just talking about the future and how important it is to stick together. Isn't that right?"

Stenberg nodded. Even managed to force a smile.

"I'm reluctant to leave two such stylish gentlemen, but my company's waiting." Carina LeMoine nodded toward the rest of the room. "Why don't we have lunch together soon? I'll ask Lina to arrange something."

"Sure. Definitely." Stenberg squeezed out another smile.

"I actually meant Karl-Erik, but of course you and I should meet up again soon as well, Jesper."

Fuck, straight into the trap. Stenberg tried to look untroubled, but he could feel his cheeks blush.

"Well, then, *au revoir*, gentlemen." Carina LeMoine flashed her perfect teeth.

Just as she turned away, Stenberg got the impression that she winked at him. He looked at Karl-Erik to see if he'd noticed anything, but the expression on his father-in-law's face didn't give him any clues. Stenberg emptied his glass and nodded when the bartender gave him a quizzical look. He felt Karl-Erik take a gentle hold of his arm and spotted his shake of the head toward the bartender.

"John Thorning has been offered an ambassadorial post. It's all been put through the Ministry for Foreign Affairs. I haven't mentioned it to you because it was better if it looked like you weren't involved. He's asked for time to think."

Stenberg murmured in reply. His head was starting to feel heavy. No one was offered an ambassador's post just like that. Karl-Erik must have been prepared. And evidently John Thorning as well.

"The article," he said. "Per Sörensen."

"John saw through the offer. That article is his response. His way of raising the stakes." Karl-Erik leaned closer to Stenberg. "John Thorning is an enemy we can't afford right now. He could ruin more than you can imagine. Arrange to see him again next week. Play the obedient protégé for a while until we work out what it is he really wants."

"Is he still here?" Stenberg didn't really know why he was asking. The thought of having to fawn over John Thorning made him feel sick.

"No, he just left. Said he had to catch the morning ferry out to Sandhamn."

Karl-Erik straightened up and patted the top of Stenberg's arm.

"You look tired. What about going home and getting some rest?"

Stenberg shook his head.

"I just need a bit of fresh air."

He left the bar, aiming for the nearest glass door. Fortunately the balcony was empty. He leaned against the metal railing and breathed in the summer night's air. Looked down over the railing.

For a moment he thought he could see the silhouette of a figure lying stretched out on the pavement below. His stomach clenched and before he could stop himself he vomited straight over the railing and down into the darkness. Taken completely by surprise, he stood there for a couple of seconds as he swallowed to get rid of the bitter taste of alcohol and half-digested food. He clung to the railing and waited for his stomach to settle down.

A discreet cough made him turn around. Boman was standing in the doorway.

"I've been asked to drive you home, Jesper."

Stenberg wiped his mouth with his hand and glared at him. Slicked-back hair, an impeccable dark suit with the parachute regiment's pin on his lapel. The constant helper, always ready. Always on duty. Day and night alike.

"Don't you ever get tired?" he said. Tried to meet the man's unnaturally pale-blue gaze.

"Tired of what?"

"Of always doing what you're told."

Boman raised his eyebrows slightly. "There's a certain satisfaction in subordinating oneself and letting someone else make the decisions. Perhaps you should try it." He went and stood beside Stenberg, conjured a pack of Marlboros from his inside pocket, and tapped out a cigarette.

"You think I'm just a lackey, don't you?" Boman lit the cigarette between his cupped hands.

"What else would you be?" Stenberg wasn't in the mood for this discussion, but the alcohol and the headache pills he'd been taking at increasingly regular intervals were making his stomach turn somersaults, and he refused to let go of the railing.

Boman took a deep drag. Let the smoke out of one corner of his mouth and looked intently at Stenberg.

"I'm surprised you haven't worked it out. You're evidently an intelligent man." He picked a piece of tobacco from the tip of his tongue. "I'm Karl-Erik's confidant. The only person he trusts unconditionally. Sometimes he asks me to drive his car—you're right about that. But more often I help him with completely different services."

"Such as?"

Boman shrugged his shoulders.

"I keep an eye on things. I evaluate risks, solve problems. Make sure that the party's brand and reputation don't get soiled. If I worked in the private sector, I'd probably have a smart office and title. Something to do with risk management or security." He took another drag. "But both Karl-Erik and I prefer to keep a low profile. To exert influence without being seen."

Stenberg's stomach had calmed down slightly. He straightened up and brushed the front of his jacket.

"Why are you telling me this?"

"Because I wanted to explain to you that you and I have something in common. The Cedergren family gave me a job when my career in the military came to an end. Welcomed me into the family, were prepared to overlook my little . . . peculiarities."

Boman gave a wry smile.

"I'm not cut out for an average life. If it weren't for the Cedergren family, I'd probably be dead. I'd have drunk myself to death or fired my service pistol at my temple out of sheer boredom. But Karl-Erik gave me a role, made me feel I could do something important. All I can offer him in return is my absolute loyalty."

Boman took a last drag on the cigarette before flicking the butt off into the summer darkness.

"The way I see it, you got an even better deal. The princess, and perhaps even the whole kingdom. But that means you have to behave and not forget for a single moment who made all this possible."

The wiry little man took hold of Stenberg's elbow.

"Time to go home and get some rest." His grip wasn't aggressive but almost tender. Even so, something in Boman's tone made Stenberg realize that it wouldn't be a good idea to object.

Twenty-Seven

Jesper Stenberg leaned his head in his hands and rubbed his temples. He had carpet-bombed his headache with acetaminophen when he got home the previous evening, then in the morning switched to Karolina's stronger migraine tablets from the back of the medicine cabinet. But the only effect he noticed was a numbness in the end of his nose and fingertips. And his stomach was also starting to make ominous warning signs, so any thought of lunch was out of the question. He looked at the clock. Just over two hours to go, then he could go home with an easy conscience. It was Friday, after all, and no state-run organization could be expected to go on working after three o'clock.

He had fallen asleep on the way home, although he was only faking to start with. He couldn't bear the idea of having to listen to another installment of Boman's lecture about how much they both owed the Cedergren family. Boman was clearly trying to stress his own importance, not least to himself. If Stenberg knew the party and its members at all, Boman's work would consist mainly of making parking tickets disappear and stopping visits to porn clubs from appearing on parliamentary credit card accounts.

His computer and cell phone beeped simultaneously, reminding him that it was social media time. Which meant that he ought to be tweeting, or at least blogging a few lines about the previous day's party. Post a couple of the press pictures that were already waiting in his in-box. Or why not a selfie with the prime minister?

In truth, Stenberg would rather not be reminded about

230

yesterday evening at all. He poured a fresh glass of water from the crystal carafe. There were plenty of excuses for his behavior: the nightmares, lack of sleep, alcohol, stress. The little mind games that his boss and Carina LeMoine had been playing. John Thorning's newspaper article and Karl-Erik's so-called advice, which had begun to look more and more like undisguised orders. He had made a fool of himself. Karl-Erik had no doubt called Karolina that morning a matter of minutes after he had got into his Security Police car. He'd have talked about their conversation, spiced it up with Boman's testimony, and explained how *concerned* he was. Stenberg loathed the way his father-in-law used that word. The way he lingered over the second syllable ever so slightly too long.

I'm conceeerned about Jesper . . .

He would have to fall into line. Book another meeting with John Thorning and listen to the old bastard's supercilious pontificating. And as soon as that meeting was over, his father-in-law would want a report. A chess duel for the over-sixties with him as the key piece.

Stenberg almost lost his grip on the glass and spilled some water in his lap. *Fucking hell!* He stood up and tried frantically to wipe the water from his suit trousers. Just as he realized how ridiculous he was being, there was a knock on the door, and before he had time to answer, Oscar Wallin was standing in his room. Wallin looked at him, then at the stain in his crotch. Stenberg let his hands fall to his sides.

"I just wanted to wish you a good weekend," Wallin said. "I've got a meeting out of the office this afternoon and then I'm heading off to the country. Summer in the archipelago, that's something else, isn't it? We all need a place where we can relax, disconnect from all our worries. John Thorning said the same thing. They've got a place out in Sandhamn, but I'm sure you already knew that. He went off there this morning."

Stenberg stared at Wallin without saying anything.

"I'll have my phone with me if anything crops up," Wallin

went on in the same brisk tone. "Have a great weekend, and see you on Monday!"

As soon as the door closed behind Wallin, Stenberg clapped one hand over his mouth and rushed toward the little basin in the corner of the room. He didn't quite make it before the contents of his stomach forced their way out between his fingers and sprayed across the front of his jacket.

Twenty-Eight

He woke up slowly. He was in no hurry to open his eyes and lie there in the darkness for a few seconds, listening to the sounds. The fibers of the wooden walls and floor twisting as the morning sunlight warmed them. The cries of the seagulls circling over the little jetty below the house. Farther away was a boat on a Sunday outing, the sound of its motor so faint that he could only just make it out. His senses always felt sharper out here. As if the clean air blew away all distractions. Made him see things in a new way.

He kept his eyes closed and breathed in through his nose. The familiar smell of scrubbed wooden floors and rag rugs. The smell of the archipelago filtering through the old windows. Brackish water, seaweed, damp rocks slowly drying in the sun.

But then he noticed something else. A faint smell he couldn't quite identify. Sharp, almost acrid. The drains, maybe? He'd run all the taps and flushed the toilet the moment he arrived and hadn't seen any worrying signs of leaks. Anyway, this smell was more reminiscent of tobacco smoke. Time to find out what it was that needed repairing. He opened his eyes and looked up at the whitewashed boards in the ceiling, filled his lungs with air, and tried to get up.

The pain came out of nowhere, squeezing like a tight band around his chest and constricting his throat. He gasped for breath and contorted his body to try to make the pain stop, but the band kept getting tighter, pinning him to the mattress. His hands clasped to his chest, he could feel his heart buzzing against his sternum. It was vibrating like a pneumatic drill instead of methodically pumping oxygen around his body.

A heart attack, he thought. *A fucking heart attack.*

Suddenly it felt as if the ceiling were several hundred meters above him. His field of vision was shrinking, becoming a narrow tube. He had to get out of bed, find his medication. Then call for help. He managed to roll onto his side, saw the jar of pills and his phone on the bedside table. His fingers closed around the jar and he pulled it toward him and got the lid off with his teeth. He put three pills in his mouth and chewed to break them up. His mouth filled with a dry, bitter dust that he tried desperately to swallow.

The pain in his chest was getting even stronger. The tube was getting narrower; the ceiling was out of sight now. He realized he was dying. That the oxygen in his brain was running out and that everything—pain, fear, panic—would soon be over. In a way, it was a strangely comforting thought.

Twenty-Nine

Jesper Stenberg was having trouble not laughing. His smile was making his face hurt as he got up from his heavy desk chair.

"A terrible tragedy, of course. John was my role model in many ways. A good friend. Our thoughts are with his family . . ." he heard himself say into the phone. Then a lot more nonsense that seemed appropriate but which was gradually drowned out by his own thoughts.

He ended the call with one last expression of sorrow and was halfway out of the room by the time the receiver settled back into its cradle. He walked with light, almost airy steps toward the far end of the corridor.

He forced himself to stop outside Wallin's door and take a couple of deep breaths. Then he threw it open without knocking.

Wallin had his feet crossed on the edge of his desk. It took a couple of seconds before he slowly removed them.

"Have you heard?" Stenberg said, even though he could read the answer from Wallin's arrogant expression. The day was just getting better and better.

"Heard what?"

Stenberg drew the moment out. For the first time in months he felt completely present. As if time had slowed down slightly, giving him the chance to enjoy every aspect of his triumph. He glanced around at Wallin's office. Photographs on the walls, a number of them of himself and Wallin together. Diplomas from various courses and colleges. In the middle of the wall was a picture that he had noticed before. A quotation that reminded him of the one Karolina had had installed in his own office.

Only those who dare to fail greatly, can ever achieve greatly.

An almost perfect summary of Wallin's situation. He had dared everything—and now he had failed.

"John Thorning," Stenberg said as calmly as he could. "He died yesterday morning. Had a massive heart attack out at his summer cottage. A terrible tragedy, of course. John was a close friend."

He saw the color drain from Wallin's face, could almost see the thoughts whirring through the man's mind as he tried to figure out the consequences. He decided to give him a bit of help.

"Listen, now that we're talking, there was something else I was going to mention. After the election the police are going to be placed under a Home Office minister. A new post, one which brings us into line with the rest of Europe. In purely organizational terms, the police shouldn't be too close to prosecutors and courts. In formal terms the Home Office minister will report to me, but as of the last day of September he or she will be responsible for all police matters."

Wallin was completely pale by now.

"Naturally, I'll recommend you to whoever gets appointed, and I'll make sure you get a suitable position with the National Police Committee, where your abilities can be used to best advantage," Stenberg went on. "Everyone's already aware of the work you've done with the reorganization. And I don't think there's anyone who could question your loyalty."

Stenberg paused for a few seconds. This conversation was immensely satisfying, and he wasn't in any hurry.

Wallin sucked his lips in. His Adam's apple bobbed up and down.

"So there'd be no job for me here in Justice? An inquiry or something like that?"

Stenberg enjoyed the moment. He waited just long enough for a spark of hope to ignite in the other man.

"I've thought about it, Oscar. And we simply don't have a position that would do you justice."

Oscar Wallin stared at the screen in front of him. He had called the duty officer and found out as much as he could. But nothing he had learned had done anything to improve his own position.

John Thorning had been found by his daughter-in-law shortly after two o'clock on Sunday. His wife, who was at their home in Spain, had tried to call him a number of times that morning, and because their daughter-in-law happened to be closest, she was the one who ended up going out to the summer cottage. John was lying in bed with his eyes open, and his daughter-in-law, who was evidently a sensible woman, realized at once that he was dead. The police patrol that was dispatched reached the same conclusion, and the doctor on call simply had to fill in the necessary paperwork and sign a death certificate.

There was nothing to indicate that Thorning's death was anything but natural, and there was no sign that anyone else might have been in the house. In all likelihood there would be no further police investigation and no autopsy. Unless the family, in the midst of their grief, insisted upon one, which Wallin doubted.

John Thorning was dead. Just as dead as his own future career. Stenberg had been crystal clear on that point.

He had been hoping that, over time, Stenberg would come to realize the importance of keeping him by his side. That everything he had done thus far had actually been for the good of them both. To promote their mutual agenda. Even the meetings he had had with John Thorning. Naturally, it had been a way to gain a degree of political protection until Jesper came to his senses. But once that happened, they would have been able to use his new friendship with John as a way of approaching their adversary and obtaining inside information. But he had never had the chance to explain that to Jesper. And now it was too late.

The sound of his cell phone buzzing made Wallin jump. His mother's picture appeared on the screen but he decided not to take the call. His voice mail took over and the ringtone stopped, then started again almost immediately. Just as well to get it over and done with.

"This isn't a good time, Mom. I'll call you later," he said as soon as he pressed the green button.

"Don't use that tone with me, Oscar. This is important." Her voice was harder than usual.

Wallin took a deep breath. "What's happened?"

"I've just had a phone call from the bank. The woman who rang was very nice, but she told me that forty thousand kronor have been withdrawn from a brand-new credit card that's been issued in my name, and she wanted to check if everything is okay."

Wallin pinched the bridge of his nose.

"In our family we never have credit card debt," his mother went on. "Your father was very particular about that. I explained that it must be fraud. The woman at the bank said that we'd have to report it to the police and then contest the debt. I tried to explain that my son is a police officer, one of the most important in the country, but I could tell from her voice that she didn't believe me. Not even when I told her your name."

"No?" Wallin pressed his fingertips against his forehead. His pulse was drumming in his temples. He knew exactly who was behind this, and why. *Fucking little bitch!*

"I want you to sort this out, Oscar. At once, before we get a bad reputation at the bank. Surely it ought to be easy for someone working directly for the minister of justice. Or perhaps you'd rather I ask your father for help. He's got plenty of contacts. Important people . . ."

A strong smell of smoke, presumably from the steamboats over by the City Hall, suddenly drifted into the room, and Wallin glanced over at the window. It was closed, but he could definitely smell it, and imagined he could even hear the rumble and crackle of the fire consuming the dry wood deep inside the bowels of the boat.

"Mom," he said, noting that his voice sounded very different now. "There's no need for you to worry. I'll sort it out."

Thirty

Natalie felt her heart start to beat faster. Oscar Wallin was standing in her doorway. On the threshold of her home, for fuck's sake. His face was completely white, and his words were accompanied by a fine spray of saliva.

"I have no idea what you're talking about," she said. "Has something happened to your mother?"

Wallin took a step forward and ended up closer to her than felt strictly comfortable.

"A forged credit card, almost forty thousand withdrawn on it," he repeated. "Do you understand what that means for her? For me?"

Natalie shrugged her shoulders and tried to hide the fear that was getting steadily stronger. "What's that got to do with me?"

"Don't play stupid, you little bitch!"

"Think about what you're saying . . ." Natalie heard the quiver in her voice. Her heartbeat moved up into her throat.

Wallin took another step forward, forcing her to retreat farther into the hall. Obviously she should have left the security chain on before she opened the door, but she hadn't anticipated this particular scenario. The bills wouldn't start descending on Mrs. Wallin for several weeks, and by then Natalie would be long gone.

"You've crossed the line," Wallin hissed. "I'll crush you like a fucking insect." His eyes were wide-open, his teeth bared, as if he were thinking of biting her.

"For God's sake, calm down . . ." Natalie didn't sound anywhere near as cool as she hoped.

Wallin closed the door behind him. Felt for something in his jacket pocket.

"I'm not alone . . ." she said, a bit too quickly.

Wallin stopped for a moment, then craned his neck as if he were listening for sounds within the apartment. But all he could hear was the noise of the television.

"You're lying," he said. "Who the hell would you have here?"

Natalie gasped. Wallin had pulled his hand out of his pocket. He was holding a black oblong object that looked a bit like an electric razor. A tiny blue spark glistened between the electrodes at the end.

Fear squeezed all the air out of her. She held her hands up in front of her. "Oscar, for fuck's sake . . ."

A sudden clatter inside the apartment made Wallin start. The sound of a dishwasher being opened. Wallin blinked a couple of times and looked like he'd just woken up. He closed his mouth and looked around. And saw Atif's big running shoes on the mat beside his feet.

"Like I said"—this time Natalie managed to keep her voice steady—"I'm not alone. I have no idea what's happened to your mom or who's ripped her off. Have you got any proof? Anything that leads you to suspect me? Because you wouldn't just show up here and start yelling accusations at me, would you?"

Wallin didn't answer. He quickly put the Taser back in his pocket, his eyes darting between Natalie and the running shoes. The color of his face slowly returned to normal. More noise from the kitchen, a bit louder this time.

"I'll interpret your silence as a no," Natalie said. "You have no proof whatsoever that I'm behind the attempt to defraud your mother."

Wallin went on glaring at her. His jaw was clenched, his lips barely visible. Then he turned on his heel and left the apartment without a word.

Natalie closed the door behind him and slowly locked it.

She put the safety chain on, leaned against the doorframe, and breathed out.

"What was that about?" Atif asked, peering out into the hall. To judge by the expression on his face, he hadn't heard much of the conversation. The television must have drowned it out.

"Nothing," Natalie mumbled. "Just an old acquaintance."

· · ·

Oscar Wallin was sitting completely still inside his car. The key was in the ignition and the radio was on, playing a piece of classical music he recognized. Mozart, his father's favorite composer. Sometimes he could still conjure up the image of the professor as he sat in his armchair in front of the record player. "Mozart was a genius, Oscar. But he'd be nothing without his father, Leopold. Just another child prodigy without goals or direction. That shows how important it is to have role models, doesn't it?" The professor put one hand on his son's head. Patted him absentmindedly, as if he were a dog.

But the memory always became distorted toward the end. The professor grew older and lost his hair, and now there was a different boy next to his armchair. A fire burning in the hearth. The flames reflected in the windows, so that it looked like the fire was actually in the garden. Tall flames reaching for the night sky.

Wallin changed stations in the middle of the piece and took a GPS tracker out of the glove compartment. He turned a switch and a small green diode flashed a couple of times. Then he pulled the sun visor down and caught his own reflection in the little mirror.

They thought they could trample all over him, treat him like a dog. That was partly his own fault. He had been too kind, too forgiving. Had thought there were still rules and that everyone was sticking to them. But he knew better now, knew what it was going to take for a man who wanted to win. Who was prepared to fail badly in order to achieve great success.

He opened the door and started to walk down the street. It took less than two minutes to find Natalie's car. And even less time to attach the GPS tracker under the mud flap.

Thirty-One

Natalie looked out across the parking lot in front of the gates of the preschool. Half the places were taken, but none of the vehicles were any of the cop cars she had seen at the gas station or during her discreet little walks around the residential area where Cassandra and Tindra lived. By now she knew their routines. Knew that the police car that picked Cassandra up from work would stop outside the small gate to the preschool and the two cops would accompany her into the square building on the other side of the play area.

The men were on their guard, but they were looking out for Atif, a two-meter-tall thug with half an ear missing. She was about as far from that description as it was possible to get.

In other words, this job ought to be pretty straightforward, no harder than walking around the area where Cassandra lived with Nordic walking poles and pretending to exercise, the way she'd spent most of the past weekend. Even so, she could feel her hands shaking slightly. Wallin's visit the previous evening had unsettled her. He'd threatened her before, but he'd never previously visited her home. And he'd never waved a fucking Taser in her face before either.

She should really be delighted. Aside from filling her travel kitty, she'd managed to do exactly what she'd set out to. She had kicked Wallin right where he was most sensitive. But his rage scared her. What would have happened if Atif hadn't been in the apartment? As luck would have it, she wasn't planning on staying in the country long enough to find out, and until it was time to leave, she wouldn't be opening her front door for anyone.

She looked at her watch. Five minutes to five. High time to go in. She got out of the car. The heels of her low pumps echoed against the asphalt of the little parking lot. Jacket and dress. Dark-framed glasses, makeup, hair loose. No one who had seen her in the various exercise outfits she had worn on her reconnaissance circuits would recognize her.

In the playground she walked around some Hula-Hoops that were lying in the middle of the path. In the distance she could hear children laughing and yelling. She opened the door and found herself in a corridor. For a moment she was unsure of which way to go, then turned left. She reached several rows of hangers and tiny lockers with little photographs and name badges above them. She found Tindra Nygren's sign and beneath it her mother's name. Her jacket and backpack were hanging from the hooks beneath the locker. So now she just had to wait.

There was a chair a short distance away in the corridor, and she got out a pen and some papers from her briefcase. She sat down and pretended to fill them in.

Cassandra appeared exactly six minutes later. A slim, toned cop came in a meter or so behind her but luckily stopped by the door. The cop glanced briefly at Natalie and quickly dismissed her as just another mom picking up her snotty little darling.

Natalie stood up. She went over to the locker next to Tindra's and pretended to sort out the clothes inside.

"Cassandra," she said quietly without looking up.

The other woman stopped and for a moment looked frightened. But Natalie's appearance seemed to calm her down.

"H-Hi," she said. "You're Linnea's mom, aren't you?"

Natalie shook her head.

"Of course not, how silly of me. Elin's mom, I mean." Cassandra smiled weakly and Natalie couldn't help noticing how exhausted she looked. Her eyes seemed simultaneously tired and wary.

Natalie shook her head again, then took a quick look at the cop by the door.

"I'm a friend of Atif's. He asked me to talk to you."

The name made Cassandra start. The fear was back in her eyes.

"Here." Natalie carefully handed over an envelope. She kept her hand too low for the cop to see. Cassandra looked at her outstretched hand as if there were a bomb in it.

"Take it," Natalie said. "This is just to tide you over, to make sure you're okay."

She waved the envelope and thought how ironic it was that she was giving away Oscar Wallin's mother's money.

"Atif wants to help the two of you," she went on. "Get you out of the country. Start again somewhere else." She saw movement from the corner of her eye. But it was just one of the teachers saying hello to the cop before smiling at them as she passed.

"Iraq?" Cassandra shook her head. "Forget it. I'm not going to go around in a burka."

"You're probably thinking of Saudi Arabia. But I don't think either of those countries is very likely."

"Doesn't matter." Cassandra snatched the envelope and dropped it in her handbag. "Who are you, anyway? His girl-friend?"

Natalie recognized the mocking tone all too well. Attractive girl talking to plain girl. Treating her as an object of pity because she hadn't done too well in the looks lottery.

"A friend, like I said," Natalie said.

"Oh, okay. A friend who happens to be a girl." Cassandra smiled in a way that did nothing to reduce Natalie's irritation. "Tell Atif that if he cares about us, he'd give Susanna and Eldar what they want. Then everything will be all right."

Cassandra's confidence seemed to be growing with every sentence. Her smile revealed a perfect row of white Hollywood teeth.

Natalie forced herself to smile back. She held her breath for a couple of seconds.

"Now listen. This is how it is. Atif escaped from one of Sweden's most secure prisons and managed to get hold of a pretty big bundle of money along the way. The first thing he should have done is get away from here. That's what I would have done, and no doubt you as well."

Her voice was tense with dislike, and she had to pause before going on.

"Do you know why they blew Abu Hamsa's head off?" She studied the other woman's reaction with satisfaction. "No? Well, because he was stealing money from other criminals, and he spent that money on you. At least, that's what some people will think. Nasty bastards who are already in a bad mood and are now wondering how much you knew—and if you might be sitting on a nice little stash as thanks for all the blow jobs you gave the old man. So guess what's going to happen ten minutes after the police stop watching you?"

Natalie could see the other woman shrink as she followed her reasoning to its conclusion. All her self-confidence drained away and fear came back with full force. Natalie almost felt sorry for her, and felt ashamed of herself for kicking someone who was already on the ground. But Cassandra had been asking for it.

"Everything Atif has done is for your sakes," Natalie said quietly. She waited until the other woman looked up at her. "For you and Tindra. So if you're even half as smart as Atif says, you need to listen really fucking hard now."

Thirty-Two

This time the Thorning family had pulled out all the stops, in marked contrast to their response when Sophie died. They'd used all the contacts they had to pull together a memorial service for four hundred guests in Gustaf Adolf Church in just a few days. This would then be followed by coffee for a select number of guests in the cavalry mess at K1, the Östermalm barracks. John Thorning had been a romantic militarist, just like Karl-Erik, so a color guard was a pretty safe bet. Maybe even a military band, considering the amount of money John had donated to the Royal Guards over the years. A fitting farewell to the Great Lawyer.

For the third time in just a few minutes, Stenberg realized he was smiling. He quickly rearranged his features, then glanced at Karolina, who was sitting beside him in the backseat of a car that was slowly cruising through the flow of guests arriving at the church.

But if his wife had noticed anything, she wasn't showing it. Karolina looked fantastic. A black two-piece and a little pillbox hat, the veil of which stopped just above her perfectly straight nose. She was wearing suitably subdued pink lipstick instead of the usual red. Her heels were just the right height. As always, she radiated elegance. Her clothes, her posture, the way she spoke. That little thing she did with her chin when a topic of conversation seemed to interest her particularly.

Karolina seemed to feel him looking at her, because she turned to him and gave him a cool little smile. "How does it feel, Jesper?"

247

"Good," he said. "Well, obviously it's all very sad." He gestured toward the black-clad figures outside the car.

"John was your mentor," Karolina said slowly. "One of the most important figures behind your success. He meant a great deal to you."

Stenberg nodded. *Mentor, important figure, meant a great deal.* The words led him into the correct emotional register and at last he managed to adopt an appropriate expression. Sad, concerned, empathetic.

"A terrible tragedy," he murmured. And heard, to his satisfaction, how genuine it sounded.

The car pulled up in front of the church and Becker jumped out. Stenberg saw him nod to the suited bodyguard who was already waiting on the steps. Then he noticed the two dark Security Police vehicles parked in front of them. The prime minister was present, naturally. And the entire party entourage with him. Carina LeMoine and presumably her puppet, his very own recently appointed national police chief. All the supporting troops, everyone who—now that his problem had shuffled off this mortal coil—would propel him onward and upward. All the way to the top.

Becker opened the door for him, and Gustavsson, the bodyguard who had driven the car, did the same for Karolina. Subdued organ music curled out of the open doors of the large church.

Showtime, a little voice in his head said, and Stenberg had to make a real effort to keep his smile from breaking out again.

• • •

Stenberg had methodically worked his way through the front three rows. He signed the book of condolences in front of the lit candle and the photograph of John, conveyed his sincere condolences to John's widow and sons. Then he shook his boss's big paw and his father-in-law's somewhat cooler one, and air-kissed Carina LeMoine. He hesitated momentarily in

248

front of Eva Swensk. Did you air-kiss the most senior police officer in the country when she also happened to be in full uniform with sparkling new epaulettes? There couldn't have been many people before him who'd had to ask themselves that question. He decided that the answer was no, and held his hand out for a firm shake. In her eyes he could see the expression of gratitude and respect that he had every right to expect.

"Good to see you again," she said. "Even if the circumstances are naturally very sad."

While Karolina made small talk with Eva Swensk, Stenberg caught sight of Oscar Wallin, who was lurking in the shadows toward the back of the church. Wallin's presence surprised Stenberg somewhat. Was Wallin actually rather masochistic? Did he wear a hair shirt under those impeccably ironed tailor-made shirts that in all likelihood came from the same Östermalm tailor as his own?

On an impulse he left Karolina and went over to him. Wallin raised his eyebrows slightly but made no attempt to retreat.

"I didn't know you and John were so close, Oscar."

Wallin pulled an inscrutable grimace. "I wanted to show my respects. Someone has to, after all."

Stenberg clenched his teeth. "I've been thinking. Maybe it would be a good idea if you moved back to Police Headquarters at once. To give you a chance to work your way back into the organization again."

Wallin didn't answer. Instead he looked over at the group Stenberg had just left. "It's odd."

"What?"

"The way people you trust and respect can suddenly appear in a very different light. Almost from one day to the next."

Wallin smiled, a cold, reptilian smile that Stenberg had never seen before. He looked over at the other group again.

"He looks happy, your father-in-law. Extremely happy, given

that he's attending a memorial service for a dead man. Things are going well for Karl-Erik now. And you, of course."

Stenberg reached out a hand and patted Wallin on the shoulder.

"I'll make sure the national police chief takes good care of you. Get you a good job, like I promised. Something that suits your abilities and ambitions."

Wallin turned his head and Stenberg couldn't see the expression on his face. But that didn't matter. This match was over. He had won, and no one could change that.

"Do you know what else is odd?" Wallin's voice was still surprisingly calm.

"No, what?"

"The way all the obstacles are disappearing, one way or another. John here, for instance"—Wallin gestured toward the table holding the photograph and book of condolences—"who happened to die after that article. Just before campaigning enters its final phase and he could do any real damage. Very practical for you, wouldn't you say? If one were inclined toward conspiracy theories, one might almost say that John's death is in many ways reminiscent of his daughter's."

Stenberg felt a vein start to throb next to his right eyebrow. "What are you trying to say, Oscar?"

"Only that it seems to be very dangerous to get in the way of your career. Lethal, in fact."

• • •

The Royal Guard, who had been lined up along the walls during the priest's eulogy and the obligatory speeches from John's lawyer friends, walked out slowly to the notes of the final piece of music. Family and friends followed along slowly behind them.

"Shall we go, Jesper?" Karolina leaned toward him to make herself heard above the organ. Rousing him from his thoughts.

"Of course." He stood up and gently ushered her out of the pew and toward the exit, where there was already quite a crowd.

Becker appeared in front of them out of nowhere to clear a path for them.

The ceremony had been admirably short. Evidently both the speakers and the priest had recognized that the congregation was made up of important people who had appointments to keep and decisions to make. But Stenberg had only been half listening. Wallin's insinuations had unsettled him. Both Sophie and John Thorning were dead, and they had both threatened his position in some way. But Sophie had been unstable and prone to suicidal thoughts. The fact that she had finally carried out her threat wasn't really that much of a surprise. And John had just turned sixty-nine. He was already on his cardiologist's danger list after a warning murmur a couple of years ago. A long working life full of late nights, too much whiskey, and unhealthy meals had finally taken its toll. Considering his daughter's tragic suicide and the stress of being general secretary of the Bar Association, as well as running one of the country's most prestigious legal practices, it was almost astonishing that John's heart hadn't given out sooner. Even so, Stenberg couldn't drop the thought. What if someone had cleared John Thorning out of the way? Someone who thought he constituted a serious threat to the party . . .

Becker led them on purposefully. His colleague Gustavsson fell in behind them, sealing them off from the crowd. They emerged into the fresh air and Stenberg took the opportunity to take a couple of deep breaths and tug at his shirt to stop it from sticking to his back. He looked around for Wallin but could see no sign of him. Just as well. Once again Wallin had planted a thought in his head, one he was going to have to work to get rid of. Idle nonsense from an embittered man.

Karl-Erik had somehow managed to get out before them. He and Nisse Boman were talking to a uniformed man with a somber, stony face. As they approached he exchanged a quick handshake with the man, who walked away.

"Well, then," his father-in-law said. "That's done. Sad busi-

251

ness. The Thorning family really has had its fair share of trag-edies." He smiled in a way that was probably supposed to look sad. Stenberg found himself staring at his father-in-law, but the gray eyes behind his glasses weren't giving anything away.

"Who was that you were talking to?" Karolina asked.

"Oh, just an old acquaintance I haven't seen for a while. Erik Ohlén, remember him? He, Nisse, and I all did our paratrooper training together. Erik's in charge of the Military Intelligence and Security Service. I'll introduce you sometime."

Karolina said something that Stenberg didn't catch. Karl-Erik seemed just as calm and relaxed as he usually was. Even so, there was something that made Stenberg react. A dissonant note in his father-in-law's voice.

It's odd, the way people you trust and respect can suddenly appear in a very different light. Almost from one day to the next, Wallin whispered softly inside his head.

Stenberg felt himself drifting off and forced himself back to the present. From the corner of his eye he saw Nisse Boman watching him.

"I thought I might skip coffee," Karl-Erik said. "I've never really liked that sort of occasion. I've booked a private table at the Grand, if you'd care to join me? Two members of the Law Council will be coming as well. It could be a very interesting discussion."

Stenberg opened his mouth to decline the offer, but Karo-lina was quicker.

"Of course we'd like to. Wouldn't we, Jesper?"

Stenberg forced a smile. "Of course."

"How are you feeling?" Karl-Erik said. "You look a little pale. Perhaps there's been a bit too much death for your taste as well?"

• • •

The food at the Grand Hôtel was exquisite. Arctic char with dill potatoes, a dry white wine that Stenberg could have identified without listening to the sommelier. Karl-Erik's choices were predictable. No surprises. No risks.

But instead of enjoying the bouquet, Stenberg quickly emptied his glass. The wine blended with the aperitif that was already sloshing about in his stomach. He could feel Karolina looking at him. Ordinarily he would have looked up and nodded to her to show that he was going to take it easy. But nothing was the same as usual today.

They were in a private dining room, just as his father-in-law had promised. Heavy curtains, thick carpet, oil paintings on the walls. The serving staff in their white uniforms slipped in and out of the room. Fast, discreet.

He glanced at his father-in-law. Karl-Erik and Karolina were engaged in an intense discussion with the members of the Law Council. In some regards, the three men were almost comically similar. All around sixty, all in dark suits, white shirts, and black ties. But Karl-Erik had fewer double chins than the others, and no visible signs of encroaching baldness. Karl-Erik's posture was like a steel spring, the eyes behind his dark-framed glasses alert and engaged. Stenberg had always regarded his father-in-law as something of an auditor. Slightly dull and prone to admonishing people. That was a view that many in the party seemed to share. Karl-Erik was no leader, not like the prime minister, who was the sort of man who used his whole hand to point things out and wasn't afraid of flattening people, whether or not it was necessary. There were plenty of people who disliked, perhaps even hated, the prime minister. And who were waiting for a suitable opportunity to exact payback for past injustices. No one had strong views of that sort about Karl-Erik Cedergren. Karl-Erik kept on good terms with everyone, challenged no one, and sought consensus as far as possible.

He was the person who stepped in once the dust had settled. The person who smoothed things over, soothed hurt feelings, bolstered battered egos, and helped everyone move on. Over the years he must have built up an immense store of reputational capital, both within the party and the apparatus of the state, especially if he used Boman to clean away troublesome mistakes and blunders discreetly.

Karl-Erik wasn't regarded as a threat. But perhaps that was actually a huge underestimation. In an age when everything was about rapid decision making, Twitter storms and revelations, and deals being revealed and concluded in less than a week, Karl-Erik was still working long-term. A cunning old spider who was slowly and methodically weaving a web that was large enough to catch not just one fly but all of them.

Soon the prime minister would be forced to step aside, and the party would enter a new phase. A phase that Karl-Erik had spent his entire professional life preparing for and had even dragged his own daughter into. Because the final little detail that was required for Karl-Erik's spider's web to be finished was a crown prince. Someone who would be granted power, no matter what the cost.

Stenberg realized he was staring at his father-in-law. Karl-Erik looked up and met his gaze for a moment. Gave him a slightly wry smile. A smile that was neither triumphant nor even irritating.

John Thorning had realized that Karl-Erik was the man behind Stenberg's cometlike career. Judging by the newspaper article, John would rather see him fall, would rather sink his own protégé, than let himself be outmaneuvered and sidelined by Karl-Erik. John Thorning had seen through Karl-Erik. Had challenged him. And now John was dead.

Stenberg raised his wineglass to his mouth, but all that was left was a little drop at the bottom that wasn't going to come close to quenching his thirst. He looked at the waiter and saw that the man was already on his way over to him. Karolina's eyes were burning into the back of his neck, but he chose not to look in her direction. Instead he carried on observing his father-in-law. Studied the man's restrained body language, trying to work out what thoughts were going through his head. For almost twenty years he and Karl-Erik had socialized and spent time together. But just then, at that moment, Stenberg doubted he knew the other man at all.

Thirty-Three

Atif got off the subway at Farsta strand. He kept his eyes on the platform, not giving in to the temptation to look up at any of the security cameras on the roof. His cap and sunglasses weren't a foolproof disguise, and it would be stupid to tempt fate now that they were so close.

Freedom was just a few hours away. They had four tickets booked on the evening flight to Zürich. As soon as the banks opened the next morning he would empty Gilsén's anonymous numbered account. Then it was just a matter of working through the checklist:

1. Pay Natalie, thank her for her help, and say good-bye.
2. Transfer payment for the large house in Abu Dhabi for which he had submitted a bid.
3. Transfer money to his aunt's account so she and his mother could get there.
4. Buy tickets for himself, Cassandra, and Tindra. Business-class, with Etihad.
5. Leave Europe for good.

Once he had passed the barriers and emerged into freedom, he checked the time. Ten minutes until Natalie put her part of the plan into practice. He ought to be there with her instead of running a simple errand, but Natalie had forbidden that. She said that under no circumstances was he—regardless of whether or not he was in disguise—to show himself in the vicinity of the apartment on Grimstagatan. She said his presence would make the entire operation ten times more risky than if she did it all herself, and she was right, of course.

Even so, that morning he had hesitated again. Wondered if Natalie was planning to trick him somehow. She was smart, much smarter than he was or anyone he knew. Considering that she'd made a living from lies and deception, it seemed reasonable to question her motives. But he didn't really have any choice. He glanced as his watch. Three minutes, then his, Cassandra, and Tindra's futures were entirely in Natalie Aden's hands. And all he could do was mutter a quiet prayer that nothing would go wrong.

· · ·

Natalie looked at the time. Two minutes to go. She ran her ChapStick over her lips, tried to get her hands to stop shaking. Nerves, she thought. Nerves were her biggest enemy right now. They could force her to make a mistake, to make ill-considered decisions. She had to calm down. Follow the plan.

On the seat beside her lay four cell phones, all pay-as-you-go, impossible to trace. The car was ready: Atif had stolen the new license plates the night before from an extended-stay parking lot. She took a quick look at the rearview mirror and concluded that her horn-rimmed glasses and combed-back hair made her look completely different. What with the green paramedic's outfit she had ordered online, the person in the mirror was practically a stranger, or at least a very distant acquaintance.

One minute: time to focus.

She quickly went through her checklist again. Cassandra had received the parcel, a box covered with the Ellos home-shopping logo that not even the most suspicious cop could object to. Natalie had checked on the courier's website and had seen that Cassandra had signed for it in capital letters, the way she was supposed to if everything was okay.

Natalie looked at her watch again. Thirty seconds to go. She picked up one of the phones. *One, one, two, so easy to do . . .*

257

"SOS one one two, what's the nature of the emergency?" the operator said.

"There's a fire!" she shouted at the phone, trying to sound shrill and hysterical. "A really bad fire. Please hurry!"

"Try to calm down," the operator said. "A fire, you say. What address?"

"Grimstagatan, number 161. Come quickly—please!" Natalie cut the call off. Then she picked up the next phone.

Same number, different operator.

"SOS one one two, what's the nature of the emergency?"

"Hello," she said, in as low and nasal a voice as she could manage. "I just thought I should let you know that there's smoke coming out of the building on the other side of the road. I live at Grimstagatan . . ."

• • •

She opened the front door and her nose immediately detected the acrid smell. She encountered the first tendrils of smoke on the first-floor landing. She ran up the last two flights. The smoke was thicker there and made her eyes sting. She heard a door open below her, then agitated voices shouting in a language she didn't understand.

"There's a fire," she called. "Everyone needs to get out!" She repeated the message in both Arabic and English.

She knocked lightly on Cassandra's door. It opened at once and for a moment Natalie thought she'd been found out, that her plan was blown and the woman with the shoulder-length red hair who opened the door was a police officer who was about to arrest her. Then she saw that the woman was wearing the same paramedic's outfit as she was. She recognized the large glasses she had put in the Ellos box and realized that the woman in front of her was Cassandra.

"Your hair . . ." she couldn't help saying.

Cassandra shrugged. "Trimmed and dyed. You said I should try to make myself look different."

Natalie's expression showed how impressed she was. Then she glanced quickly at her watch again. The sound of sirens was echoing off the buildings: big gas-powered horns approaching at speed.

"Are you ready?" she asked. Cassandra nodded. On the floor in front of her was the orange backpack that had also been in the Ellos box, now packed with essentials, hopefully. Tindra looked out from behind Cassandra's legs. The black dress made her look even smaller than she was.

Natalie crouched down. "My name's Natalie. I'm friends with your uncle Atif. I'm going to take you and your mom to him, but first we have to play a pretending game. But there's nothing to worry about really, okay?" She held out a transparent breathing mask. "You put this over your nose and mouth, just like you do at the doctor's."

The girl nodded. "Mom's told me." She took the mask and pulled the elastic strap over her head and put it on.

"Good girl." Natalie nodded at Cassandra. "Get ready."

She stood up and looked out through the peephole. The emergency vehicles must have arrived; the sirens were deafeningly loud outside. From out in the stairwell came the sound of heavy footsteps and the clatter of equipment, then doors opening and voices speaking loudly in several different languages.

Cassandra pulled the black hijab over Tindra's hair and as far down her forehead as she could. Then she picked the girl up in her arms.

"I'm Darth Vader," Tindra twittered through the breathing mask. It covered half her face and made the little voice sound hollow.

"You certainly are, sweetheart," Natalie murmured. She couldn't help smiling. She quickly grew serious again.

She exchanged a quick glance with Cassandra before looking through the peephole again. Four firemen stomped past on their way to the attic. The smoke had gotten a bit thicker.

"Okay, then," she said, picking up the backpack and pulling

it on. "Just say when you can't carry her anymore and we'll swap. We walk straight out. Don't look around. Don't talk to anyone. We're two paramedics on our way out with a child suffering from smoke inhalation, and no one's going to stop us. Okay?"

She waited until Cassandra nodded reluctantly at her.

"All right, let's go!"

The stairwell was full of smoke now. From the attic they could hear the sound of metal against metal. A sledgehammer or some other heavy tool striking a steel door. The sound echoed in the stairwell, bouncing off the concrete walls.

They encountered the first cops one floor below. A man and a woman: Natalie recognized them from her reconnaissance. All of their attention was focused on the upper floors, and they passed without so much as pausing. On the next floor they encountered a team of paramedics in similar green outfits as they were wearing, and with matching orange backpacks. Natalie greeted them in what she hoped was a collegial way.

"Any more?" one of the paramedics called, pointing upward.

Natalie nodded. "Top floor." She turned back toward Tindra and Cassandra to indicate that she was in a hurry.

They continued downstairs, but the staircase was temporarily blocked by agitated people and they were forced to stop. The noises up above changed character, becoming a painful metallic creak as the steel door and its frame reluctantly let go of each other. Another minute or so, maximum, then the firemen would be in the attic and would find the smoke flare Cassandra had put there and understand that the fire was deliberate. Behind the sound of the sledgehammer, Natalie thought she could hear the cops banging on the door to Cassandra's apartment. Time was running out. They needed to get away from there immediately.

Someone touched her arm. Natalie turned her head and found herself standing face-to-face with one of the handsome cops from the gas station. The man was staring at her; his lips were moving slowly but the cacophony of hammering, banging, and shouting made it impossible to hear what he said. Natalie's heart skipped a beat. She felt Cassandra tuck herself and Tindra behind her back.

"What?" she yelled. Trying to win a bit of time. The cop was standing in front of them now, blocking their way. His colleague was standing on the next step down. For a moment she considered turning and pushing Cassandra and Tindra back up the stairs again, but there were already two cops up there. They were stuck, caught in a trap.

The noise from the attic turned into something resembling a scream. Then suddenly there was silence up there. The handsome cop's lips suddenly formed audible words.

"Follow me!" he shouted. "I'll help get you out." He gesticulated to his partner to proceed upstairs.

Natalie nodded, glanced quickly over her shoulder at Cassandra, and set off after the man's broad shoulders. He efficiently forged a path through the agitated crowd milling about in the stairwell, enabling them to get through. First Natalie with the backpack, then Cassandra with Tindra in her arms.

They reached the foot of the stairs and forced their way out through the front door, out into the fresh air. Another group of firemen was waiting out there, concentrating on their comms radio.

The handsome cop turned to Natalie. He barely looked at Cassandra and Tindra.

"Where's your ambulance?"

"Around the corner." Natalie gestured with her free hand.

"Is it far? I can carry the girl if you like."

"Don't worry, we'll be fine." Natalie took a quick step to place herself between the cop and Cassandra. For a brief moment the cop seemed to be wise to them. His eyes narrowed slightly.

"Thanks for your help." Natalie forced a smile. "We need to get this little one away from here."

She pulled Cassandra and Tindra with her toward the corner of the building. The cop's eyes burned into their backs.

"Don't look back," Natalie hissed through her teeth, as much to herself as to Cassandra. "Just keep walking."

Just as they turned the corner, she heard one of the firemen's comms radios crackle at top volume. "They've found a smoke flare up in the attic."

Natalie shoved Cassandra in the back. "Run," she said. "Run!"

Thirty-Four

It was hot inside the little smoke shop. The air was almost still and the feeble fan the owner had set up on the counter wasn't doing much to improve things.

"Sorry." The man on the other side of the counter shrugged.

"What do you mean, 'Sorry'?" Atif said.

"The passports aren't ready. The printer broke and I had to order some replacement parts. Won't get them until Monday. You know, 3-D printers are complicated things."

"And you're telling me this now?"

The man shrugged once more. The rings of sweat under his arms were well on their way to conquering the chest of his stained shirt.

"You didn't leave a number the last time you were here. I tried calling Zio Erdun but all I got was his idiot grandson. I thought you'd rather I didn't leave a message with him. The new passports are difficult. Far more security features. They take much more work. But, believe me, you'll thank me when you're standing there at customs."

Atif tried to control his anger. Without the passports, their whole plan fell apart. There were other ways of getting across Europe and off to the east. If he'd been on his own he probably would have dared to attempt such a road trip, but now he had Cassandra and Tindra to think about. Getting fake passports—good ones that couldn't really be differentiated from the real thing—and flying across the continent was still the best option, no question. But the risk was greater now. They'd have to stay in Stockholm while every cop and something like half the criminals in the city were trying to find them. Hundreds of eyes searching for them. He clenched his fists, then opened them slowly. He fought an urge to wipe the grin off the shrugging fool on the other side of the counter.

• • •

Natalie opened the back door of the VW Golf. She helped Tindra and Cassandra into the backseat before dumping the backpack in the trunk. Only when she got in the driver's seat did she realize that her shirt was soaked with sweat.

"There are water bottles in the pockets in the doors," she gasped, but got no answer.

She looked quickly in the rearview mirror. There were no cops running after them.

She turned the engine on, put the car in first gear, and pulled away from the little courtyard. Resisted the temptation to put her foot down.

"Keep your heads down," she said to the pair in the back. "The sunshades cover the side windows, but you're still visible through the windshield.

They reached the main road and were approaching the place where one of the cop cars was usually parked. Natalie looked around. Cassandra was lying down in the backseat with her arms around Tindra.

The unmarked car, a blue Passat, was still there, unfortunately. She had hoped that all the cops would drop what they were doing and head to the apartment. But clearly one of them had been smart enough to hold back. She tried to keep her eyes fixed firmly ahead, but it was almost impossible not to glance at the Passat as she drove past.

There were two people sitting in it; both of them seemed to be looking at her car. One of them was holding a microphone to his mouth. Just as she passed she saw the unmarked car's headlights switch on.

Shit!

She looked in the rearview mirror and saw the police car lurch into motion. Natalie changed to a lower gear and put her foot down. But her car didn't stand a chance. The Passat was gaining on them fast as blue lights started to flash at the front of the car. Embarking on a car chase in a battered old Golf with a child on board was hardly an option. Better to just give up.

She indicated left and slowed down. But instead of following suit, the Passat pulled out into the other lane and continued to accelerate. It swept past so fast that Natalie hardly had time to react before it was way ahead of her. Astonished, she started to speed up again. She saw the Passat's brake lights go on, then the driver performed a sharp left turn and disappeared from view along a narrow cycling path.

She accelerated and made her way onto the motorway. She slipped in among the rest of the traffic and headed back toward the city. One kilometer or so farther on, a whole row of police cars with flashing blue lights and sirens came toward them. None of them made any attempt to slow down or turn around.

Relief washed over her, then turned to delight. *We're going to make it! We're fucking well going to make it!*

After another kilometer or so she turned around.

"You can sit up. We're safe now."

       • • •

When Atif opened the door for them, Natalie realized at once that something was wrong. She saw the somber look in his eyes before they filled with joy at seeing his little niece again. Even so, she couldn't stifle her surprise when he told her what had happened.

"What do you mean, 'no passports'?"

She could hear how stupid she sounded. What exactly hadn't she understood in what he'd said?

"So we can't fly out tonight? Is that what you're saying?"

Great. One more obvious statement of fact and she'd have a

hat trick. She pressed her lips together and tried to synchronize her thoughts and speech. This couldn't be happening!

Atif squirmed. Tindra had her arms wrapped tightly around his neck. She hadn't let go of him since they got inside Natalie's apartment. In spite of the seriousness of the situation, he looked as if all he wanted to do was sit there with a silly grin on his face.

"We'll just have to lie low for a few days before we can leave," he said. "It doesn't really change anything."

"What are you talking about? For fuck's sake, it changes everything!"

Tindra looked up from Atif's arms.

"You're not allowed to swear," she said. "Mommy said."

Natalie opened her mouth to explain that she'd swear as much as she fucking wanted, that this was her fucking home and that Tindra's mommy was too busy smoking her fucking cigarettes under Natalie's fucking fan in the kitchen to bother about anyone's language. But she stopped herself at the last moment.

"You're quite right, Tindra," she said instead. "I promise to do better."

Natalie glared at Atif. Tried to gather her thoughts.

"How long?"

"Monday, the guy thought."

Natalie thought about Wallin's visit. What would happen if he showed up again? That wasn't out of the question, given how crazy he'd seemed. What if he caught sight of Cassandra or Tindra? He wouldn't even have to break into a sweat to get his revenge.

She looked at Atif and the little girl, who were still hugging on the sofa. She heard Cassandra poking about in the kitchen. The kitchen fan was weak and the smell of smoke was already invading the living room. A cigarette would have been great just then, would have helped calm her down.

According to their original plan, they should have been

halfway to Arlanda by now, all four of them. And by lunchtime tomorrow she'd have had her money. Cash in hand, just as she'd been promised. Free to go wherever she wanted. Make a fresh start, far away from Sweden, far from the parents who barely spoke to her, and, not least, far from Oscar fucking Wallin.

The thought of being shut inside an apartment that reeked of smoke at the height of summer with three wanted individuals for the duration of a holiday weekend while Wallin lurked around the corner wasn't exactly appealing. She needed to rethink things, come up with a different plan. Preferably straightaway.

"You can't stay here."

"Why not?" Atif said.

"Too big a risk. I'll see if I can come up with something else," she added, before he had time to protest.

Thirty-Five

Stenberg drank a mouthful of chamomile tea. The fog outside the kitchen window was easing as the morning sun rose steadily higher. The birds out in the garden were already in full swing with their morning serenade, even though it wasn't yet six o'clock. He couldn't claim to be quite as awake.

He thought he'd sleep better now that John Thorning was no longer disturbing his thoughts. That the nightmares about Sophie would disappear again now that no one was reminding him about her. And for the first few nights he did sleep better. But after the memorial service, Wallin's comments, and that meal at the Grand, the dreams were back. Sophie was still tormenting him, waking him in the middle of the night.

But the dream was slightly different. Instead of putting the car in reverse and driving back into the garage with Sophie's dead body on the hood, he gets out of the car. Looks up at the building and the open window up above. Thinks he sees the silhouette of a wiry little man leaning out. The man's unnaturally blue eyes meet his, and he nods faintly at him, as if there is an understanding between them.

A necessary sacrifice.
It was her or you.
You had no choice.
We had no choice . . .

When he turns around and looks in the car, past Sophie's shattered body, he sees John Thorning sitting in the backseat. Staring at him accusingly.

Then he woke up. Had to lie there quietly listening to Karolina's calm breathing while his thoughts formed a swirling maelstrom, dragging him deeper and deeper.

Was Wallin right? Had someone gotten John Thorning out of the way? If so, there was only one suspect.

Former soldier and loyal underling Nisse Boman. What was it he had said about the Cedergren family? That he owed them everything—that they had chosen to ignore his little peculiarities. Could one of those peculiarities be that he was capable of murder? Killing a man in a way that couldn't be detected? Or maybe even pushing a young woman out of a window?

Up until the memorial service Stenberg had never thought of Sophie's death as anything but suicide. But Oscar Wallin had ignited his paranoia. And now he couldn't get it back under control, even though he kept repeating the same mantra: *There's no evidence at all to suggest anyone else was involved in either Sophie's or John's death.* Their deaths were two separate, very tragic events that had nothing to do with him. He needed to put the past behind him. Focus on the future instead: onward and upward.

Prime Minister Jesper Stenberg.

He drank some more tea and looked out at the garden. The fog was almost completely gone now, and the sun was shining in a clear blue sky.

"No evidence at all," he muttered to himself.

• • •

Wallin gestured to Julia to sit down beside him on the green bench. "I heard Regional Crime had a busy day of it yesterday."

She sat down and crossed her legs. The tall trees in the little park in front of Rosenbad, together with the cool breeze blowing off Riddarfjärden, offered just enough relief from the summer heat. Wallin held out a bag of cherries to her but she shook her head.

"Six detectives watching the apartment, but Kassab's sister-in-law and niece still manage to disappear. Not the force's finest hour." He popped a cherry in his mouth.

"They had help from outside," Julia said. "Probably a woman dressed as a paramedic. We're trying to find a potential suspect among Kassab's acquaintances."

"Description?"

"Average height, a little on the heavy side. Red hair, possibly, but that's slightly unclear."

"Is that all you've got? In that case Kollander's probably clearing his desk already. Abu Hamsa, Gilsén, Kassab's escape, and now this."

He smiled and spat the stone out. Julia followed it with her eyes as it bounced over the pavement. She felt practically cross-eyed. She must have passed the overtime limit a good while back. All she really wanted to do was go home and get a couple of hours' sleep before carrying on with her and Amante's investigation. But Wallin had suggested meeting, and she hadn't been able to say no.

"I'm actually more surprised that the details of Kassab's escape haven't leaked to the press. Pärson doesn't usually neglect an opportunity to replenish the coffers," Wallin continued.

"He wouldn't dare leak it. Not right now, anyway."

"No?" Wallin raised one eyebrow.

Julia shook her head. "Pärson himself was involved in questioning Kassab. Amante reported to him, not Kollander. And if heads start to roll . . ." She ran one hand across her throat.

"I see. Say what you like about Pärson, but at least he's not stupid."

Wallin shook the bag and then looked down, evidently searching for a particularly juicy cherry.

"Before we talk about Sarac, I've actually got a bit of information that I think could be helpful in the Abu Hamsa case. But it's strictly confidential. You mustn't let anyone know who you heard it from, is that clear?"

"Of course." Julia leaned closer.

"It just so happens that I knew Abu Hamsa fairly well. You could say that we had dealings with each other."

"You mean he was one of your informants?"

"Well . . ." Wallin smiled. "I never name my sources, but you could say that we had a mutually beneficial relationship."

He picked another cherry from the bag and held it up to the light to inspect it.

"The murder was arranged by Abu Hamsa's daughter, Susanna, and her husband, Eldar Jafarov. They did it to save themselves when Abu Hamsa's deal with Gilsén was uncovered. Abu Hamsa and Gilsén had to die, and the money would be repaid to the defrauded gangsters. And in return Susanna and Eldar would be allowed to keep both their lives and control of Hamsa's businesses. A purely commercial agreement. The only problem was that Kassab got in the way. Now Susanna and Eldar are in the shit. They need to get hold of Kassab—and Gilsén's money—to fulfill their part of the bargain. Otherwise they'll end up going the same way as Abu Hamsa. Keep an eye on Eldar and Susanna and eventually you'll find Kassab. If he and his family haven't already left the country, of course."

He held the bag out once more.

"Nothing comes close to Swedish cherries. Are you sure you don't want one?"

Julia shook her head and tried to take in what Wallin had just said. She needed to tell Pärson about this right away. Make it sound like it came from her own sources—which, in the strictest sense, was absolutely true. Then she had to get him to suggest and decide to authorize surveillance of Susanna and Eldar. That idea couldn't come from her, not the way things stood at the moment, because he'd only reject it. But if Wallin's tip-off turned out to be correct, Pärson would have no choice but to bring her back into the fold. An apprehended cop killer would trump any toes she was supposed to have stepped on.

"How's your private detective work going, anyway? Are you any closer to solving the mystery?"

She put aside all thoughts of Pärson and gave Wallin the short version of what they'd found out. The abandoned office, the laptop, her phone call with Frank Hunter.

"Hunter and Sarac swapped identities and secrets?" Wallin sucked a cherry stone thoughtfully. "That explains a few things. But you still don't know what was in the e-mail Sarac sent."

"No. Except that it was sent to someone who wasn't happy to be issued with an ultimatum."

"No, evidently not." Wallin spat the stone out. Then he methodically folded the paper bag into a little parcel. "I share your conviction that Pärson should be kept out of this for the foreseeable future. You need to go straight to Kollander. But obviously you need hard evidence before you do that."

"We've got Hunter's testimony," Julia said tentatively. She already knew what the response would be.

Wallin shook his head. "You know as well as I do that all you've actually got is a short telephone conversation with an unidentified man who you think might be the individual who helped Sarac to escape. A man who can no longer be contacted and whose identity is probably fake."

He looked at her for agreement. Reluctantly, Julia had to admit he was right. She had been hoping that the case would open up—that something would appear and move things along. But days had passed and Pärson had kept her fully occupied. Now over a week had passed since her conversation with Hunter, and they hadn't made any more progress. In fact, it had been several days since she last spoke to Amante, which was almost enough to make her feel guilty.

"You'll have to soldier on for a bit longer," Wallin said. "Get ahold of some evidence that can't be called into question. As soon as you've got it, call me. Okay?"

"Okay."

Wallin tapped the folded bag against his thigh a couple of times.

"There's one other thing that's been bothering me slightly."

"Just one?" Julia couldn't help smiling, but Wallin didn't respond.

"Amante," he said, and her smile quickly faded.

"What do you mean?"

"I've done a bit of discreet research among some old colleagues of mine in The Hague and eventually managed to find out what happened. It wasn't easy: someone's tried to put a very tight lid on it, and for good reason. Did you know that Amante set fire to his office down on Lampedusa?"

Julia swallowed. "No."

"His wife left him for a close friend of theirs. Apparently she and the friend had been having an affair while Amante was down in the Mediterranean. When he found out, he lost it completely. He set fire to his room and tried to commit suicide by hanging himself with his belt. But a couple of his colleagues saved him. His stepfather sent him to an expensive clinic in the Alps. He pretty much came straight from there to the Violent Crime Unit."

Julia didn't know what to say. She could see Amante's face in front of her. The miserable look in his eyes, his pathetically empty apartment. His tone of voice when he spoke of what had happened on Lampedusa.

"So his appointment to the unit was simply because his stepfather wanted to keep him occupied? No hidden agenda?"

Wallin pulled a face that was hard to interpret. "Right now I'm not sure I'd rule anything out. Amante has undoubtedly shown himself to be pretty useful. Without him you wouldn't have got this far, would you?"

"No," Julia said, then realized that it was completely true.

"My suggestion is that you keep working together. At least for the time being." Wallin stood up, looked at the time, and then up toward Rosenbad. "But I'd advise you to be careful. In my experience, people like Amante usually go to pieces completely, sooner or later."

Wallin smiled at her, and for a moment looked almost human.

"I'd think it would be a great shame if he dragged you down with him, Julia."

• • •

When Oscar Wallin got back to his office, he put down the cup of coffee he had picked up on the way, opened the GPS website, and logged in. A large map of Stockholm opened on the screen. There were a number of thin red lines across it that flashed up time and date symbols when he moved the cursor over them. A little red dot indicated where Natalie's car was at that moment.

He'd already compared the car's movements with the locations of the cash machines and, to his disappointment, hadn't found any conclusive matches. He had hoped she had more credit cards in his mother's name that she would continue to use. Give him some firm evidence to hand over to the Fraud Unit. So far he hadn't been as lucky as that. But the thought that he knew where she was, that he had her under observation, was still strangely satisfying.

He sipped the coffee and clicked at random over Natalie's tracks. The previous day she had been out in the western suburbs but hadn't been anywhere near an ATM dispenser. He moved the cursor again and the name of a street appeared in a little box. Grimstagatan.

It took him a second or two to remember where he had heard that name before, but when he did he almost choked on his coffee. Of course. A woman dressed as a paramedic had helped Kassab's family to escape. Average height, rather heavily built, possibly red hair. It was too good to be a coincidence.

He quickly pulled up the report of Kassab's disappearance. The bridge where the prison van had gone through the railings was only a kilometer or so from Natalie's apartment. The trail of blood had led in that direction, and Kassab had needed someone to patch him up. Someone who had done it before . . .

Bloody hell!

Wallin pushed his chair back, put his feet up on his desk, and folded his hands behind his head. Natalie hadn't been alone in her apartment the other day, but the company she had been keeping was almost too good to be true. All he had to do was pick up the phone and then his mother's worries—and those of Regional Crime, perhaps even the national police chief too—would be over. The question was: How did that benefit him?

He looked at the red dot again. Saw it start to move across the screen.

"Where are you off to now, Natalie?" he whispered to himself. "And who have you got in the car with you?"

• • •

Natalie turned into the narrow unpaved road and drove down it for five hundred meters or so until it ended in an improvised parking lot between some trees. She parked the car and let Atif out of the backseat. She led the way down the path toward the cabin. The sun was high in the sky, the birds were singing, and the only sign of human activity was the distant sound of a motorized lawn mower.

"Not bad, eh?" She opened a window to let out the stale air inside the main room. She took the chance to quietly brush some dead flies from the windowsill.

Atif remained silent, just stretched and massaged his neck. The drive had taken ten minutes, which was at least eight too many for his long frame to be bent double in the backseat of a Golf.

"'Be prepared.'" He pointed at the large plank of wood above the stove into which someone had carefully burned the Scouts' motto, flanked by two fleurs-de-lis.

"Exactly. I was at a party here a few years ago. You just have

275

to call a guy and book it. The nearest house is a couple of hundred meters away, on the other side of the trees. Not overlooked by anyone, no nosy neighbors, and plenty of space for Tindra to run around."

She pointed at the water glittering beyond the pine trees.

"I seem to remember that there's a little jetty down by the lake if you feel like taking her for an evening swim."

She smiled. The girl was the best way to get at Atif; she'd figured that out the moment she saw them together. His normally stony face softened in a way she rather liked. His body language and voice got softer too.

Cassandra had made the same observation. Her first meeting with Atif had been frosty in the beginning, but as Atif warmed up, so did Cassandra. She had even sat down on the sofa with him and Tindra. For a while they looked like a proper family, and for some reason that bothered Natalie more than the smell of smoke Cassandra spread through the apartment. Another reason to get them out of there as quickly as possible.

"So, what do you say? I can go and get some food, then call home and pick the girls up. You spend the weekend lying low here, I pick up the passports on Monday, then we're back on track."

Atif walked around the house and peered out through the little leaded windows, one after the other. He grunted something she didn't catch. But she decided to interpret it as a yes. Three days, she told herself. Then it would all be over.

Thirty-Six

Julia parked behind the run-down office building, in the same place as when she and Amante were there together. She had picked the keys up from him but made it very clear that she wanted to be alone in Hunter's hideout this time. The main reason was that she needed to concentrate, to shut out all distractions, and right now that was what Amante was, especially after what Wallin had told her the day before.

Inside the neglected premises everything looked exactly the way it had when she and Amante had first found it. The sleeping bag and camping mat on the floor, the table and chairs in the middle of the room. The only thing missing was the laptop. Both Hunter and Sarac had stayed there at different times. That explained why she had had trouble detecting a rhythm before. There were two of them overlapping, and neither of them was particularly obvious, seeing as both men had regarded this place as a temporary hideout.

She pulled out one of the rib-backed chairs and sat down gently. Pärson seemed to have believed the information she gave him about Abu Hamsa's murder. He had gone off to see Kollander about putting together a surveillance team, just as she had hoped. But he hadn't included her in the operation, not that she had been expecting him to. He had at least been good enough to let her have Saturday off, though.

And she had nothing better to do than come out here. Amante had said he'd conducted a thorough search of the room. This wasn't a crime scene, and there was no external memory device containing the picture they were looking for.

So, what was she really hoping to find? Peace of mind, perhaps? Sarac wasn't just anyone. He was a colleague, a famous police officer, but also someone who had sacrificed everything in the hunt for what he thought was justice.

Someone had stripped Sarac of everything he possessed, even his humanity, and she was determined to look under every stone, follow the tiniest clue, until she found the culprit. But the truth was that they were stuck. This was all that remained.

She stood up, switched the light off, and lowered the blinds. As she did so, she glanced out at the big parking lot, where grass was already poking through cracks in the asphalt. Everything seemed quiet outside.

She crouched down in the gloom and lit her flashlight. Shone its beam over the floor.

There were plenty of footsteps in the dust, most of them around the table and chairs in the middle of the room and over by the mattress. Two clear tracks heading to the toilet, the little kitchen, and the front door, but no individual prints.

If she closed her eyes she imagined she could almost see Hunter moving around in there. To start with, mostly shuffling between the mattress, toilet, and kitchen. Then, as his injured leg healed, moving more smoothly. Daring to go out to buy food. And then a laptop. Then he was gone long enough to recruit Eskil at the nursing home. But she was after Sarac, not Hunter. She needed to find his rhythm.

Julia squeezed her eyes shut a bit more, so she could just see the outline of the room. The table where he had sat in front of the computer, the kitchen cupboard where he left his sleeping pills. She shut her eyes completely, tried to think.

If Sarac was really planning to kill himself, why had he left the pills in the cupboard?

Because he no longer needed them.

Sarac left the room to do something where he was expecting to be killed. Perhaps that was even part of his plan—one last sacrifice to make the killer step out of the shadows.

She summoned up the image of Sarac's body again. His grinning skull. And suddenly she imagined she could hear a faint sound. A thin, emaciated Sarac knocking tentatively on a door. Hunter opening it. Then Sarac sitting on one of the chairs, listening carefully as Hunter reveals his secret. Then it's his turn. The camera on the tripod is rolling, Sarac stares into its lens. His mouth moves. Weak yet still very focused, he says what Hunter wants to hear.

Your secret in exchange for mine.

The next sequence in her head shows Sarac alone at the little table. Hunter has gone, Sarac has moved in, is using Hunter's computer, his sleeping bag. Looking at the picture or pictures Hunter has given him as he toys with the bag of sleeping pills. She sees him sitting at the table, typing on the computer. Pressing "send" . . .

You betrayed me. Pay your debt.

Julia kept her eyes tightly shut for a few seconds more. Then she opened them and was back to reality.

Sarac would have kept a digital backup. A cloud account or something like that. But so far the IT guy hadn't found any trace of one on the laptop. She'd begun to doubt that Sarac would rely on digital storage. The more time she spent in that spartan room, the more convinced she became that what she was looking for was there after all. That Sarac had left something else behind besides the sleeping pills.

She got to her feet and went over to the little kitchen. Pulled out the top drawer. She found some mismatched cutlery and cooking utensils.

She stood still for a few moments staring down into the drawer. On top of the cutlery there was an old potato peeler. The garbage bag had contained packaging from noodles, but she hadn't seen any trace of potatoes. But the peeler was on top in the drawer. She shone her flashlight at it.

There was a trace of fine white powder at the end of the curved blade. She frowned and ran her finger over it. It left a

279

small streak of white powder on her fingertip. She rubbed her thumb against her finger. Lifted them to her nose.

Plaster?

Her heart started to beat faster. She tried the nearest plaster wall. Pushed in the tip of the potato peeler and twisted it. The plaster was old and porous, and as she twisted the peeler, a small plug appeared in the middle of the curved blade. The hole it had covered was no bigger than her little finger, and it was almost impossible to see the opening if you didn't know exactly where to look.

She looked around. Four walls, a finite number of square meters to search. But she knew from experience that people usually hid things as far from the door as possible. So she started in the far corner. She found the little round mark just above the baseboard after no more than a couple of minutes looking.

Her hand was shaking slightly as she inserted the potato peeler, but the plaster plug came out without resistance. She bent over and shone her flashlight in the hole. She could see something flat and blue in there. It took her a couple of tries before she managed to remove the object. A tiny memory card, no bigger than the nail of her little finger.

· · ·

The penultimate trip to the Scout cabin. At least, that's what Natalie hoped. It would all be over the day after tomorrow. She would dump the Golf in the extended-stay parking lot at Arlanda Airport and throw the parking ticket away without a backward glance. The apartment and her secondhand Ikea furniture were the landlord's problem. She hadn't decided if she was going to send her parents a postcard once she was settled or if she simply wouldn't bother. Disappoint them one last time.

She had bought some candy and a comic book for Tindra while she was getting the rest of the shopping. She liked the girl; she reminded Natalie a bit of herself at that age. Plucky, inquisitive, a bit precocious. Not without a sense of humor. She had already known what she wanted to be. A doctor, just like Daddy had been in the old country. But things had turned out very differently. So now she'd given up. Her fate was in her own hands, and she was creating her own future.

She parked the car outside the cottage, unloaded the bags, and went around the corner. Cassandra was sitting on the bench outside the door, smoking. She nodded as Natalie approached.

"Have a seat." Cassandra gestured toward the bench. "Cigarette?"

Natalie shook her head. "I've given up, but thanks anyway."

She still hadn't gotten used to Cassandra's new hairstyle and color. She must have cut off at least half of her blonde hair before dying it. Cassandra seemed to know what she was looking at.

"You told me to try to look more common. So I tried to go for the same look as you."

Natalie raised her eyebrows and tried to think of a suitably cutting retort. But Cassandra realized her mistake.

"Okay, I didn't mean it like that . . . You've helped us so much, me and Tindra. I really do appreciate it. Please forgive me. I can be such a fucking bitch."

Cassandra smiled warily. The hard expression on her face softened briefly.

"After Adnan died I was forced to do things so we could survive. And things didn't exactly improve when Atif was sent to prison. But you keep going. Play tough." She stubbed the cigarette out in the flower bed. "Am I forgiven?"

Natalie nodded. They sat in silence for a few moments. A group of magpies flapping about in the trees on the other side of the clearing caught their attention.

"Magpies . . ." Cassandra said.

"What?"

"Nothing. Just an old nursery rhyme my grandmother used to tell me. 'One for sorrow, two for mirth. Three for a wedding, four for . . .'"

She stopped.

"Four for what?" Natalie asked. "What do four magpies mean?"

Cassandra hesitated before replying.

"Death."

One of the magpies let out a chattering call. The eerie sound echoed between the treetops.

Natalie stood up. "Where's Atif?"

"He's down by the lake with Tindra, swimming. I was thinking of joining them in a bit. Do you want to come? It would make Tindra happy; she likes you."

Natalie shook her head again. Even if there didn't seem to be any ulterior motive behind Cassandra's offer, she had no desire to show off her love handles alongside Cassandra's gym-trained figure and plastic tits.

"Time of the month," she lied, aware that that would stop any attempt to persuade her.

"Ah. But you'll come along anyway? Atif wants to talk to you about tomorrow."

• • •

Atif was sitting on the jetty when they got to the lake. Tindra was racing in and out of the water and was evidently getting him to score her different jumps.

"What about that one, Amu? What score does that one get?"

"An eight."

"An eight? But you gave the last one a nine!"

"Okay, nine, then." He nodded to Natalie as she and Cassandra sat down beside him.

"Is everything set for Monday?"

"Yes, I'll phone tomorrow and double-check that the passports will be ready. If I get the green light, I'll pick them up in the afternoon and then come and get you. The plane takes off at nine o'clock. And we've got rooms booked at a hotel at the airport in Zürich."

"Good," Atif said. "What about the bank?"

"I've made an appointment to see someone on Tuesday, as soon as they open. We should be done by lunchtime at the latest. Your plane leaves at eight o'clock that evening. You'll be in Abu Dhabi early the next morning."

Atif nodded slowly.

"How about you? Where are you going to go?"

"Haven't decided yet." She shrugged and wondered why she was lying. Thailand—that was the plan. Buy a bar in Pattaya, somewhere like that. But suddenly the idea didn't feel quite so appealing anymore.

She looked out across the small lake. The sun was going down as a couple of dragonflies danced across the surface.

Tindra clambered up the steps. She focused for a few moments, then jumped again. Feetfirst, with her hands flapping in the air. For an instant the girl hung in the air like the dragonflies. Hovering between the evening sky and the surface of the water. Then gravity caught up with her and pulled her down into the dark water. One second, two. Then the little head surfaced.

"What about that one, Amu? What score?"

"A ten," Natalie said before anyone else had time to say anything.

• • •

Julia stuck the memory card in the socket, then waited as the cursor turned into a little hourglass. For a moment she worried that it wasn't going to work, that the memory card was protected by a password, or that the reader she had bought from the Elgiganten store minutes before it closed wasn't the right one. But then a new window opened. Three small, unnamed JPEG files. She clicked the first one.

The picture filled the screen and made her gasp for breath. A naked woman's body lying facedown across the hood and windshield of a car. The metal had buckled and the window had shattered, showering the inside of the car with glass.

The next picture was taken from the side. The woman's injuries were visible: crushed white skin, shattered eyeballs.

Julia knew exactly who the woman was. She'd seen the pictures when she was going through the case last winter. Sophie Thorning, moments after she jumped from the window of her penthouse apartment. The same apartment she herself had searched as a favor for Wallin.

But why had Hunter given Sarac pictures of Sophie's body? Okay, so the two pictures made for uncomfortable viewing, but there had to be fifty similar photographs in police records. Sophie Thorning had jumped and was found by a guy delivering newspapers as she lay dead on the hood of a dark-colored Volvo. End of story.

So why had Sarac been murdered? Whose secret had cost him his life?

She opened the third picture. The same angle as the first, Sophie's dead body on the hood, but this time taken from a greater distance. Disappointed, she looked at the picture for a few seconds without seeing anything that she hadn't already seen in the other photographs. She tried to concentrate on one detail at a time. The body, the blood, the car.

And then she suddenly noticed what it was that wasn't right. *Fuck!*

Thirty-Seven

Atif lay quietly listening to the small breaths from the bunk below his.

If he ignored the drama that had preceded them, the past two days had been among the best of his life. He and Tindra had played croquet out on the grass and gone swimming several times each day, and in the evenings the little girl curled up on his lap and wanted him to read her favorite story, the one about the princess who vanquished the dragon and rescued the prince. And when the story was over, he and no one else got to put her to bed in the bunk bed she had decided they should share.

Sometimes, mainly when she didn't want to do as she was told, Tindra was so like her father that it made Atif's heart ache. The same dark look in her eyes, the same stubborn expression, the same ability to somehow manipulate her way to a tiny victory before giving in. But Tindra also resembled her mother. She had her hair, her cheekbones. Cassandra was a beautiful woman when she let her guard slip. She was still angry with him, blamed him for everything that had happened—which wasn't altogether fair, given that she had been Abu Hamsa's mistress. But, for the sake of domestic harmony, Atif was prepared to shoulder the blame.

Cassandra had done what she had to in order to protect her family, just as he had. She was already starting to thaw, especially when she saw him together with Tindra.

He carefully changed position and looked over the side of the bed. Tindra was lying curled up with her teddy bear close to her cheek. Her blonde hair was draped across her pillow. He loved her so much, it actually hurt.

In just over twenty-four hours they'd have their passports and would be on their way. On their way to a place where none of them would have to be scared anymore. A place where they'd be safe.

· · ·

Oscar Wallin studied the little red dot on the GPS map, as he had done in practically every spare moment in recent days. Natalie's car was currently stationary a block or so from her apartment, in the same place it had been parked since late yesterday evening. It was only just after nine o'clock, so at a guess Natalie was spending her Sunday morning in bed. She had mostly been shuttling between her home and one and the same address, with just one detour to a supermarket.

He had looked up the address on Google Earth. It was a Scout cabin in the southern suburbs, fairly remote. The perfect place for an escaped killer and his family to hide.

Wallin was actually rather surprised that they hadn't already fled, hadn't left the country as soon as Natalie got them out of Cassandra Nygren's apartment. But there could be any number of reasons why they were still there. It certainly made the whole thing considerably more interesting for him.

He still hadn't told his colleagues where to find their escaped convict. Naturally, he would be happy to see Natalie behind bars, but the longer Kassab was on the run, the worse things were getting for Kollander and, by extension, the national police chief. That bitch Swensk was more than welcome to sweat a bit longer. So he was biding his time, watching the red dot on the map. Enjoying the feeling of complete control.

· · ·

Julia Gabrielsson was having trouble hiding her eagerness.

"Do you see what's wrong?"

"You mean apart from the fact that the pictures depict a woman's shattered body?" Amante turned pale and looked away from the five photographs Julia had spread out on the kitchen island.

He really didn't look well: his robe was threadbare and the smell from his vest suggested that he probably hadn't showered for a while. Perhaps she shouldn't drag him into this, but after careful consideration she had realized that she couldn't go to Wallin without talking to Amante first. She owed him that much.

"No, I can't."

"Look again!" Julia pointed at the photographs. "Four of the pictures are from the police investigation. The fifth is from Sarac's memory card."

Amante shut his eyes for a few seconds and seemed to pull himself together. Then he looked at the pictures again, longer this time.

"The body's lying slightly differently in this one." He pointed to one of the pictures. "One arm is a bit higher up the windshield, at a different angle."

"Good. Ignore the body for a bit and concentrate on what's around it."

Amante did as she said, then suddenly stiffened.

"It's not the same car," he said. "That's a BMW. Very similar, but it's not the same car as the one in the other pictures."

Julia mimed applause. "Bravo! If you look through a magnifying glass, you can also see that the car's parked on concrete rather than asphalt. In a garage, not on the street."

"But what does it mean?"

"To begin at the beginning, Detective Superintendent Oscar Wallin asked me to have a look at this particular case. It was last winter, toward the end of November. A young woman, Sophie Thorning, had jumped from her window and landed on a car twenty meters below. She had a history of mental illness, and Sophie's stomach was full of whiskey and psychoactive

287

drugs. But her father evidently wasn't happy with the investigation. And because John Thorning was both the minister of justice's erstwhile mentor as well as general secretary of the Bar Association, they humored him. I looked through the case and discovered a few little things that didn't seem to make sense."

"Such as?"

"It looked like someone had cleaned Sophie's apartment very recently: the sheets and towels had been changed but the old ones couldn't be found, that sort of thing. I got the feeling someone had been there either just before or maybe even as Sophie jumped, and that the presence of this person had been carefully wiped away. I found a fragment of glass with some blood on it. I hoped that might lead somewhere, but it turned out to be Sophie's own blood, so that was as far as I got."

"Nothing else unusual?"

"No. I went through the autopsy report with a fine-tooth comb, but there was nothing but a hell of a lot of cuts and injuries caused by the fall. An unusually large number, in fact. Now that I've seen these pictures, I understand why."

She tapped the photograph of the BMW gently.

"Sophie fell twice. The first time she landed on the wrong car. This car. A car that belonged to a person who shouldn't have been there. So someone moved her."

"Who?"

"Someone who was fast, discreet, and who had no moral objections to doing a thing like this."

"You think it was Frank Hunter?"

Julia nodded. "It must have been. Hunter was a security consultant, so presumably cleaning up someone else's mistake was nothing new for him. He took some before-and-after shots of Sophie and kept them in case they ever became useful."

Amante scratched his stubble.

"And once Sarac had exchanged his secret for Hunter's, he contacted whoever had been driving the car, to make him accountable. He sent him the note and pictures, and then he was

288

murdered." Amante held up the photograph. "The registration number of the BMW is visible. I'm guessing you've already run it through the system."

"The car is leased to Thorning & Partners. John Thorning's law firm."

Amante started. "What, you mean her father was in the apartment? How does that work?"

Julia shook her head.

"I was just as confused as you. But then I called the leasing firm down in Hammarby Harbor. Thorning & Partners leases a total of fifteen executive cars from them. They're all BMWs and they get changed every other year. This particular one is last year's model, so it's still in use. It's currently being driven by the company's head of finance, but at the time of Sophie Thorning's death it was being used by one of the firm's other employees."

She paused and took a deep breath.

"Who?" Amante said. "Who was driving the car?"

"Jesper Stenberg. Sweden's minister of justice and our ultimate boss."

Thirty-Eight

"Fantastic that you could come at such short notice." Stenberg's father-in-law squeezed his hand and gestured toward the interior of the restaurant. "We'll sit inside where we can talk in peace and quiet."

Karl-Erik had called him in person just an hour or so ago. Had asked for an urgent meeting, said it was important. And even if Stenberg had considered saying no, mostly to point out that he wasn't at his father-in-law's beck and call, there was something in Karl-Erik's tone that made him ask his secretary to rearrange his schedule. Now he was even more curious. A lunch meeting at short notice at a ridiculously expensive restaurant on a Monday definitely wasn't his father-in-law's usual style.

Karl-Erik turned to Boman, who, as usual, was standing just a meter or two behind him.

"Nisse, take care of the gentlemen from the Security Police. Make sure they get something to eat, will you?"

"Of course. Good morning, Jesper, nice to see you looking a bit brighter." Boman winked at him in passing. Stenberg ignored him.

Karl-Erik opened the double doors leading to a private dining room. Another of Karl-Erik's little *chambres séparées*.

Inside, Karolina was already waiting at the table. Stenberg was brought up short, but recovered quickly and leaned over to kiss his wife. He was expecting her to turn her cheek to protect her lipstick, but to his surprise she kissed him on the mouth and held her lips there for several seconds. Her eyes were twinkling and she seemed to be in an excellent mood.

"Do you want to tell him or shall I, Daddy?" she said as soon as Stenberg had sat down. "You don't think we should order first? Poor Jesper hasn't even gotten anything to drink."

The waitress appeared, and Stenberg was about to ask for mineral water, but his wife got in ahead of him.

"Champagne," she said. "Don't you think, Daddy?"

Karl-Erik nodded contentedly from the other side of the table.

Stenberg frowned. He was still trying to work out what was going on. The waitress came back with glasses, a bottle, and a bucket of ice.

"It's all done now," his wife said when they all had something to drink in their glasses. "Daddy's just come from a meeting with the prime minister. He's going to appoint you as his official running mate in the election tomorrow evening. You're going to be the party's crown prince."

Karolina flashed her most beautiful smile. Stenberg tried to find the right words. The prime minister and his father-in-law had had a meeting without him. Had decided his future without his involvement. But he had to rise above that humiliation. Tell himself that it was just another little sacrifice on the way to something bigger. Everything he and Karolina had dreamed about was on its way to coming true. He was on his way to the very top. Even so, he felt strangely distant. Cold. As if he were actually staring into an abyss.

"Wonderful," he managed to say.

"Cheers, Jesper!" his father-in-law said. "A toast to you, the party, and the future!"

• • •

Julia pointed toward the little brown sofa that had once stood in her father's study at home. "Sit down!"

Amante sat down obediently. She wasn't used to having visitors, especially not colleagues, even though she lived only a few blocks from Police Headquarters. The apartment on Pontonjär-

291

gatan was her refuge. But he had called her at work a quarter of an hour earlier and had asked to see her at once.

For understandable reasons she couldn't take him up to her office or to any of the restaurants or cafés in the immediate vicinity, especially not at lunchtime. If Pärson found out that she was seeing Amante, and during work time at that, she would doubtless slip a few notches farther down his blacklist.

She really ought to have said no, explained that she didn't have time. Should have said they could meet up after she finished work, whenever that was. But she was far too curious to wait that long. So now he was sitting in her living room, on the sofa that still smelled faintly of the wax her father used to rub into it.

Amante glanced tentatively at the photographs above the television. Her parents' wedding, her father as a young man in full uniform in front of a patrol car, a picture of her when she graduated from the police academy.

He looked a bit brighter today, better than when they had last met. He had showered, put on some fresh clothes, and made an effort to shave, probably with a disposable razor, seeing as he still had a bit of bloody tissue paper stuck to his neck. But the rings under his eyes and the glassy stare were still there. She wondered if he was getting any sleep.

"Coffee?"

He looked as if he needed it. But he shook his head, so she went on:

"What have you found out? Did you find someone in the department who could help?"

"Yes. Here's the minister of justice's diary." Amante put some printouts down on the coffee table. "David Sarac last used his computer on February twenty-eighth, so it's reasonable to assume that he was killed that day, or possibly sometime in the following few days. That fits reasonably well with the length of time the body spent in the water. He sends the document and photograph on the twenty-sixth, and receives an answer via the Inkognite server by the twenty-eighth at the latest. Do we agree on that?"

"Absolutely."

"Jesper Stenberg was away on business from February twenty-third. First a couple of meetings in Brussels, then a trip to his former workplace in The Hague, the International Criminal Court, then, finally, a meeting of EU justice ministers in Paris. He didn't get home until the evening of March third. If we seriously suspected the minister of justice of having murdered Sarac, he appears to have an alibi. Unless Sarac was killed later than we think." Amante paused for a moment. "Just to be clear: Do we really think that the minister of justice might have killed and dismembered someone?"

Julia had thought about that a lot in the past twenty-four hours. She had read all she could find about Stenberg's career and family, plowing through numerous articles and online discussion boards, and had even watched a few clips of him on YouTube.

"No," she said. "I don't think Jesper Stenberg killed Sarac and chopped him up."

"Okay, what do you base that on, apart from his apparent alibi?"

"To start with, I don't think he's capable of it. Like the pathologist said, it takes a particular mentality to do what our perpetrator did to Sarac's body. A will of iron, absolute commitment. Stenberg isn't the type. He's slippery; he's used to talking while other people do the dirty work."

Wallin's face popped into her head. The vein in his temple, his bitter smile. How was he going to react when she told him what she'd found out?

"You mean he commissioned someone?"

"Maybe. Or . . ." She didn't really know how to express what she was thinking without sounding like an idiot. ". . . or perhaps he didn't actually know anything. About the e-mail from Sarac, or the photograph."

Amante looked at her quizzically. "You're going to have to explain that a bit more."

Julia bit her top lip.

"Jesper Stenberg is a highflyer. He did a few years in The Hague, then got a job with a prestigious law firm, Thorning & Partners. He was given a few high-profile cases, became the media's golden boy, and ended up being offered the post of minister of justice. But if you take a closer look at his résumé, it isn't quite as impressive as you might expect. His references from The Hague are okay but not brilliant, and in his big cases for Thorning & Partners, Stenberg was backed up by a whole team of other lawyers. There were actually a couple of critical articles about that specific point when Stenberg was appointed last autumn. Their authors implied that Stenberg's résumé had been tailored toward the job of minister of justice, and that his family connections were more significant than his actual abilities."

"You mean Stenberg's father-in-law was behind it?"

"That's what some people have claimed. Others say that John Thorning was involved too. And now there's a lot of speculation that Stenberg is likely to be appointed chair of his party and therefore quite possibly our next prime minister."

"So how does this tie in with Sarac's murder?" Amante asked. "Apart from the fact that Stenberg has a lot to lose."

She paused again. She knew what she was about to say was going to sound crazy.

"I'm sure you read that article in *Dagens Nyheter* recently—the one criticizing Stenberg's plans for the legal system. I've had a look at the authors of the article, and one of them works for Thorning & Partners. A couple more have close connections to the firm. John Thorning has a reputation for playing rough. I can't imagine that any of those lawyers would have put their names to that article without his approval."

"So, why would John Thorning agree to his protégé being given a public mauling?"

"Good question. The only answer I can come up with is that the two of them had fallen out for some reason. That the article was a warning shot, a little taste of the damage John Thorning could do to Stenberg and his career."

"If Thorning hadn't died, you mean?" Amante looked at her. The same mournful, inscrutable expression as always.

"Well, what I really meant," she said after a brief pause, "is that someone might be protecting Stenberg. Getting rid of anything that could stop him reaching the top. Anything and anyone . . ."

Amante was still staring at her. For a moment she thought he was going to stand up and walk out. And why not? He was suspended and obviously wasn't doing too well. They were investigating a case that was no longer theirs, the murder victim's body was missing, and their main line of inquiry seemed to point at the minister of justice. And she'd just taken the lead in the competition for biggest tinfoil hat in the room. But instead he remained where he was on the sofa.

"A lot at stake . . ." he muttered. "More than we can imagine, just like Hunter said."

He said nothing for a few seconds.

"Let's say I buy your theory. Someone's protecting Stenberg and is prepared to commit murder for his sake. So, how does the chain of events look, from beginning to end?"

Julia took a deep breath and collected her thoughts.

"I've been turning this over in my mind and here's what I think happened. We can prove some of it, but other parts are qualified guesswork, and some of it's sheer speculation."

"Your reservations are hereby noted. Go on, then." Amante winked at her. For a couple of moments he looked almost normal.

"Okay. Stenberg and Sophie Thorning studied law at the same time. They were part of a wider circle that also included Karolina Cedergren, Stenberg's future wife. Stenberg and Karolina eventually get married. Villa in Danderyd, two daughters, dog, all that."

She paused for breath.

"But at some point Stenberg starts having an affair with Sophie Thorning. Probably after he started working at Thorning & Partners, but it could really have been at any time."

"I'm with you so far."

"Sophie's suicide occurred in November of last year, the weekend before the prime minister appointed Jesper Stenberg as minister of justice. Stenberg had probably been offered the post before the weekend, to give him a chance to consider it. Talk it over with family and so on. But as soon as he gets the offer, he realizes that his relationship with Sophie Thorning poses far too great a risk. and he rushes over to see her and put an end to it."

Amante looked thoughtful. "That sounds logical," he said.

"Well, all that is really just guesswork. But listen to the rest."

Julia stood up and started to walk back and forth in the living room.

"During Stenberg's visit, Sophie Thorning kicks up a fuss. She doesn't want to break up and they have an argument. One of the neighbors in the building claimed to have heard raised voices, but because he's halfway to being an alcoholic, his statement was dismissed. Either way, Stenberg leaves the apartment. Sophie Thorning is distraught, and she's far from stable anyway. Do you remember the photograph of the BMW, the surface it was parked on?" She laid the photograph down. Pointed at the pale area visible at the bottom of the picture.

"Yes," Amante said. "Concrete, not asphalt. Probably a garage."

Julia nodded. "I've checked, and there's a large subway garage beneath Sophie's building. The ramp leading up to the street comes out right beneath one of the windows of Sophie's apartment. When Stenberg is leaving, she jumps to her death and lands on the hood of his car."

"Intentionally?" Amante said. "Was she that crazy? Is it even possible to judge a fall that precisely?"

Julia shrugged. "Maybe, maybe not. It doesn't change the

result. Stenberg's mistress, the daughter of his mentor and benefactor, is lying dead on the hood of his car just days before he's due to be named minister of justice. So, once the initial shock dies down, he makes a drastic decision. Instead of calling the police and emergency services, he reverses back down into the garage, tucks the car away in a corner, and calls Frank Hunter."

"How do you think they knew each other?"

"Probably from The Hague. I've checked and, sure enough, Stenberg was working for the ICC at the same time that Hunter was working at the International Criminal Tribunal for the former Yugoslavia. The two courts are based on the same block, and I'm guessing there's a fair bit of interaction. Or else they just met in one of the cafeterias and realized that they were both Swedish. All it takes is an exchange of business cards. A favor done in one direction, a promise to call if you ever need help, no matter what with."

"Sounds a bit tenuous," Amante said, "but not impossible. So Hunter arrives at the scene. He puts Stenberg in a taxi. And then what?"

"First, Hunter hides the body and the car down in the garage. Then he cleans the apartment. Removes anything that could be traced back to Stenberg. Towels, sheets, anything like that. He writes a suicide note on Sophie's iPad and sends it out by e-mail. Then he goes and gets the body. The elevator goes all the way from the garage straight up to the apartment. He drops Sophie from a different window of the apartment, so that she lands on another car. All that remains is to remove Stenberg's battered BMW from the scene and get it repaired and cleaned up. Then golden boy Jesper Stenberg can calmly accept his new job as head of the Swedish judicial system. Not a cloud in the sky, if only Sarac hadn't been obsessed with justice and Hunter needed to swap some information to find out the identity of Sarac's informant. And those two guys deciding to dive after their lost anchor."

"Wow." Amante raised his eyebrows. "Not a bad theory. I'm guessing you've thought of some other possibilities as well."

Julia shrugged her shoulders.

"The alternatives are either that Stenberg killed and dismembered Sarac on his own, or that he hired someone to do it for him. Neither of those fits Stenberg's personality. He doesn't seem to have a particularly cool temperament. He could probably talk his way out of Sophie's suicide, if you get what I mean. 'It wasn't my fault, she was already unstable, I just happened to be in the wrong place at the wrong time. Why should I be punished because she was crazy?'"

Amante nodded.

"But to go from that sort of rationalization to hiring a professional hit man—or, even worse, doing it himself and then going home and patting his children with the hands he just used to chop someone up with—that seems a very big step. Stenberg wasn't capable of cleaning up after Sophie's suicide. Can you imagine him taking a chain saw to Sarac's face?"

Amante slowly shook his head. He seemed to be digesting everything she had said.

"What do we do now? How do we prove that your theory is true? Is it time to talk to someone higher up?"

"Not yet. There are still far too many suppositions and uncertainties for us to take this any further. That photograph of Sophie Thorning's body would ruin the minister of justice's career if it was made public. The risk is that it would become the focus of attention and everything else would be forgotten."

For a moment she imagined Pärson's face if she were to show him the picture of Sophie's body on the hood of Stenberg's car. The wheels would be spinning inside his fat head as he tried to calculate the market value of a government minister's career.

"But if we're going to solve the actual murder, we're still missing both a perpetrator and a murder scene." Amante frowned and fell silent for a few seconds. "But I think I may have an idea about the latter."

· · ·

Nisse Boman intercepted Stenberg as he crossed the creaking floor outside the dining room.

"Excuse me, Jesper. Just a quick word."

"Yes?" Stenberg carried on walking toward the large front door of the restaurant. He looked demonstratively at his heavy wristwatch.

"Let me start by congratulating you. Excellent news both for you and for the family."

Stenberg forced himself to look into the man's pale eyes. "Thank you, Nisse."

"I can imagine that things are going to be very different from now on. There'll be much more attention focused on the family, both desirable and undesirable."

"Really?" Stenberg stopped. What was the little man getting at?

"Of course you've got protection from the Security Police." Boman nodded toward the two bodyguards who were waiting by the door. "But Karolina and the girls haven't got anyone to keep an eye on them. I was thinking, that might be a good idea from now on. There are some crazy people out there."

Stenberg nodded. He hadn't actually thought that far.

"What do you suggest?"

"I can get ahold of a couple of calm, sensible guys from the Paratroop Regiment with experience in this sort of assignment. We could just call them chauffeurs. The party will cover the cost, obviously. What do you say?"

Stenberg's first instinct was to say no. That he didn't want Boman or any of his trusted associates anywhere near his family. But on the other hand Karl-Erik had presumably already agreed to the idea. And if he were to refuse without having a very good justification, it would look like he was putting his family at risk. And what could he say, anyway? That he suspected Boman had murdered both John and Sophie Thorning?

And that the whole lot, his accumulated suspicions and nightmares, was pretty much based on one spiteful comment from Oscar Wallin?

"Good idea, Nisse," he said instead.

He started to walk away, then changed his mind mid-step. He turned back to Boman.

"I appreciate you looking out for my family's safety."

"No problem." Boman looked almost friendly for once. "Like I said, I'd do anything for the Cedergren family."

That's what's worrying me, Stenberg thought.

Thirty-Nine

Julia put her foot down and jerked the car into an unnecessary overtaking maneuver. The car heading toward her in the other lane flashed its lights at her as she pulled back in at the last moment. The automatic transmission changed gears, making the engine quieter, and she saw Amante slump back into his seat.

"Tell me in more detail," she said. "How did you figure out which building it was?"

Amante cleared his throat. "Well, like I said, I went through all the properties in the vicinity of where the body was found during those first few days when you asked me to call around to see if there were any witnesses. I checked Google Maps and tried to work out which buildings had a clear view of the ice where Sarac's body was dumped. Then I found out which ones were residential buildings before I started calling around. As you know, that didn't give us anything: a lot of the properties are summer cottages, and none of the permanent residents had seen anyone out on the ice, apart from people skating when the weather was good enough."

He let go of the handgrip above the door and flexed his fingers a few times.

"But if your theory is right, then Sarac thought he had contacted Stenberg personally. So the murderer must have chosen a location that had some association with Stenberg and therefore seemed plausible. And why not somewhere that's uninhabited in winter and that also works perfectly if you want to get rid of a body? When you put that together with the place where the body was found, you end up with . . ."

"Källstavik," Julia said. "The party's training center."

"The grounds cover over fifty hectares," Amante went on. "There are a number of individual houses spread out around the property, and several of them are rented to senior party bosses. Stenberg doesn't have a house of his own there, but his father-in-law has one that's used by the whole family. Two cottages for guests, a woodshed, and a boathouse. The boathouse is down by the lake, of course, just seven or eight hundred meters as the crow flies from where Sarac's remains were found."

Amante sounded eager, almost excited. And suddenly Wallin's words of warning were back in her head. *In my experience, people like Amante usually go to pieces completely, sooner or later.*

She pulled onto the road's shoulder just before the turning to Källstavik and switched the engine off.

"There's something I've been wanting to ask you. Something I need to know before we go on."

"Sure." He looked at her. The usual gloomy look in his eyes had been replaced by something else—something she couldn't quite put her finger on.

"What's the real reason you ended up at Violent Crime?"

Amante looked away and Julia almost said something more. But instead she kept quiet and sat him out. She could practically feel his gloomy mood returning.

"I had a breakdown. On Lampedusa. My wife left me; I was drowning in bureaucracy. And the dead bodies . . ." He paused. "They just kept coming. More boats pretty much every day."

Amante fell silent for a few moments.

"I went to pieces. I tried to commit suicide but failed, as you can see. Then I spent a couple of months in the Alps, at a rest home." He made air quotes. "When I got out, my stepfather got me a job at Violent Crime on the condition that I sorted my life out and stopped embarrassing him."

"I understand," Julia said. She felt suddenly guilty for dragging up his past. Even so, she wanted to ask more. Find out if he was okay to go on. Or if he was likely to drag her down with him when he fell.

Amante almost appeared to read her mind.

"I'm fine," he said. "Just drive, Gabrielsson, so we actually get there sometime soon."

. . .

The man behind the counter in the little smoke shop grinned stupidly at Natalie.

"Like I told your boyfriend the other day, I'm missing some parts for the printer, and they haven't arrived yet. So I haven't been able to finish the passports yet. You'll have to wait a bit longer."

"But I called you yesterday. You said they'd be ready today."

"Not me. You must have spoken to my brother. We sound very similar. Must have been a misunderstanding."

Natalie glared at the man. He smiled back. Two of the guy's front teeth were gold, which didn't exactly make him look more trustworthy.

"How long do you think it'll take?"

"*Inshallah* . . ." The man threw his hands out and looked up at the grimy ceiling, where a little spherical camera stared down at Natalie. "A few days, I'd say. Toward the end of the week, something like that. Give me your number and I'll call you as soon as they're ready."

Natalie went on glaring at the man as she tried to work out all the things she'd have to sort out.

"I'll call you tomorrow, okay?" she said.

She left the shop and began to make a list in her head. Buy more food, rearrange their flights, the hotel, her appointment at the bank in Zürich. She crossed the street and walked slowly toward the supermarket parking lot where she'd left the Golf. She might as well buy the food while she was there.

. . .

It wasn't until she reached the fruit section that Natalie was sure. She'd got herself a cart and had been cruising up and down the aisles rather aimlessly, the way everyone does in a shop they're not familiar with. At one point she almost ran into a dark-skinned man with a baseball cap and neatly trimmed stubble. For a moment she got it into her head that he was a cop in plain clothes. He actually reminded her of the handsome cops she'd watched at the gas station, so she looked at him slightly longer than usual. She calmed down when she saw the word *THUG* tattooed on his knuckles. It was always convenient when people chose to label themselves like that.

She went on with her shopping but couldn't quite shake the feeling that she was being watched. It got stronger as she walked about. She changed direction abruptly a couple of times, and when she spotted the man again by the bananas, she was sure. The guy in the baseball cap wasn't a cop. But all the same he was following her.

She continued on to the clothing department. She picked up a few garments at random, parked her half-full cart in plain sight, and went into one of the little changing rooms. She took off her jacket and sunglasses, then let her hair down over her shoulders. She looked at the result in the mirror: not perfect, but good enough. Common, as Cassandra had put it. Not the sort of person anyone would notice.

Cautiously she left the changing room, made a wide detour around the cart, which Cap Man was bound to be watching like a hawk, and made her way back outside through the entrance in case he had an accomplice watching the cash registers.

This wasn't good, not good at all.

• • •

Julia let the car roll slowly along the gravel road. The house used by the Stenberg family lay partway up a hill covered with oak trees, half-hidden by vegetation. A dark-colored car was visible in the drive.

"Keep going toward the water," Amante said.

The track came to an end at a little turnaround surrounded by pine trees. They got out of the car. In front of them lay a jetty with a little boathouse alongside, jutting out into the water. A weak breeze was blowing off Lake Mälaren, carrying with it the smell of inland water.

"Locked." Julia tugged slightly at the heavy padlock holding a heavy steel bar in front of the door. "Maybe we could get in from the other end?"

They walked out onto the jetty but found that the far end was covered by a rolling door that ended half a meter above the water.

"The ice formed in the middle of December and lasted until the end of March," Amante said. "I checked with the weather service when we started our investigation. In February it would have been possible to raise this door and walk or ski straight out across the lake. All you'd need is a sledge to transport the body, and the chain saw. To cut a hole in the ice," he clarified when she raised a quizzical eyebrow.

He pointed across the water. Far away on the horizon, the other side of the lake was just visible as a strip of green.

"The body was found some seven hundred meters in that direction. It wouldn't take an experienced skater with the right equipment and pulling a sledge more than half an hour at most. In the middle of the night no one would have noticed, and it wouldn't have taken much wind to cover the tracks through the snow. And the hole didn't have to be any larger than this." He formed a circle with his arms. "I'd guess it would have frozen over again in a couple of days. And with that, Sarac was—"

"Out of the way," Julia muttered.

She looked out across the water, then back at the boathouse between the water and the trees. At the edge of the woodland was what looked like an old stone wall.

"We have to get in there," she said.

The water was cold, or at least colder than she'd expected.

She'd rolled her jeans up and left her shoes and socks on the edge of the water, and had only taken a couple of steps before realizing that she'd gotten it completely wrong. The water was already over her knees and there was some way to go before she reached the far corner of the boathouse. The channel had to be deep enough for a reasonably large boat with its outboard motor down. That meant one and a half meters, maybe more. And she wasn't quite one meter seventy centimeters tall. Wading out and ducking in under the door wasn't going to work.

She hesitated for a few seconds, then looked up at Amante, who was still on the jetty, fiddling with his phone. She took out her own phone and put it between her teeth, then fell gently forward and started to swim. The chill of the water made her shiver, but after a couple of strokes her body got used to it.

She couldn't find a ladder and had to climb up onto the boat itself to get out of the water. It was a motorboat, covered, between four and five meters long, several years old. Stenberg's father-in-law clearly knew how important it was not to appear flashy or excessively wealthy. She jumped across to dry land and found a light switch next to the locked door. She wrung as much water as she could out of her clothes and slipped her phone into her back pocket.

She stood still for a moment, trying to absorb her impressions. There was a strong smell of lake water and oil. Something else too, something more chemical. Chlorine, she guessed, used to clean algae from the boat.

About a third of the area of the boathouse was occupied by water. On the landward side was a gentle concrete slope that led up to ground level. Two old railway ties on struts formed a workbench along one side, and in the middle of the space was an empty trailer and some sort of winch that she assumed was used to pull the boat out in the autumn. Everything looked both well used and properly maintained. As if the owner took care of his possessions and took pride in not buying new things unnecessarily, just as her dad had done.

She climbed over the trailer and went across to the workbench. The impression of fastidious order grew stronger. Above the bench the tools hung in neat rows. On the wall careful outlines had been drawn, showing exactly where each tool belonged. Wrenches, hammers, various types of files, a large flashlight. She bent down and looked under the bench. A pressure washer, an industrial vacuum cleaner, a couple of plastic tubs. Everything you needed to maintain a boat. But no chain saw, nothing at all that could be used to dismember a body. But, considering how meticulous the perpetrator seemed to have been, perhaps that wasn't altogether surprising. Even so, she felt a little disappointed.

"Julia!" Amante called from outside. "Are you okay?"

She went over to the door.

"I'm fine. Just give me a couple more minutes."

She climbed back across the trailer again to return to the workbench, but stopped halfway. Her attention was caught by something on the ground.

When she bent down, she discovered, despite the weak light, a groove in the porous cement floor. Then another one. Julia felt her pulse speed up. She fetched the flashlight and a thick pencil from the workbench. She climbed up onto the trailer and shone the flashlight down through its metal frame. There were a number of grooves of various sizes in the floor, and she realized that she was going to have to move the trailer in order to take a good look. She released the handbrake and, with an effort, managed to move the trailer just enough to clear the floor area. Then she jumped up onto one of the wheels, shone the flashlight at the floor, and counted out loud to herself.

Thirteen grooves, some more visible than others, forming a sort of pattern around a space in the middle. She jumped down onto the floor again, got down on her knees, and drew parallel lines stretching away from both sides of the grooves, then a large oval around the gap at their center. She finished by drawing a circle above the groove at the top. She hopped back up onto the trailer and shone the flashlight at her handiwork. She shivered, not only because of her damp clothes.

The rough drawing on the floor looked like a human body. Each major joint was marked by a groove in the floor.

Thirteen very decisive cuts, one for each joint. All the way through, right through muscle and bone.

We were right, she thought. *This is where Sarac died. He was sawn into pieces on this floor before his body parts were wrapped in plastic bags and dragged out onto the ice. The perpetrator cleaned up after him, used chlorine to destroy any traces of DNA. Presumably he had pressure-cleaned the floor several times before he was happy. But he couldn't do anything about the grooves left by the chain saw in the floor.*

"Amante," she said, raising her voice, but got no answer. She felt in her pocket for her cell phone. She opened the camera function and aimed it at the floor. But before she had time to click the button, the door was thrown open wide. She turned around, thinking that Amante had somehow managed to pick the lock. But the man she saw in the doorway was someone else altogether. And he was holding a pistol in his hand.

Forty

Natalie slowly drummed her fingers on the steering wheel. She had set off to drive to the Scout cabin to tell Atif what had happened. Explain that they wouldn't be leaving that evening after all. But after a kilometer or so she changed her mind, pulled into a gas station, and decided to call him on his pay-as-you-go cell phone once she'd had a chance to think things through.

Passport Guy and his brother had shafted them, that much was obvious. Somehow they had realized there was more money to be earned by informing on them. Because she'd called the shop before she showed up, they knew it wasn't going to be Atif himself picking the passports up. They evidently assumed she was just some dumb bitch who was going to lead them straight to his hiding place, but now she'd managed to shaft the bastards instead. Now all they could do was wait for her to call again, which she obviously wasn't going to do.

But that didn't solve their problem. Without passports they were stuck. Okay, so they could squeeze into her car and drive to Switzerland, hoping they didn't get caught in a random check at one of the borders. But as soon as Cassandra and Tindra were forced to use their real passports, they'd be finished. Alarm bells would start to ring, the trip would be over, and she would get charged with aiding and abetting a criminal. Besides, Atif didn't have a passport at all. And the thought of heading off on a road trip across Europe really didn't appeal to her. She wasn't at all sure her battered little Golf or her own sanity would survive a trip like that.

Natalie put some ChapStick on her lips. She had to come

up with some sort of solution to this. But how? She leaned her head back against the headrest and looked out across the forecourt of the gas station. She caught sight of one of the security cameras above the pumps. A little black sphere, the same sort she remembered seeing not that long ago. Suddenly she had an idea. Maybe there was a chance after all. But it would take a lot of nerve and intelligence—and a hell of a lot of luck.

• • •

Julia was crouched on the step of the boathouse. Amante was sitting beside her with his hands tied behind his back, as hers were. Her wet clothes were making her shiver in spite of the mild breeze. But it wasn't her own condition that worried her. She could see Amante's chest rising and falling heavily as beads of sweat trickled down his temples. He was staring down at the ground.

"Couldn't you untie his hands?" she said to the bodyguard watching them while his colleague talked on the phone a short distance away. "You've seen our IDs. I've explained why we're here. For God's sake, we're colleagues. Can't you see he's not well?" She nodded toward Amante, whose eyes were still fixed glassily on the ground.

The guard pretended not to hear. His colleague, a tall, well-built man with prominent features, walked slowly toward them. It became possible to hear part of his phone call.

"Okay, so you can confirm that they work for you. And that this is a case of wires getting crossed?"

A short silence as the person on the other end spoke.

"Okay, I get it. If you've got the all-clear from Command, then there's no problem. We'll draw a line under the whole business."

The man sought to make eye contact with his partner, then jerked his head toward Julia and Amante. Their guard pulled out a bunch of keys and gestured for them to stand up. Julia had to nudge Amante to get him to his feet.

"Here." The man held his phone out to Julia as soon as her hands were free. "He wants to talk to you."

Julia took the phone and walked a few meters away, then turned away from them before she spoke.

"Sorry to drag you into this. Pärson would have burst an artery if I'd called him. He thinks I'm shut away in my room looking through databases. And—"

"I assume this relates to your investigation," Wallin said drily. "I've spoken to the duty officer at the Security Police. He and I, and our bodyguard colleague Becker, have all agreed that it was a misunderstanding. That you, on my initiative, were investigating a tip-off but that we should obviously have informed the minister of justice's personal protection team before we set off to the site."

"Th-Thanks," Julia said. She realized her teeth were chattering.

"Don't mention it. Now I want you to get back in your car and drive back into the city as fast as you can. In precisely ninety minutes I want to see you, and you alone, in my office, when I will require a thorough explanation of precisely what the two of you were doing out in Källstavik. All the details, no holding back. Is that understood?"

Julia looked at Amante, who was already getting back in the car. His movements were jerky, as if he was on autopilot.

"Understood," she said.

• • •

The man in the smoke shop didn't seem to recognize Natalie at first, possibly because she was wearing a long, light-colored raincoat instead of the dark, waist-length jacket she had been wearing just a few hours before. But then their eyes met and he put two and two together. His eyes darted to the cell phone a little way down the counter.

"Hello again," she said. "Do you remember me, the girl with the passports?"

311

"Er, hi. Did you forget something?" The man pulled his phone toward him. He was trying to act casual but wasn't really succeeding. He and the man in the cap had called off the search for the day. He clearly hadn't counted on her turning up in the shop again.

"No, it's about something else. Something I wanted to show you. Come with me."

She stepped behind one of the low shelving units containing sweets and porn magazines. And glanced up at the little spherical camera in the ceiling.

The man behind the counter glared at her. He was holding his phone in his hand and didn't seem altogether sure what to do.

"Come on, hurry up," she said. "It's important!"

He walked around the counter and stopped a meter or so away from her.

"Closer," she said.

The man took a step forward. Then another one. Natalie opened her coat. She saw his eyes open wide when he caught sight of her tattered clothes.

"Let me explain," she said, the way she'd practiced in front of the mirror in her apartment. "You're going to give me the passports, right now, without calling or texting anyone. If you try anything stupid, or say you haven't got the passports, I'm going to start screaming and pulling these shelves down. I've got a friend standing outside, and when she hears me screaming she's going to call the police and tell them you're trying to rape me. I'd guess the cops would be here within five minutes, and they'll find me here in a state of shock with my clothes in tatters."

She nodded toward the pants, blouse, and bra she'd carefully prepared at home on her kitchen table.

"Obviously my friend will back me up, and the recordings from your cameras will support us. That would certainly be enough to get you taken into custody. I'd imagine the cops would take the opportunity to conduct a thorough search of both the shop and your home."

312

She flashed her most beautiful smile at him. She could almost hear the thoughts going around in his head.

"Look . . ." he said. "You c-can't . . ."

Natalie turned to the camera with a look of horror on her face. Then she threw herself at the man and they collided. She pulled down a row of porn magazines in the process.

"No, no, stop it!" she yelled.

The man just gawked. She threw herself at a shelf, making it sway.

"Let go of me!" she cried. Louder this time. "Let me go, for fuck's sake!"

The man held his hands up. "Stop it!" A bead of sweat was slowly trickling down his forehead. Then another one.

Natalie tackled another shelf, pulling down a load of chocolate bars and cookies.

"Stop it, you're hurting me! I don't want to! Get the fuck off me!"

The door opened and an elderly woman stopped in the doorway. She stared at Natalie, then at the shopkeeper. Natalie winked at him and took a deep breath, getting ready to let out another scream.

The man's face was white, and his eyes darted between Natalie and the old woman.

"For fuck's sake, stop it," he hissed. "You can have the passports. Just stop it!"

• • •

Julia Gabrielsson was sitting in one of the visitors' chairs in Wallin's office. Her clothes were still damp in the places where the car's seat warmer and air conditioner hadn't managed to dry them during the drive back into the city. She'd considered stopping at home to change but realized she wouldn't meet Wallin's deadline if she did. And pissing him off even more after he'd helped her wouldn't be a good idea.

Amante hadn't said much during the journey. He mostly

stared ahead blankly and barely showed any sign of life until she told him about the marks in the cement floor. Being apprehended and cuffed had evidently triggered something inside him, something he had trouble dealing with. Julia felt embarrassed to admit it, but it was actually a relief to be able to drop Amante off outside the apartment. And now here she was, making damp stains on Wallin's leather armchair.

"So, to sum up," Wallin said slowly, "your theory is based upon the assumption that a security consultant named Hunter gave Sarac information about the minister's involvement in Sophie Thorning's suicide. Then, when Sarac tried to contact the minister, he was murdered in the boathouse out at Källstavik, a boathouse that is used by the minister of justice's extended family. Am I right so far?"

Julia nodded. She wanted to say something else, but Wallin went on before she managed to remember what it was.

"But all you've got by way of evidence, rather than guesswork, theories, and half-truths, are a few grooves in a cement floor?"

Julia shook her head.

"We've got the message from Sarac, and the pictures."

Wallin smiled sardonically. "Yes, you do. But if I've understood correctly, it isn't possible to determine who the message was sent to, much less who might have read it. And as far as those pictures are concerned . . ."

He gestured toward his screen, where Sophie Thorning's dead body was in full view.

"They're certainly unpleasant, but can we be sure they aren't fakes based on pictures from the original investigation? It wouldn't be that hard for someone who's good at Photoshop to change the make of the car, the surface it's standing on, and the license plate."

"The body's in a different position," Julia said quickly. "One arm is at a completely different angle. And her legs aren't in the same position."

Wallin shrugged his shoulders. "Same thing there. Probably not that difficult for a talented designer to do in Photoshop."

Julia opened her mouth to protest but stopped herself. So far Wallin had been cautiously supportive. He had bought her theories even though she lacked firm evidence. But his attitude seemed to have changed. Was he trying to protect himself and distance himself from her in case rumors of their antics out at the boathouse spread up the chain of command? Or were there other reasons behind his sudden coolness?

"Well, I still think the pictures look genuine," she said. "Two cars, two falls. That would explain the extensive injuries described in the autopsy report. Impact injuries sustained immediately before and after death are difficult to distinguish from one another. Unless you know exactly what you're looking for."

Wallin pulled a face that was difficult to interpret.

"Anyway," Julia went on, "who'd be interested in Photoshopping those pictures? No one's likely to have confronted Stenberg with fake pictures, are they?"

Wallin leaned back in his chair. His expression softened somewhat.

"That's an ass-backwards argument, Julia. You're assuming that the minister of justice was confronted with something, possibly even blackmailed by Sarac, and for that reason the pictures have to be genuine. But set that aside for a moment. Suppose instead that the memory card containing those pictures was left in that office specifically to connect Sarac's death with Stenberg."

Julia shuffled slightly on the chair, making the leather squeak beneath her wet pants as she tried to work out what Wallin was trying to get at.

"You think this might be some sort of conspiracy? That someone's trying to frame Stenberg? Isn't that a bit far-fetched? I appreciate that you work for the minister of justice and feel obliged to defend him . . ."

Wallin held one hand up. "I don't think anything right now.

315

All I can conclude after hearing your story is that it is a series of suppositions held together by some highly dubious evidence. Some of which you aren't even in possession of."

"So what are your thoughts?" Julia still wasn't entirely sure of the turn their conversation had taken.

Wallin gestured toward his computer again.

"These pictures, for instance. Who found the memory card in Hunter's hideout?"

"I did."

"The first time you were there?"

"No, the second time."

"Had anyone else been there in between those visits?"

She hesitated before replying. "As far as I know, no one but Amante. He searched the room while I was at work."

"I see. And who found out about that room in the first place? Who got hold of the keys? The phone number of the man you believed was Hunter?"

"Amante," she said. She suddenly realized what Wallin was getting at. "You mean Amante planned the whole thing? Hunter's identity, his hideout, the laptop, those pictures? That none of this is real, and Hunter was really some sort of actor? Why would Amante do that?"

"Amante appeared out of nowhere. As luck would have it, the morning after the remains of the body were found. And I already know it was his stepfather who arranged that."

"Yes, but Amante got the job because he needed help. He had a breakdown. Lampedusa, the divorce—he told me about all that himself . . ."

She noticed Wallin's skeptical expression before she had even finished the sentence.

"Besides, you were the one who told me about his suicide attempt and the fire," she added. She could hear the doubt that had crept into her voice. She didn't like it.

"You could be right," Wallin said without sounding convinced. "Maybe I'm too susceptible to conspiracy theories.

Maybe Amante showing up was a complete coincidence, like you say. But, either way, all the evidence or suspicions pointing at Minister of Justice Stenberg have passed through Amante's hands. You can't deny that."

Julia didn't answer.

"The boathouse and your little excursion to Källstavik—that was his idea as well, wasn't it?"

She nodded reluctantly. Wallin said nothing for a few seconds as he drummed his fingers on the edge of his desk.

"I can think of an alternative theory," he said thoughtfully. "One that we at least need to consider before we move on: Amante shows up at Violent Crime for the reasons you've outlined. He ends up in the middle of the investigation into a dismembered body found near Källstavik. Because of the connection to the party, the media begin to take an interest in the case. Amante explains the details to his stepfather, a man who looks likely to replace Stenberg as minister of justice if the opposition wins this autumn's election. An idea begins to grow. What if the dismembered body could somehow be linked to the government or, better still, to the party's rising star?"

Wallin paused, as if to assure himself that Julia was following his reasoning.

"Linking Stenberg to Sophie Thorning's suicide wouldn't seem too far-fetched, considering that they worked together and had known each other for a long time. All it would take would be enough plausible details for the newspapers to bite. The story has everything, after all: sex, suicide, blackmail, a dismembered body. Not to mention a government minister. And the chase would be on. Even if it later turned out that the story didn't stand up to scrutiny, it would certainly be enough to cause the party, and Stenberg, very serious problems just in time for the election. No smoke without fire and all that."

"Wait a minute . . ." Julia began, but Wallin held his hand up before she could go on.

"I know what you're thinking. Amante got himself suspended for his mistake with Kassab, and everything seems to have ground to a halt. But instead of dropping the whole thing, they go ahead with the plan. Because by now someone else has been drawn into it. Someone with considerably more credibility than Amante. A talented homicide detective with an excellent track record. An almost perfect messenger for the story they want to plant, wouldn't you agree?"

This time Wallin waited for her to reply. But her brain seemed to have seized up and she couldn't think of anything sensible to say.

"What do you say about that theory, Julia? Is it really any worse, or any less plausible, than the one you outlined a little while ago? Remember, I did warn you about trusting him."

Julia swallowed a couple of times. A bitter taste filled her mouth. Could Amante have been manipulating her? Pulling her strings and making her do what he wanted? Amante's behavior had certainly become increasingly odd during the course of the investigation, as if he was under great pressure. She had believed that was because of the case and his shock at being exposed once again to dead bodies. But she could easily be wrong. If Wallin's theory was right, then she would have to re-evaluate absolutely everything. Every lead, every word Amante had uttered. She tried to fast-forward through the previous three weeks to find a pivotal moment. A litmus test that could differentiate between truth and lie.

"There is one way to find out the truth," she said slowly. "If your theory is right, then the saw marks I found in the boat-house floor a couple of hours ago are also fake, made by Amante or someone he knows, to reinforce the connection to Stenberg. The entire boathouse looked extremely clean. But the cement on the floor is porous, and a body being cut up there would have left loads of DNA evidence. If we conducted a proper forensic examination, I'm pretty sure we'd find at least something in those grooves. Even if the body is gone, a DNA trace could be compared with the sample on file at the National Forensic

Centre. If it's a match, then the case is solved. Our theory holds. Sarac was dismembered in the boathouse at Källstavik, and the blackmail letter and pictures are probably genuine."

"And if not?" Wallin said. "If there's no trace of DNA in the boathouse?"

Then I'm nothing more than a puppet, a puppet dancing when someone else pulls the strings, Julia thought. *As well as a pretty shitty judge of character.*

Forty-One

Oscar Wallin sat down on one of the armchairs in front of the head of Regional Crime's oversized desk. He noted that, unlike on previous visits, he hadn't been offered coffee or anything else to drink. Kollander hadn't even shaken his hand, just nodded to him to have a seat.

"So, how are you getting on?" Wallin said. "Have you found Atif Kassab yet?"

Staffan Kollander leaned back in his chair. The wall behind him was covered with the framed badges of different foreign police forces, all hung with impressive, millimeter-perfect precision that must have taken hours to get right.

"Does that question come from you or the minister of justice?"

Wallin shrugged. "Does it make any difference?"

"A couple of months ago I'd have said no. Whereas now . . ."

Kollander let the sentence die as he brushed an invisible speck of dust from one of his cuffs, but Wallin was more than capable of finishing it. The head of Regional Crime saw him as a loser, and no one wanted to swim too close to a drowning man.

"It's probably best not to draw any hasty conclusions," he said, trying to make it sound as though the comment amused him.

He reminded himself of why he was there. Kassab had been hiding in that Scout cabin for several days now and might move on any time. Disappear off the map. And after careful consideration he had decided it was time to tip Kollander off about where the escapee and his family were hiding and who was protecting them. Maybe he could build up some new alliances by helping the cretinous Kollander sort things out. But he had other things to worry about. More important than an escaped convict. A possibility of restitution.

"Like I said on the phone, I was thinking of offering my help in the Kassab case. Some people are saying that your career depends on whether or not you manage to catch him." Wallin attempted a disarming smile but could tell he hadn't quite succeeded. That last sentence was unnecessary.

There was a knock on the door and Pärson walked in. The fat man nodded to Kollander before sinking into the other armchair. He didn't even grace Wallin with as much as a glance.

"Good to see you, Pärson," Kollander said. "Deputy Police Commissioner Wallin here says he can help us with the Kassab case." His voice was neutral, but even so, there was something in Kollander's tone that Wallin didn't care for. Pärson was hardly likely to show up in his boss's office without being summoned, so the two of them had evidently already spoken.

"Really? How?" Pärson grunted. "We've got twenty detectives on the case, there's a national alert, and Kassab is the subject of an international warrant. National Crime is helping, and we've got the Rapid Response Unit on standby in case they're required."

He shifted his heavy frame and glared at Wallin.

"Anyway, haven't you already got your hands full? Rumor has it that the only investigations you'll be dealing with in the future concern the force's postal expenses." The corners of Pärson's mouth twitched. "A great shame, for such a well-liked officer as yourself."

Wallin breathed in slowly through his nose. Once again he tried to remind himself of why he was there. To build alliances, think strategically. Free up his time for other things.

He saw Pärson wink at Kollander. Only a few months ago they'd have rolled out the red carpet. They'd have given him anything he wanted, scared of what he could do to their careers.

Now they were having fun at his expense and not even trying to hide the fact. A seriously overweight gossip of a commissioner and a bone-dry pedant of a desk jockey, both of a lower rank than him, saw fit to make fun of *him*.

Was this the sort of alliance he had imagined? The sort of cooperation he wanted to build his future on?

Wallin stood up abruptly.

"Well, never mind, then. Thank you, gentlemen, for taking the time to see me," he said as amiably as he could.

They could go to hell, the both of them. He might even give them a bit of a nudge in that direction. He nodded to the two men and left the room, then took the elevator all the way down to the garage and managed, as luck would have it, to avoid running into any other gleefully malicious colleagues.

His cell phone rang the moment he sat in the driver's seat.

"Oscar, it's your mother. The woman from the bank has called again. They've found another card, with a debt of almost fifty thousand. I thought you said you were going to take care of this."

"I am."

"In that case, I suggest you try a little harder. Your father was always very particular about settling bills on time. In this family we always do the right thing. Always, do you hear?"

Wallin clenched his jaw so tightly, he could hear his teeth creak. Natalie. How dare she ignore him? Carry on even though he'd warned her? Even though he was watching her?

"Don't worry, Mom," he said. "I'll take care of it. There won't be any more, I promise. Have a cup of tea and try to calm down, and I'll phone you this evening."

He ended the call before she had time to reply, threw the phone down on the passenger seat, and punched the steering wheel with his fists. Once, twice, three, four, five times. He didn't stop until his hands hurt and he was wet with sweat.

They were underestimating him. Thought they could walk all over him. Stenberg, Kollander, Pärson, even Natalie. But enough was enough. Time to show them who was really in charge.

He pulled out the pay-as-you-go cell phone he kept in the glove compartment, switched it on, and pulled up a number. He wound his window down a little to clear the condensation from the windshield. Or possibly the faint smell of smoke he thought he could detect inside the car. The smell of wood slowly being consumed by fire.

"This is Oscar Wallin," he said when the woman at the other end answered. "Your father and I did a fair amount of business together. You might remember me. I can help you get rid of a problem. But you'll have to do the same for me."

·   ·   ·

The Sniper was sitting on his camp bed in the little basement room. From the den he could hear the sound of the video game that the three men played pretty much around the clock. Could hear them squabbling. When he had moved in it had sounded good-natured, but it had grown more and more irritable and volatile. The three men on the sofa saw themselves as soldiers. They kept their guns out to show that they were ready to fight. But none of them understood what a challenge it was simply having to wait. Wait for an attack that might come at any moment, or perhaps never. That was why they were drinking more, smoking more cigarettes, arguing more volubly about the video game.

He preferred to take refuge in the Bible. He read the passages Father Ivor had underlined over and over again.

Blessed is he whose transgression is forgiven, whose sin is covered.

They had said it would be no longer than a week before the danger passed. A week when he would have to live in the little cubbyhole in the basement. Just over two weeks had passed already. He had done his job, exactly as agreed. Abu Hamsa was dead. But something had gone wrong, and now they were all in danger.

He should have gone home. Explained to them that his debt was paid the moment Abu Hamsa died. But he knew that wasn't true, that he couldn't leave until everything was finished here, one way or another. Eldar Jafarov was a gorilla, the sort of man who mistook fear for respect. Who thought it was something that could be instilled, not earned. Eldar's uncle had been the opposite. One of the finest men the Sniper had ever known. A man who had saved his life several times. Seb Jafarov was dead, blown to pieces by a land mine many years ago. But the Sniper's debt to him remained. Forced him to sit here, waiting patiently and reading his Bible.

Blessed is the man unto whom the Lord imputeth not iniquity, and in whose spirit there is no guile.

In the other room the game went quiet and he heard Susanna's voice. Then the sound of movement. The clatter of guns and bulletproof vests, voices full of expectation, excitement.

A quick knock, then Susanna was standing in the doorway. She was beautiful, he thought. In a cruel way, rather like a bird of prey. The beauty of a creature whose entire existence was devoted to ensuring its own survival.

"We've received a tip-off," she said. "From an old associate of my father's. He says he knows where Cassandra and Tindra are hiding. Atif is probably there too."

The Sniper nodded and slowly put his Bible away.

"I've got a special assignment for you," she said. "Something I had to promise in return. There's someone else who has to die."

Forty-Two

The passports were in her inside pocket, her suitcase in the trunk. There was a fresh bundle of notes in her wallet, courtesy of Wallin's mother. All that remained was a quick detour to the Scout cabin to pick up her passengers, then it was next stop Arlanda. Passport Guy's duplicity had cost them half the afternoon, but they could still catch the evening flight to Zürich and all be somewhere safe within a matter of hours.

She was approaching the turnoff. Natalie clicked the turn signal on, then drove onto the narrow gravel track. By this time tomorrow she'd be on a plane to Thailand, and everything would be over.

She parked the car in the usual place. Atif met her in the doorway, looking over her shoulder. He was holding a pistol by his hip, as if he didn't want to make a fuss about having a gun. She had told him what had happened with the passports over the phone, and it had obviously unsettled him.

"You're sure no one followed you here?"

"Quite sure."

He scanned the garden, listening. Then he turned to her and discreetly slipped the gun into his waistband. She handed the passports over. Something approaching a smile crossed his face, but he didn't say anything.

Cassandra appeared at Atif's side.

"Have you got them?"

Atif gave her two of the passports. She opened them, quickly leafed through the pages as if she didn't entirely believe him. Then she looked up. The relief in her face was unmistakable. Her chin trembled and for a moment it looked as if she was going to cry.

Cassandra took a step forward, put her arms around Natalie, and hugged her. Hard, as if she really meant it.

"Thank you. You've saved our lives," she whispered in Natalie's ear.

Natalie swallowed and didn't really know what to say.

"Time to go," Atif said. He picked up a bag that was standing in the hall, opened the door, and began to walk toward the car.

• • •

When Atif was halfway to the car, he heard the sound of an engine approaching. It wasn't any of the neighbors' cars. After a few days there he knew how they sounded. This one was larger, the sound more muffled. He looked up at the trees hiding the track, trying to spot any movement.

The sound of the engine stopped abruptly and everything went quiet. All he could hear was the chirping of crickets. He stood still for a few moments, listening for any noises from the track. He thought he could make out car doors opening and closing.

He put the bag down, turned around, and walked back to the cabin. He walked carefully so as not to give himself away. He shut the door behind him and locked it.

"We've got a problem," he told Natalie.

"Yes, I kind of realized that." She nodded toward the pistol, which was back in his hand.

"Take the girls into the back room. Lock the door and stay there. If you don't hear anything within five minutes, climb out of the window and go down to the jetty. Swim across the lake if you have to."

"What about Tindra?"

"She can do it, she's a strong swimmer."

"But isn't it better to—"

Atif shook his head. "We haven't got time to argue. The track is blocked and we don't know which direction they're coming from, except that it's unlikely to be from the lake. So that's the safest escape route."

"Okay, what about you? What are you going to do?"

He didn't answer. They looked at each other for a few moments.

"Take care," she said.

Atif realized to his surprise that she was blushing slightly. All of a sudden he didn't know what to say.

"Okay" was the best he could come up with. Then realized how empty it sounded.

He slipped out through the door and heard Natalie lock it from inside. The garden was completely open except for a few log benches arranged around a campfire. The only decent hiding places were inside the cabin or among the trees between the cabin and the jetty. Neither of those was any good. He could hear rustling from the bushes leading up to the track. A branch snapping under someone's foot. If they were cops, they probably wouldn't come much closer. They'd wait until it got dark instead. Keep an eye on the cabin, find out if he was really there before calling for backup. He was a cop killer, and that demanded dogs, helicopters, a rapid response team. But he had a feeling that the men approaching the cabin weren't cops. And that they weren't planning to wait.

He crept slowly toward Natalie's car. Lay down on his stomach and crawled underneath it. He pressed himself as close to the ground as he could. He didn't have to wait long. Two dark-clad figures appeared up by the track. Well-built men, one of them holding a shotgun, the other a pistol. They moved slowly, at a crouch, stepping carefully, like soldiers advancing. Another branch snapped in among the bushes. The men on the track stopped and whispered to each other.

Two attackers on the track, at least one more making his way through the bushes toward the garden, where he'd have a clear line of sight across the grass to the side of the cabin. But he'd have to go a fair way to be able to see around the corner to where the path led down to the lake.

The men on the track started moving again. They approached the car slowly. But their attention was focused on the cabin and the garden. They didn't see him lying there. Atif felt his pulse quicken. He tried to take deep, silent breaths to calm it down. Adrenaline would make his hands shake, and the battered Zastava he had taken from the Somali was already hard enough to fire.

The men were holding their weapons as if they knew what they were doing. Pointing them toward their target instead of up in the air or down at the ground, the way people did in films. As they got closer their upper bodies disappeared from view, and all he could see were their boots and the bottom of their legs.

When they reached the car the men split up to go around it. They were taking short steps as they approached the cabin.

Atif shot the first man's foot from a distance of mere centimeters. He was almost touching his leather boots with the barrel of the pistol when he fired. He didn't wait to see the result and crawled over to his left instead. He heard a howl behind him as he fired two rapid shots at the second man's feet and banged his head on the bottom of the car. He'd missed, or at least thought he had.

He grabbed the rear axle and pulled himself out behind the car. He pressed his back against the bumper. There was another howl, then a pistol shot rang out. It cut straight through the body of the car and came out the other side, just centimeters from Atif's head. Crouching down, he went around the right-hand side of the car and saw the man whose foot he had shot trying to stand up. Atif fired another two shots, and at least one of them hit. The man staggered but, weirdly, didn't fall. Instead he turned and raised his gun toward Atif.

Atif squeezed the trigger again. Nothing happened. The damn pistol had jammed. He threw himself behind the car again. A bullet hissed past, half a meter away, then another one.

The man he had just shot yelled something at his partner, then fired another shot in Atif's direction.

Atif tugged at the bolt of the battered pistol. A cartridge that had got stuck in the chamber came loose and bounced up toward him before disappearing into the gravel.

Another shot, a dull, flat thump, unlike the distinct cough of the pistol, and the car lurched, sending a shower of plastic and fragments of metal over Atif's hiding place. He felt a sting at the back of his neck, then a warm, familiar sensation slowly spreading down his back. The pain was a two, more irritating than anything.

He didn't bother to investigate the injury. His surprise ambush had failed. His two attackers were still able to fight, the third man was bound to be rushing toward them through the bushes, and now he was trapped behind the car. His heart was pounding uncontrollably in his chest, and his hands were shaking.

Another shot turned the rear right-hand corner of the car into a fog of plastic and metal. Atif threw himself in that direction. He saw a dark silhouette just a meter or so away and fired, then landed flat on his side on the gravel. He heard a scream of pain, then the thud of a body falling. He rolled toward the ditch behind him, feeling the rush of air as a bullet flew past his face. Then another one, which didn't.

The shot felt like being punched, almost sounded like it too, but strangely enough he didn't feel any pain. He rolled down into the ditch and pressed his fingers to his cheek. He could feel the hole, the flap of skin, the stumps of teeth inside. The same on the other side where the bullet had exited.

Stumbling steps were approaching on the track. He managed to raise his gun, then realized that he'd lost track of how many shots he had fired.

A dark shape appeared at the edge of the ditch. Atif saw a pistol aimed at him and fired his own without thinking. The cracks of the two pistols came so close together that they sounded like a single shot.

Forty-Three

The Sniper was lying in position on the camping mat. He'd un-folded the rifle's supports, adjusted the telescopic sight, taking the distance, wind, and angle into account. The exchange of fire made him scan the facade of the cabin through the sight, but because the gunfight seemed to be taking place on the other side of the building, he was only able to hear it.

He went back to looking at the two small, dark windows. For some reason Father Ivor's voice appeared in his head.

Do you have regrets, my son?

He would probably regret this—he knew that already. But he had no choice. He owed it to Seb to complete his mission.

Do you have regrets?

The Sniper screwed his eyes shut a couple of times and managed to make the voice in his head stop. He returned to studying the little windows through the telescopic sight.

• • •

"We have to go! Right now!" Cassandra's eyes were wide open. Her voice muffled by terror.

The gunfire outside had made them all instinctively curl up on the floor, Cassandra with her arms around Tindra, and Natalie with her arms around both of them. Natalie looked at her watch. Her chest felt tight with fear, making it hard to breathe. Five minutes, Atif had said. That had passed already. She stood up, went over to one of the windows, and tugged at the catches. But the window was stuck.

There was a crash from the main room. She guessed it came from the front door.

Then one catch came loose. The sharp metal cut into her thumb. Someone yanked at the handle of the bedroom door.

"Open up, for fuck's sake, Cassandra!"

"That's Eldar," Cassandra said. "Susanna's husband. Atif must be . . ." She wrapped her arms even more tightly around Tindra. Buried the girl's head against her chest.

"Open the fucking door!"

The handle rattled up and down, and the flimsy door bowed as the man outside pulled at it.

Natalie made one last attempt at the window. But the top catch refused to budge. She heard the bedroom door creak and realized it was going to give way at any moment.

She ran over and put her shoulder to it, waiting for the handle to go up before quickly turning the key and shoving with all her might. As Eldar pushed the handle down and pulled once more, the door flew open and he staggered backward. Natalie flew at him, colliding with his chest. She knocked him back and over one of the heavy benches, with her on top of him.

"Run!" she yelled at Cassandra. "Now!"

She thrust her fingers into Eldar's face, trying to scratch his eyes. The hand clutching the pistol came flying toward her, and she only half managed to duck. The blow struck her on the ear, making her feel giddy. It would be a matter of seconds before Eldar regained his balance and began to pummel her with considerably more force and better aim.

She heard Tindra scream out loud, and as she reflexively turned her head, Eldar grabbed her by the jaw with his left hand and lifted her up. He squeezed and her vision started to fade. She waved her arms wildly, reaching toward his face. But Eldar was much too strong. She saw him taking aim to smash her in the head with the pistol. She closed her eyes and waited for the blow. For the darkness.

331

But instead Eldar let out a howl of pain. She opened her eyes and saw Cassandra clinging to his right arm, sinking her perfect white teeth into the hand holding the pistol. But Eldar refused to relinquish the gun, braced himself against the floor, and struggled to his feet, with Cassandra hanging from his right hand and Natalie still on his lap. His grip on her throat was getting tighter. Her feet left the ground and her field of vision narrowed. She flailed with her arm and touched something with the back of her hand. One of the big, glazed Höganäs pots on the table.

Eldar jerked his body and sent Cassandra flying as if she were a rag doll. He took aim again to hit Natalie in the head with the pistol. She met his gaze, saw the rage and hatred in his eyes. Then the surprise as she smashed the pot against his head.

The pot must have had a crack in it already. It shattered, and in her hand she was holding a long shard. Eldar's head fell back, blood pouring from a deep wound in his forehead. But he didn't fall, just shook his head, straightened up, and raised the pistol a third time.

Cassandra screamed, a scream so shrill that it was painful to hear, and Natalie struck again, helplessly, because her strength was almost gone. She hit Eldar above his left eye, and the long, sharp piece of pottery forced its way in until her knuckles were touching his brow.

She felt his whole body twitch, and the hand that was clutching her throat let go and fell to his side. She struggled to get free, to reach the floor. Cassandra was still shrieking. She didn't stop until Natalie managed to get to her feet.

"The window," she gasped, almost absentmindedly wiping the blood from her face with the sleeve of her sweater. "We have to get out of here."

• • •

The Sniper had watched the commotion through the telescopic sight. A door opening, bodies moving about inside the cabin. A fight was clearly taking place, but he couldn't tell who was who. He had been in similar situations before. Knew it paid to be patient. To wait for the right moment.

The noise had died down and he moved his finger back to the trigger. Placed the crosshairs in the middle of the window. Father Ivor's voice was louder than before, almost strong enough to make him lose his concentration. As if his old mentor were right behind him.

Do you have regrets, my son?

His pulse was suddenly throbbing in his throat, temples, eyes. It was making him feel sick. He held his breath, forced his nausea back into his stomach while trying to slow his heart rate the way he usually did. But this time his normal routine failed him.

He spotted movement in the window. It flew open. He saw a red-haired woman appear in the sights. The moment he squeezed the trigger, a microsecond after it was too late, he regretted it.

• • •

Atif flew into the main room of the cabin. He swept the room with the hand holding the pistol. Eldar's dead body lay spread across the big dining table. Tindra was curled up behind an armchair.

"Amu!" The girl threw her arms around his neck and hid her little face against his shoulder. It almost made him forget the pain.

He carried Tindra over to the door of the little bedroom. He stopped in the doorway. Cassandra was lying on her back, her mouth open, eyes staring blankly at the ceiling. A pool of blood was slowly spreading out across the pine floorboards, forming a striped pattern.

"It came from outside," Natalie sniffed as she knelt by the body. "There was nothing I could do."

The window was wide-open. Moving slowly back and forth in the evening wind, as if it were waving good-bye.

Forty-Four

Oscar Wallin was half lying across his desk. The police radio beside him was tuned to the operations channel. Four dead bodies so far, one of them a woman. He already knew who. Knew that the stupid little bitch would never fuck with him or his family again.

In half an hour the media would be awash with hastily put-together reports. They'd be broadcasting live from the crime scene. Another gangland massacre in the backyard of the Regional Crime Unit, and in all likelihood the final nail in the coffin of Staffan Kollander's career. And for Pärson, the fat bastard.

Natalie, Kollander, Pärson, all knocked out in one single stroke of genius that could never be traced back to him. He reached out to switch the radio off, but stopped with his finger on the button. Why was he hesitating?

He certainly had other things to concentrate on. Julia Gabrielsson had outdone herself and had provided him with the tools he needed to regain admittance to the center of power. In an odd way he felt proud of her. She was his protégée, and his strategic investment in her was now paying a higher dividend than he had ever dared imagine. Julia was very different from all the idiots he had been forced to work with on the force. She was smart, driven, and dependable, rather like him. Together they could go far, toward a brighter future. All that was needed was one last push. Or sacrifice, depending on how you looked at it.

So, why didn't he just switch off the police radio?

Probably because of the little dot that was moving slowly across the map on his screen. Heading northeast along the motorway, toward Arlanda. At a guess it was Kassab, or possibly Cassandra Nygren, who had managed to get away and was fleeing for his or her life.

It wasn't really any of his concern now. But he hated loose ends.

Wallin took his pay-as-you-go cell phone out of his pocket. Before he had even pressed the buttons, he decided that this would be the last call he would make with it. He'd get rid of it at the same time as he deleted the tracking program from his computer, and Natalie Aden from his memory.

Susanna answered on the first ring.

• • •

"What are we going to tell her?" Natalie said quietly, so that Tindra—who was leaning on her chest—didn't wake up. It probably wasn't necessary. The air blowing through the bullet holes in the car doors was almost as loud as her voice.

"Nothing," Atif said over his shoulder. "We stick to what we said in the cabin: that her mom climbed out through the window. That she had to do it to save Tindra from the bad men. That Cassandra asked you to take care of her for the time being."

"We can't do that, can we? She has a right to know the truth."

"Yes, she does. But not now, not until she's safe. Tindra's been through enough already."

Natalie didn't answer, just looked out through the window. Ten more minutes and they'd be at Arlanda. Everything had changed. She'd never be able to return home even if she wanted to. The cabin was full of her fingerprints. The man she'd rented it from would be able to identify her. Obviously they should have set fire to it, but whoever had shot Cassandra was still out there somewhere. Their only option had been to grab their

335

things, get in her shot-up old Golf, and get out of there as fast as they could.

They passed the first patrol car about a kilometer from the junction with the road. It would take the police a long time to secure the scene, get a forensics team out there, and run all the findings through their system. But she guessed that she'd be as wanted as Atif by tomorrow evening, at the very latest. She held her right hand up. It was shaking.

"How do you think they found us?" she said. "Could they find us again?"

• • •

The Sniper had packed his gun and camping mat away with the usual five practiced movements. He crept carefully around the little lake, through the forest, and up among the houses where his rental car was parked. He had driven almost thirty kilometers from the Scout cabin when his cell phone rang.

"Eldar's dead," Susanna said. Her voice was cold, more factual than sad. "The other two as well. Kassab managed to escape."

"I'm sorry," the Sniper said. He wondered about adding something about Eldar being a good man, but decided against it.

"How far are you from Arlanda?"

He looked up and saw a road sign.

"Quarter of an hour, max."

"Good, they're already there. Put an end to this."

Forty-Five

Jesper Stenberg splashed water on his face, then straightened up and looked at himself in the mirror above the basin. Karolina and his mother-in-law had taken the girls down to the jetty. That had given him a chance to have a power nap in the guest cottage before his next mangling. He had been woken by the phone. It was the national police chief herself no less, informing him of another gangland shoot-out, this time in the southern suburbs of Stockholm. But he had lost interest in details of that sort. Before too long, the person he appointed as home minister would be in charge of the police and the fight against organized crime. He was on his way toward a different goal altogether.

"Prime Minister Jesper Stenberg," he said, trying it out in front of the mirror. He changed the emphasis slightly: "*Prime* Minister Jesper Stenberg." That sounded better.

It was going to happen tomorrow. The first step toward the absolute pinnacle. A press conference at Rosenbad. The prime minister would give a short election speech, and then it would be time for him to climb the podium to be presented as the prime minister's running mate and the future of the party. All he had ever wished for. The question was: What had his elevation cost? And did he really want to know?

He had turned the matter over in his mind repeatedly and arrived at one possible conclusion. The only possible conclusion.

Sophie had committed suicide. John had died of a heart attack. Wallin's insinuations, Boman's unpleasant talk of unconditional loyalty, and his own increasingly confused nightmares were all very irritating. But none of that constituted evidence of

337

any sort. And without evidence there was nothing he could do. Which left him with two choices: decline the offer and throw away all the work he and Karolina had put in, all the sacrifices they had made to get this far. Or say yes to the job and move on. Use his new position to do good. For the good of the country.

He wiped his face on one of the guest towels. Time for yet another run-through of his speech with his press secretary. A familiar feeling began to spread through his body. Something he hadn't felt for ages. A feeling of absolute presence.

• • •

There were only a couple more flights due to leave that evening, so the terminal was almost empty. Atif would have preferred to go through security at once, get all the way to the gate before they stopped for food or rest. But Natalie had forced him to sit down and wait on the benches outside the restrooms. She must have been in there for a good ten minutes now. Not that there was anything odd about that. He remembered the first time he had killed someone. How he had thrown up once the adrenaline kick ebbed away. It was actually pretty impressive that she had held it together this far. But Natalie was tough, probably one of the toughest people he knew. She'd even had the sense to patch his injuries up out in the airport parking lot.

You can't go into the terminal building with a bloody great hole right through your face, now, can you?

He touched the neat bandage covering one of his cheeks. Then the other one. Although her hands had been shaking, the pain hadn't flared up until after she patched him up. A four, which the painkillers were turning into a three.

Tindra was lying with her head on his lap. She had barely woken up when they made their way from the car to the terminal. Which wasn't that strange either. She must be completely exhausted. But now they had to gather their strength. Make one last effort in order to get to safety.

"Is this seat free?" a voice said in English.

Atif looked up and saw a black-clad man, about the same age as him, ordinary looking, carrying a rolled-up newspaper in one hand. The man indicated the bench opposite.

"Sure," Atif mumbled.

The man sat down. Looked at him for a few seconds.

"Pretty girl," he said. "Your daughter?" His English was good, with just a trace of an accent. Eastern European, maybe? Russian?

"Niece."

The man went on looking at him. His gaze was friendly, but there was still something in it that Atif felt he recognized. Something very familiar.

"Can I ask you a question? It might sound a bit strange . . . but I'm genuinely interested in your answer."

Atif frowned. Almost fifteen minutes had passed since Natalie disappeared. She ought to be back soon. He glanced over toward the women's restroom. Then at the man opposite.

"Okay," he said.

"Do you ever have any regrets?"

Atif was taken aback. "Regrets about what?"

The man shrugged his shoulders.

"This life. The fact that we became the people we did. The things we've done . . ."

"I've done many things I've regretted," Atif said, to his own surprise. Tiredness must have lowered his guard.

The man nodded slowly. "Me too. Once I shot a man from a distance of seven hundred meters. I lay hidden on a forest slope for over twenty-four hours waiting for the right moment. Killed him when he went out onto his balcony to get some air. Ten bodyguards couldn't stop me."

Atif stiffened. He gently lifted Tindra's head and slid out sideways. No sign of Natalie. The man had come from the direction of the toilets. He looked at the rolled-up newspaper. Wondered what sort of weapon it was hiding.

"There are only a few people on the planet who could do

339

something like that," the man went on. "So I should have felt proud. I suppose I did, for many years." He paused and met Atif's gaze again. "But not anymore. Now I've started to . . ."

"Have regrets," Atif said.

The man nodded. Then smiled weakly.

The two men sat in silence for several seconds, looking at each other across the narrow gangway.

"Did you kill her?" Atif said. Tried to keep his voice calm.

"Did I kill who?"

"Natalie." Atif nodded toward the toilets. "Did you kill her?"

The man pursed his lips.

"That was my task. Kill the red-haired woman. Susanna promised her source that she'd do that in exchange for him telling her where you were." He pulled an apologetic face. "But I made a mistake, didn't I? Killed the wrong woman back at the cabin. The girl's mother . . ."

Atif knitted his hands. Tindra stirred anxiously beside him.

"Susanna's husband and I are old acquaintances," the man said. "His uncle and I fought together. We were friends . . ."

"Eldar's dead," Atif said bluntly.

The man raised his eyebrows slightly. "Yes, I heard. So, in a way, perhaps you could say that we're quits?"

Atif shook his head. Felt the pain from the wound to his cheeks increase as his blood pressure rose. He leaned forward.

"You killed an innocent woman," he whispered. "We're not quits. Not by a long shot."

The man nodded slowly.

"I thought that was how you'd see it."

He laid the newspaper in his lap. Atif pressed his soles to the floor, got ready to move.

"Susanna will never give up," the man said slowly. "Even if you kill me, and the person she sends to replace me, and the one after that."

"Susanna is finished. Without the money there's no deal. Her creditors will turn on her for breaking her promise."

"You underestimate her. She had her own father killed, sacrificed him to save herself. Now Eldar is dead and the grieving widow will find a way of exploiting that fact to get out of the trap. Blame Eldar, make another deal with the same people. Whatever she offers, it will involve you and therefore everyone you care about. None of you will be safe. It doesn't matter where you hide."

He leaned closer.

"I have regrets." His voice was quiet, almost a whisper. "I regret things I've done, things I didn't do. This is my last job. I'm never going to take another life. But for people like you and me, it makes no difference how much regret we feel. Our punishment has already been meted out. All we can do is put as much as we can right. I've done what I can. The rest is up to you."

He slowly unrolled the newspaper and passed it to Atif. Then he stood up and walked calmly away.

On the back of the paper was an address and a simple sketch of a building, along with six digits followed by a roughly drawn square. It took a few seconds before Atif realized what it all meant.

"Who was that?"

Atif looked up. Natalie was standing in front of him, a bit pale, but otherwise unharmed.

He stood up and came close to throwing his arms around her but stopped himself at the last moment.

"Who?" he managed to say.

"That guy you were talking to." She pointed over her shoulder toward the man, who was slowly walking off through the terminal.

"No one special," Atif muttered. "He just wanted to give me his newspaper." He gestured for Natalie to sit down opposite him and rolled the newspaper up. The man's words echoed inside his head. *Susanna will never give up. It doesn't matter where you hide.*

"Change of plan," he said. He tried to keep his voice neutral. "You and Tindra have to travel on your own."

Natalie started. The tiredness in her eyes was suddenly replaced by confusion.

"Without you? Why? How?"

"You go ahead, I'll give you the codes to the numbered account. Take Tindra to Abu Dhabi and see that she, my mom, and my aunt settle into the house okay. You speak Arabic; it'll be fine. You can keep half the money. If Gilsén was telling the truth, that should be seven or eight million. Enough to make you a millionaire."

"But what are you going to do here? Everyone's looking for you."

"There are a couple of things I need to sort out before I leave."

"And you've only just realized that, an hour before the plane takes off?"

He kept his eyes on her.

"I didn't think it would be necessary. I'd hoped to avoid it, but now I realize it has to be done. Otherwise none of us is safe."

Natalie sat there without saying anything for several moments.

"What about Tindra?" She gestured toward the girl, who looked like she might be about to wake up.

"I'll explain it to her. It won't be a problem. She likes you, Natalie. Trusts you . . ." He found himself swallowing, involuntarily.

Natalie looked at the girl, then back at Atif. "I like her too," she said slowly.

Atif picked Tindra up in his arms. Held her tight.

"Why do you have to go, Amu?" Tindra said into his neck. She must have heard what he'd just told Natalie. He gulped and did his best to keep his voice steady.

"Sometimes that's just how it is. But Natalie will look after you. And I'll see you soon."

"With Mommy and Grandma and Khalti? In our new house with the swimming pool?"

He nodded. He couldn't bring himself to put the lie into words. He felt Natalie looking at him.

"Good-bye, my darling . . ." His voice cracked and he ended up hugging the little girl instead, as hard as he dared.

"Good-bye, Atif," Natalie said when he stood up. She carefully ran her knuckles over the bandages on his cheeks. "It's bled through on one side. The wounds should really be sewn up. You ought to get that vet to take a look at you."

Atif could see that her eyes were wet.

"Take care of yourself." She stood on tiptoe and kissed him on the chin. He put his arm around her back and held her for a few seconds. Closed his eyes.

Go with them, a little voice in his head was saying. *Be with them. Why not?*

Because I'm the tiger, he thought. *I'm the monster.*

Forty-Six

Dusk had started to fall, and Julia had gotten almost halfway back to Källstavik, when Pärson called.

"There's been a shooting at a Scout cabin in the southern suburbs. Abu Hamsa's son-in-law and two of his men are dead. Kassab's sister-in-law too. Full alert. I want you there right away. I don't give a damn about time off and overtime limits. Kollander and I are on our way, along with everyone else." Pärson rang off before she had time to protest.

Shit. She pulled over onto the shoulder. Wallin had promised to get ahold of a reliable forensics expert to examine the boathouse the following morning. Because he had access to the minister of justice's diary, he knew that Stenberg was out there with his family. But they would probably be heading back into the city by tomorrow morning at the latest, to prepare for a press conference at Rosenbad. And then there'd be nothing to get in the way of a discreet examination of the cement floor.

But the thought of waiting until morning didn't appeal to her. The Security Police guards who had caught her and Amante were bound to have written a report about the incident, possibly even mentioned it to someone in Stenberg's inner circle, which could mean, at worst, that the perpetrator realized that they were on his trail. Even if it sounded far-fetched, she wasn't willing to take the risk. So the boathouse would have to be watched overnight. She had a thermos, night-vision binoculars, and sandwiches with her in the car. Her pistol and bulletproof vest. But now she was going to have to change her plans if she was the slightest bit interested in keeping her normal job.

She sat and thought for a few moments as she irritably tapped her foot on the floor of the car. Then she started the engine, did a tight U-turn that made the tires squeal, and started to drive south.

• • •

Atif stopped the car a couple of streets from his destination and walked the rest of the way. Finding the right address was no problem. He kept his distance and found a suitable vantage point a few hundred meters from the house.

The big villa was lit up from all sides, and well guarded. Wall, automatic gate, cameras. And, as if that wasn't enough, two not particularly inconspicuous plainclothes cops sitting in a car not far down the street. Even so, he had to get in.

He ran his tongue over the insides of his cheeks. Felt the rough edges of the wounds, the uneven surface of congealed blood. The taste of iron. He was tired. Far more tired than he cared to admit. More than anything, he felt like going back to the car, leaning the seat back, and sleeping for a while. Recharge his batteries.

But he had no choice. This had to happen this evening.

He closed his eyes for a few seconds and tried to summon up an image of the starry sky above the desert. For once, he succeeded. He imagined them there. Tindra, his mother, his aunt. Natalie. Safe. Secure. Thanks to him.

• • •

The rear of the house faced a patch of woodland. Just as on the drawing, a path led to a door in the high wall. The quickest way out if you wanted to walk the dog or just leave the property a bit more discreetly. Beside the door was an entry phone with both a keypad and a camera.

He tapped in the code that had been written on the newspaper the man at the airport had given him, ending with the hash key. The lock whirred and the door swung open. He pulled the pistol from his belt and held it by his side as he crossed the garden as quickly as he could, in the direction of the back steps. He knew he could be seen by the security cameras. But that no longer mattered.

He was barely ten meters away when the back door flew open and Susanna stepped out. She was holding a shotgun in her hands, aimed directly at him. Atif stopped. Kept his pistol pointing at the ground. She wasn't going to shoot him, at least not yet, he told himself. Susanna still needed Gilsén's money.

"I was wondering when you were going to show up." Susanna's voice was cold as ice. "Or, rather, I was hoping you would."

"I've got something you want," Atif said. "And you've got something I want."

One corner of Susanna's mouth lifted in a crooked smile. The shotgun was still pointing straight at Atif's chest.

"And what might that be?"

"The man who told you where we were, the man who demanded that Natalie had to die. I want to know who he is."

• • •

Stenberg was sitting in a wingback chair in front of the open fire in the spacious living room of Karl-Erik's cottage. Although *cottage* was hardly the right word for a building covering almost two hundred square meters. The stone wall around the fireplace was full of hunting trophies. Deer antlers. Even a stuffed elk's head glaring at him with eyes of dark glass.

He had never really understood the point of hanging the remains of dead animals on walls as decoration. But, on the other hand, there were plenty more things about his father-in-law that he didn't really understand.

"So, are you ready now?" Karl-Erik handed him a glass of whiskey, then poured himself one.

"You'd have to ask Cecilia about that."

His press secretary nodded on the other side of the coffee table. "You're ready. Top marks in both presentation and emotion."

"Good," Karl-Erik said. "Thanks for your help, Cecilia. It must be time to call it a night." A statement, not a question.

Stenberg's press secretary gathered her things and left the room. Obeyed without so much as a glance in Stenberg's direction.

"We're going to have to replace her," his father-in-law said as soon as the door had closed behind her. "Cecilia has done a good job, but you're going to need someone more experienced at your side from now on. Same thing with your undersecretary of state. But that's a more strategic matter; it can wait a few months. You and Karolina are going home this evening, aren't you? Do you want me to get Boman to drive you?"

Stenberg shook his head. "The Security Police can take us. I thought it best to sleep in my own bed tonight, so I'm fully rested and alert tomorrow."

"Good thinking, Jesper." Karl-Erik smiled contentedly and sat down in the armchair next to Stenberg's. "Tomorrow is a big day. Not just for you and Karolina, but for the whole family. As you know, we have held important posts before. But as of tomorrow you will be our brightest star."

Karl-Erik patted his hand lightly, and the intimacy of the gesture took Stenberg by surprise.

"I have a small confession to make. I'm sure you remember the first time Karolina introduced us. You'd been studying law together for a couple of years by then, hadn't you?"

"Two and a half," Stenberg said. And had been sharing a bed for just under one of them, he thought, even if Karolina hadn't dared to tell her doting father that.

"Exactly. You seemed very polite, pleasant, and intelligent. I remember that clearly. Even so, I have to admit that I was a little doubtful about Karolina's choice of partner."

Stenberg was somewhat taken aback. Enough for his father-in-law to notice.

"You seemed a little . . ." Karl-Erik swirled his whiskey as he searched for the right words. ". . . lacking in focus. A talented

347

young man with great expectations but who didn't quite have the strength or desire to develop. Who consciously set the bar low and wasn't trying to achieve his full potential."

The topic of conversation surprised Stenberg, and he wasn't sure if he was expected to say anything.

"But Karolina was convinced you were the right person to go for, both personally and professionally," his father-in-law continued. "Happily, it turned out that she was right and I was wrong. She's her father's daughter."

Karl-Erik patted Stenberg's hand again.

"What I'm really trying to say is that I'm proud of you, Jesper. Proud of the man you've become, and what you . . . what *we* have achieved together. You, Karolina, and I."

Stenberg thought he could see a shimmer in his father-in-law's eyes. Karl-Erik looked away for a few moments. When he looked at Stenberg again, his usual expression was back in place.

"You've sacrificed a lot to reach this point. I'm well aware of that. Sometimes you have been obliged to do things you would have preferred not to do. Make decisions you would rather have avoided. And have probably acquired a few enemies along the way."

Karl-Erik fell silent for a few moments.

"But you've done so without hesitation. You've kept your eye on the larger prize and not allowed yourself to be distracted. And tomorrow it's time for you to receive your reward."

Our *reward*, Stenberg thought. Our *reward, for* our *sacrifices. Surely that's what you mean?*

Karl-Erik nodded, almost as if he could read Stenberg's thoughts.

"We're standing on the threshold of the future, Jesper. That's why it's vitally important that there's nothing that could trip us up. No little detail, no matter how insignificant, that could cause a problem."

Stenberg felt his father-in-law's eyes bore into his. And go on into his head. He almost blinked and looked away to escape.

But he stopped himself. Instead he tried to adopt an expression that was as blank and vacuous as that of the elk on the wall above them.

"I don't know what sort of detail that might be. The party went through my background before I got this job, and I can only assume that the press has done the same. I haven't got any skeletons in my closet. Or perhaps it would be more accurate to say . . ."

He was surprised he managed to say the words without his gaze wavering even slightly.

". . . that *we* don't have any skeletons in *our* closet. Because we haven't, do we, Karl-Erik?"

Forty-Seven

Omar Amante waited up by the main road for the cars to leave. First the big Security Police Volvo with Stenberg and his wife. Then, a quarter of an hour later, a dark Audi that he guessed was the father-in-law's. To be on the safe side, he waited another ten minutes before slowly rolling down the road toward the boathouse with just his sidelights on.

He'd considered calling Gabrielsson before heading out there. But the truth was that he felt ashamed. He hadn't actually realized what a poor state he was in—not until he saw the crazed look in his reflection in the bathroom mirror when he got home. Lack of sleep, fixation on his work, and the thoughts of dead bodies that wouldn't leave his head. The handcuffs had almost tipped him over the edge. But he had stopped himself. Hadn't tumbled over the way he did once before.

Lampedusa. He wanted to tell her what had happened there. Everything this time. How his colleagues had pulled him down from the noose. How he had struggled when they leaped on him and cuffed his hands and feet. The smell of smoke. The sound of his voice screaming insults until the doctor put the needle in his arm. It couldn't happen again. Wasn't going to happen again.

The boathouse was their only real lead, the only thing that could take them closer to the murderer. And for that reason he was going to guard it. Sit and wait until Gabrielsson got a forensics expert out there, which he knew she would. Because Gabrielsson was the best police officer he had ever worked with.

The look she had given him as they parted outside his door

had stuck in his head. She felt sorry for him, which was the last thing he wanted. So he had to prove to her that he could still function. Which meant he had to think like a detective.

He ascertained that the place up by the house where the cars were usually parked was empty, and the only illumination visible up there came from the outside lights. Even by the boathouse a lamp was spreading a semicircle of light around the door. He reversed the car as far as he could into one corner of the turnaround, where it was well-enough hidden by some wild roses that no one would see it unless they were pretty close. He turned the engine off and made sure the interior light was switched off. Then he got out the flashlight he'd bought on the way and walked over to the boathouse. The door was locked, like before. There was no sign that anyone had tried to get in.

Just as he was getting back into the car, he thought he heard a noise. A branch snapping in the woods. He sat still and listened for a while, trying to work out exactly where the sound had come from, without success. There was a barking noise in the distance. A peculiar sound, like a dog, yet somehow different. A deer, maybe?

He sank back in the driver's seat and left the door ajar. He reached for his flask. It was almost midnight. In three or four hours' time dawn would break through the grainy summer night. Three or four hours, no problem. The bark sounded again. Closer this time. He couldn't help shuddering at the harsh noise.

• • •

He must have dozed off for a while. Five, ten minutes, maybe. The dregs in his coffee cup had had time to go cold. Not a good idea to fall asleep at his post. Good thing there was no one around to notice. He opened the car door a little more and tipped the coffee out onto the ground. He blinked hard several times to wake himself up. He listened closely for the deer, but the barking sound had stopped.

351

His bladder was making itself felt and he got out of the car. Walked around it, stopped behind the trunk, and took aim at the nearest clump of grass. He closed his eyes and smelled the mixture of fresh urine and forest. Then he heard the deer bark again. A rattling, warning sound, no more than twenty meters away in among the dark trees. He jerked and suddenly felt very uneasy. The hairs on the back of his neck rose up against the frayed collar of his tennis shirt. He started to turn around but he wasn't quick enough.

White, glowing pain spread from the back of his neck. Flashed through his body, to his head, his consciousness. And turned to darkness.

• • •

The plane was over an hour late when it finally took off from Arlanda. Natalie waited for the clunk of the landing gear retracting before she let herself relax. Her body felt numb, almost as if it didn't belong to her. Her hands were still shaking, and the bitter taste of bile refused to budge in spite of a double dose of chewing gum. Inside the restroom in the terminal she had lain curled up next to the toilet bowl, throwing her guts up and sobbing like a child.

She had killed another human being. Taken a life. But it could just as easily have been her lifeless body draped over the bench in the cabin. Game fucking over!

Just a few short weeks ago she had had a perfectly okay life. An apartment, a job, almost an average life. Now she was sitting here, everything she owned in a small carry-on in the locker above her head. She had left everything behind her, fleeing with a dead woman's fake passport in one hand and a small child she'd only known a few days in the other. She looked at Tindra, half expecting to see that she was asleep. But instead the little girl was crying. Tears were running down her cheeks, but the only sound emerging from her lips were little gasps. Natalie put her arm around her. Leaned her head back against her shoulder. Felt the warmth and moisture from her cheek.

"Everything's going to be okay," she murmured softly.

She stroked the girl's hair. Realized that her hand had stopped shaking.

. . .

It was the noise that woke him. A crunching sound, accompanied by a muffled bass note that kept getting louder.

Amante opened his eyes and tried to get up, but his hands were tied behind his back. The pain triggered by his movement almost overwhelmed him, as if his body's entire electrical system had been switched on at the same time, overloading his pain sensors.

He gasped for breath. The smoke in the confined space was starting to make him cough. Then his brain realized what the sounds, heat, and smoke meant. Where he was and what was happening. He was lying tied up in the trunk of a car. His own car. And on the other side of the thin metal, a fire was raging.

Panic made his body contort, summoning all available muscle power to break free. He tugged and pulled so hard at the rope that the skin on his wrists tore. His feet kicked out in all directions. Right, left, upward. He struck the lid of the trunk with a loud thud that made the metal bend. He kicked again, this time with both feet. Now he could just make out shimmering light in the gaps around the trunk lid. He kicked again, and again.

Smoke billowed in through the gaps. Merged with his memories, making him panic more. He screamed. And kicked again.

The lid flew open, letting a wall of heat into the trunk. The light blinded him, but as his eyes got used to it he realized where he was. He was tied up inside the burning boathouse.

Flames were licking the walls around him. In places, they had already reached the roof. He clambered out and somehow managed to free his hands from the rope.

The noise of the flames was deafening, getting louder with each passing second. He had to do something, had to try to get out before the wall of heat reached the gas tank. But he just stood there, paralyzed, every muscle in his body hard as stone, while the fire devoured the oxygen around him. The heat was starting to melt the soles of his shoes, and his clothes were scorching his skin. He heard the tires and windows of the car explode as the metal began to buckle.

He opened his mouth, roaring as loudly as his lungs could manage. And threw himself right into the cauldron of flame to his right, where the water ought to be.

His clothes caught fire, then his hair. The skin on his back. He leaped. And fell.

Forty-Eight

"The call came in just after three o'clock," Wallin said in a sub-dued voice. "According to the officer in command, the building was completely ablaze when the fire brigade arrived. Their initial priority was making sure the fire didn't spread to the forest. It was sheer luck that one of the firemen saw something floating out in the water."

A nurse walked past and Wallin leaned a bit closer to Julia. A distinct smell of smoke was coming off his clothes, making her nose twitch.

"I headed out there at once, but there wasn't much to see. It's going to take a while before the ruins cool down enough for Forensics to start their work. It was a stroke of luck that a neighbor had borrowed the boat, otherwise he wouldn't have . . ."

Wallin gestured toward the locked door of the intensive care unit a short distance away. Julia didn't say anything. Her whole body felt numb, her head full of thick sludge. When was the last time she got a decent night's sleep? She couldn't remember.

"What do you think he was doing out there?" Wallin said.

"You mean, do I think he's responsible for the fire?"

Wallin held his hands up in halfhearted protest. "I didn't say that. But can we at least agree that someone set light to the boathouse to destroy evidence?"

"But what evidence? Actual evidence that proved Sarac was dismembered there, or fake evidence that suggests some sort of conspiracy? If there was any biological evidence of Sarac

355

left there, it's been destroyed now. And the cement floor will probably have cracked in the heat."

She tried to gather her thoughts, but it was pretty much impossible. If anything, her head seemed to be getting more sluggish.

"We agree on that much, anyway," Wallin said. "There's something else I should tell you. I've checked with people I know at the Security Police, but no one's willing to say where Sarac's body has gone or even which unit took it. Officially they're referring to the need to keep the investigation confidential, but unofficially my guess is that the body's been cremated."

"Who do you think did it?"

Wallin shrugged. "Someone who's one step ahead of us."

"We've still got the pictures and the blackmail letter."

"Yes, but we still don't know who it was sent to. And even if the pictures are genuine, they only link Stenberg to Sophie Thorning's death. They'd cost him his career, but they aren't enough to catch a murderer."

"They provide a plausible motive," she said in the absence of a better argument.

"True. But what good is that when we have no body, no murder weapon, and no crime scene?"

"So what do we do, then? Just give up?" Her voice cracked slightly at the end of the sentence and she cleared her throat.

"Not yet. There's one more thing I want to check. Lie low for the time being. Don't talk to anyone!"

She nodded. Wallin turned and started to walk toward the exit. She would have liked to do the same; it felt like she'd completely run out of energy. The shoot-out in the Scout cabin had kept her busy all night, and just as she was on her way home, Wallin called and she headed straight for the Karolinska University Hospital instead. But she couldn't just leave Amante to fight for his life in there. She had to see him.

A doctor came out through the double doors; it looked like he'd pressed the button to open them automatically. When he disappeared around the corner, she darted forward and caught the doors just as they were closing.

At first she thought she was in the wrong room. That the man inside the plastic tent was someone else. If it was actually a man. The body in the bed surrounded by tubes looked more like a mummy, a corpse that had been embalmed and wrapped in bandages in advance of its final journey.

But then she noticed an eye in the bandage covering the head and face. It opened, and a thin, bandaged arm rose in her direction. Julia gasped. She knew she shouldn't be there, that she had acted on a foolish impulse. Even so, she took a step forward. She needed some sort of clarity.

"Omar," she said. "It's me, Julia."

Amante raised his arm a few more centimeters toward her, and for a moment she came close to holding his hand.

"I'm so sorry," she said.

"Fffff . . ." Amante hissed. He seemed to want her to move closer. One of the machines beside the bed began to bleep.

Julia took another step toward him. She leaned over. Smelled the cream they had covered his body with, and beneath it the smell of burned flesh.

"F-Find him," Amante whispered in her ear.

Forty-Nine

Jesper Stenberg was standing in the spacious walk-in closet he shared with his wife. He inspected his reflection in the mirror as Karolina adjusted his tie. Power red, in a perfect double Windsor. Tailor-made white shirt, hand-sewn Italian shoes, and the Brioni suit she and the girls had given him for his birthday. As the icing on the cake, the heavy cuff links his in-laws had given him, and which he actually thought made him look a bit old-fashioned. But he didn't have the heart to say anything. Today was Karolina's day too. The reward for all her sacrifices.

"Take everything off again and hang it in the travel case so it doesn't get creased in the car. I'll find a bit of concealer for the rings under your eyes. You were up during the night again. From tonight on, you'll sleep better, I promise."

Stenberg nodded distantly. Even though he'd showered and shaved, his head still felt heavy. The nightmares were refusing to give up without a fight, replaying the moment of Sophie's death over and over again, then Boman's face looking out from her window high above.

He looked at his wife. Admired her lithe, gym-trained body as she walked through the room. Sophie Thorning had been short and slight. White porcelain skin, blonde hair. Firm buttocks, perfect breasts. A body made for sex. Karolina's body was more reminiscent of her father's. Straight-backed, broad shoulders. Dark hair, high cheekbones. She carried herself elegantly. She pulled off the difficult trick of being tall without it becoming her single memorable feature. He admired his wife, admired her self-control, her style, her strength.

Karolina seemed to sense him looking at her. She turned her head and smiled at him. But in his sleep-deprived state, her smile turned into John Thorning's smug grin. John Thorning, whose suited corpse was slowly rotting in his expensive oak coffin.

Isn't it odd the way all obstacles disappear, one way or another?

Stenberg shook his head gently. He needed to steer his brain away from thoughts like that, mustn't let it sink into paranoia.

Karolina was right. That evening they would turn over a new page. Enter a new, happier era. He owed it to her to put the past behind him. That was how he had to look at it. He would do it for her sake.

Stenberg straightened his back. A double espresso, then his brain would start working normally again. Karolina would set him on the right track. Toward the future.

• • •

Natalie had sought out a quiet corner of the vast hotel lobby before calling Atif. She didn't really want to leave Tindra alone in the room, but she didn't have any choice.

"You wanted me to call when everything was done."

"Yes. Did it all go okay?"

"All according to plan. I've transferred the money and paid for the house and all the plane tickets. Your mom and your aunt and her family are traveling the day after tomorrow."

"Good. What about Tindra? How is she?"

"As well as can be expected, considering everything she's been through. She keeps asking for her mom, and she's sleeping a lot."

The line went silent for a few moments.

"How are you doing?" she said. "Have you sorted out the things you mentioned?"

"One of them. I'm hoping to get the second one resolved this evening."

"You sound tired. You're being careful, aren't you? Tindra needs you. We need you," she added, after a short pause.

There was a click on the line and he was gone. She knew there was no way of knowing over the phone, that it was just wishful thinking. But she was still sure she had heard him smile.

. . .

Julia had driven straight home and fallen into bed. She shut her eyes and waited for sleep to put a stop to the maelstrom of thoughts in her head. She gave up after three-quarters of an hour or so. She just lay there instead, staring at the ceiling.

Wallin was right. Someone was one step ahead of them. Someone who had found out that they were taking an interest in the boathouse and had gone out there to make sure there were no loose ends. But was that person Amante? She doubted it, not only because she had heard what he whispered in the hospital. She had called one of the forensics experts, and it looked like the car inside the boathouse was Amante's, so if he was a pyromaniac, he was an incredibly inept one.

Julia was more and more convinced that he had gone to Källstavik for the same reason that she had set off there: to watch the scene, make sure no one destroyed the evidence. Presumably he had been inexperienced enough to park near the building and thus present an easy target.

Amante was her colleague and was maybe even on the way to becoming her friend. She put her arm over her eyes and tried to suppress the image of his burned body. She only half succeeded.

She sat up and looked at the time. Just past twelve. She went out into the kitchen and made herself a cup of coffee.

Trying to burn Amante alive was clearly a risky strategy for the perpetrator. Yet he had evidently thought it was sur- mountable. It wasn't too hard to realize why. Amante had been suspended from duty, the car was his own, and he had recently been treated for a nervous breakdown. Add to that the fact that Amante had previously been apprehended at the scene, and you could easily mistake him for a mentally unstable individual with an unhealthy fixation on the minister of justice. Someone who might well be capable of burning himself alive in his boss's boathouse in his frustration at being suspended. Unless perhaps Amante's stepfather would rather deal with the matter more discreetly, so that his unstable stepson's slip-up didn't affect his own political ambitions. Either way, there was no way Pärson, Kollander, or anyone else would let her dig any deeper.

Wallin was right, as usual. Without the evidence of the boathouse, all that was left was a blackmail letter without a recipient, and a few digital photographs that may or may not have been manipulated. And her own conviction. Hers and Amante's, she corrected herself. And actually, as of today, Oscar Wallin's as well. Because Wallin had implied that he believed her, hadn't he? That he was thinking of helping her somehow?

Wallin was her only hope now. Her only chance of getting justice for Sarac and Amante.

Fifty

Atif was dreaming about the tiger again. But this time it lies on top of a cracked lump of concrete. The ground around it is frozen; the branches of dead trees stretch out above ruins covered by snow.

The tiger's breath rises like smoke from its mouth. The beast is looking at him, its head tilted slightly.

What are you frightened of? it seems to be saying. *Come closer.*

The tiger is wounded—he can see that now. There's red around its nose, and a large bloodstain is slowly spreading across one of its sides. A gunshot wound.

"Who shot you?" his dream self asks, but he already knows the answer. "It was Susanna, wasn't it?"

The tiger raises its head slightly. Sniffs tentatively at the dry, cold air.

But you're not dead, he thinks. *Not yet. Not until you've finished your hunt.*

With an effort the tiger stands up, then jumps down from the concrete block and disappears among the ruins.

He woke up because he was freezing. The windows of Natalie's Golf had misted over, and he opened the door to let out the damp air. At the same time the pain came back to life. A definite six. He felt his stomach. His fingers came away wet. He had bled through the bandage. *Fucking hell.*

He looked at the bandage and his wet shirt. Tried to work out how much blood he'd lost in total. Possibly half a liter or thereabouts. He picked up the bottle of water from the passenger seat and drank a few gulps. The cold water made him shudder. He thought about Natalie's phone call, worried for a moment that it too had been a dream. But the call log on his phone reassured him. Tindra and Natalie were safe; they'd always be safe now. All he had to do was summon the last of his strength. Find the man he was looking for. Finish the job.

He straightened up, wiped the windshield. At that moment a garage door along the street opened and a car pulled out. Atif caught a quick glimpse of the driver as the vehicle passed him. He started the car, did a sharp U-turn, and followed the other car.

. . .

The operations room in the Violent Crime Unit. The same people as usual, Pärson and Kollander included. Julia stayed in the background. She didn't want any more work thrown her way.

"To summarize the situation after last night's events," Pärson said as the image of a cabin appeared in the projector screen behind him. "A total of four individuals were found dead in or in the vicinity of the Scout cabin."

He waved at the police officer operating the projector to change the picture. Four photographs of equal size appeared.

"The victims are: Kassab's sister-in-law, Cassandra Nygren; Eldar Jafarov; and two of his thugs whose names I'm not even going to try to pronounce. All the evidence suggests that Atif Kassab was in the cabin and was the target of the attack, but his sister-in-law somehow got in the way."

Pärson shifted his weight to the other foot, evidently not used to having to stand up.

"When the Rapid Response Unit conducted a search of Eldar Jafarov's villa in Älvsjö this morning, they found his wife, Susanna—Abu Hamsa's daughter—dead in the living room."

Another picture. Susanna was lying on the floor. The rug beneath her was dark red. She was staring blankly at the camera. Just under her right eye was a small, black hole.

"Susanna Jafarov seems to have been expecting a visitor. She

363

was wearing a bulletproof vest and beside her body was a shotgun from which one cartridge had been fired. Traces of blood on the steps suggest that she hit her target. The DNA match against Kassab's records will be ready this afternoon, but that's mostly a formality. We already have pictures from the security cameras mounted outside the property."

Pärson gestured once more to the guy operating the projector. Julia noted that he had chosen not to point out that there had been two detectives sitting outside the front of the property who evidently hadn't noticed anything going on inside the house. Hardly surprising.

The screen came to life, playing a video clip of a man moving across an illuminated backyard in a crouch. The image froze and the operator zoomed in on Atif Kassab's angular face until it filled the whole screen.

"At the risk of stating the obvious, we are looking for Atif Kassab. He's armed and is judged to be extremely dangerous. And he's wounded. We don't know how badly, but we're urging all officers to exercise extreme caution when he's found. There's already a national alert out for Kassab. We're also looking for his niece, Tindra Nygren, seven years old, who may be traveling with him, plus an as-yet-unidentified woman who rented the Scout cabin and called herself Anette. Regional Crime has been on high alert since last night. The preliminary investigation is being led by District Prosecutor Schill, and head of the operation is Superintendent Kollander here." Pärson nodded toward the head of Regional Crime. "Any questions before the head of the operation takes over?"

One officer said something Julia didn't hear, but whatever it was, it sparked a discussion. Obviously she ought to get involved and show an interest in their biggest case since Skarpö. But Pärson had given all the most interesting jobs to his buddies in the Tic Tac Club and the rest to people Kollander liked. And she didn't exactly belong to either of those groups.

As expected, not a word was said about the fire at Källstavik.

Pärson and Kollander had presumably received orders to hush it up. Kollander had now stood up and was evidently sharing pearls of wisdom. Julia quietly got to her feet and crept out, and began to walk toward her office. Her phone rang as soon as she had closed the door.

"Wallin here." He sounded much the same as usual, but she thought she could detect a note of tension in his voice. "I've managed to find an image specialist. One who's good and seriously fucking discreet. He can help us figure out if those photographs are Photoshopped or genuine. Can you get away at three o'clock?"

She looked at her watch. "Sure."

"Good, we need to meet someplace no one else knows about."

She thought for a moment. "What about Hunter's hideout? I've still got the keys."

"Perfect. See you there."

Fifty-One

They met in the parking lot in front of the office building. Julia had pulled all the tricks she knew to avoid being followed. First she checked the car to make sure there was no tracking device on it. Then she switched off the police radio and her cell phone. She headed north on the motorway with the blue lights flashing, and used an access road to pull a bold U-turn. She repeated the same maneuver ten minutes later. Then she added a few extra little tricks that pursuers tended not to appreciate. She hadn't seen a single indication that anyone was following her.

She very nearly didn't recognize Wallin at first. He wasn't wearing his suit, and was sporting a jeans-trainers-hoodie outfit that made him look almost like a teenager. Beside him stood a guy in his thirties. Blond, well built, and in a T-shirt that was slightly too tight, revealing the bottom half of a tattoo on one arm.

"Sebastian," he said, smiling in a relaxed way that made her like him at once.

"Are you going to show us the way?" Wallin gestured toward the building.

"Sure." She set off. Walked up the narrow staircase. The building seemed just as deserted as it had the last time she was there.

She unlocked the door and let them into the little room. It smelled musty. Hunter's sleeping bag was still spread out over the camping mattress. Sebastian sat down at the table and took out a laptop. Wallin walked around the room. He pointed at one of the corners.

366

"Was that where you found . . . ?"

"There." She pointed at the opposite corner.

He walked closer and inspected the little hole made by the potato peeler. He seemed quite impressed by both the hiding place and the fact that she had found it.

"Okay." Sebastian turned to look at them. "I'm ready. Which of you has the picture?"

Julia put her hand in her pocket and removed the little memory card. She hesitated briefly.

"Sebastian knows what he's doing, and he's very discreet," Wallin said.

"Absolutely. I've done several jobs for the Security Police before. I usually have to sign a bunch of paperwork."

"That won't be necessary today," Wallin said. "We trust your professionalism." He patted the man on the shoulder. And nodded to Julia to hand over the memory card. She obeyed.

Sebastian inserted the card into the slot in the laptop, then tapped some keys.

"There are three pictures. Which one do you want me to start with?"

"The one titled zero zero three," she said, pulling the other wooden chair out and sitting down next to him.

He clicked. Said nothing for a few moments. "Powerful image," he said. As a statement of fact.

He clicked again. Zoomed in and out across Sophie Thorning's body.

"My first impression is that the picture is genuine. The shadows and lighting all make sense, and there are no odd edges or changes in color."

More clicking.

"If this is a fake, then whoever was responsible certainly knew what they were doing." He looked up. Smiled at her again, not quite as broadly this time.

"So, what happens now?" Wallin was standing behind Sebastian, looking over his shoulder.

"I run the picture through a program that analyzes the pixels. Figures out if there are any color patterns that don't fit. The sort of thing that can't be detected by the naked eye."

"How long will that take?" Julia said. All of a sudden the atmosphere in the room was making her feel uneasy.

Sebastian shrugged his shoulders.

"Anything from a couple of minutes to a couple of hours. It depends what crops up."

She looked at him. Since when were IT guys in such good shape as he was? He looked like a professional triathlete. More at home on a running track or assault course than in front of a screen. Obviously that could just be her prejudice: people could look however they wanted to, of course. But he'd barely flinched at the sight of Sophie's battered body. She continued to surreptitiously watch the guy. Sebastian tapped at the keyboard some more, then raised his hands above his head and stretched.

"There. Now we just wait."

Julia nodded. The sleeve of his T-shirt slid up as he stretched, revealing the rest of the tattoo. An eagle with outstretched talons, its wings spread.

"Parachute regiment," she said.

He raised his eyebrows. "How did you know?"

"Your tattoo. I once dated a guy who had one like it. I seem to recall he was a lieutenant."

"Okay. And there was me thinking you were pretty *and* clairvoyant."

"How does a paratrooper end up doing a job like this?"

His eyes narrowed, not much, but enough for her to notice. "You mean I don't fit the template for an IT guy? Would it be better if I had scrawny arms and a Green Lantern T-shirt?"

She didn't answer, just went on studying him. As subtly as she could, she moved her chair back a little. The computer made a faint noise.

"Okay, it's done." Sebastian clicked the pad.

Wallin took a step closer. "What does it say? Is the picture fake or genuine?"

"Genuine."

"Are you absolutely certain?" Wallin said.

"Hundred percent." Sebastian looked up and met Julia's gaze. His face was hard, almost clenched.

She held her breath and felt tentatively for the pistol at her right hip. But then Sebastian suddenly flashed her a suggestive wink. His face softened and cracked into another charming smile. A facial expression that quickly switched to surprise when Wallin Tasered him in the back of the neck.

Fifty-Two

Sebastian's body twitched as if he were cramping. Then he fell heavily across the laptop. Julia was sitting frozen to her chair. For a brief moment she imagined that Sebastian had in fact presented a threat and that Wallin had realized this and rendered him harmless. But then she saw the pistol in Wallin's other hand. He raised it and aimed it straight at her face.

"Hands on the table," he said. "Nice and gently."

She did as he said and she tried to work out what was going on. Wallin walked around her, still pointing his pistol at her head. He was wearing black rubber gloves. When had he put those on?

"Keep looking straight ahead."

He pulled her jacket up, removed her service weapon, and kicked it away across the floor. Then took out the cuffs she was carrying in a little pouch at the small of her back.

"Left hand," he commanded, and she felt the cold metal against her wrist. "And the right."

He cuffed her to the back of the chair. Then went and stood on the other side of the table and put his pistol back in its holster.

"I'm sorry about this, Julia. But you and I need to talk, and I had to take certain precautions."

She finally got control of her voice. "What the fuck are you playing at, Oscar?"

"A perfectly justifiable question."

Wallin held a couple of fingers to Sebastian's neck, apparently checking how conscious he was. Then he felt in his pocket and pulled out a large, transparent plastic bag and a matchbox, which he put on the table.

"Let me explain. You and I have a unique opportunity. We've uncovered a secret, an incredibly potent one, and as I see it, we have two options. Either . . ."

Wallin slowly unfolded the plastic bag, opened the matchbox, and tipped about half the contents into the bag. A fine black powder that looked a bit like printer toner.

". . . we reveal the secret. Probably by way of an anonymous tip-off to the press, seeing as we don't know who we can trust in the police force. Jesper Stenberg goes down and drags a whole load of powerful people down with him. His father-in-law, the national police chief, possibly even the prime minister."

Wallin closed the plastic bag and shook it gently, spreading the powder around inside it.

"But once the witch hunt is over and the dust has settled, what would be left for you and me? I'd get fired because I was too closely associated with Stenberg. And you . . ." He looked up and tilted his head slightly. "Well, at best I imagine that you'd be allowed to carry on slaving away in the Regional Crime Unit. Taking orders from whatever moron replaces Pärson. Assuming the police authority doesn't find out that it was the pair of us who leaked the whole story. Because if that happens, we can probably count ourselves lucky if we get away with losing just our jobs."

Julia was frantically trying to figure out what was going on. What was Wallin getting at, and what was the plastic bag for?

"The other option is that we do the exact opposite. We protect the secret. We guard it as preciously as if it were our own. Use it to our advantage."

"You mean blackmail," Julia managed to say.

Wallin shook his head. "No, no, you misunderstand me. This isn't about blackmailing anyone but showing that their secret is safe in our hands. Safer than ever, in fact. Because we're prepared to go to great lengths to protect it."

He fell silent and held two fingers to Sebastian's neck again.

"Tasers are wonderful things. They leave very little evidence. Just two tiny scorch marks. The trick is to fire the Taser at the base of the hairline so the marks aren't spotted during an autopsy. But then you have to get your opponent to look away. Distract him somehow."

Julia straightened up.

"Amante," she said drily. "Did you use the Taser on him?"

Wallin shrugged his shoulders. "I wasn't expecting to find him out there. It looks like our little civilian was trying to play at being a real police officer, which was very bad luck for him. But in the long term his fate was unavoidable. Amante was a risk factor. One single unguarded remark to his father, Victor, and everything would come crashing down. He couldn't be left at large."

"You meant to burn him alive?" She was having difficulty keeping her voice steady. "Is that what you're planning to tell Jesper Stenberg? That you're so loyal, you're prepared to kill to protect his secret?"

Wallin snorted. "You're overestimating Jesper, I'm afraid. He's neither ambitious nor strong enough to handle that sort of loyalty. Just as you and Amante suspected, he doesn't know anything about Sarac. Other people took care of that for him. John Thorning is another example. Even Jesper has begun to suspect that his death came at a very opportune moment."

"You mean you're thinking of cooperating with the people who murdered Sarac and Thorning?" A drop of saliva flew out of her mouth with the last word.

"We could both do that. You're smart, driven, ambitious. In no more than a year or so, Jesper Stenberg will be the new prime minister. You'd be working directly for him. Imagine the possibilities you and I would have. We wouldn't have to listen to fat idiots like Pärson or incompetent bureaucrats like Kollander. Direct contact with the people in power. A place in the inner circle."

He fell silent and left the unspoken question hanging in the air. Sebastian moved slightly and let out a faint whimper.

"And if I say no?" she said.

Wallin grabbed Sebastian's body and pushed him back on his chair. Pulled the plastic bag over his head and pressed it tight over his nose and mouth. Through the plastic, Sebastian's eyelids fluttered. He gasped for breath, breathing the black powder into his nose and throat. He coughed, raised his hands, and clawed at the thick plastic that was keeping him breathing. But his body hadn't recovered from being Tasered and his movements were impotent. Julia could see the panic in Sebastian's eyes, the silent scream that had caught in his gaping mouth.

"Stop it!" she shouted. "For fuck's sake, stop it, Oscar!"

She stood up. The chair she was cuffed to went with her, making her movements slow and unsteady. Wallin kicked the table and the top of it hit her in the thighs, and she fell to the floor. She caught a brief glimpse of Sebastian's feet jerking under the table. But by the time she had got to her knees, the movement had stopped. Wallin held the bag over Sebastian's face for a few more seconds before releasing it and letting the body slump on the chair. His face was red, and there were beads of sweat on his brow.

"You're completely . . ." She couldn't find the right word. Nor the right thought. The whole room was swaying and she suddenly felt nauseous.

"I eliminated a risk. The question now is: Am I going to have to do it again?"

Wallin pulled the plastic bag off Sebastian's head. He picked up the matchbox and refilled the bag with black powder. Julia swallowed.

"The whole business of fires is trickier that you'd think. I caused my first one when I was fifteen. Burned down my dad's garden shed and scared the crap out of his new family. Dad never figured out it was me, and the police investigation never found anything. I'd done my homework; I'd read everything I could get my hands on about arson attacks. The *Nordic Crime Chronicle* was particularly good. 'How Pyromaniacs Work' was an almost perfect step-by-step guide to what to do."

Wallin closed the bag again and shook it. Julia couldn't take her eyes off his hands. That bag was meant for her. He was planning to kill her. Terror took hold of her chest, made her breathing shallower and shallower.

"Soot," he said. "If a pathologist doesn't find any in the airways of a burned body, he gets suspicious and concludes that death occurred before the fire. That's why I left Amante alive, locked in the trunk. But I underestimated his will to survive. So many poor decisions are the result of underestimating people, so I really should have known better. That's a mistake I shall have to correct. If he survives, of course."

He pulled a disappointed face.

"Do you know what I think the worst thing about the whole Sophie Thorning incident is, Julia?"

"No." She needed to pull herself together, think clearly. Try to find a way out.

"That Jesper didn't call me instead of Frank Hunter. If he'd done that, we'd never have ended up in this position. A fucking security consultant he'd had dinner with a couple of times in The Hague. He even introduced us once in the cafeteria." Wallin shook his head. "Jesper was easily impressed. He bought that whole macho soldier thing. But Hunter turned out to be both sloppy and disloyal. In the long run he ended up becoming a bigger problem than the one he was contracted to solve. Swapping Sarac's secret for Stenberg's was smart, I have to give him that. But Sarac, on the other hand . . ."

Wallin looked at Julia and seemed to be considering how to continue. He waved his hand. "It looks like whoever took care of that problem was rather better than Hunter. More ruthless, more efficient, and left very little evidence behind. Even so, you still tracked them down, which only goes to show how much

Jesper Stenberg really does need us. People who can clean up after him without making mistakes."

Wallin walked around the table with the plastic bag in one hand. He pulled her chair up so that she was once again sitting at the table. She looked at the man who had been her mentor, her ally. Or, rather, the man who had pretended to be those things. In actual fact he was a manipulative and cold-blooded murderer. And she hadn't suspected a thing. Even though she regarded herself as something of an expert when it came to judging people's characters. The humiliation she felt was almost as strong as her fear. And was gradually turning to anger.

"Now, I've got some questions for you. I want you to answer them honestly. It's vital that we can trust each other."

He raised his eyebrows and waited for her to answer. Julia said nothing. For a moment she contemplated screaming, then realized that no one would hear her. It made more sense to play along for a bit longer.

"To start with, are there any copies of the photographs? On your personal computer, for instance?"

She remained silent for a few more seconds, trying to work out what to say that could win her some more time. She decided to tell the truth.

"Yes. I've got a backup at home."

Wallin scrutinized her, then nodded slowly. "Good. I believe you. I'd have done the same. Question number two." The corners of his mouth twitched. "Have you told anyone apart from Amante about my involvement in this case? A boyfriend, lover, family members, work colleagues?"

She ran the calculation through her head but came up with the same result.

"No, no one. Amante and I kept it to ourselves. I'm single right now, and my parents are dead."

"Good, Julia. See, this is going splendidly." Wallin smiled again and looked almost friendly.

She bit her top lip so hard, she could taste blood. If she

could just reach her gun, she could blow his head off. For Amante's sake, for Sebastian's, and—not least—her own. But Wallin had kicked it away into one corner of the room.

"Third and most important question: Can you imagine continuing our collaboration? Protecting Jesper Stenberg's secret, using it to achieve good things?"

She held her breath for a few seconds. There was only one answer, and she had to make it sound credible.

"Yes," she said. "I can actually imagine continuing our collaboration."

"And why would you want to do that?"

"Because there's something I want—something I'm prepared to do practically anything for."

"And that is?"

"I want to be head of National Crime. If you can manage that, I'm in."

Wallin looked at her for several seconds. His eyes narrowed to slits.

"You lie well. Extremely well, in fact."

He kicked her chair and she toppled over backward again. He threw himself on top of her before she had even hit the floor. She drove her knee up toward Wallin's crotch but missed, and he grabbed her shoulder and knocked both her and the chair aside.

Instinctively she tried to get up on her knees. She realized too late that that was precisely what he wanted. The plastic bag was pulled over her head and she only just managed to fill her lungs with air before it covered her mouth and nose. He dragged her back, giving her an opportunity to put one foot down on the floor. She pushed off it with all her strength and jerked her head back and felt it hit his chin. His teeth snapped shut and his grip on the plastic bag loosened slightly. She managed to put her other foot on the floor and stand up, still pushing the chair backward against Wallin.

They staggered back. But the room was so small that Wallin

hit the wall long before she had time to build up any momentum. The collision wasn't hard enough to make him lose his grip. A weary thud was all she managed to accomplish before the plastic bag was pulled tight again.

"You little cunt . . ." Wallin hissed. He moved away from the wall, then jerked quickly and kicked her legs out from under her. The fall made the bag pull even tighter across her nose and mouth.

She bucked her upper body wildly and tried to stay on her knees. Her violent movements were burning up the oxygen in her blood and she was going to have to take a breath any moment now. Inhale the air that was still in the bag, and her nose and throat would fill with soot.

Her heartbeat was thudding inside her head, her lungs bursting. She had no choice, couldn't resist any longer. She had to take that breath.

The sooty powder filled her throat, making her airways cramp. The plastic sucked hard onto her nose and mouth. She felt her knees buckle. And knew it would all soon be over.

Fifty-Three

Julia was lying on her side. The bag had slipped up a bit and let in enough air for her brain to start working again. She coughed, spluttered, and gasped for breath. She tossed her head to get the bag away from her mouth.

Through the misted, sooty plastic she could see movement, as if Wallin was wrestling with someone. For a fraction of a second she got it into her head that it was Amante, but then she realized that her mind was playing tricks on her. Someone else had saved her, given her a chance of survival. She tugged at the handcuffs and finally managed to break the back of the chair apart. She untangled herself from it, slipped her cuffed hands under her backside, and tucked her legs up as tightly as she could. With a lot of effort she managed to slip the cuffs past her feet, so that she now had her hands in front of her.

She tore off the plastic bag and blinked a couple of times. The fight was still going on, and she crawled as quickly as she could toward her pistol, which was lying in the corner where Wallin had kicked it. The men were fighting almost silently. All she could hear was their groans and the sounds of elbows, knees, and fists hitting their targets. There was a crash as the table collapsed. Then a groan that turned into a gurgle.

When she reached the gun, she grasped it with both hands. She pulled the bolt back by pressing the top of the pistol against her thigh. Then she rolled over onto her back.

"Stand still!" she shouted, aiming the weapon at the two men.

The attacker had the upper hand. He was standing behind Wallin, had a firm grip around his neck and throat, and was in the process of slowly strangling him. She recognized him immediately in spite of his bandaged face. It was Atif Kassab.

Wallin's face was turning blue, and his eyes were bulging. He was still trying to break free, flailing above his head with his arms and trying to reach Kassab, but it was clear that he wasn't going to succeed.

"Let go of him!" she yelled, twisting to get a better firing angle. "Let go of him, Kassab, or I'll shoot!"

The distance was no more than a couple of meters, but she could feel the lack of oxygen making her hands tremble. What the hell was Kassab doing there just then?

Wallin stopped flailing. He evidently thought he had a better chance of survival if he kept completely still. Kassab looked at her, then at the gun in her hands.

"Do it, Gabrielsson," Wallin croaked. "Shoot him. You'll be the heroine of the force."

Kassab tightened his grip, trying to keep Wallin's body in front of him as a shield. Julia kept her aim on him and waited for his next move. But nothing happened. Her head was still clearing. Even so, the situation felt hopelessly confused. She tried to gain some time.

"What are you doing here, Kassab?"

"Wallin snitched. He told Susanna and Eldar where they could find us. Because of him, Tindra no longer has a mother. My family isn't safe as long as he . . . as long as anyone . . ."

Kassab let out a gurgle. One whole side of his shirt was dark with blood, she now noticed. She remembered the pictures from the team meeting earlier. The trail of blood at the villa.

"And Susanna Jafarov?" Julia said. "Was that for the same reason?"

Kassab didn't answer. It looked as if he was having trouble staying on his feet. His grip on Wallin's neck loosened slightly.

"What are you waiting for?" Wallin hissed. "Shoot him. You'll get a medal. The minister of justice and I will—"

Kassab tightened his grip again, enough to get Wallin to shut up. Julia was still aiming at Kassab. She looked him in the eye. Then Wallin. She saw hatred there. Hatred toward Kassab, hatred toward her. Hatred toward everything and everyone who stood in his way.

Find him, a voice whispered in her head.

"Wallin tried to burn my friend alive," she said. "Omar Amante, the one you called Vaseline. And he murdered Sebastian there, an entirely innocent civilian, and was trying to do the same thing to me. All to get power for himself. If you hadn't shown up, I'd be dead by now."

She stared at Kassab along the top of the pistol. Her hands were shaking less now. She'd be able to shoot. The distance was two, three meters at most.

She aimed at Kassab's face and began to squeeze the trigger. He went on staring straight at her. Oddly, his eyes weren't at all scared but more sorrowful. They reminded her of Amante's. And all of a sudden she realized what that look meant.

It was the look of someone who had seen far too much death but was still struggling to go on. Doing whatever was necessary, no matter what the cost. Because there was no other choice.

She eased up on the trigger and slowly lowered the gun. Then nodded slowly toward Kassab.

Wallin suddenly seemed to realize what was happening. He opened his mouth to protest, but no sound came out. His limbs jerked a couple of times as the grip on his throat tightened. Soon there was an unpleasant crunching sound as Kassab broke his neck. Julia looked away; she didn't want to watch as Kassab let Wallin's dead body fall to the floor.

Kassab slumped onto one of the rib-backed chairs. The big bloodstain had spread down his thigh and past his knee. It was nothing short of a miracle that he was still conscious. That he was even alive.

Clumsily, she holstered her pistol, got to her feet, managed to pull her key ring from her trouser pocket, and removed the cuffs.

• • •

"Can you hear me, Kassab?" she said.

Atif looked up and nodded slowly.

The blonde cop straightened up. "I'm leaving now. In five minutes I'll call for an ambulance and police. It'll be ten minutes or so before the first car gets here."

The room started to spin faster. The ceiling and floor changed places; the details dissolved and became a fog. Somewhere in the distance he thought he could hear voices, someone calling him.

"You can decide for yourself what you want to do," the cop said. He saw her lips move, but he was no longer listening.

Instead he sees the tiger in front of him. It lies on the ground as the life slowly runs out of it. Its glossy red stomach heaves up and down, slower and slower. Its head falls back.

The voices were still calling, closer now. He recognized them. Adnan and Cassandra.

"They're safe now," he murmured, and closed his eyes.

He thought about Tindra. Her breath against his neck, her little heart vibrating against his chest. Drumming fast, as fast as a bird's. He imagined her and Natalie, hand in hand beneath the desert sky as night fell slowly, releasing the stars.

Fifty-Four

The conference room on the third floor had a view of the little Rosenbadsparken, like Stenberg's own office. Heavy furniture, a thick carpet, and a smell of power that made him slightly giddy.

"Well, then, I'll see you downstairs in a moment." The prime minister shook his hand and leaned forward slightly. "A piece of advice from someone who's been around a while: Enjoy this moment. After this evening, nothing will ever be the same again."

"Thanks, I'll bear that in mind. Your advice is always highly appreciated."

Stenberg smiled his best TV smile and kept his gaze steady. He didn't even have to try particularly hard. The old man's little mind games had become increasingly predictable. Karolina was right: he was the future now, and from that perspective his boss's jibes looked pretty pathetic. An old man's way of telling himself that he still had the upper hand.

The prime minister and his entourage left the conference room. Cecilia and his father-in-law remained behind.

"What do you want to do now, Jesper?" Karl-Erik asked as Karolina silently joined them. "Does he need to go through the speech again? Perhaps that would be best. One more time, just to be sure."

Karl-Erik spoke directly to his press secretary, which, in contrast to the prime minister's comment, immediately triggered Stenberg's irritation. But before he could say anything, Karolina had put her hand on his arm.

"You've got it all under control, haven't you, darling?" She turned toward her father and the press secretary. "I've arranged for a bite to eat up in Jesper's room, and he'll need to shower and change his shirt. We want him to look smart next to the prime minister. That's the whole point, isn't it?"

Karl-Erik exchanged a glance with his daughter. For a few moments it looked as though he was going to object, but then he nodded.

"That sounds like an excellent idea, my dear."

. . .

Julia Gabrielsson was driving into the city. She passed police cars and ambulances on the way. She managed to hold down her nausea until she had driven a couple of kilometers and found a suitable parking spot. Then she opened the car door and threw up on the blacktop. She didn't stop until she could taste bile stinging her mouth.

She cleaned her face with some wet wipes she found in the glove compartment, then sank back in the seat and rested her hands on the wheel. They were shaking.

Wallin had clearly been utterly insane, but he had been right about one thing: she couldn't trust anyone. She had to make sense of this mess on her own. Going to the press and letting them bring down Stenberg for his involvement in Sophie Thorning's death didn't really feel like a viable option. Sarac's killer would escape, and she would have turned herself into a leak. No better than Pärson.

That left Wallin's second suggestion. Turning to the people who were protecting Stenberg. And explaining to them that the secret was safe in her hands.

She had just averted her eyes as another person was murdered. Would she be forced to do that again? That would mean she had let down David Sarac, and Amante, and everything she believed in.

A thought suddenly popped into her head, supported by something Wallin had said. Stenberg didn't know who was re-

383

sponsible for Sarac's murder. He probably didn't even know that Sarac had tried to contact him. But, according to Wallin, Stenberg had begun to suspect that things weren't quite right and that John Thorning's death might not have been a coincidence. So perhaps he might listen to what she had to tell him. He might even believe her. It would all depend on how she presented it.

It might work. Or it could be the death of her.

In that case you'll be in good company, Julia, a voice whispered. She looked up, almost expecting to see Sarac's mutilated face in the rearview mirror. But of course there was no one there. She started the car, put it in first gear, and drove off slowly toward the main government buildings.

. . .

"What's happened between you and Daddy?" Karolina handed him his freshly pressed shirt. "You used to get along so well."

Yes, until I realized just how ruthless Karl-Erik is, Stenberg thought.

"Sometimes your father forgets who actually sits behind that desk," he said as he fastened the buttons. "Don't get me wrong: I'm only too aware of everything Karl-Erik has done for me. But if I'd enjoyed doing someone else's bidding, I might as well have stayed at Thorning & Partners."

"John Thorning is dead." She put the tie around his neck. Her voice had that harsh note he didn't like.

He forced out a smile.

"We'll sort it out. As soon as this is over, I'll sit down with your father and smoke the peace pipe." He saw her brighten up a little.

"Good! I don't want my two favorite men to be at loggerheads. There!" She adjusted the knot. Centered it perfectly between the wings of his collar. A double Windsor, just like the one her father always wore.

There was a knock on the door and Stenberg's secretary popped her head in.

384

"Excuse me, but there's a detective from Stockholm Regional Crime, a Julia Gabrielsson, down at reception. She wants to talk to you about the fire in the boathouse last night. Says it's important."

Karolina turned toward her. "Jesper hasn't got time for distractions, Jeanette. Anyway, the boathouse is leased to my father. Ask her to make an appointment to see him."

Jeanette looked slightly sheepish. "Yes, I explained that to her, but she was most insistent. She asked me to say that new information has emerged and that the minister would want to be informed before the press conference."

Stenberg looked at the time. Forty-five minutes to go. Any moment now his press secretary would be standing at the door, wanting him to go through that ridiculous speech again. And this time Karolina would make him agree to it. Would make him dance to her daddy's tune like a good boy.

"Send this Gabrielsson up, if you would, please," he said. He ignored the look his wife gave him, went over to the window, and gazed out. He didn't turn around until Julia Gabrielsson was standing in the doorway. For a few moments it looked as if Karolina was going to stay, and he noticed Gabrielsson shuffling uncomfortably. Then his wife appeared to change her mind.

"Five minutes. I'll keep Cecilia calm in the meantime." Karolina closed the door behind her.

Stenberg gestured to Gabrielsson to sit down.

"Well, then. What's this information that you wanted to share with me in such an unconventional manner?"

Gabrielsson held her cell phone out toward him. An image directly from his nightmares. It hit him like a punch in the gut.

Sophie Thorning's battered body across the hood of his BMW. White skin, black metal, red blood. For a brief, dizzy moment he almost thought Sophie was going to raise her head and turn in his direction. Smile at him with her shattered face.

Did you think you could forget me, Jesper?

He started, and swallowed hard. Then he looked up and met Julia Gabrielsson's gaze. And realized at once that his reaction had given him away.

"I know you were there," she said slowly. "I know what happened, and I know who cleaned up after you."

Stenberg swallowed again. Glanced fleetingly at the door. Karolina and Cecilia were going to appear at any moment.

"Wh-What do you want?" he said, almost in a whisper. "You can have anything—anything at all."

"I only want one thing. Something that only you can give me. I want David Sarac's murderer."

Fifty-Five

Stenberg watched the door close behind Julia Gabrielsson. He sat motionless for a few seconds before calling his secretary. His hand was shaking and he cleared his throat to make sure his voice would remain steady.

"Jeanette, would you mind getting ahold of my father-in-law? We don't have much time, so right away, please."

There was a knock on the door and Karolina came back in. "What was that about?"

Stenberg struggled to adopt the right expression.

"The man who was badly burned in the boathouse. It turns out he's Victor Amante's son."

Karolina started. "What?"

"And the Security Police found him poking around out there the other day." Stenberg fell silent, deciding not to say anything else.

"So this Gabrielsson came all the way here just to tell you that? Couldn't she have called or, better still, let one of her bosses do it through the usual channels?"

Stenberg pulled a face to show that he agreed with her.

"Gabrielsson used to work for Wallin. She knows how important the press conference is and was worried that the information about Amante might have leaked, that one of the reporters might ask about it this evening. She decided to inform me personally, seeing as she happened to be nearby. A little overzealous, perhaps, but you have to admire her strategic thinking."

Karolina was giving him that look that usually cut straight

through him. He met her gaze and did his utmost not to buckle under it.

"Why didn't Wallin contact you?" she said.

Stenberg shrugged. "Apparently he's otherwise engaged."

There was another knock on the door and Karl-Erik walked in without waiting for an answer, as usual.

"You wanted to talk to me, Jesper?"

"Yes, I do. Have a seat." He gestured toward the visitors' chairs, then turned to his wife. "Darling, I've just remembered, I forgot to synchronize our holiday schedule with Jeanette. I don't suppose you feel like dealing with that with her?"

"Now?" She sounded confused, almost insulted at being sent out again.

Stenberg nodded. "Just as well to get it done." He winked at her to indicate that he and her father needed to talk man-to-man.

"Okay. You're sure this is the right time?" She raised her eyes questioningly.

"Definitely."

Unless you'd rather stay and watch when I knock your father off his fucking pedestal, he thought.

Stenberg locked the door behind Karolina. Then he returned to his desk.

"Not long to go now," Karl-Erik said, and glanced at his watch. "You've fought well, managed to get right to the top."

"I've had a good adviser"—Stenberg smiled—"someone who made sure I kept moving in the right direction, and helped get rid of the occasional obstacle. Like John Thorning, for instance . . ."

A little wrinkle appeared between Karl-Erik's eyebrows. Stenberg leaned forward.

"I know what happened to John Thorning and David Sarac. Why they died."

The wrinkle between Karl-Erik's eyebrows deepened, but Stenberg wasn't about to let him speak—not yet.

"On one level I can actually understand your reasoning. The calculations you made. I let you down, Karl-Erik. I betrayed you and Karolina. And you'd invested far too much, spent too many years stubbornly slaving away in the shadow of pompous idiots like the prime minister to let it all run into the sand."

He paused for a moment to moisten his lips. Karl-Erik's face was rigid. It looked like a mask.

"A short while ago I had a visit from a Detective Inspector Julia Gabrielsson. She had evidence including, among other things, an extremely compromising photograph that David Sarac is supposed to have sent me. A picture that would have ruined my career. But someone got there first and snapped up Sarac's e-mail before it reached me and arranged a meeting with him in my name. Gabrielsson told me what happened to Sarac down in your boathouse. What he was subjected to . . ."

Stenberg could feel his shirt sticking damply to his back.

"I did what you would have done, Karl-Erik. I made a deal with her. Agreed to her ultimatum."

A flicker of movement in the mask. An expression Stenberg had trouble interpreting. But he wasn't going to let himself be put off now.

"Gabrielsson is going to make sure it all disappears: pictures, evidence, the lot. She only wants one thing in return. Or perhaps it would be more accurate to say: one person."

Stenberg paused for breath. His speech was almost over now. All that remained was the final demand.

"The murderer has to take his punishment, Karl-Erik," he said in his most persuasive courtroom voice. "Julia Gabrielsson could demolish everything we've built up. We have no choice but to do as she wants. Boman . . ." He forced the words out. "We have to sacrifice Boman."

Karl-Erik got up slowly from his chair. He stood still in front of Stenberg's desk for a few seconds, his back militarily straight, his face almost the same rigid mask as before. The only difference was a tiny, barely perceptible trace of anxiety. Unless it was something else?

"Jesper," he said, "I haven't the faintest idea what you're talking about."

Karl-Erik turned around and walked over to the door, unlocked it, and left the room without looking back.

Stenberg loosened his tie and unbuttoned the sweaty collar of his shirt. He went over to the little basin, looked in the mirror for a few seconds, then rolled his sleeves up and washed his hands, all the way up to his elbows. He scrubbed so hard that his skin stung.

Fifty-Six

Julia Gabrielsson parked a short distance away at Tegelbacken. She could just make out Stenberg's windows through the tops of the trees in Rosenbadsparken. She didn't really know why she was sitting there in the car. She had done what she could. Said what she had to say. Yet she was still there. Wanted to be there when it happened.

Two big live-broadcast vans were parked in Fredsgatan, around the corner from Rosenbad. People were hurrying back and forth to the vehicles; they seemed to be laying cables. A patrol car was parked in front of them and she could see two uniformed officers keeping an eye on the media circus. She turned her car radio on, found the news channel, and pushed her seat back slightly. Nearby, some road workers began using a pneumatic drill, forcing her to turn the radio up.

A little over an hour ago a number of people were found dead in an office building in Sollentuna. The Stockholm Police have yet to issue a statement, but sources indicate that one of the bodies is that of a police officer . . .

She leaned over and lowered the volume. At the same time she thought she could see a silhouette in one of Stenberg's windows. The sound of the drill continued to echo off the buildings.

* * *

Jesper Stenberg looked out across the treetops toward Riddarholmen. At last, the feeling was back. Total, absolute presence.

He looked at the time. Twenty minutes left before he had to go downstairs, shake the prime minister's hand, and stand at the podium. Lean toward the microphones and say how happy and grateful he was to have received the boss's endorsement. That he would do his best for the party in his new role, was looking forward to the coming election campaign, blah, blah, blah. Live broadcast on both radio and television, at least fifty reporters in the room, and just as many party dignitaries and principal mourners.

Karl-Erik would be standing there, watching him. He would come to the same conclusion that Stenberg had, if he hadn't already done so. Boman was a pawn, a piece to be sacrificed to gain a better position. To win the game.

He didn't hear Karolina come into the room, didn't know she was there until she touched his arm.

"Jesper."

He jerked. Turned around. She had a serious look on her face.

"I just spoke to Daddy. He's worried about you. Said you weren't making much sense. That you were talking about John Thorning."

It took Stenberg a few moments to absorb what she had said. Then he understood. This was his father-in-law's petty act of vengeance. Revenge for having to lose his faithful servant. Dripping a couple of well-chosen words in Karolina's ear to demonstrate that she was still Daddy's dutiful instrument.

"I think your father misunderstood me," he murmured.

"I hope so. Because you can't seriously believe that he could have had someone killed. Or that Nisse Boman is some sort of professional hit man?"

His brain seized up and couldn't find any sort of comprehensible explanation.

"Well, I . . ."

"Yes?" She tilted her head. "What were you going to say?"

He took a deep breath, trying in vain to marshal his thoughts.

"How about 'Thank you'?" she said. "'Thank you, Karolina, for being such an understanding wife. For letting me have an

392

affair with that whore Sophie Thorning ever since we were at university. Thank you for playing dumb, for pretending not to notice the furtive glances, or the smell of her cunt when I crept into bed shamefaced at night.'"

The corners of her mouth turned up into a contorted smile he had never seen before.

"I let you do it, and do you know why? Because I knew that Sophie would arrange for you to become one of John's protégés. That was the price I paid to get John Thorning on our side. A reasonable price, until she started to threaten our family."

Stenberg opened his mouth but still couldn't manage to utter a single word.

"Do you know, there's an app that scans keys?" Karolina continued. "It takes ten seconds, then you can order a copy on-line. So easy to do on one of the many occasions Sophie asked me to look after her handbag."

She stroked his cheek.

"I used to go around to her apartment when she was away. I'd walk through the rooms, look in drawers, lie on her bed. Imagine the pair of you fucking in it. But when you were offered the post of justice minister, I realized that the risk had grown too big. I let you think I was going out with the girls, then I went around to Sophie's to talk to her, explain that it was all over. But when I was standing outside the door I heard voices. I realized that you were already there, doing the same thing. I heard what she screamed at you. She could have ruined everything we'd worked for, all the sacrifices we'd made . . ."

She paused, then lowered her voice.

"After you left, I went into the apartment and saw her standing by the open window, leaning out. It wasn't difficult to . . ." She threw one hand out. "It was only later that I realized Sophie was planning to yell at you when you drove out of the garage. And that she'd actually landed right on your car."

Stenberg gasped for air. It felt like the room was slowly starting to revolve counterclockwise. He closed his eyes and tried to sort his head out, but failed. The silhouette in the window from his dreams popped into his mind. But it was no longer Boman standing up there, leaning out and looking him in the eye. It was Karolina.

"When the e-mail from David Sarac appeared in the in-box of your computer at home, I was furious. Not so much with you, but myself. I'd been sloppy; I'd put us in unnecessary danger. So I arranged to meet him in the boathouse. He was never supposed to appear again, but when he did, all I had to do was make a discreet phone call to the national police chief. Ask her to make sure that the investigation into the unidentified body at Källstavik didn't cause any problems for the party. Especially not now, before the election. Eva Swensk is loyal: she knows who she's got to thank for her job, and how to make sure that a case ends up buried deep within police bureaucracy."

"John Thorning," he said. His voice sounded like a whisper. The room was still spinning. Everything felt unreal, almost like a dream.

"John was a bit more difficult. But we couldn't just leave him, not after Daddy had made a fool of himself offering him that ambassadorial post. Another mistake that I had to put right." She smiled again. "Do you know, there are certain substances in migraine medication that you really shouldn't take if you suffer from angina?"

"You switched his pills," Stenberg said incredulously.

"It was actually a bit more complicated than that. John's medicine came in capsule form. I'd seen him take it on a few occasions. So I ground up some of my migraine pills with a pestle and mortar and kept the powder in a little bag in my handbag. When I was dancing with him at the party, I got him to take off his jacket, which contained the bottle of pills. I went into the toilet and emptied the capsules, then filled them with the powder. After that, it was just a matter of waiting. It actually happened quicker than I expected."

"But what if they'd done an autopsy?"

"Really, Jesper. John was almost seventy. He had a hectic lifestyle, he'd already had one heart attack, and he was taking medication for angina. Why would they conduct an autopsy? And even if they did, it would only look like he'd taken a few of his wife's migraine pills."

Stenberg shook his head disbelievingly. "You can't be serious?"

"I did what needed to be done, Jesper. I kept my eye on the prize, thought about the fantastic future that lay ahead of us. That still lies ahead of us."

She took hold of his arm and shook it gently.

"I can explain to Daddy. I'll tell him that what you said was a joke, some sort of misunderstanding. He'll believe me. After all, people hear what they want to hear, don't they? And you don't have to worry about that Gabrielsson either. All you have to do now, Jesper . . ."

She raised her hands toward his neck and, to his own surprise, he found himself jerking back slightly. Then he realized she was reaching for his tie to straighten it.

". . . is go downstairs and give the best speech you've ever made. Make the words sound genuine and heartfelt, the way only you can. Talk about all the things you'll be able to do for the party, for the country."

She pulled his tie tighter than necessary. Looked him right in the eye without taking her fingers from the knot. His collar dug into his neck and throat, and forced him to swallow hard. There was a flicker of movement outside the window. A chalk-white seagull was hovering out there, almost motionless. Staring at Stenberg with its empty, dead eyes.

"Can you do that, Jesper?" she said.

• • •

The knock on the driver's-side window took Julia by surprise. Made her heart start beating unnaturally hard.

A man in a suit was standing outside the car, gesturing to

her to open the window. He was waving something that looked like police ID.

"You can't stay here," he said. "No parking."

"I'm police too." She held up her own ID. "Regional Crime. What department are you?"

The man smiled at her. He looked pleasant. Familiar too, but she couldn't quite remember why. The pneumatic drill that had been quiet for a while started up again, forcing the man to lean closer to her.

"Personal Protection," he said.

"Oh, so you've got one of the ministers." She nodded toward Rosenbad.

"That's right."

"Which one?" she said. At that moment she realized where she'd seen the man before.

• • •

Jesper Stenberg stood quite still at the podium as the cameras flashed. The prime minister had just introduced him. All eyes were on him now.

He could hear every sound, see every nuance of color, in the fireworks display taking place in front of him. He knew that this moment would engrave itself on his memory—would be there for the rest of his life.

He looked at the audience, trying to find some familiar faces. But the spotlights and flashes were blinding him, turning the people in front of him into dark shapes with barely discernible features. He thought he could see his father-in-law's stern expression, and Oscar Wallin standing over by the door. But then another flash blinded him and Wallin was gone. He screwed his eyes up and suddenly thought he could see John Thorning sitting next to David Sarac in the front row. Then more flashes made the two men disappear into the darkness.

Ghosts in your mind, Jesper. Pull yourself together, for God's sake.

He looked down at the podium. Saw the sheet of prompts. The letters blurred and formed a sludgy mess.

"Thank you," he heard himself say. "It truly is a great honor for me to be standing here . . ."

He looked up and turned to the closest television camera. Sophie Thorning was standing right beside it. White dress, white shoes.

He could still see her falling.

See her hang between ground and sky, with her eyes open wide, her mouth gaping, for a moment almost weightless. And then he heard the sound when she stopped being weightless. A muffled, awful sound—a sigh, rather than a bang. The sound of something breaking. Something that could never be mended.

A necessary sacrifice.

It was her or you.

You had no choice.

". . . and therefore it is a matter of great regret that I must for personal reasons decline the prime minister's offer," he went on.

The whole room seemed to stop.

"Sadly, my wife is suffering from a serious illness. Karolina has always been my main support in life, my rock. She has made huge sacrifices for my sake, more than anyone has any right to expect. Now that she is facing a great challenge, it is therefore no more than right that I do the same for her. Mental illness isn't something that is often talked about, but Karolina and I have decided to be completely open. Our hope is that we can help show that mental illness is a problem that can afflict any-one. An illness that can be treated, and that ought not to be a source of shame."

He changed camera and adjusted his voice and body lan-guage.

"Before I finish, I'd like to ask you to respect our desire to be left in peace as far as possible. Karolina, I, and our daughters would like to thank you in advance for your consideration at this difficult time."

397

Stenberg smiled his very saddest smile. Questions rained down on him, forming a maelstrom of voices. He tried to catch sight of Karolina. He found her in the second row, only a few meters from where he had imagined he'd seen Sophie Thorning. She was looking at him, meeting his gaze. She nodded slowly. When the next flash went off, she was gone.

• • •

An agitated commentator's voice took over on the radio and Julia turned the volume up.

"Bloody hell," Becker said, leaning against the door of her car. "The Stenberg family has certainly been keeping that quiet. I only saw Karolina Stenberg an hour or so ago, and she seemed the same as usual. We even spent a few minutes talking about exercise. She said she was going to ski in the Vasa cross-country race next year."

Julia got out of the car to stretch her legs and looked up toward Rosenbad again. Something toward the top of the facade caught her eye. A curtain billowing in the wind.

For some reason the piece of fabric filled her with unease. She pointed up at the building and shouted to make herself heard over the sound of the pneumatic drill.

"Look, am I wrong or is that Stenberg's window open up there?"

Becker looked to where she was pointing. He started to walk with long strides toward the building. Julia half ran after him, more out of instinct than for any actual reason. There was something not quite right.

She caught up with him as they entered the park. A moment later they saw the body by the wall.

Karolina Stenberg was lying on her stomach. Her head was turned to one side, her eyes staring blankly at them, almost in surprise, as the pool of blood slowly spread across the pavement.

Becker threw himself down on his knees beside the body. He felt Karolina's neck and yelled something into the microphone fastened to his wrist. He was rattling off orders that Julia couldn't hear. The sound of the pneumatic drill had gotten even louder, echoing between the buildings in a rhythm she could feel in her gut.

She stared at Karolina Stenberg's outstretched hand. It was large, its fingers long and strong. The hand of someone who could handle practically any tool.

People came running out from the entrance. Guards, police officers, followed by journalists. The first camera began to click. Firing off flashes. It was joined by others.

Julia took a few steps back from the growing crowd surrounding the body and looked up at the window. The curtain was still fluttering mournfully up above. There was a hint of a figure, a man leaning out of the window slightly.

Their eyes met. For a moment time seemed to slow down. Movement and sound switched to slow motion. The drill went on drilling. Hammering down through the asphalt and concrete like a racing metallic heart, before it suddenly stopped. Pausing time for an instant of utter silence.

Then Jesper Stenberg slowly nodded to her from the window, and time started to move once more. Turning the scene into a cacophony of voices, movement, and flashing lights.

Julia turned and started to walk away. A mild wind was blowing off the water, carrying with it the sound of faint laughter.

Julia told herself that it belonged to David Sarac.

Epilogue

The tiger's body is lying stretched out in the clearing. Its shaggy coat is spattered red with blood. Its eyes stare blankly up at the night sky. At heavens and stars it can no longer see.

The little girl is on her knees on the soft ground. She slowly runs her hand over one of the tiger's paws. Then she bends down and kisses it on the nose.

"Thank you," she whispers. "Thank you for saving us."

She gets to her feet and turns toward the red-haired woman standing behind her, and takes her hand. Then she looks over her shoulder.

"Are you coming, Amu?" She holds her free hand out toward him. It's so small, so beautiful. Possibly the most beautiful thing he's ever seen.

"I'm coming, Tindra," he murmurs.

• • •

The words were still ringing in his head as the plane's landing gear hit the scorching-hot tarmac and woke him from his slumber.

THANKS

There are always a lot of people involved in the creation of a book. Some are easy to thank, like my family, publisher, editor, and agent. Or all the brilliant people who translate my stories into a myriad different languages. Others are harder to thank, because I am prevented for various reasons from giving your real names. But that doesn't change my appreciation of your help.

Anders de la Motte
Malmö, 2015